Graham, Heather LP
  The Presence

The Presence

*Also by Heather Graham
in Large Print:*

Apache Summer
Dark Stranger
Dead on the Dance Floor
Haunted
Hurricane Bay
Night of the Blackbird
Picture Me Dead
Rides a Hero
Every Time I Love You
Lord of the Wolves
Queen of Hearts
Quiet Walks the Tiger
A Season for Love
Tempestuous Eden
Tender Taming

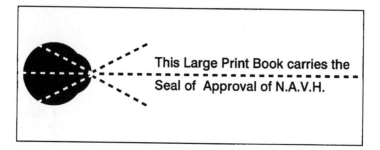

This Large Print Book carries the
Seal of Approval of N.A.V.H.

The Presence

Heather Graham

Thorndike Press • Waterville, Maine

Published in 2004 by arrangement with Harlequin Books S.A.

Thorndike Press® Large Print Basic.

The tree indicium is a trademark of Thorndike Press.

The text of this Large Print edition is unabridged.
Other aspects of the book may vary from the original edition.

Set in 16 pt. Plantin by Al Chase.

Printed in the United States on permanent paper.

Library of Congress Cataloging-in-Publication Data

Graham, Heather.
    The presence / Heather Graham.
        p. cm.
    ISBN 0-7862-7086-1 (lg. print : hc : alk. paper)
    1. Young women — Crimes against — Fiction.   2. Serial murders — Fiction.   3. Scotland — Fiction.   4. Castles — Fiction.   5. Large type books.   I. Title.
PS3557.R198P74 2004

                                                    2004059424

For Rich Devlin, Lance Taubald, Leslie and Leland Burbank, Connie Perry, Jo Carol, Peggy McMillan, Sharon Spiak, Sue-Ellen Wellfonder, Kathryn Falk and Rubin, with much love — and to great memories of streams and castles in Scotland.

As the Founder/CEO of NAVH, the only national health agency solely devoted to those who, although not totally blind, have an eye disease which could lead to serious visual impairment, I am pleased to recognize Thorndike Press* as one of the leading publishers in the large print field.

Founded in 1954 in San Francisco to prepare large print textbooks for partially seeing children, NAVH became the pioneer and standard setting agency in the preparation of large type.

Today, those publishers who meet our standards carry the prestigious "Seal of Approval" indicating high quality large print. We are delighted that Thorndike Press is one of the publishers whose titles meet these standards. We are also pleased to recognize the significant contribution Thorndike Press is making in this important and growing field.

Lorraine H. Marchi, L.H.D.
Founder/CEO
NAVH

* Thorndike Press encompasses the following imprints: Thorndike, Wheeler, Walker and Large Print Press.

Prologue

Nightmares

The scream rose and echoed in the night with a bloodcurdling resonance that only the truly young, and truly terrified, could create.

Her parents ran into the room, called by instinct to battle whatever force had brought about such absolute horror in their beloved child.

Yet there was nothing. Nothing but their nine-year-old, standing on the bed, arms locked at her side, fingers curled into her fists with a terrible rigidity, as if she had suddenly become an old woman. She was screaming, the sound coming again and again, high, screeching, tearing, like the sound of fingernails dragged down the length of a blackboard.

Both parents looked desperately around the room, then their eyes met.

"Sweetheart, sweetheart!"

Her mother came for her unnoticed and tried to take the girl into her arms, but she was inflexible. The father came forward, calling her name, taking her and then shaking her. Once again, she gave no notice.

Then she went down. She simply crumpled into a heap in the center of the bed. Again the parents looked at one another, then the mother rushed forward, sweeping the girl into her arms, cradling her to her breast. "Sweetie, please, please . . . !"

Blue eyes, the color of a soft summer sky, opened to hers. They were filled with angelic innocence. The child's head was haloed by her wealth of white-blond hair, and she smiled sleepily at the sight of her mother's face, as if nothing had happened, as if the bone-jarring sounds had never come from her lips.

"Did you have a nightmare?" her mother asked anxiously.

Then a troubled frown knit her brow. "No!" she whispered, and the sky-blue eyes darkened, the fragile little body began to shake.

The mother looked at her husband, shaking her head. "We've got to call the doctor."

"It's two in the morning. She's had a nightmare."

"We need to call someone."

"No," her father said firmly. "We need to tuck her back into bed and discuss it in the morning."

"But —"

"If we call the doctor, we'll be referred to the emergency room. And if we go to the emergency room, we'll sit there for hours, and they'll tell us to take her to a shrink in the morning."

"Donald!"

"It's true, Ellen, and you know it."

Ellen looked down. Her daughter was staring at her with huge eyes, shaking now.

"The police!" she whispered.

"The police?" Ellen asked.

"I saw him, Mommy. I saw what that awful man did to the lady."

"What lady, darling?"

"She was on the street, stopping cars. She had big red hair and a short silver skirt. The man stopped for her in a red car with no top, like Uncle Ted's. She got in with him and he drove and then . . . and then . . ."

Donald walked across the room and took hold of his daughter's shoulders. "Stop this! You're lying. You haven't been out of this room!"

Ellen shoved her husband away. "Stop it! She's terrified as it is."

"And she wants us to call the police? Our only child will wind up on the front page of the papers, and if they don't catch this psycho murdering women, he'll come after her! No, Ellen."

"Maybe they can catch him," Ellen suggested softly.

"You have to forget it!" Donald said sternly to his daughter.

She nodded gravely, then shook her head. "I have to tell it!" she whispered.

Ellen seldom argued with Donald. But tonight she had picked her battle.

"When this happens . . . you have to let her talk."

"No police!" Donald insisted.

"I'll call Adam."

"That shyster!"

"He's no shyster and you know it."

Donald's eyes slid from his wife's to those of his daughter, which were awash in misery and a fear she shouldn't have to know. "Call the man," he said.

He was very old; that was Toni's first opinion of Adam Harrison. His face was long, his body was thin, and his hair was snow-white. But his eyes were the kindest, most knowing, she had seen in her nine years on earth.

He came to the bedside, took her hand, clasped it firmly between his own and smiled slowly. She had been shaking, but his gentle hold eased the trembling from her, just as it warmed her. He was very special. He understood that she had seen what she had seen without ever leaving the house. And she knew, of course, that it was ridiculous. Such things didn't happen. But it had happened.

She hated it. Loathed it. And she understood her father's concern. It was a very bad thing. People would make fun of her — or they would want to use her ability for their own purposes.

"So, tell me about it," Adam said to her, after he had explained that he was an old friend of her mother's family.

"I saw it," she whispered, and the shaking began again.

"Tell me what you saw."

"There was a woman on the street, trying to get cars to stop. One stopped. She leaned into it, and she started to talk to the man about money. Then she went with him. She got into the car. It was red."

"It was a convertible?"

"Like Uncle Ted's car."

"Right," he said, squeezing her hand again.

Her voice became a monotone. She repeated some of the conversation between the man and woman word for word. Perspiration broke out on her body as she felt the woman's growing sense of fear. She couldn't breathe as she described the knife. She was drenched with sweat at the end, and cold. So cold. He talked to her and assured her.

Then the police arrived, called by neighbors who were awakened by her screams.

The two officers flanked her bed and started firing questions at her, demanding to know what she had seen — or what had been done to her.

Despite the terror, she felt all right because of Adam. But then huge tears formed in her eyes. "Nothing, nothing! I saw nothing!"

Adam rose, his voice firm and filled with such authority that even the men with their guns and badges listened to him. They left the room. Adam winked at her and went with the men, telling her that he would talk to them.

A month later, the police came back to the house. She could hear her father angrily telling them that they had to leave her alone. But despite his argument, she found herself facing a police officer who kept asking her terrible questions. He described horrific things, his voice growing rougher and rougher. Somewhere in there, she closed off. She couldn't bear to hear him anymore.

She woke up in the hospital. Her mother was by her side, tears in her eyes. She was radiant with happiness when Toni blinked and looked at her.

Her father was there, too. He kissed Toni on the forehead, then, choking, left the room. An older man in the back stepped up to her.

"You're going to move," he told her cheerfully. "Out to the country. The police will never come again."

"The police?"

"Yes, don't you remember?"

She shook her head. "I'm sorry . . . I'm really sorry. I don't know who you are."

He arched a fuzzy white brow, staring at her. "I'm Adam. Adam Harrison. You really don't remember me?"

She studied him gravely and shook her head. She was lying, but he just smiled, and his smile was warm and comforting.

"Just remember my name. And if you ever need me, call me. If you dream again, or have a nightmare."

"I don't have nightmares," she told him.

"If you dream . . ."

"Oh, I'm certain I don't have dreams. I don't let myself have dreams. Some people can do that, you know."

His smile deepened. "Yes, actually, I do

know. Well, Miss Antoinette Fraser, it has been an incredible pleasure to see you, and to see you looking so well. If you ever just want to say hello, remember my name."

She gripped his hand suddenly. "I will always remember your name," she told him.

"If you ever need me, I'll be there," he promised.

He brushed a kiss on her forehead, and then he was gone. Just a whisper of his aftershave remained.

Soon her memory faded and the whole thing became vague, not real. There was just a remnant in her mind, no more than that whisper of aftershave when someone was really, truly gone.

1

"Imagine, if you will, the great laird of the castle! The MacNiall himself, famed and infamous, a figure to draw both fear and awe. Ahead of his time, he stood nearly six foot three, hair as black as pitch, eyes the silver gray of steel, capable of glinting like the devil's own. Some say those orbs burned with the very fires of hell. His arms were knotted with muscle from the wielding of his sword, his ax, whatever weapon fell his way in the midst of battle. It was said that he could take down a dozen men in the opening moments of a fray. Passionate for king and country, he would fight any man who spoke to wrong either. Passionate in love, his anger could rage just as deeply against a woman, if he felt himself betrayed.

"Imagine then, being his beloved, his bride, his wife, burdened with the most treacherous of advisors, men determined to find a way to bring down a man so great in battle, to further their own aims. Imagine her knowing that she had been betrayed, maligned and that her laird husband was returning from the blood of the battlefield . . .

intent upon a greater revenge. There . . . there! He would come to the great doors that gave entry to the hall."

Toni stood at the railing of the second-floor balcony, pointing to the massive double doors, high on sheer exhilaration. A crowd of awed tourists were gathered below her in the great hall entry, staring up at her.

This was really too good, far more than they had imagined they could accomplish when she and the others had set their wild dream about procuring a rundown castle and creating a very special entertainment complex out of it. So far, David and Kevin had rallied their crowd magnificently by playing a pair of hapless minstrels in the reign of James IV, when the current structure had been built upon the Norman bastion begun by thirteenth-century kings. Ryan and Gina had done a fantastic job playing the daughter of the laird and the stable boy with whom she had fallen tragically in love during the reign of Mary, Queen of Scots. Thayer — the wild card in their sextet — had proved himself more than capable of portraying a laird accused of witchcraft in the time of James VI. And they had all run around as kitchen wenches or servants for one another.

Beyond a doubt, the crowd was into the

show. Below, they waited. So Toni continued.

"Alas, it was right here, as I stand now, where, tragically, Annalise met with her husband, that great man of inestimable prowess and, unfortunately, jealousy and rage. Believing the stories regarding his beautiful wife, he curled his fingers around her throat, squeezing the life from her before tossing her callously down the staircase in a fit of uncontrollable wrath. Since he was the great laird of the castle, his servants helped him dispose of the body, and Laird MacNiall went on to fight another day. He was, however, to receive his own just rewards. Though he had bested many, and countless troops had been slaughtered beneath his leadership, Cromwell was to seize the man at last. He received the ultimate punishment, being castrated, disemboweled, decapitated, dismembered and dispersed. His pieces were then gathered by his descendants, and he now lies buried deep within the crypt of these very stone walls! Ah, yes, his mortal remains are buried here. But it's said that his soul wanders, not just around the castle itself, but through the surrounding hills and braes, and he is known to haunt the forest just beyond the ruins of the old town wall."

Her words were met with a collective "Ooh!" that was most encouraging. Toni flashed a smile to Gina, hovering in a room off the second-floor landing, watching. Any minute now, Ryan would come riding into the main hall.

"They say he roams his lands still, hunting for his wife, anxious to see her face, filled with love and lust . . . and a fury seizes him each time he would hold her in all her spectral beauty!"

She glanced at Gina, frowning. Ryan should have made his appearance by now.

Gina looked at her and shrugged, then lifted her hands, indicating that Toni should finish up, however she could manage.

"That night the great laird of the castle came bursting through his doorway!"

As if on cue, a fantastic flash of lightning suddenly tore through the darkness, followed by a massive roar of thunder.

The doors burst open . . . and a man appeared.

Toni inhaled on a sharp breath of disbelief. It wasn't Ryan. The man was on the biggest black stallion Toni had ever seen. She thought that the prancing animal might breathe fire at any instant.

And the rider . . . He was damp from the

18

rain, but his hair appeared to be as black as pitch. And though he was atop the giant horse, he appeared massive himself. If his eyes had glowed like the devil's just then, she didn't think that she could have been any more surprised. He was the great Laird Bruce MacNiall, the warrior in mantle and kilt, just as she had described him.

Again lightning flashed and thunder rolled and roared.

Toni let out a startled scream, and a collective squawking rose from the audience.

Perfect! Toni thought. It was time to announce that the laird has come home, in all his glory — and wrath. But for once in her life, words failed her. Like the others, she was mesmerized, watching, afraid to breathe, thinking she must have conjured a ghost.

He dismounted from the stallion with such ease that anyone there with a question would still be in the dark as to what a Scotsman wore beneath his kilt. He looked around the great hall with dark, narrowed eyes and a jaw of concrete.

"Who is running this charade?" he demanded harshly.

The spellbound crowd still seemed to believe it was all part of an act.

David, down with the crowd, jumped to

life. "The lady at the top of the stairs!" he informed the stranger, pointing up to Toni. Then he did his best to vacate the place as quickly as possible. "And there we are, at the end of the show. Ladies, gentlemen, thank you for your attention!" he said.

The crowd burst into applause, staring at the newcomer as they did so.

The stranger's scowl deepened.

"Thank you again," David said. "And now let's adjourn into the kitchen, where we'll have the promised tea and scones!"

As Toni watched the crowd disappear, she heard Gina whispering frantically to her. "What is it? What the hell . . . ?" She stepped from the bedroom, moving out on the landing. "Is it Ryan? What on earth has he done now?"

"It's not Ryan," Toni murmured beneath her breath. Kevin had followed David and the crowd into the kitchen, but not before looking up the stairs and glaring at her, lifting his hands in a "what the hell . . . ?" motion himself. Thayer must have gone out to help Ryan, since it appeared that Toni and Gina were alone with the irate stranger, who was now slowly striding his way up the stairs.

"Oh, God!" Gina breathed. "You said you made him up!"

"I did!"

"Then who or what is walking up the stairs? Never mind — I can tell you. It's one very angry man."

He was angry? Suddenly Toni, who had been so stunned and awed herself, was angry, as well. Who the hell was he, charging in on them? They had a lease option on the castle, and whatever he might be, Great Britain had laws, and he surely had no right here.

"Hello," she said, determinedly putting ice and strength into her voice. "Can I help you?"

"Can you help me? Aye, that you can!" he snapped. Now that he was close, she could see that his eyes were gray, a dark stormy gray, right now. "Who in the hell are you people and what in God's name do you think you're doing here?" If his eyes were a storm, his voice was the thunder that cracked through it. He was a Scotsman, definitely — it was clear from the burr of his words — but his clean, crisp enunciation suggested that he had traveled, as well, and spent a great deal of time in other places.

"Who are we?" she said, frowning. "Who are you?"

"Bruce MacNiall, owner of this castle."

"The MacNialls are all dead," she told him.

21

"Since I am a MacNiall, I beg to differ."

Behind her, Gina groaned. "Oh, Lord! It sounds as if there's been some terrible mistake."

"There's been no mistake," Toni said softly to Gina. "There can't be!" To the stranger who had arrived in perfect theatrical form, she said, "We have a rental agreement, a lease-purchase agreement, as a matter of fact."

"Whatever you have is not legal," he said crisply.

"We honestly believe that it is." Gina stepped forward, smiling ruefully and trying the polite approach. Gina was petite, with a wealth of lustrous brown hair, and green eyes that surveyed the world with intelligence and an easy courtesy. Her forte was public relations. "This," she continued politely, "is Antoinette Fraser. Toni. I'm Gina Browne. Honestly, sir, we've gone through all the right steps and paid a handsome sum for the right to be here. We're registered and have a license as tour guides. I can't begin to imagine why you've suddenly burst in here tonight. The people in the village, including the constable, know that we're here. If there was a problem, why are you appearing only now?"

"I have been traveling. The constable

didn't throw you out because he hadn't had a chance to talk to me, and find out if, for some reason, I had decided to rent the place. I just arrived back in the village this evening, and learned that my home was being turned into the Pete Rose Circus!"

"Oh! Really!" Gina sucked in air.

Toni looked at her, smiling grimly. Gina looked stricken, and certainly she felt the depth of the insult herself. "I quite enjoy the Pete Rose Circus," she said. Arms crossed over her chest, she turned back to the stranger. "Look, we're truly baffled by your sudden appearance, especially since we didn't know that you existed and because we do have legal forms. Perhaps people here keep their own counsel, but surely someone might have mentioned you to us! And . . . we walked right in here, without even having to acquire keys — we found a set on a hook by the door. Perhaps you're out of town too frequently, Mr. MacNiall."

"It's Laird MacNiall," he said, his tone dry. "And I could hardly expect to come home and find —"

"Aha!"

The roar of the word sounded along with a new clatter of hoofbeats, cutting off Laird MacNiall. Ryan Browne had at last arrived, sword drawn, risen in his stirrups. He realized almost immediately that the room was emptied of people and filled with a huge black horse. He reined in swiftly, his eyes following the steps until they fell upon the upper landing, and he stared at the three of them.

"The great laird returns to his castle?" he said weakly. "Where he finds . . . ?"

The black stallion let out a wicked-sounding snicker. Ryan's horse, their handsome roan named Wallace, shied. "Another great laird with a bigger horse! Okay. . . . This great laird is leaving," he said quickly, getting the gelding under control. "But I'll be back," he promised.

He turned and left, the roan clattering its way out of the castle.

"I really will have the lot of you arrested," Bruce MacNiall said. It was more like a growl than a spoken comment. "How dare you burst in here, mocking Scottish history? Americans!"

"Excuse me, I think that we've explained all this. We have a lease, a legal document," Toni said. "And we're not mocking Scottish history, we're here because we love it."

"Listen to me one more time, you addled woman! I own the place, and it has never been for sale or lease!"

It simply couldn't be, yet his irritated aggression was so vehement that Toni found herself suddenly afraid that something could be really wrong. Gina looked stunned, and equally worried.

Toni stepped up to the plate, ready to do battle. "You're wrong," she informed the man claiming to be the living MacNiall. "We have an agreement."

"The hell you do!"

"We should have you arrested, since you're doing your best to destroy the tour," Toni told him, aware that she was taking a slight step back despite her words. "And you've certainly no right to call me an addled woman. We have papers that prove we have leased the place. Now you say that *you* own it! It was filthy and in horrid disrepair. It was obvious that no one had given the least care to this place in years. We've been through here repairing electrical connections, replacing wires, plastering and painting — just to keep the place from falling apart completely. The first day, David and Kevin shored up the front wall. We've worked our asses off to make it livable."

"I told you, I've been out of the country."

"All of your life?" she said sharply. "Because if not, you should be ashamed. This

25

place is incredible. If I had owned it since birth, I'd have never let it come to this!"

"My castle is not your concern," he said icily.

"But it is, because for the next year — at the least — it's *our* castle," she said tightly.

"No, it is not," he said. "I own the place and I did *not* lease it!"

Toni was forced to feel another moment's unease. There was definite conviction in his voice.

"I can see that you've put time and work into the place," he told Gina. "For that, I'm sorry. But the place is not now, nor ever will be, for rent. I would have stopped you, but as I said, I've been out of the country."

"Well, that's just amazing," Toni said, stepping in before Gina could reply. "In this day and age, one would have thought that someone in this little village might have known where you were and called you, or at least said something about you when we were buying the paint and materials!"

"Right!" Gina said.

At that moment Ryan came striding back into the great hall. Being Ryan, however, he paused. "Great horse!" he said, staring at the stallion. "What a beautiful animal."

Bruce MacNiall started back down the stairs. "He's a mix of long and careful breeding."

"Draft horse . . . look at the muscle and the size! And there's Arab in the history somewhere. He's almost got the legs of an American Thoroughbred," Ryan said.

Bruce MacNiall kept walking down, talking to Ryan as easily as if they were friends meeting at a horse show. "Good eye," he commented. "The mare was a cross between an American Thoroughbred and one of our own stallions. He is something. He's got the strength of a Belgian, the grace of an Arab and the dignity of a Thoroughbred."

"Majestic," Ryan agreed.

Toni and Gina stared at one another, then followed MacNiall's path down the stairs. The men were both standing at the stallion's head, admiring the length of his neck and the wide set of his very large eyes.

"Excuse me, but we have a problem here," Toni reminded them.

"Yeah, what's up?" Ryan said. He flashed a smile. "Has Toni's invention come to life? I'm Ryan, by the way. Ryan Browne. Gina's husband."

"Pleasure, but I'm afraid that I've been very much alive and well for quite some time," MacNiall said, staring at Toni. She seemed to be the one capable of really drawing his wrath.

Ryan cast his brown gaze toward Toni worriedly. "Didn't the rental company tell us that the family had died out?"

"They did," Toni said.

"They lied," MacNiall informed them. He stared straight at Toni. "Either that or you're lying." His words didn't seem to include the others, only her. "And you are all trespassing. Which you should know, because it's obvious that you've gotten hold of family history *and* local lore and rumor."

"I did not lie!" she protested indignantly.

"Well then, you 'imagined' an incredible facsimile of the truth," he said.

She shook her head. "I knew that a family named MacNiall had owned the place, but that was it. Bruce is a common enough Scottish name. Since we have been working our butts off here, we didn't really get a chance to question the community on the past!"

"Six-three, pitch-black hair, gray eyes . . . like the devil's own," Gina murmured, staring at the man, then looking at Toni.

"I swear, I made it all up!" Toni said irritably.

"We do have documents," Ryan said.

Toni bit her lip. Ryan's approach might work better than her own.

"All right, look, maybe you have some kind of documents — an agreement, a lease, whatever. The point is —" he paused to stare at Toni "— no matter what you have, I'm afraid that you've been taken in. Unfortunately, it does seem to be something that happens to Americans now and then. They believe in the almighty Internet, and don't really research what they're doing. This is Europe."

He was beyond irritating. Toni looked at Gina. "Imagine that. This is Europe."

"You've been taken, and that's that," MacNiall said flatly to her. "In American? Screwed, Miss Fraser."

Toni stared at the man without blinking, feeling her facial muscles grow tense. "Gina, perhaps you could show the nice man our documents."

"Oh, yes! Of course!" Gina turned and went flying down the hallway.

MacNiall shook his head, looking at her.

"We put so much into this — years of saving!" Ryan said with dismay.

MacNiall wasn't budging. "I'm sorry," he said flatly.

"Everything," Ryan murmured.

"Wait a minute, we have to find out the

truth here. There's no reason we should vacate simply on this man's say-so," Toni stated. "He's claiming that we have no right to be here, but how do we know that he really has a right to be here?" The man had called her a liar. She stared straight at him and smiled sweetly. "There are a lot of penniless gentry running around Europe, as we all know. Maybe *Laird* MacNiall is unaware that government powers have taken control of the property because of nonpayment of taxes or the like?" she suggested.

For a moment, she could well imagine the man strangling her in truth. He did, however, control his temper. His eyes scorned her to the core as he said, "I assure you, that is not the case."

Gina came running back down the hallway, their lease agreement and licenses in hand.

"Look, Mr. MacNiall . . . *Laird* MacNiall."

Papers fluttered. They all started scooping them up, including MacNiall.

MacNiall righted and studied the documents, shaking his head. "I grant you, they look good. And your licenses and permits appear to be in order. You simply haven't any right to this place because you were taken in by fraud. I'm very sorry about that, but —"

30

"Bruce?" A sudden shout came from down the stairs. "Everything all right?"

The new voice came from the entryway. Toni saw that the village law had arrived in the form of Constable Jonathan Tavish. They'd met briefly in town. He was a pleasant man in his early thirties, with sandy hair and a beautiful voice. His R's rolled almost hypnotically when he spoke. Though he hadn't mentioned that there was a living descendant of the once great lairds, he had seemed to view their arrival and their plans with worry and skepticism.

Her heart began to sink, and yet, inside, a voice was insisting, *No! This just can't be!*

"Everything is just fine, Jon," Bruce said, eyes coolly set upon Toni once again. "But perhaps you could assure these *nice* people that I am indeed the owner of the property."

"The Laird MacNiall," Tavish told them solemnly. "Owns the castle, half the village and the good Laird above us all knows just what else."

Toni stared at the man incredulously. Now her heart seemed to thump straight downward into the pit of her stomach. The stunned confusion remained, and once again her temper soared.

Toni suddenly found herself furious with the constable. How could the man have let

31

them all do this without saying a word if there might have been a problem? "Constable Tavish, if this is all true, sir, you might have informed us that there was a living MacNiall who rightfully owned the property and wasn't known to rent it out!" Toni said, trying very hard to keep her voice level.

The constable looked at her, grimacing ruefully. "If I've added to your confusion and distress, lass, I am, indeed, sorry. You never suggested to me that you weren't aware that Laird MacNiall existed. And until I saw Bruce, I couldn't be certain that he hadn't rented the property . . . though I definitely found it a surprise that he might have done so," Tavish said.

A crack of lightning showed them that Tavish had not come alone. Behind him was Eban Douglas, a man who had introduced himself as the jack-of-all-trades for the place. They'd explained that they'd put just about everything they had into the rent on the castle and for the repair materials. He'd seemed very pleased, but then again, he always seemed pleased. He was a small, wizened man with tufts of white hair on his skeletal face. Gina referred to him as Igor, and was convinced that he might have made a fortune in life performing as Riff-Raff for the *Rocky Horror Picture Show.*

He'd actually talked to them a great deal. At times, he'd appeared to help. And never once — in any way, shape or form — had he mentioned that there was a Laird MacNiall who still owned the place.

Despite that — and his rather creepy appearance — he had certainly seemed decent enough. Toni had seen him working about the grounds and had assumed that he was paid by the agency that had rented the castle to them.

A shopkeeper in town had told them that he lived in a little carriage house just beyond the hill in back, a piece of landscape created by the fact that the moat that had surrounded the castle no longer existed.

"You, Eban!" Toni said. "Why didn't *you* tell us about Laird MacNiall?" she demanded.

"Y'didna ask," Eban told her, then grimaced. "I didna know myself — perhap His Lairdship had decided such folks as yerselves might ha been good fer the old place." He shrugged. "After all, y'were doin' a fine job of settin' 'er ta rights, that y'were!"

"Well, thank you for that acknowledgment, at least! I think we've been really good for it," Toni said, feeling her jaw clench.

"Ah, then, back to the buses!"

David, who had apparently been charming the guests in the massive kitchen, came bursting back into the hallway, the large group of tourists behind him.

"Now, now!" David said as his group began to splinter. "The buses are waiting!" But he had lost control, and their guests began to mingle before leaving, stopping by Toni, Gina, Ryan and Bruce. The four of them, including Bruce MacNiall, received glowing compliments for their performances.

"Oh, it was great!" a woman named Milly — from Chicago, if Toni remembered correctly — cooed to Bruce MacNiall. "I mean, it was all just so wonderful. And then you on this magnificent beast here — pure magic! Thank you so very much. I'll never, ever, forget this trip to Scotland. What a dream fulfilled it has been!"

"Thank you, dear," Kevin said, quickly sweeping up behind her to draw her away.

"I loved it!" Milly said.

"Buses are waiting!" Kevin said cheerfully. "Mustn't hold them up!"

"Really!" Milly called to Bruce MacNiall as she was ushered out.

He had the grace to slightly incline his head to her. "I'm delighted that you're enjoying Scotland," he said.

The crowd moved on, passing by the constable and Eban, the tourists chatting and boisterous as they moved out to the courtyard, ready to board their buses.

Thayer, however, was now in the room.

"My cousin! He is a Scotsman!" Toni said. Her words sounded defensive, as though, because Thayer was a Scot, they couldn't possibly be in a mess here.

"A Scotsman, or an American of Scottish descent?" MacNiall queried.

"Glasgow, born and bred," Thayer said, frowning. He stepped forward, offering a hand. "Thayer Fraser, sir. I've overheard just a bit of this. And I'm *really* sorry regarding this and my own confusion. We may well be at your mercy. Toni did the paperwork from the States after finding this rental through the Internet. The agreements went through a rental agency, a corporation. But we had a lawyer — and I saw the ads for the place myself, down in Glasgow."

MacNiall shook his head. Toni once more felt a fierce irritation. Again, the men's club was meeting, and she and Gina were entirely ostracized. MacNiall was decent enough about horses, and give him a fellow Scotsman and he could almost resemble polite.

"There's definitely a problem, I'm afraid."

"Aye, but they been good, Bruce, really good a fixen 'er up!" Eban announced suddenly.

"We really have put a lot of hard work into it," Ryan said.

Apparently the tourists had been loaded back onto their buses. David and Kevin came back into the hall. For a moment, they were all a tableau, at an impasse. David moved up awkwardly. "Laird MacNiall?" he murmured. "David Fulton, and my friend, Kevin Hart. We're only beginning to understand the gist of what went wrong, but, honestly, no group could have put more toil and loving effort into making improvements here. If you'll take some time and look around, you'll see what very real elbow grease has gone into our stay here."

Then, to Toni's amazement, Bruce MacNiall uttered an oath beneath his breath, and made what to him must have been a very generous statement. "All right. It's Friday night. Jon is here with us and can validate who I am, but the legal offices are in town and they won't be open again until Monday morning. Until then, I believe you'll have to stay."

"We'll have to stay because we paid a

great deal of money to be here, and we have legal documentation," Toni said stubbornly.

Gina jabbed her with an elbow to the ribs. She winced, realizing that maybe she was pushing it. But she wasn't going to blindly believe this man, or even the local-yokel constable, when she had brought the agreement to an attorney, and he had read over the deal.

"We do have an attorney!" she murmured.

"Solicitor," Thayer murmured to her softly. "We have *solicitors* here."

"I get the feeling he knows what an attorney is," Toni murmured back softly.

Jonathan Tavish cleared his throat. "Ladies and gentlemen, I'm truly sorry now that I didn't try to stop you. As I said, I didn't know for certain that Bruce hadn't decided to rent out the old ancestral place. But I am afraid that someone knew about the castle — and how much Bruce traveled — and took you for a soaking." He cleared his throat and looked at Bruce with an uncomfortable shrug.

"Should I take those papers now? Not much I can do on this till Monday, though. Law enforcement spends the weekends goin' after the dangerous fellows running around out there, I'm afraid. All the law offices are closed."

"We'll keep the papers until Monday," Toni said. Gina stared at her, but the papers were all that they had. She wasn't letting them out of their own keeping.

"Fine," Tavish said. "When you come in Monday, bring all your papers." He cleared his throat. "If you say that everything is in order for the night, Bruce, I'll be going."

Bruce MacNiall inclined his head toward the constable, as if he weren't just the laird here, but world royalty. "Thanks, Jon," he said. "Come Monday morning, we'll get these papers they're talking about into the hands of the proper authorities. Hopefully they'll be able to track down the frauds who soaked them for their money."

"Hopefully," Jonathan Tavish agreed. He gave a smile that seemed to offer some sympathy to the group. "Don't feel too badly. Won't be the first time Americans have been taken in. And it won't be the last. We'll see what we can do."

"Thank you," Thayer said.

Jonathan Tavish gave them all a nod.

"Good night!" Gina called cheerfully.

"And thank you," Kevin added.

"I'll be movin' along, too, then, lest y'be

38

needin' me," Eban Douglas said, looking at Bruce MacNiall.

"I think I can manage, Eban," MacNiall said.

Eban turned and left. He didn't have a hunched back, nor did he limp, but he somehow gave the appearance of both.

"Do you, uh, stay here when you're in town?" Ryan asked politely.

The answer was a little slow. An ironic smile seemed to twitch MacNiall's lips. "With the ancestral home filled with unbelievers? Indeed."

"Want me to see to the horse? I did some work in the stables. He isn't usually there, is he?" Ryan asked. "I only ask because the stables were in serious disrepair, and this fellow is so obviously well tended."

"He was boarded in my absence."

"How long were you gone? Twenty years?" Toni muttered.

Once again Gina jabbed her fiercely in the ribs.

"I'll take him out, bed him down," Ryan offered.

Toni wanted to knock him in the head for the offer, but she knew that he wasn't being subservient. Ryan simply loved horses. And she had to admit that the animal was magnificent.

"Sure," MacNiall said. "Thanks. His name is Shaunessy."

"Shaunessy?" Toni couldn't quite help herself. "Not Thor, Thunder or King?" Gina's third strike against her rib cage nearly caused her to cry out. She winced. "Shaunessy," she said. "Great name."

Ryan came to lead the horse out. "I'll give you a hand!" Kevin offered quickly, and they departed.

"There's tea!" David said suddenly into the awkward silence. "And scones. Great little scones."

"Wow, tea! I'd love tea!" Gina said. "You'd love tea, too, Toni!" Gina grabbed Toni's hand. "And we'd love for Laird MacNiall to join us so we can explain about how and why we rented the place . . . talk about all the work we've done here, and find out about Laird MacNiall, while we're at it?" She looked at him hopefully.

"Since you've been so kind to let us stay while we get to the bottom of this, would you be willing to join us, Lord MacNiall?" Thayer asked.

"Thanks. I had a long flight in today, a lot of business and a long drive, only to find out that the castle had been . . . inhabited," MacNiall said. "I'll just retire for the night, if you don't mind. Please feel free to enjoy your tea, however. And the hospitality. Until Monday."

"Until Monday?" Toni said, and her reward was a final jab from Gina. This time she protested, staring at Gina. "Ow!"

"Good night!" Gina said, "and thank you."

"Your papers," MacNiall said, handing them back to Gina.

"Thank you," Gina said again. "And thank you for . . . for letting us stay until Monday. Until this is all straightened out. I don't know where we'd go, especially at this hour."

He inclined his head. "I sympathize with your situation," he said. "Good night, then." He took one long last look at Toni and turned away.

Toni opened her mouth, about to speak, but Gina clamped a hand over her mouth, desperately whispering, "Just say, 'Good night, Laird MacNiall!' "

MacNiall looked back, all six feet three inches of him. His eyes now appeared to be more of a true blue, and as sharp as a summer's sky. Something strange ripped through Toni. She was caught, frozen. She felt as if she knew him, knew the way that he looked at her.

Had known him before.

And would know him again.

A tremor ran down her spine. Ice. Fire. *She had invented him!*

He was just a man, she told herself — irritating, superior and angry that they were in his house.

Not true. If his hair were a little longer, his clothing a bit different, just a bit different . . .

"Good night," he said.

The ice and fire, and a feeling of foreboding so intense she trembled, became too much, far too intense. She turned herself and hurried down the stairs. Ran.

Yet a voice whispered to her all the while.

You can't run away. You can't run away.

And something even softer, an afterthought.

Not this time . . .

Interlude

When Cromwell Reigned

From his vantage point, MacNiall could see them, arrayed in all their glittering splendor. The man for whom they fought, the ever self-righteous Cromwell, might preach the simplicity and purity one should seek in life, but when he had his troops arrayed, he saw to it that no matter what their uniform, they appeared in rank, and their weapons shone, as did their shields.

As it always seemed to be with his enemy, they were unaware of how a fight in the Highlands might best be fought. They were coming in their formations. Rank and file. Stop, load, aim, fire. March forward. Stop, load, aim, fire. . . .

Cromwell's troops depended on their superior numbers. And like all leaders before him, Cromwell was ready to sacrifice his fighting man. All in the name of God and the Godliness of their land — or so the great man preached.

MacNiall had his own God, as did the men with whom he fought. For some, it was simply the God that the English did not face. For others, it had to do with pride, for their God ruled the Scottish and Presbyterian church, and had naught to do with an Englishman who would sever the head of his own king.

Others fought because it was their land. Chieftains and clansmen, men who would not be ruled by such a foreigner, men who seldom bowed down to any authority other than their own. Their land was hard and rugged. When the Romans had come, they had built walls to protect their own and to keep out the savages they barely recognized as human. In the many centuries since, the basic heart of the land had changed little. Now, they had another cause — the return of the young Stuart heir and their hatred for their enemy.

And just as they had centuries before, they would fight, using their land as one of their greatest weapons.

MacNiall granted Cromwell one thing — he was a military man. And he was no fool. He had called upon the Irish and the Welsh, who had learned so very well the art of archery. He had called upon men who knew about cannons and the devastating results of gunpowder, shot and ball, when put to the proper use. All these things he knew, and he felt a great superiority in his numbers, in his weapons.

But still, he did not know the Highlands, nor the soul of the Highland men he faced. And today he should have known the tactics the Highlander would use more so than ever. For MacNiall had heard that these troops were being led by a man who had been one of their own, a Scotsman from the base of the savage lands himself.

Grayson Davis — turncoat, one who had railed against Cromwell. Yet one who had been offered great rewards — the lands of those he could best and destroy.

Like Cromwell, Davis was convinced that he had the power, the numbers and the right. So MacNiall counted on the fact that he would underestimate his enemy — the savages from the north, ill equipped, unkempt, many today in woolen rags, painted as their ancestors, the Picts, fighting for their land and their freedom.

Rank and file, marching. Slow and steady, coming ever forward. They reached the stream.

"Now?" whispered MacLeod at his side.

"A minute more," replied MacNiall calmly.

When the enemy was upon the bridge, MacNiall raised a hand. MacLeod passed on the signal.

Their marksman nodded, as quiet, calm and grim as his leaders, and took aim.

His shot was true.

The bridge burst apart in a mighty explosion, sending fire and sparks skyrocketing, pieces of plank and board and man spiraling toward the sky, only to land again in the midst of confusion and terror, bloodshed and death. For they had waited. They had learned patience, and the bridge had been filled.

Lord God, MacNiall thought, almost wearily. By now their enemies should have learned that the death and destruction of human beings, flesh and blood, was terrible.

"Now?" said MacLeod again, shouting this time to be heard over the roar from below.

"Now," MacNiall said calmly.

Another signal was given, and a hail of arrows arched over hill and dale, falling with a fury upon the mass of regrouping humanity below.

"And now!" roared MacNiall, standing in his stirrups, commanding his men.

The men, flanking those few in view, rose from behind the rocks of their blessed Highlands. They let out their fierce battle cries — learned, perhaps, from the berserker Norsemen who had once come upon them — and moved down from rock and cliff, terrible in their insanity, men who had far too

48

often fought with nothing but their bare hands and wits to keep what was theirs, to earn the freedom that was a way of life.

Clansmen. They were born with an ethic; they fought for one another as they fought for themselves. They were a breed apart.

MacNiall was a part of that breed. As such, he must always ride with his men, and face the blades of his enemy first. He must, like his fellows, cry out his rage at this intrusion, and risk life, blood and limb in the hand-to-hand fight.

Riding down the hillside, he charged the enemy from the seat of his mount, hacking at those who slashed into the backs of his foot soldiers, and fending off those who would come upon him en masse. He fought, all but blindly at times, years of bloodshed having given him instincts that warned him when a blade or an ax was at his back. And when he was pulled from his mount, he fought on foot until he regained his saddle and crushed forward again.

In the end, it was a rout. Many of Cromwell's great troops simply ran to the Lowlands, where the people were as varied in their beliefs as they were in their backgrounds. Others did not lay down their arms quickly enough, and were swept beneath the storm of cries and rage of MacNiall's

Highlanders. The stream ran red. Dead men littered the beauty of the landscape.

When it was over, MacNiall received the hails of his men, and rode to the base of the hill where they had collected the remnants of the remaining army. There he was surprised to see that among the captured, his men had taken Grayson Davis — the man who had betrayed them, one of Cromwell's greatest leaders, sworn to break the back of the wild Highland resistance. Grayson Davis, who hailed from the village that bordered MacNiall's own, had seen the fall of the monarchy and traded in his loyalty and ethics for the riches that might be acquired from the deaths of other men.

The man was wounded. Blood had all but completely darkened the glitter of the chest armor he wore. His face was streaked with grimy sweat.

"MacNiall! Call off your dogs!" Davis roared to him.

"He loses his head!" roared Angus, the head of the Moray clan fighting there that day.

"Aye, well, and he should be executed as a traitor, as the lot of us would be," MacNiall said without rancor. They all knew their punishment if they were taken alive. "Still, for now he will be our captive, and we will try him in a court of his peers."

"What court of jesters would that be? You should bargain with Lord Cromwell, use my life and perhaps save our own, for one day you will be slain or caught!" Davis told him furiously. And yet, no matter his brave words, there was fear in his eyes. There must be, for he stood in the midst of such hatred, that the most courageous of men would falter.

"If you're found guilty, we'll but take your head, Davis," MacNiall said. "We find no pleasure in the torture your kind would inflict upon us."

Davis let out a sound of disgust. It was true, on both sides, the things done by man to his fellow man were surely horrendous in the eyes of God — any god.

"There will be a trial. All men must answer to their choices," MacNiall said, and his words were actually sorrowful. "Take him," he told Angus quietly.

Davis wrenched free from the hold of his captors and turned on MacNiall. "The great Laird MacNiall, creating havoc and travesty in the name of a misbegotten king! All hail the man on the battlefield! Yet what man rules in the great MacNiall's bed-chamber? Did you think that you could leave your home to take to the hills, and that the woman you left behind would not consider the fact that one day *you will fall?* Aye, MacNiall, all men must deal with their choices! And yours has made you a cuckold!"

A sickness gripped him, hard, in the pit of his stomach. A blow, like none that could be delivered by a sword or bullet or battle-ax. He started to move his horse forward.

Grayson Davis began to laugh. "Ah, there, the great man! The terror of the Highlands. The Bloody MacNiall! She wasn't a victim of rape, MacNiall. Just of my sword. A different sword."

Grayson Davis's laughter became silent as Angus brought the end of a poleax swinging hard against his head. The man fell flat, not dead — for he would stand trial — but certainly when he woke his head would be splitting.

Angus looked up at MacNiall.

"He's a liar," Angus said. "A bloody liar! Yer wife loves ye, man. No lass is more honored among us. None more lovely. Or loyal."

MacNiall nodded, giving away none of the emotion that tore through him so savagely. For there were but two passions in his life — his love for king and country . . . And for his wife. Lithe, golden, beautiful, sensual, brave, eyes like the sea, the sky, ever direct upon his own, filled with laughter, excitement, gravity and love.

Annalise.

Annalise . . . who had begged him to set down his arms. To rectify his war with Cromwell. Who had warned him that . . . there could be but a very tragic ending to it all.

2

Gina caught up with Toni at the bottom of the stairs.

"What are you doing?" she asked in dismay.

"What am I doing?" Toni echoed. Now that she was away from him; from the way that he looked at her, the trembling had stopped. The strange moment was gone. He was just a man. Tall, wired, muscled, imposing — and irate that they were in what he claimed to be his property.

"Gina!" she said, determined that they would not be groveling idiots, no matter what the situation turned out to be. "Do you hear yourself? You're thanking him for throwing us out on Monday, after all this!"

"Shh!"

Gina pulled her along, anxious that Laird MacNiall not hear any more of her comments. They moved from the great hall, through a vast dining area and then through another door to the kitchen, a large area where a huge hearth with antique accoutrements still occupied most of the north wall.

There were concessions to the present,

however, including the modern stove, freezer, refrigerator and microwave. The huge island counter in the center of the room, set beneath hanging pots and pans, was surely original, and at one time had certainly hosted huge sides of venison, boar and beef. Now cleaned and scrubbed, it was a dining table with a multitude of chairs around it.

The fact that MacNiall hadn't joined them had opened the floodgates of emotion. Thayer, Gina and Kevin all accosted Toni immediately.

"How the hell did this happen?" Kevin demanded.

"We all saw the agreements! And signed them," Toni reminded them. She looked around. These were her friends, her very best friends. Gina and Ryan, whom she'd met three years ago while working at a Florida tourist attraction. And David Fulton! Tall, dark and handsome, with the deepest dimples and warmest smile in both hemispheres, David had been Toni's friend in college. Brokenhearted by the loss of a lover, he'd quickly rallied when he and Toni had gone to a concert with Gina and Ryan, and he had met Kevin — who had immediately fit in.

Toni had been the loner in their group,

but in a strange way that had changed when they had come to Scotland together six months ago. They had visited a castle bought by some of its clan members, who had then opened the house to visitors for whatever money they could bring in, thus affording to restore the place. And their wild scheme had hatched. If others had done it, why couldn't they? It was possible if they pooled their resources.

And that was where Thayer had come into the picture to complete their group of six. Thayer was her cousin, a Fraser. A distant cousin, Toni assumed, since their respective grandfathers had been cousins, which made Thayer . . . exactly what, she wasn't sure. He was certainly intelligent and attractive, but he was something even more important to their enterprise — an authentic Scot. Not only was he fluent in Gaelic, he understood the customs and the nuances of doing business in the small community. He acted as their interpreter — in more ways than one.

Her friends and her kin stared at her, almost accusingly. She stared straight back.

"Think about it! Maybe he doesn't have a right to be here. We just don't really know, do we?"

"Well, not positively," David murmured, but he spoke without conviction.

That MacNiall might be in the wrong, and they were the ones with the right to the place, was a nice hope. Unfortunately, none of them really seemed to believe it. Toni didn't even believe it herself.

"The constable said that MacNiall owned the place," Thayer reminded her wearily.

"So? Constable Tavish is a local. He has loyalties to an old family name. We really don't know the truth. Our lawyer may be American, but he still knows the law. We need to get more serious legal advice, and get it fast."

"Legal advice from the States may not help us now," Kevin reminded her.

"Thayer?" Toni said.

He shrugged, shaking his head. "I saw the ads for the place in Glasgow, and I saw the same thing on the Internet that you did. And yes, I read the rental agreements, just as we all did. Gina, can I see the papers?" he asked.

Gina set them down before him.

"Even *Laird* MacNiall said that they look real or proper or . . . whatever!" Toni murmured.

"Yeah, they look legal," Ryan said bitterly. "Tons of small print."

"We actually rented from Uxbridge Corporation," Thayer murmured. "We're going to have to trace it down. When you sent the euro-check, Toni, was there an exact address?"

She groaned, sinking into one of the chairs.

"What? What is that groan for?" Ryan demanded.

"The address was a post office box in Edinburgh," she admitted.

"Okay!" Kevin said, reaching over to squeeze her hand and give her some support. "That will give the police a trail to follow, at least."

"It will help the police," David said softly, offering Toni a half smile despite his words. "But I'm not real sure what it will do for us."

"Toni, why didn't you want the constable to take the papers tonight?" Gina asked, frowning. "Wouldn't it have been better for him to have gotten started on this as quickly as possible?"

"Those papers are all we have," Toni said. "What if I'm right and this man has lost his family castle yet still has illusions of grandeur in his head? If the constable is his loyal subject, our papers could disappear."

"She has a point," David said.

"She has a point, but this fellow isn't broke. You can't be broke and own a horse like that," Ryan told them.

"Sorry, but it looks like we'll have to suck up to this guy if we want to make it through the weekend," Thayer said.

"Maybe he borrowed the horse," Toni said.

"Oh, honey, come on. You're just getting desperate here," David said softly.

"Well, hell, it is desperate!" Toni said.

"Everything we've saved has gone into this!" Gina breathed, sinking into a chair, as well.

"Maybe we can arrange a new rental agreement," Toni said.

"With what?" Thayer asked. "We put a fortune into this. Unless one of you won a lottery before you left the States . . . ?"

"No. But I still say we have to have some rights!" Toni insisted.

"The sad thing is," Kevin told her, "unfortunately, people who have been screwed don't generally have a right to anything. They're just . . ."

"Screwed," David said.

Toni shook her head, rising. She felt a pounding headache coming on. "I'm going to go to bed. Tomorrow afternoon, I'm calling the lawyer in the States. He can give us some advice, at the very least." She started toward the door, then turned back. "I am sorry, so very sorry. At best, this is really a mess."

"Amazing," Gina said suddenly.

"What?" Toni demanded.

"That he looks just like your MacNiall — the one in your phony family history. I mean . . . it's incredible that you could invent a man who existed down to the last detail."

"No, not to the last detail. The MacNiall I invented died centuries ago," Toni said bitterly.

"Yeah, but apparently, there was one of those, too," Gina said.

"Look, I don't believe it, either!" Toni said.

"Toni," Kevin said softly.

"Yes?"

"We don't blame you just because you were the one who found it on the Internet and got us all going. We all — every one of us — read the agreements."

She hesitated. They were staring at her sorrowfully. And despite the denial, she felt a certain amount of blame. Sure, they'd all wanted to do this, all been excited. But she'd pushed it. She'd been the one to do the actual work. But what had there been to question?

She bit her lip, feeling a little resentful

and a lot guilty. If this really was totally messed up, to herself, at least, she would be the fall guy.

"Thanks," she said.

"Get some rest. We'll all get some rest. When we're not so tired and surprised, we'll be much better at sucking up!" Kevin said cheerfully.

Toni nodded, gave him a weak smile and departed.

In the great hall, she paused. They had been so happy here. This place had truly been a dream. And they had been like kids, so excited.

She hurried up the stairs to the upper landing. There were rooms on the third floor, as well, but the main chambers were here. Servants had once slept above. Her group had chosen rooms in the huge U that braced around the front entry to the main keep of the castle. Hers was to the far right and she had assumed that it had once been the master's chamber. It was large, with both arrow slits and a turret with a balcony that looked out over the countryside. After claiming the room she had discovered that it also had the most modern bath, and that the rug and draperies were the cleanest in the castle. Still, she remembered uneasily that her room also contained the huge wardrobe that had been locked tight — something to explore at a later time.

As she walked to the room, she felt a growing wariness. She hesitated, her hand on the antique knob, then pushed the door open.

There was a naked man in her bedroom. Nearly naked, at any rate.

A fire was beginning to burn nicely in the hearth. The dampness was already receding. A reading light blazed softly near the huge wing-backed chair before the fire.

The chair was occupied. Bruce MacNiall was seated, already showered, his hair wet, smooth and inky-black, his form covered in nothing but a terry towel wrapped around his waist. He was reading, of all things, the *New York Times*.

"Yes?" he said, looking up but not setting the paper aside. "Don't you knock in the States?"

"Not when I'm entering my own room."

"Oh?"

"I've been living in here," she informed him.

"But it's not your own room, is it?" he queried.

"So . . . this was your room," she murmured.

"*Is* mine."

Suck up! They had all warned her. But she was tired — and aggravated.

"If you're the one in the right," she reminded him, regretting her words at once.

"I do assure you that I am," he said solemnly.

"At this particular moment, I don't really have any legal proof that you're telling the truth, so I'm not entirely convinced that it is your room, that you have the right to claim it from me," she said. "You'll note my things at the dressing table. They do look like mine, unless you customarily wear women's perfume, mascara and lipstick."

He stared at her politely, and maybe a bit amazed.

"My wardrobe, you'll notice," he pointed out. "Since you're ever so observant, I'm sure you noted that when you came in and made yourself so thoroughly at home, you had no place to actually hang clothing since the wardrobe was locked."

He had won from the beginning and she knew it. She didn't know why she was still arguing. She loved this room though, and she was settled into it.

Maybe she was just incapable of giving up a fight, or accepting the fact that they could have been taken, that their dreams had been dashed.

"My suitcases," she said, pointing to the side of the bed.

He set the paper aside and rose suddenly. She prayed the towel wouldn't slip.

"Would you like me to help you gather your things?" he asked politely.

There was something about the man that irritated her to such an extent that she couldn't keep her mouth closed — or prevent herself from behaving with sheer stupidity.

"No. I'd be happy to help you relocate, though."

"You really do have . . . what is it the Americans say? Balls," he told her.

She flushed.

"I'm not relocating," he said flatly.

"Unless you have the deed to this place right here and now," she said sweetly, "neither am I."

He stared at her a long moment, and she found herself flushing.

"Do you think I keep my important papers under a mattress or something?" he queried. "My documents are in a bank vault." He shrugged, then took his seat before the fire once again, retrieving his paper. "If you're staying in here, do your best to keep quiet, will you? I have a hell of a headache coming on."

"You *are* the headache!" she murmured beneath her breath.

He had heard her. Once again, his eyes met hers. "I believe that you're supposed to be *sucking up* to me, Miss Fraser. I am trying to be patient and understanding. I've even offered a helping hand."

"Sorry," she said swiftly, though she couldn't help adding a soft, "I think!"

But she had lost and she knew it. Now she just had to accept it. She entered the room, slamming the door behind her. After gathering up what she could hold of her toiletries, she headed back to the hall.

"Next door down is the bride's chamber for this room. It's very nice," he told her absently, studying his paper again.

"I've seen it. I got down on my hands and knees and scrubbed in there — just as I did in here."

"Yes, very nice, actually," he told her. "Good job. As I said before, I can help you move your things."

"Wouldn't want you to have to get dressed," she said.

"I don't have to get dressed, actually. Just go through the bathroom."

"These two rooms share that bath?" she murmured. She felt like an idiot. She knew that. She'd also cleaned the bathroom!

"This is a castle, with some modernization — not the Hilton," he said. "Most of the rooms share a bath. Since you've been living here, surely you know that."

She only knew at that moment that she wished she had chosen a room on the other side of the U.

He rose and grabbed one of her suitcases. "Through here," he said, walking down the little hallway to the bath, and through it.

The next room was one of the nicer ones, not as large as the one she had vacated, but there was a fireplace, naturally — *it was a castle, not the Hilton* — and a wonderful curving draped window. "Widow's walk out there," he pointed out. "You'll love it, I'm sure."

"Naturally, I've seen it," she snapped.

"Right. You cleaned that, too."

"Yes, we did."

"Lovely."

He deposited her suitcase on the floor.

It was fine, it was lovely. But . . . *it attached to his room.* How did she know that the man wasn't . . . *weird?* What if, in the middle of the night, he came through the connecting doorway? No, there were other vacant rooms. She should choose one of them.

He must have read her mind, for a small

smile of grim amusement — and a touch of disdain — suddenly played upon his features. "Rest assured, you can lock your side of the bathroom door."

"I should hope so," she murmured.

"Really? Seems I'm the one who should be concerned about locking doors. Have no fear, Miss Fraser. There's really not a great deal for you to worry about. From me, at any rate."

His look assured her that he found her less appealing than a cobra. For some reason, that was disconcerting.

Because the bastard looked good in a towel? she mocked herself. More than that, he had assurance and self-confidence. Sharp, intelligent eyes, well-sculpted, masculine, handsome features. And his other assets were well sculpted, too.

"I'll keep my door locked, too," he assured her.

"You do that," she said sweetly.

He turned and walked back through the connecting bath. The towel, amazingly, remained just as it had been tied.

Toni shut the door in his wake. She leaned against it, wondering how such a brilliant night could have possibly ended in such disaster. And how she had not only invented a historical figure who had actually existed, but one with a seriously formidable, modern-day descendant who was here, in the living — near naked — flesh?

Fear trickled down her spine, but she ignored it. It was very late now, and she was determined to get organized and get some sleep. And that was that.

She looked around, trying to forget the man on the other side of the door and keep herself from being cowed by him in any way. Surveying her surroundings, she decided it was more than just a fine room. Really. It was a *better* room.

She moved away from the door, telling herself that she liked it just fine, that she was going to move right in — even if it did prove to be just for the next few nights.

So determined, she went about arranging her toiletries and unpacking some of her belongings. But despite her resolve to settle in and get some sleep, she was restless and disturbed. First, this really was one total mess. She couldn't believe that they had been taken by some kind of a shyster. But worse, it bothered her that his family history, which she thought she'd made up, had turned out to be true.

Finished with hanging a number of her garments, she gathered up her toothbrush, toothpaste and flannel nightgown and headed for the bathroom. She hesitated at the door, then decided that for whatever length of time she'd still be in the castle, she had to take showers. She gritted her teeth, knocked tentatively and heard nothing. She went in. The shower-tub combination was to her left, and a large vanity with double sinks to her right. The last time anyone had redone the bathroom had been many years ago, but it was still decent with artistic little bird faucets and a commode and bath and shower wall that had surely been state-of-the-art at the time.

The doors to the master's chamber and the bride's room were directly opposite one another. She stared at the door to the other room for several seconds, then walked over to it and tapped on it.

"Yes?"

She opened the door and peeked in. He was still in his towel, deeply engrossed in the paper, and he had a fire going. The entire room seemed much warmer than hers.

A little resentment filled her until she remembered that there was a fireplace in her new room. She could build her own fire.

"I was going to use the shower. I just wanted to make sure that you didn't need it." *And that you don't intend to barge into the bathroom.*

She had a sudden, absurd image of him riding the great black stallion into the tiny bathroom.

He arched an ebony brow. "My apparel would seem to show that I've already bathed," he said.

"Right. Well, I'll unlock the door from this side when I'm done."

"Yes, please do," he said, and looked back at the newspaper.

She couldn't resist. "The *Times*, huh? You apparently like American newspapers better than American people."

"I usually like Americans very much," he said. There was the slightest accent on the second word he spoke.

She closed the connecting door and locked it, swearing beneath her breath. The situation was bad enough. If there had to be a living MacNiall, why couldn't he have been eighty, white haired and kind!

Fighting her irritation, she stripped and stepped into the shower. The hot water didn't last very long; she was probably the last one getting to it that night.

Still swearing beneath her breath, she stepped out, towel-dried quickly and slipped into a flannel gown. In her room, she debated the idea of attempting a fire.

She'd had one herself in the other room, but David and Kevin had built it for her. Despite her Chicago homeland, she'd never built a fire.

Using the long matches from the mantel, she tried lighting the logs in the hearth. But nothing happened. Some kind of kindling was needed. Perhaps a piece of newspaper or something. Looking around the room, she saw nothing to use.

Lightning suddenly flared beyond the gauzy drapes that covered the door to the widow's walk. It was an actual balcony, she thought, not a little turret area, as was found in the master's chambers.

Immediately after, thunder cracked. The wooden door that led outward to the old stone area swung in with a loud bang as the wind blew it open with a vengeance. She hopped up and hurried over to the door. It was a nasty night, not the kind she had imagined here!

She closed the door with an effort and bolted it. Staring through the slender openings of the arrow slits, she saw another flash of lightning. She should count her blessings that they hadn't been thrown out that night.

She gave up on the fire and curled into the canopied bed, then hopped up again. The only light switch for the room was apparently right next to the bathroom.

With it out, she was plunged into a darkness so deep it was unnerving. Shaking her head, she opened the bathroom door, turned the light on, hesitated, then left the door on her side of the room ajar — she would have killed herself trying to get into bed in the pure ink that had filled the room.

Was she being an idiot? No, this fellow truly had no interest in her. Maybe she should be insulted, she thought wryly. At five-nine, with deep blue eyes and light hair that had deepened over the years to a dark blond, she was usually considered to be attractive. But apparently not to the ogre in the next room.

Bruce MacNiall. She *must* have heard the name somewhere.

Lying in the great bed, she shivered as she hadn't shivered in years.

No! It was not some kind of precognition coming back to her. She had stopped all that years ago, closed her mind, because she had willed that it would be so!

Still . . .

She tossed and turned, wishing that there was a television in the room. Or a fire. Watching the flames would have been nice.

Her mind kept racing, denying that this

could be happening when they had tried so hard to do things right. There had to be a mistake. There had to be something to do!

How had she come up with the name Bruce MacNiall?

At last, she drifted to sleep.

Bruce had just lain down when he heard the ear-piercing scream. Instinct brought him bolt-awake, leaping from the bed. A second's disorientation was quickly gone as he heard a second cry of terror.

It was coming from the next room.

He raced through the connecting bathroom to see his uninvited guest sitting up in the bed, pointing in front of her, a look of terror on her face.

"Miss Fraser . . . Toni! What is it?"

He realized only then that she wasn't really awake. Racing to her, he took her by the shoulders and gave her a gentle shake. Her reaction stunned him. She jerked from his hold and leaped with an incredibly lithe and agile motion to her feet and stared down at him.

She was a rather amazing sight, mane of gold hair caught in the pale light, shimmering like a halo around her delicate, refined features. Her eyes were the size of saucers, and in the soft-colored flannel gown, she might have been a misplaced Ophelia.

Something hard inside him wondered just what new act she was up to now. Something else felt a moment's softness. The terror in her eyes seemed real. For the first time she seemed vulnerable.

"Toni," he said firmly, stretching out his arms to catch her around the middle and lift her down. "Toni! Wake up!"

She stared at him blankly.

"Toni!"

With a jolt, she blinked and stared straight at him.

He thought she was going to scream again. Instead, she blinked once more and quickly stepped back, eyeing him up and down. Luckily he had donned a long pair of men's cotton pajama pants.

"I think you were dreaming," he said.

She frowned, flushed and bit her lower lip. "I screamed?"

"Like an alley cat," he informed her. He stepped back himself. In this pale light, in this strange moment, he suddenly realized just how arresting a woman she was. Not just beautiful, but fascinating. Eyes so intensely blue, bone structure so perfect and refined, her mouth so generous. Her features seemed carefully drawn, as if they had been defined by an artist. And despite the vivid color of her hair and her eyes, there was a darkness about them, as well.

"I woke you," she murmured. "My deepest apologies."

"I wasn't actually sleeping, but I am surprised you didn't wake the entire castle. Or maybe you did," he added. He couldn't refrain from a dry smile. "Maybe they're creeping down the hall now, afraid to come in and find out what's happening." He left her and walked to the door, opened it and looked out. Then he shrugged. "Well, castle walls have been known to keep the sounds of the tortured from traveling too far."

She still stood there, tall, elegant, strangely aloof. He found that he was annoyed to be so concerned. She seemed to be the head of this wretched gang that had the gall to "invent" history and entertain others with their perception of the past. "Are you all right?" he asked her.

"I just . . . I'm fine. And I'm truly sorry." Her words were sincere. Her eyes were still too wide. And she seemed to be afraid of something.

Him? No. Something in her nightmare?

Bruce hesitated. Leave! he told himself. He didn't want them here. Lord, with everything else going on . . .

She shivered as she stood there. That was his undoing.

"The wretched room is freezing. Why didn't you build yourself a fire?" he demanded.

"I . . ."

The uncertainty seemed so unlike her. She'd been a tigress, arguing with him before. Impatiently he strode to the fireplace, dug behind the poker stand for kindling, laid it over the logs and struck a match. Hunkered down, he took hold of the poker to press it deeper into the pile of wood. He wondered if that had been a mistake, if she was going to think that he'd turn and take the poker to her.

But she was still standing, just as he had left her. To his sincere dismay, he felt a swift stir of arousal. The flannel should have hung around her like a tent, but it was sheer enough for the light to play with form and shadow. And there was that hair . . . long, lustrous, blond, curling around her shoulders and breasts.

"A drink. You need a drink," he told her. Hell, he needed one.

She lifted a hand suddenly, obviously regaining some of her composure. "Sorry, I don't have any."

"Thankfully you didn't jimmy the wardrobe," he told her. "I'll be right back."

He went back through the bathroom and opened the wardrobe, found the brandy and poured two glasses from the left-hand shelf. Returning to the bride's room, he found that she had taken a seat in one of the old upholstered chairs in front of the fireplace.

He handed her a glass. She accepted it, her blue eyes speculatively on him. "Thanks," she told him.

"They say it will cure what ails you," he told her, lifting his glass. "Cheers."

"Cheers," she returned. A little shiver snaked through her as she took a long swallow. "Thanks," she said again.

He set his glass on the mantel, hunkered down and adjusted the logs again. A nice warmth was emanating from the blaze now.

He stood, collected his glass again and took the chair by her side.

"So . . . do you want to talk about it?"

A twisted smile curled her lips. She looked at him. "Sure. It was you."

"Me! I swear, I never left that room," he protested.

"I know. It was very strange. It was as if I had wakened and . . . there you were. Only, it wasn't really you. It was you — as you might have been — in historical costume. It was very, very real. Absolutely vivid."

"So I was just standing there, in historical costume? Well, I can see where that might be a bit unsettling, but those screams . . . It sounded as if the devil himself had arrived."

She flushed slightly.

"You were in more than costume."

"Oh?"

"Were it a picture, the caption might have read, 'Speak softly and carry a very big and bloody sword,' " she said.

"Ah. So I was about to lop off your head. Sorry, I may be irritated and rude, but I do stop short at head-lopping," he told her, then turned, getting comfortable in the chair. "Don't you think you might have gotten a bit carried away with your historical fiction?"

"I have to admit, I've scared myself a bit," she murmured. "I made up a Bruce MacNiall, only to find out that he exists. Well, in the here and now, that is."

Bruce shook his head, wary now. "You must have known some of the local history."

"No, not really. We hadn't ever been to this area when we decided to attempt this venture," she assured him.

It sounded as if she was telling the truth. And yet . . .

He swirled the brandy in his glass, studying the color. Then he looked at her again. She couldn't be telling the truth.

"There was a Bruce MacNiall who fought with the Cavaliers. He opposed the armies Cromwell led and beat them mercilessly many times. At first, he even survived Cromwell's reign. But he and some other Scottish lairds kept at it, wanting to bring Charles II back from Europe and see him crowned king. He was eventually caught when one of the lairds supposedly on his side turned coat. That man was killed by MacNiall's comrades, but unfortunately MacNiall rode into a trap and was caught himself. He had defied the reigning power, which was Cromwell. You know the penalty for that. He received every barbarity of the day that was reserved for traitors."

She turned to him, blue eyes enormous. Then she closed them and leaned back, looking ashen.

"Hey, sorry. It's history. I didn't get the sense that you had a weak stomach."

She shook her head. "I don't," she said flatly, and he realized that the particular history he was giving her was more disturbing to her than it was to him.

She looked at him. "He didn't murder his wife in a fit of jealousy, did he?"

Bruce shrugged, watching her closely. "No one knows. There was some rumor that she kept company with a certain Cromwellian soldier — whether true or a pure invention, I don't know — and that she disappeared from the castle. It's historical fact that MacNiall was castrated, disemboweled, hanged, beheaded and generally chopped to pieces. But as to his wife, no one knows for certain. She disappeared from history, right when he was caught. He was trapped in the forest. And executed there, after a mock trial. At the time he died, he had a teenage son running with Charles II in France. Very soon after MacNiall's execution, Cromwell died, and the people, very weary of being good, were anxious to ask him back to take the throne. Charles proved to be a very entertaining king, and a truly interesting man. He might have dallied with dozens of mistresses, but he steadfastly refused to consider a divorce from his wife. So after him, his brother became king, and that was another disaster for history to record."

"It's . . . horrible!" Toni said.

He smiled grimly. "From what I hear, you didn't mind fleecing the public with such a horrible story."

"But it wasn't true when I told it!" she protested.

He waved a hand in the air impatiently. "Say you're telling me the truth —"

"Are you accusing me of lying?" she demanded indignantly. The anger was back in her eyes.

"I don't know you, do I?" he asked politely. "But even if you think you're telling the truth, it's quite possible that you heard the story somewhere else. Because you made it up to a tee."

She waved a hand in the air. "The land belonged to the MacNialls. And if there is anyone famous in Scottish history, it's Robert the Bruce. Bruce. A very common name here!"

"Aye, that's true. But you went a step further."

"How?"

He stared at her. She was either the finest actress in the world, or she really didn't know.

"MacNiall's wife," he said slowly, watching her every reaction.

"You just said that history didn't know about her!"

"Aye, that's true enough."

"Then . . . ?"

"Her name," Bruce said softly.

"Lady MacNiall. That would be fairly obvious!" she said disdainfully.

"No, Toni. Her first name. Her given name. Annalise."

3

Could anyone act so well, or even lie with such aplomb?

"What?" Her eyes were saucers, and her color was as close to pure white as he had ever seen on a human being.

"Annalise. Our famous — or infamous — Bruce MacNiall was indeed married to an Annalise."

She shook her head. "I swear to you, I had no idea! It has to be . . . chance. Coincidence. Okay, the most absurd coincidence imaginable, but . . . I honestly have never heard this story before. Stories like it, sure — your ancestor wasn't the only man to meet such a fate."

He wondered if she was trying to convince him or herself.

"Aye, that's true enough," he said. She was an audacious interloper in his home, he reminded himself. And yet . . . At this particular moment, he couldn't add to her distress. She needed some color back. Hell, she could pass out on him at any moment. She could be such a little demon, as self-righteous as Cromwell himself. But right now, she was simply far too vulnerable, and that vulnerability was calling out to whatever noble and protective virtues he might possess.

"Yes, it's true!" she said, desperately clinging to his words. "I've been to Edinburgh. I've seen the tomb built for Montrose, who was a Cavalier and who sided with the king, finally meeting his end in such a manner. And there were others . . . but I had no idea there was really a MacNiall! Or," she added, wincing, "an Annalise. Look!" She sat up straight, finding her backbone again, and stared at him with sudden hostility. "We did not come here to mock your precious history or your family. I am telling you, I did not know about your MacNiall or that he might have even existed!"

"Well, he did," he said flatly, and stared at the flames, anger filling him again. He loved this place. Granted, he hadn't given it much attention lately. Though he'd always intended to do so, there was always something else that needed to be done first. And now, with everything that had been going on . . .

"Don't you understand?" she demanded. "There's never been anything the least disrespectful in what we wanted to do. Every one of us came here and simply fell in love with the country. Unfortunately none of us is independently wealthy. Gina, however, is a marketing genius. She decided that she could take all of our talents and market them. That way, we could acquire a castle, work hard and give some of the magic to the public."

"Stupid idea," he murmured hotly, looking at the fire again.

"It's not a stupid idea!" she protested. "You saw how the people came."

"The locals will never enjoy such a spectacle."

"Maybe not, but the shows aren't intended for the locals. They will help the economy all around, don't you see that? People who come to the castle for the history, the splendor or even the spectacle will spend money in other places. It will be good for local stores, for restaurants . . . for everyone around."

"I don't agree," he said, fighting the rise of his temper again.

"Then you're a fool."

"Oh, really?"

"Indeed, a blind fool!" She turned toward him, no longer ashen, passion in her voice, fire in her eyes. "You saw those people when they left here! They were thrilled. And they loved Scotland. Don't you want people to love your country?"

"Not a mockery of it," he told her.

"I told you, we're not mocking it!" She shook her head, growing aggravated. "Others give tours of the closes and grave-yards in Edinburgh. People are fascinated. We like to think that we've come far from doing horrible things to one another, even under the pretext of law. We're not saying that the Scots were especially brutal, we're explaining that it was just a different time!"

"Voyeurs!" he said roughly, waving a hand in the air. "And that's Edinburgh. A big city. We're talking about a small village here."

"It's hard these days to buy a castle in the middle of town," she said sarcastically.

"Many people don't want to be reminded of mayhem and murder," he said.

She let out a sigh of exasperation. "Don't you ever do anything for fun?" she asked him. "Have you ever seen a movie? A play? Gone to the opera?"

He looked at the fire again. "The point is, this is a small, remote village. It could be a dangerous place for tourists to wander."

"Dangerous!" she said dismissively.

He felt tension welling in him.

"There are forests, crags and bogs. Hillsides. Crannies and cairns. Places where the footing is treacherous at best," he said. "Places that are remote, dark and, aye, believe me, dangerous." His own argument sounded weak even to him.

Maybe he was a fool for being so suspicious, wary . . . when he need not be. But the lasses were gone, were they not?

Gone. Two of them. Found dead. Here.

"What are you talking about?" she demanded.

He had no intention of trying to explain what had happened, or why he was so concerned. Even Jonathan Tavish thought it was a problem for others, for big-city authorities. After all, the women had not disappeared from here. They had just been found here.

"Antoinette *Fraser*," he said suddenly, determined to change the subject. "So . . . your father was Scottish, or Scottish-American?"

"He was half, but born here. His dad married during the war. On his side, my grandmother was French. My mother was Irish."

"Was?"

"I lost her my first year of college."

"I'm sorry."

"Thanks."

"And your father?"

"I lost him, too," she said softly. "A few years ago. His heart gave out. I think that he missed my mother, actually."

"I'm sorry again."

"Thanks." She hesitated, then asked, "If you are the laird, then . . . ?"

"Indeed, my parents went together. An automobile accident in London."

"I'm sorry," she murmured.

"Thank you," he acknowledged. "It was over a decade ago, now."

"You still miss people," she said.

"Indeed, you do." He didn't want the two of them growing morose together, so he brought a small smile to his lips. "Still . . ." he murmured.

"What?"

"You couldn't have bought a castle in Ireland, eh?"

She halfway smiled, but her eyes flashed. He realized that he had been breathing in her scent. She really was a stunning woman. Brilliant as an angel one second, claws extended, blue fire in her eyes the next.

She shouldn't be here.

He looked at his brandy glass again and swirled the liquid. "The truth of the matter is, I didn't rent this castle to anyone. I do own it, and you are trespassing." He added the last very quietly, and swallowed more of his brandy. The warmth was delicious.

She was quiet for a moment, then said, "I'll admit to having the sinking feeling that we were taken by a British scam artist."

"Might have been an American. They are here, you know, in vast numbers."

Ah, yes, that goaded her temper again. Was he doing it on purpose? Enjoying the rise of her breasts, the flash in her eyes? Wondering what it would be like to suddenly strike a bargain for total peace, draw her in front of the fire and find some real truth in those generous, sensual lips?

"If something was pulled off, it was done by someone over here," she said vehemently.

He realized that he was actually enjoying watching her trying to control her temper.

"You've got to understand! We've sunk a fortune into this!" she told him.

"Aye, that I do believe. I've seen the work."

She frowned, staring at him. "How do you know exactly what I made up?" she demanded. "You didn't ride in until . . . well, it was almost as if you'd ridden in on cue!"

"I'd meant to stop it before it started," he told her. "Eban had heard you rehearsing, and though he was pleased with all the work being done, he wasn't pleased to hear the family slandered."

"But you said the story I made up was true!"

"I never said that Bruce MacNiall strangled his wife."

"She did disappear."

"She disappeared from the pages of history."

Lightning suddenly filled the sky again, followed with rocketing speed by thunder that caused the castle to shake. Startled, Toni let out a little scream, jumping to her feet. Seeing him, she flushed, lost her balance in her attempt to regain her seat quickly and toppled over — directly into his lap.

Long elegant fingers fell against his bare chest. The silky soft sweep of her hair caressed him. Warm and very solid, her scent, that of lavender soap and femininity, caused an instant physical reaction in him that he prayed wasn't evident through the sheer fabric of his pajama pants.

"Oh, God! I am so sorry!" she swore, struggling to get up. Trying to brace against his knee, she missed. Her flush deepened to something of a painful crimson, and her apologies came out in a garbled stream.

"It's all right!" he expelled, plucking her

up, setting her on her feet and remaining vertical himself. "It's very late. If you're sure that you're fine . . ."

"Yes, yes, I'm fine," she said, looking toward the window. He had the strange feeling that she was expecting to see someone there. Or that she was afraid that she would.

"You know, I'm not exactly tired, but I can see that you are. Go to sleep. I'll get the newspaper and study the pages here, in this chair. That way, if you have a nightmare about me being in your room, you won't panic, because you'll know that I'm here," he said.

"I'm a big girl. Really," she told him.

"I'd rather read the paper than fall asleep to another scream," he told her.

"It's all right," she said, tossing back a length of hair. "I don't want you to feel that we're any more of a burden than you already do."

"So go to sleep," he said.

"I won't scream again, really."

"I'm going for the paper," he told her.

When he returned, she was still standing there uncertainly. There was a conflict of emotions in the deep blue of her eyes. She obviously wanted to tell him to jump in a lake, but she was doubting her own rights.

90

For her own sake, and that of her friends, she didn't want him as angry again as he had been when he had first arrived.

Yet . . . he sensed a strange touch of fear in her, as though she really didn't want to dream again. That she would prefer a living, flesh-and-blood stranger in her room to being alone in it with her dreams.

"Look, I'm serious!" he said. "Go to bed, get some sleep. I'll be here."

"You're going to sleep in the chair all night?"

"Frankly, there's not a lot of night left. When the dawn breaks, I'll head over to my own bed. If you wake up then, it will be light so you won't panic. It always works that way."

"How do you know?" she demanded suspiciously.

"Because people never panic in the daylight. You know, the light of day. Reason and sanity. They go together."

She stared at him uncertainly, then headed for the canopied bed.

"This isn't fair to you," she said, turning her back to him.

"Go to sleep."

She crawled on top of the bed and pulled the covers around her.

He shook out the paper and took a seat

before the fire. But though he tried to read, he couldn't pay attention.

He glanced over to the bed. So much for her having difficulties sleeping. Her eyes were closed. She was on her side, facing his way. An angel at rest. Ivory features so artistically sculpted. Full, dark lips, parted just slightly. Arms embracing a pillow.

Oh, to be that pillow!

She had to be a shyster, he told himself angrily. No matter how innocent or vulnerable she appeared, she couldn't have just made up his history, not down to the name Annalise. He had to take care around her, despite the fact that she could twist something deep inside of him. Or maybe because of that.

Annalise.

Impatiently he tried to read again, but then he gave up, folded the paper and simply watched her sleep, doing his best to stretch his length out comfortably in the chair.

After a while, he dozed.

Then . . . he awakened with a violent start.

He didn't scream; he made no noise. But his dream had been no less the terrible.

He had seen her . . . facedown, hair flowing in the bubbling water of the little brook in the forest. Facedown . . . as he had found the murdered girl.

He reached for his brandy glass and swallowed the pinch of deep amber remaining within it. He gave himself a fierce shake. Looking to the window, he saw that the dawn was breaking at last. Silently he rose. One more brandy and maybe he could get a few hours of sleep. One more brandy . . . and he might quell the tension that was ripping up his insides.

He walked to the door of the dividing bath and then paused. He returned to the bedside.

She slept, an angel still. That spill of hair . . .

It might have been any hair.

He hardened his jaw and swore softly, decrying his own nonsense. It was fucking dawn. He needed to get some sleep.

Thayer Fraser shivered as he walked along the path, heading down toward the stream, valley and forest. "A nice brisk walk in the lovely morning air!" he said, speaking aloud. "Actually, that would be fucking cold morning air!" he added. His voice sounded strange in the silence of the very early morning as it echoed off the stone walls of the run-down castle. Eerie, even.

At the base of the hill, he turned back. Most folks outside the country didn't know that there were still many such places as this castle — smaller castles, family homesteads, not the great walled almost-cities-within-cities such as the fortified castles at Edinburgh and Stirling. They could be found, and some of them poor, indeed, much smaller than many a manor house. And naturally, in a far sadder state of being.

He stared up at the stone bastion, beautiful against the sky this morning. There was not a drop of rain in sight, not a single cloud. Ah, yes! This was the stuff of postcards, coffee-table books and calendars, the kind of thing American tourists just had to capture in a million and five digital pictures!

So far — though they all claimed to be in the bad times together, just as they were in the good — they were all secretly blaming Toni. For she had been the one to find the property on the Internet. She had been the one to write to the post box. And she had been the one to receive the agreement, bring it to her lawyer and then pass it on to all of them.

So, yes . . . they were blaming Toni. But pretty soon they'd be looking at him.

After all, he was Scottish, born and bred. He'd seen the advertisements in Glasgow, and had told Toni that it looked fitting for their purpose.

"Shite!" he muttered aloud.

He looked to the forest. Hell, he'd actually never known what they called the damned place. They should understand that. Most Americans had never seen their own Grand Canyon. Why should he be supposed to know about every nook and cranny of Scotland?

Hopefully they would continue blaming Toni, his American cousin. His kin. With her wonder and exuberance, she had convinced them that they could do it. He could remember first meeting her, how pleased she had been to meet a Fraser, an actual — if slightly distant — member of her father's family. He'd been bowled over by her. Indeed, he'd found her gorgeous, stimulating, though she'd rather quickly squelched any thoughts of more than a brother-sister relationship between them.

It wasn't as if he didn't have enough blokes for friends in Glasgow, but she and her American group had been a breath of fresh air. In Glasgow, it was too easy to get into the old work by day, live for the pub at night mentality. The Americans had nothing on the Scots when it came to alcoholism and drug addiction. The working class was the working class, and therein lay the pub, the delights of escape, drugs — wine, women and song.

And though Toni might not want a hot roll in the old hay with him, she trusted him. Liked him. Relied on him.

He smiled grimly. Oh, aye! Americans, God bless them, just loved to look back to the old homeland. Give them an accent and they were putty.

He stared at the forest again, a sense of deep unease stirring in him. He never had known the damned name of the place, and that was a fact.

The forest was still as dark as a witch's teat in the glory of dawn. Dense, deep, remote. And he realized that he was just standing there, staring into it. Time had passed, and he hadn't moved. He'd been mesmerized.

It was an effort to draw himself away, to shake the sudden fear that seized him. It was almost as if he had to physically tear himself away from the darkness, as if the trees had reached out, gripped him . . . and held him tight.

"Fooking ass!" he railed against himself as he turned and hurried back to the castle.

Jonathan Tavish sat at his breakfast table,

morosely stirring the sugar in his tea.

His home might be old by some standards — built around 1910 — and it might have a certain thatched roof, quaint charm. But it sure as hell wasn't any castle.

Through the window, he could see the MacNiall holding, just as he had seen it all of his life. A dilapidated pile of stone, he told himself.

But it wasn't. It was the castle, no matter what else. It was Bruce MacNiall's holding, because he was the MacNiall, and in this little neck of the world, that would always mean something, no matter how far the world moved along.

Bruce had been his friend for years.

"Wonder if he knows what I've felt all these years?" Jonathan asked out loud. "You're a decent chap, Laird MacNiall, that y'are! Slainte, my friend. To your health. Always."

He smiled slightly. Aye, he could have told the Americans easily enough that there was a Bruce MacNiall. Then again, why the hell should he have done so? Bruce had never seen it necessary to explain his absences from the village, or suggest that Jonathan keep an eye on things or, heaven forbid, ask his old chum to keep him informed when he was away. And that was often. Bruce spent time in Edinburgh, confiding often enough with Robert, his old friend from the service, delving into matters though he'd been out of it all long enough himself. Of course, with the events of the last year or so . . .

Then there were his "interests" in the States. Kept an apartment there, he did. Well, money made money, and that was a fact.

Hell, who had known when he would return this time. It was all legitimate that he hadn't said a word to the new folk about there being a real Bruce. And those folk had, amusingly enough, done real work at the place. Bruce sure hadn't kept up the place. In fact, there were times when it seemed that he hated the castle and the great forest surrounding it, even the village itself.

That, of course, had to do with Maggie. . . .

"Well, old boy," he said aloud softly, "at least you had her once. She loved you, she did. She was my friend, but she loved you."

Maggie had been gone a very long time. There was no sense thinking about those days anymore.

Impatiently Jonathan stood, bringing along his tea as he walked to the window.

There it was, the castle on the hill. Bruce's castle. Bruce was the MacNiall. The bloody MacNiall. *Laird* MacNiall.

"To you, you bloody bastard! These are not the old days, my friend. I am not a subject, a serf, a servant. I'm the law here, the bloody law."

He stared at the castle and the forest, the sun shining on the former, a shadow of green darkness enveloping the latter.

"The bloody law!"

A crooked grin split his lips.

"Y'may be the MacNiall, the bloody great MacNiall, but I am the law. I have that power. And when it's necessary for the law to come down, well . . . friend or nae, I will be that power!"

4

"What are we going to do about *tonight?*" Gina asked Toni.

They were alone in the kitchen. Gina had been the first up. Ever the consummate businesswoman, she had apparently been worrying about the tour they had planned for Saturday night since waking up. In fact, she might not even have slept.

Toni was still feeling fairly haggard herself. When she woke, she had found the chair empty and the dividing doors shut. She'd tapped lightly at the bathroom door, but there had been no answer. She had entered, locked the other side, gotten ready and unlocked it. She hadn't heard a sound and assumed that he was at last sleeping. The night seemed a blur to her now.

Even the absolute terror that had awakened her seemed to have faded. And yet . . . something lingered. A very deep unease.

"Toni, what on earth are we going to do?" Gina repeated.

"Maybe he'll just let us have our group in," she said.

Gina folded her hands in front of her on

the kitchen table, looking at Toni. "We could have had our butts out on the street last night. You have to quit aggravating the guy."

"Wait just a minute! I was actually in the right last night. How did we know — until the constable came — that he really was who he said he was."

"You have to quit being so hostile to him," Gina insisted.

"I talked to him again last night. And I wasn't hostile," Toni told Gina.

Gina instantly froze. "You . . . talked to him again?" She sounded wary and very worried.

"I told you, I wasn't hostile!"

David, looking admirably suave in a silk robe, walked into the kitchen. "Did I hear that Toni was talking to our host again?" He, too, sounded very worried.

"Hey, you guys! This isn't fair. When he came bursting in like Thor on a cloud of thunder, I assumed we were perfectly in the right," Toni said, exasperated. "And we were. We did everything right."

"Well," David said, opening the refrigerator, "for being right, we're looking awfully wrong. We have tourists coming in tonight. What are we going to do?"

"What else? I'm going to get on the phone

and cancel," Gina said. She laid her head on the table and groaned. "Where am I going to get the money for refunds?"

David smoothed back his freshly washed dark hair and shut the refrigerator. "Wow, we sure have made this home. Do you think it's still all right if I delve into the refrigerator?"

"Yes, I'm sure," Toni said. "It is our food in there. There wasn't a thing in the place when we arrived, except for a few tea bags!"

"Hey, I know. I'm going to whip up a really good breakfast. Think Laird MacNiall will like that? You know, Toni, you're going to have to be careful when making things up from now on. This guy turned out to be real, and you have his ancestor being a murderer! From now on, invent characters that are noble and good."

"Hey, Othello was noble, and he killed his wife," Toni said.

"That breakfast doesn't sound like a bad idea," Gina said.

"We should make Toni cook," David said.

"No!" Kevin protested, standing in the kitchen doorway. "We'll definitely get kicked out if we do that." He grinned, taking the sting out of his words, and surveyed the kitchen. "Imagine this place if we had a few more funds! I'd love to see baker's rows of copper pots and pans and utensils."

"It's not our place anymore," Gina reminded him.

"Soft yellow paint would bring in the sunlight," David mused.

"How the hell can you be so cheerful this morning?" Gina asked him.

"I'm eternally and annoyingly cheerful, you all know that," Kevin said. "Things will work out. Hey, whoever made the coffee did a full pot, right?" he asked, moving to the counter.

David closed the refrigerator door and leaned against it, looking at Kevin. "Think that Scottish lairds like eggs Benedict?"

"Shouldn't we do something with salmon?" Kevin countered.

"Good point," David agreed.

"I'm glad you two can worry about breakfast," Gina murmured. "What are we going to do?"

"We're going to sit down like the good friends we are and figure a way out of this," David said flatly. "Where's your husband, Gina?"

She shook her head. "He wasn't in the room. He's out somewhere . . . walking, playing in the stables, Lord knows."

Thayer came walking into the kitchen, bearing the newspaper from Stirling, the nearest major city. He set it on the table, offering them all a grimace. "Good morning, we can at least hope."

"Maybe, but only if we start over with the coffee. Gina, did you make this?" Kevin asked, tasting the brew. "What did you use, local mud?"

"It's strong, that's all," Gina protested.

"So, what do we do?" Thayer asked.

"We'll wait for Ryan and then figure out what we can do. Of course, we have until Monday before we need to worry about where we'll sleep!" Gina sighed. "I should call the travel agency in Stirling and start canceling the arrangements for tonight."

"Sixty people at twenty-five a pop — pounds sterling," Thayer said woefully. "My place in Glasgow is small, but if we buy a few pillows we'll be fine."

"We all quit our jobs," Kevin reminded him.

"And we can get new ones," David said.

"There has to be some recourse here," Toni said.

"Toni has been talking to Laird MacNiall again," Gina warned, trying to keep emotion from her voice.

"I wasn't fighting with him!" Toni protested.

"Well, you didn't exactly offer him warm and cuddly Southern hospitality," David reminded her.

"I'm not Southern!"

"You could have faked it," Kevin said.

"Actually, you are from the south — the south side of D.C.," David offered.

She glared at him. "Look, I had a conversation with him, and he wasn't miserable at all," Toni said.

David gasped suddenly and walked around to her, looking down into her eyes. He squeezed her shoulders. "You didn't . . . I mean, Toni, we're in trouble here, but you don't have to . . . you don't have to offer *that* kind of hospitality, no matter how dire things are looking!"

"David!" she snapped, feeling a flush rise over her cheeks. "I didn't, and I wouldn't! How the hell long have you known me?"

Gina giggled suddenly. "Hey, I don't know. In the looks department, he's really all right."

"What she really means is," Kevin teased, "if it weren't for Ryan, *she'd* do him in a flash."

Gina leveled a searing gaze at him. "The

105

breakfast better be damned good."

"Look!" Toni said. "I talked to him but I didn't sleep with him. He was in my room, but . . ."

"What?" David demanded, drawing out the chair at her side and looking at her, his dark eyes very serious.

"It seems that I was in his room, so I moved into the next one," she told him. "We had to talk and we were both cordial, okay?" she said.

"You just talked to him . . . without . . ."

"Being bitchy?" Kevin asked bluntly.

"Dammit! I was polite."

"Okay, okay!" David said.

That was it. She was offering no further explanations of how she might have gotten into a *cordial* conversation with the laird. "And now I'm thinking that if we ask really politely, maybe he'd let us do tonight's performance so that we can recoup some of our losses."

"She's got a good idea there," Thayer said.

"Omelettes!" Kevin said suddenly. "Salmon and bacon on the side. So who gets to ask Laird MacNiall if we can do the tour tonight?"

"Toni," David said, suddenly determined. "She has to ask him. She's the one who's talked to him."

"Toni? Oh, I don't know about that," Thayer protested. He looked across the table as she glared at him. "Sorry! But you seem to have a hair-trigger temper with the guy. It's kind of like sending in a tigress to ask largesse of a lion!"

Toni groaned. "I don't have a hair-trigger temper. Ever. He was very aggravating last night, and I thought that I was defending us."

"You were," David assured her.

"All right," Gina said. "Toni, you ask him."

"Ask him what?"

They all jolted around. Bruce MacNiall was standing in the kitchen doorway with Ryan. This morning, he was in jeans and a denim shirt. Apparently, he hadn't been sleeping. His ebony hair was slightly windblown and damp.

"I've got to get dressed," David said. "Excuse me."

"I might have left the water running," Thayer murmured. "I'll be right back."

"Got to plan the menu!" Kevin said, hurrying for the door. "Mr. MacNiall . . . Laird MacNiall, we're going to cook a great . . . uh . . . brunch. In thanks for your hospitality, whether intended or not."

Ryan, staring at all of them as if they'd

lost their senses, came striding in, heading for Gina and Toni. "The countryside! My God, I thought I'd taken a few good rides, but you should see the sweeping hills! There is nothing like seeing this place through Bruce's eyes!" Ryan loved both horses and free spaces. His work the last several years as a medieval knight at the Magician's Court right outside Baltimore had seldom allowed him a chance to spend time with his beloved animals that wasn't part of training in closed-in spaces. He must have been happy.

"Why don't you tell me about it upstairs, sweetheart?" Gina said, rising.

"Why upstairs?" Ryan demanded.

"Toni wants to talk to Laird MacNiall," Gina said. She rose, caught hold of his shirtsleeve and dragged him along with her, smiling awkwardly as she passed Bruce MacNiall.

Toni was left alone at the table. Bruce was aware that his arrival had caused an exodus, and he was evidently somewhat amused. Especially since it had been so very far from subtle.

"They're afraid of me?" he queried.

Toni inhaled. "Well, it seems that we're all realizing that you do actually own this place and that we have been taken."

"Good," he said, striding toward the counter.

Toni winced. "The coffee is a bit . . ."

He'd already poured a cup and sipped it.

"Like mud. It will do for the moment," MacNiall said. He turned and leaned against the counter, looking at her. "What are you supposed to ask me?"

"Well . . ."

"Well?"

He might be in jeans and tailored denim, leaning against a counter with a coffee cup, but she could well imagine him in something like a throne room, taking petitions from his vassals.

She stared at him a minute, determined that she wasn't going to be so intimidated. They weren't living in the feudal ages, after all.

"We had booked a large tour group for to-night. We don't want to have to cancel."

"*What?*" His question was beyond sharp. It was a growl.

Maybe she shouldn't have been quite so blunt. He had slept in a chair in her room last night, but that hadn't made them bosom buddies.

"Look," she said impatiently, wondering what it was about him that goaded her own temper so severely. "You know that we're really in a mess here. And if you take a good look around, you'll have to admit that you owe us."

"I owe you?" The words were polite, but it was quite evident that he found the mere idea totally ludicrous.

So they were right! she thought with a wince. She was quick to become defensive and then offensive with the laird. But she had gone this far with a brash determination. There was little to do other than play it out.

"Yes," she said with conviction. "We've worked on walls, done masonry, fixed electric wiring . . . scrubbed on our hands and knees! Quite frankly, we're more deserving of such a place — at least *we've* put love and spit and polish into it. How you could own such an exquisite piece of history and . . . let it go like this, I can't begin to imagine."

She could see the outrage and incredulity slipping into his eyes. Though he didn't move, every muscle in his body seemed to tense, making his shoulders even broader.

Inwardly she winced. Great, she thought. So much for playing it out!

She was supposed to be talking him into allowing them to operate their tour, not offending and angering him.

"So now you're an expert on maintaining

a Scottish castle," he said.

She stared into her cup. A sudden and vivid recollection of falling into his lap came to mind. Her fingers against his flesh, pressing into his . . . lap. The easy way he rose and simply deposited her down . . .

Last night his behavior had been courteous — and kind. She realized then that she was attracted to him, and somewhat afraid of him, as well. And her hostility toward him had everything to do with her inner defense mechanism.

Ryan suddenly burst back into the kitchen. Toni was certain that he hadn't been far away, that he'd been listening in.

"Toni isn't explaining this very well," Ryan said, turning toward her with a fierce frown. "We really did do a lot, and not just cosmetic work. We did some structural work, as well. Honestly —"

"Yes," Bruce said, staring at Toni.

Her heart quickened.

"Pardon?" Ryan said.

"Miss Fraser wasn't particularly eloquent in her plea, but I do see that you've done a lot of labor here. And I quite understand that you're in a bad position. Your group can come. Apparently you're going to need the money." He poured his coffee down the drain and exited the kitchen.

Ryan stared at Toni in amazement. Then he bounded toward her, drawing her from the chair, grinning like a madman. "Yes! Yes!"

Gina came in behind her husband. They hugged one another, dancing around the kitchen.

In a moment Thayer was back in, and then David and Kevin. They were so pleased, Toni wondered if they realized that they hadn't gained anything but a single night. And though it would keep them from sleeping on Thayer's Glasgow apartment floor for the next week, it would far from recoup their investment.

"We're going to cook up the best breakfast in the world," David said.

"We might want to start by brewing a new pot of coffee," Toni told them, and she couldn't help a grimace toward Gina. "Laird MacNiall just dumped yours down the sink."

"Really!" Gina said.

"So your coffee sucks!" Ryan said cheerfully, kissing her cheek. "You're still as cute as a button."

"Get out of here, the lot of you," Kevin said. "Shoo! We have to cook."

Toni rose to leave, and as she did so, she glanced at the paper Thayer had left on the table when he'd first come in. The headlines blazed at her: Edinburgh Woman Still Missing. Police Fear Foul Play.

"Wait! Not you, Toni," David said.

She looked over at him. "What do you mean, not me? You all insult my cooking!"

"But you're the best washer, chopper and assistant we've ever had," Kevin told her sweetly. "And then there's the table. We should set it really nicely."

"Wait, I get to wash, chop and be chef's grunt?"

David set his arm around her shoulders, flashing her a smile, his dark eyes alive and merry. "Think of it as historical role-playing. Everyone wants to be the queen, but you have to have a few serfs running around."

"Serf you!" she muttered.

"The others will have to clean up," he reminded her.

"All right, there's a deal," Toni agreed. She walked over to the table and picked up the newspaper, sliding it under the counter so that she could go back for it later.

"Laird MacNiall?"

Bruce had been at his desk — where, he had to admit, the lack of dust was a welcome situation — when the tap sounded at his door. Bidding the arrival enter, he looked up to see that David Fulton was at his door.

"Aye, come in," Bruce told him.

Fulton was a striking fellow, dark and lean. His affection for Kevin was evident in his warmth, but he also seemed to carry a deep sense of concern for the rest of his friends, as did they all.

Bruce was surprised to discover he somewhat envied the repartee in the group. The gay couple, the married couple, Toni Fraser — and even her Scots cousin. They were a diverse group, but the closeness between them was admirable. Riding with Ryan that morning, he had gotten most of the scoop on the group, how they had met, and how they had first begun the enterprise as a wild scheme, then determined that they could make it real.

"We're really grateful to you," David said. "Anyway, we like to think that we've prepared a feast fit for a king — or a lord, at the very least. Would you be so good as to join us?"

Bruce set down his pencil, surveyed the fellow and realized his stomach was growling. He inclined his head. "Great. I'll be right down."

He waited for David to leave, then opened his top drawer and set the sheets he'd been working on within it, along with the daily news.

He didn't close the drawer, but studied the headline and the article again, deeply disturbed. The phrase *all leads exhausted* seemed to jump out at him.

Jonathan Tavish was fine enough as a local constable, but he hated giving up any of his local power, and he just didn't have the expertise to deal with the situation that seemed to grow more dire on a daily basis.

Down in Stirling, Glasgow and, now, Edinburgh, they believed that the girls were seized off the streets of the main cities, then killed in other locations and finally — with the first two, at least — left in the forest of Tillingham because it was so lush and dense that discovery could take years.

Bruce's question was this, were there others, sad lives lost and unreported, decaying in the woods, their disappearance unnoted? And now, another.

Stirling, Glasgow and Edinburgh. The killer was striking all over, yet in Scotland, the distances were certainly not major. The first three abductions had taken place in large cities. But if he had found it easy enough to seize women off busy streets, would he grow bolder and seek out quieter locations?

He drummed his fingers on the desk. Thus far, the local populace had not felt the first whiff of panic. But thus far, the girls reported as "missing" had not been what the locals would consider "good" girls. Not that the people here were cold or uncaring; it was quite the opposite. But since the victims had been known to work the streets and to have fallen into the world of drugs, the average man and woman here did not worry.

It was sad, indeed, tragic. Hearts bled. But women who fell into the ways of sin and addiction left themselves open to such tragedy.

But MacNiall didn't feel that way. There was a killer on the loose. And no matter what the state of his victim's lives, he had to be stopped.

And he had the power to stop him? MacNiall mocked himself.

He had come home — as far as Edinburgh, at least — when Robert called and told him that there had been no leads on the case and he was just about at wits' end. Then, just two days after arriving in Edinburgh, Robert had told him of a new missing persons report.

The strange thing was, he'd felt an urge to return even before he'd gotten the phone call. Actually, he'd wanted to ignore the haunting sense that he'd needed to be here. But after speaking to Robert, he'd taken the first flight out of New York.

So here he was. Yet, really, why? There were fine men on the case, and he wasn't an official anymore.

But they needed . . . something. Hell, they needed to realize what they were up against.

Bruce was afraid that all available manpower would not be put on the case until the killer upped his anger or his psychosis, or until the "wrong" victim was killed.

By then, God alone knows what the body count could be.

He pressed his fingers against his temples, remembering the other reason he was actually anxious to have the group gone — his dream. How could he explain having such a strange dream?

Then again, maybe it wasn't so strange. After all, he had found the first body. That vision would never leave his mind.

And now maybe it was natural to meet a woman, find her irritating beyond measure and then sexy as all hell. . . . And then fear for her.

Annoyed with himself, he snapped the drawer shut and rose to join his uninvited guests in the kitchen.

The setting was a wonder to behold. Toni was certain that Bruce MacNiall thought as much, because he paused in the doorway. And for once, he certainly wasn't angry. He gave that slight arch to his brow and curl to his lip that demonstrated amusement, then he wandered in and took the seat left for him at the head of the table.

Everyone was there, seated and looking at him. "I'm sorry. I didn't realize that I'd kept the rest of you waiting," he said pleasantly, taking the napkin that had been arranged into an elegant bird shape from his plate.

"Almost hate to use this," Bruce said, looking around the table.

"Please, they're nothing to fold," Kevin said. "I've worked in a number of restaurants. That's the fate of most theater majors. Actually, though, I'm a set designer."

"So Ryan told me," Bruce said.

"We each have special and unique talents," Gina said.

"I've heard a few," Bruce said.

"That's right, you were out riding with our Ryan," Thayer said, clapping his hand on Ryan's back. "He's our master of horse and arms! There's not an animal out there our boy can't ride."

"Yes, Ryan is quite skilled," Bruce agreed.

David lifted a hand. "Costumes," he said.

"Yes, and he juggles," Kevin said. "He's really a fantastic actor, as well, but we are the technical whizzes."

"And they're both so humble and modest," Toni said sweetly.

"Sorry, modesty never gets us the job," Kevin reminded her.

"Touché," she agreed.

"And you? What were you doing in Glasgow?" Bruce asked Thayer.

"Piano bar," Thayer said ruefully.

"I'm marketing and promotions, and whatever else is needed," Gina said. "The jill-of-all-theatrical trades, but my major was actually on the business side."

"Ah." Bruce stared at Toni then, waiting.

"Writer," Toni said, certain that he thought her one hell of a storyteller all right.

"Now you see," Kevin said. "Her imagination is legendary."

"So it seems," Bruce mused, staring at her.

"Our Toni is far too modest. She wrote a one-woman show on Varina Davis — she was the one and only first lady of the Confederacy — and spent six months performing it for sold-out audiences in Washington, D.C., and then Richmond. She writes, acts, directs, sews and is a regular vixen with a paintbrush. Naturally, we do whatever is needed."

"Like scrubbing floors," David said.

"And cleaning latrines," Thayer added.

"Sewing, wiring, flats, paints . . . we've done it all," Toni told him.

"And what part of the States are you from?" MacNiall asked them, looking around at the group again.

"I'm from Iowa, originally," Gina said. "Toni's from the D.C. area, David's a native New Yorker, Ryan is from Kentucky and Kevin's from Philadelphia."

"We went to college together," Toni murmured.

"NYU," David offered.

"Most of us went to college together. Toni, Ryan, David and I went to college together," Gina corrected softly. "Then, when Ryan got his job with the Magician's Castle, I moved to Baltimore. Toni moved nearer to D.C., but we stayed close. When she wanted to mount her Queen Varina show, I spent time down there to help her, David did her costume and set. We met Kevin about that time, almost two years ago, and then we finally met Thayer and dragged him in on the scheme the last time we were in Scotland."

"And that was . . . ?"

"Just about six months ago, right?" Ryan said, looking for agreement from the others. "We were at a castle owned by the Menzies family. Clan members had bought it, done some renovations and then opened it for tours."

"Ah," MacNiall murmured, still watching them. Toni wondered what he was thinking. He looked at Thayer. "You were in Glasgow and you just got roped in?"

"I had tried to meet Thayer when we were here just before that. We've vacationed in Scotland at least four times since college," Toni informed him. "But every time I was in the country, Thayer had a job somewhere else. When we finally met . . ."

"It was as if you'd known one another all your lives?" Bruce MacNiall suggested dryly.

"Actually, yes," Thayer said.

"I see."

"I wasn't roped into anything," Thayer said, offering Toni a small smile. "Their idea was a good one."

"Aye, it might have been," Bruce MacNiall conceded, surprising Toni. "What I saw was wonderfully dramatic."

"You know, we've got a problem tonight," Ryan said.

Toni realized that he was looking at her. "Yes?"

"I really had trouble going from costume to costume, and then doing the whole horse in the great hall thing last night. Of course, it worked, because —" he stared at Bruce and smiled weakly "— because Bruce showed up, but otherwise you'll have to stall more."

"She can't stall. The timing was great. Suspenseful. We'll lose them if she has to pad what is a perfect speech!" Gina protested.

"You want Bruce MacNiall to ride into the great hall as he did last night?" Bruce asked. "I can do that for you again. Is that it?"

They were staring at him incredulously.

"You would do that?" Gina said.

"Hey, you're here, and I already think I'm insane myself. Why the hell not?" he returned.

"There's a little more to it, as written," Gina said.

"Oh?" Bruce queried.

David grinned. "You're supposed to dismount, walk up the stairs and strangle Toni."

"Ah." Bruce stared at Toni again, a smile teasing at his lips. "I think I can handle that."

"You only pretend to strangle her, you know," Thayer interjected.

"And that might be a lot harder!" Kevin said, winking at Toni.

She wasn't particularly amused. "I don't really see how we can ask *Laird* MacNiall to join in with us. He's already doing us such a tremendous favor," she said very sweetly.

"I don't mind at all," Bruce MacNiall said, rising. "This was a feast, ladies and gentlemen. If you'll excuse me, though, I'd like to get into the village before your evening events."

They watched as he left.

"Well, there you go. The chap isn't really half bad after all," Thayer said. "We'll have to keep an eye on him, though, when he's up there strangling Toni, eh?"

To Toni, his accent seemed to accentuate a real danger for some reason. But the others were laughing, so it was probably just in her mind.

"Ryan, you've just been shoved out of your big moment," David said.

"Hey, that's okay. It's worth it just to watch that horse of his come racing in and stop on a dime," Ryan said. He grinned, glancing across the table. "I will miss getting to strangle Toni, though."

"Ha, ha," she said and rose, stretching. "Well, let's see . . . under the artistic direction of Mr. David Fulton and Mr. Kevin Hart, I did the washing, chopping and table adornment. Ryan, you can rue your lost opportunity to strangle me while you wash the dishes with your lovely wife and Thayer."

"Me? But I got to shovel out major horse shite already today!"

"Hey, horses are your thing, and you're the expert. As for KP, we're all in on it. So! Ta-ta, cheerio and all that! I'm off!" And with a smile, she made her exit.

Bruce entered Jonathan Tavish's office after a brief tap against the doorframe. Jonathan looked up and arched a brow. "Bruce, I thought you'd be guarding the family jewels, what with that houseful in the old estate."

"Hardly an estate, and totally a crumbling castle," Bruce said, taking a seat. "Actually, the more I walk around the place, the more amazed I am. They've taken care of a ton of minor things that I've put off for years."

"It's tough when you're keeping up with too much," Jonathan agreed. He grinned.

"Now, if you were just among the local peasant law-keepers, you'd be here year-round, pluggin' up holes at any given time. So . . . it seems you're not quite as angry as you were when you first learned about your guests?"

Bruce angled his head slightly as he surveyed his friend. They were close in age, had known each other since childhood. They shared a passion for this little neck of the world, though they didn't always agree about how it should be run. Bruce was the local gentry, as it were, and Jonathan was the local law. But because Jonathan was local, and had always been local, he seemed to maintain a chip on his shoulder where Bruce was concerned.

One day, maybe, Jonathan would run for the position of provost. As such, he could implement more of his own ideas. Thus far, though, he seemed to like being constable.

"I've cooled down some, yes," Bruce said. "Since no one threw them out in my absence, I thought another few days couldn't hurt too much."

"Ah," Jonathan teased. "It was the blonde, eh? What a beauty — and what absolute hell on wheels!"

"She does have a way about her," Bruce agreed. "But this isn't the first time I've heard about this happening."

"Your castle being taken over?" Jonathan said, puzzled.

Bruce shook his head. "This sort of thing in general. People going through what they think are private enterprises or legitimate rental agencies and winding up in a similar circumstance. I really want to find out what happened in this situation."

"Like you said, it happens too often."

"Yes, but *this* time it happened to be *my* castle that was taken over."

"Come Monday, you can let those folks see all your records. They can bring their documents down, and we'll get someone on it right away. Unfortunately, sometimes — especially in this age of the Internet — people can clean up their trails." He lifted his hands. "I might have gotten started on it already, but they didn't want to hand over the documents."

"It's all they've got to prove anything."

"Great. They don't trust the law."

"Well," Bruce said, offering a certain sympathy. "They don't trust me, either."

"Ah, there we are! In the same boat, as they say."

"Right. But actually, that's not why I'm here," Bruce said.

"Oh?"

126

Bruce tossed the newspaper on Jonathan's desk.

"Oh, that."

"Aye, oh, that!"

Jonathan shook his head. "Bruce, they're not local girls disappearing."

"But in the last year, two bodies have been found in the forest."

"If you haven't noticed, it's a big forest," Jonathan reminded him.

"Have you had men out searching?" Bruce demanded.

"This girl just disappeared," Jonathan reminded him. "But yes, I've had men out searching."

"Right. The last two girls who disappeared wound up in our forest. We should be looking for this latest lass. I'm willing to bet my bottom dollar that's where she's going to be."

"Careful with that kind of prophecy, Bruce," Jonathan warned, sitting back. "People will begin to think you know more about these disappearances and murders than you should. They do keep occurring when you're actually in residence." He raised a hand instantly. "And that doesn't mean a damned thing. I'm your friend and I know you. I'm just telling you what someone else might think."

"Bloody hell!" Bruce cursed, his tone hard. Jonathan's suggestion was an outrage, and he was both startled and angry.

"Sorry, Bruce, I didn't mean anything by that. It's just that you're getting obsessive. I understand, of course. But you're not what you were, Bruce. Time has gone on. Just because you struck it lucky once in Edinburgh doesn't make you an expert."

Bruce prayed for patience. "I'm not claiming to be an expert. But murdered women being discovered in Tillingham Forest does bother, seriously. And it should bother the hell out of you."

"I know my business, Bruce."

"I'm not suggesting that you don't."

"How can I stop a madman from kidnapping women in other cities? If you haven't noticed, we've miles of dark roads around here, not to mention that whole companies of fightin' men used to use that forest as a refuge! And again, this girl has just been reported as missing. She's an Irish lass, might have just taken the ferry home."

Bruce rose. "If she isn't found in a few days' time, I'll arrange for a party myself to search the forest."

"Bruce, mind that MacNiall temper of yours, please, for the love of God!" Jonathan said. "I told you, we've taken a look in the forest. We'll go back and search with greater effort if she isn't found in the next few days."

"Good." Bruce rose and started for the door.

"Hey!" Jonathan called after him.

"Aye?" Bruce said, pausing.

"Did you close down your haunted castle tour for this evening?" Jonathan asked.

"Actually, no. I'm joining it," Bruce said.

"You're joining it?" Jonathan said, astonished. "You've never acted in your life!"

"Well, that's not really true, is it? We all act every day of our lives, don't we?" Bruce asked him lightly.

"Ach! Go figure!" Jonathan said, shaking his head. "It's the blonde."

"It's the fact that they are in a rather sorry predicament," Bruce said. "And they did do a damn good job repairing a few of the walls. See you on Monday."

He exited the office, leaving the newspaper on Jonathan's desk. He knew what the front page carried — a picture.

She was young, with wide eyes and long, soft brown hair. She had originally hailed from Belfast, Northern Ireland. Apparently, she'd intended to head for London. But she'd never made it that far, discovering drugs and prostitution somewhere along the way instead. She'd gotten as far as Edinburgh, and been officially reported as missing when a haphazard group of "friends" realized that they hadn't seen her in several days.

News could die quickly, unless it was really sensational. The missing persons report on the first girl had run in the local papers and then been forgotten. Until Bruce had discovered her body in the forest while out riding, facedown, decomposed to a macabre degree.

He'd missed the notice about the second disappearance. But there had been no missing the fact of where the body had been found — Tillingham Forest. Eban had found the second victim there, months later.

Prostitutes. Drug addicts. The lost and the lonely. They'd needed help, not strangulation.

He sat in his car for a minute, staring out the windshield. He was parked right in the center of town, where a fountain sat in the middle of a roundabout. Atop the fountain was the proud statue of a Cavalier. There was no plaque stating his name, or the dates of his birth or death, or extolling his deeds. But the locals all knew who the statue portrayed — the original Bruce MacNiall. And tonight, he'd play his ancestor.

A sudden irritation seared through him. "You'd think they'd give you the benefit of the doubt, old boy. But let time go by and now you're a hero — suspected of killing the love of his life!"

There really was no proof that Bruce MacNiall had killed Annalise, but it made for a good story. And just as some historians saw the Stuart champion as a great hero, others saw him as a fool willing to risk the lives of far too many in his own pursuit for glory.

The idea of Bruce MacNiall having killed his wife didn't sit well with him. And still, he had said that he'd play the part. Life sure had it ironies.

"Well, old fellow!" he muttered, "I've never heard it proved that you did any such thing, but it's entertainment these days, eh?"

He threw the car into gear and started toward the castle on its tor.

Entertainment! Was someone killing prostitutes for fun?

He drove by the forest and slowed the car to a crawl. He knew that to find anything within it, they'd have to delve deep into the woods and the streams.

His heart ached for the girl. He knew she

was already there, decaying in the woods. And he had known it as a certainty last night, when he had dreamed about seeing a body floating facedown.

Except . . . in his dream, it had been the body of Toni Fraser.

5

"Hey! What are you doing out here?"

Toni turned to see that David had come out to the stables. She was a little surprised. David liked horses well enough, but usually when they came to him or happened to be where he was. Ryan was the expert rider in their crew.

She had been stroking the gorgeous black nose of Bruce MacNiall's huge Shaunessy. The animal was mammoth and, she was certain, an amazing power when ridden. He was also well mannered and seemed to enjoy affection. Amazingly, he seemed to have nothing against Ryan's gelding — at least, not so far as sharing the same living quarters.

"I was just out exploring," Toni told David, "and thought I'd come down here. I love that fellow Ryan bought — he's a great horse for the money. But this guy —" she indicated Bruce MacNiall's huge black "— he's really something. Of course, I still love our horse best, but . . . he is gorgeous."

"Yes. And imposing, just like his master."

"The great Bruce MacNiall, who happened to ride in *after* we put our blood, sweat and tears into his place!" Toni commented.

David grinned. "That's *Laird* MacNiall to you, so I understand," he teased.

She waved a hand in the air.

"Well, the situation is pretty sad," he murmured. He strode across the stables then, coming to her side. He searched her eyes. "You okay, kid?"

"Well, as okay as any of us," she told him.

David gave Shaunessy a stroke on his velvet forehead. "Don't feel that you are to blame, no matter what happens. We all rushed into this. And if it seems that we're giving you a hard time, it's mainly teasing — or the fact that it's human nature to want to blame someone else!"

She touched David's face, then gave him a hug. They'd met her first year in college, painting sets for a university production of *Aida*. They'd been best friends ever since. She loved him like a brother.

"Okay, so we came here . . . only to find out that we've been duped. But seriously, it's not all that bad. We put a lot of sweat and elbow grease into it, but blood and tears? That's a bit dramatic."

"All right, maybe I am being a bit dramatic. You would have thought that the damned constable would have said something to us, though."

"Apparently he believed that the great laird had rented the place," David said. "MacNiall's been out of town. I guess no one knew where to reach him to find out what was up."

"Don't they use cell phones in this country?" Toni murmured.

"I've gone away without feeling the need to tell anyone where I was going. And I definitely don't give my cell number to everyone," David said.

"Well, whatever, it was convenient," Toni murmured. "However you want to look at it, we've put an awful lot into the place. The sad thing is, I don't think any of us needs to wait till Monday to accept the fact that we've been screwed royally."

"Yeah, but MacNiall's being pretty decent now. Hell, he's not just letting us bring in our tour group tonight, he's going to take part in what's going on."

"Right," Toni murmured.

"So . . . ?" David's dark eyes were questioning.

She grinned, knowing the look that he was giving her very well. "So . . . ?"

"Come on, kid. Come sit on a haystack

and tell Uncle David all about it. Hey, this may be the only time in your life when you're invited to a haystack for purely platonic reasons."

She laughed and allowed him to lead her to a pile of hay, which David pushed around a bit to create a formation that was almost like a prickly love seat. It was actually rather comfortable.

"It's almost like a shrink's office, huh?" David said.

"I wouldn't know," she told him. "I haven't seen a shrink — yet."

"But something is bothering you, and I think it goes beyond being in the middle of financial disaster."

She shook her head. "David, the thing is, I really thought that I made up my story about Bruce MacNiall's ancestor."

He lifted a hand, shaking his head at her. "All right, so you made up something real. Dr. David will work on it. Hmm, let's see. Six months ago, we were here doing an extensive tour. In Edinburgh, we saw that really beautiful marble tomb built in honor of Montrose — monster to some, brilliant hero to others. We knew that the castle we were renting had been a MacNiall holding. And Bruce is a pretty common name. I don't think there's anything unusual about all this falling into place."

"Except that I learned a little more about the man — and his wife — from the current Bruce MacNiall," Toni said.

"He strangled his wife?"

"No — at least, it's not known that he did. She disappeared from history — that's how Bruce described it."

"Hmm," David said as he chewed on hay. "Sadly, my dear, many husbands have done in their wives. And many women have disappeared. Things don't really change, no matter where you go. We've got our problems in the States, big time. There was even an article in the paper about women disappearing around here, too."

"Well, the good thing is, if Lady MacNiall disappeared, she did so centuries ago," Toni said, but she felt uneasy. She had seen the headlines herself.

"There you go."

"The bad thing is, her name was Annalise."

David stared at her, arching a brow high. "No kidding?"

"According to Bruce."

"You know, Toni, maybe you did hear this story somewhere along the way in life and just don't remember," he suggested.

She was silent.

"Hey, it's all right. Really. And apparently this guy doesn't have a Lady MacNiall, so there will be no skeletons in the closet, right. He really is something, though, huh?"

"Yes." Toni was surprised to feel herself coloring a little.

David smiled, finding another blade of hay to gnaw. "There were lots of sparks flying when you two were arguing last night."

"I'm known to send off sparks now and then."

"Usually only when you're defending friends or the downtrodden!" David said with a laugh. Then he looked at her seriously. "You aren't still raving mad about this guy, and we all think that he's right — despite the fact that we don't want to. So . . . something else is bothering you."

It was a simple statement from a man who knew her far too well.

She glanced his way, hesitated, then said, "I had the most awful nightmare last night. And I screamed bloody murder. That's why he and I wound up talking."

"Okay . . ." David said slowly. "Talking to him upset you?"

"No. The nightmare upset me."

"You remember it?"

"Yes, it was terrifying. But the strange thing is that Bruce — or his ancestor — was the nightmare."

David arched a brow so she continued. "He was just . . . there. It was as if I had opened my eyes and seen him, huge, in full battle regalia, standing at the foot of my bed. And he was dressed like a Cavalier. He looked like our Bruce, except that his hair was longer and kilted, he had something like half-armor on, there was a sheath of some kind at his ankle with a knife and he was carrying a sword."

"And standing at the foot of your bed?"

"Yes."

"All right, let's analyze this. Why was he so terrifying?"

She stared at him. "He was at the foot of my bed!"

"And that's all?"

"Well, what if you woke up and found a ghost at the foot of your bed?"

"I'd wake Kevin, and knowing Kevin, he'd be all excited and try to talk to the fellow."

She knew that he was trying to tease her, to make her feel better. But she knew more.

"He was carrying a sword," she said.

"Well, if you dreamed about a Cavalier

who fought many battles, naturally he'd be carrying a sword."

"It was dripping blood."

"Toni, you were a theater major who has written a number of plays. You're imaginative. I'd expect no less from you than a dream in living color with complete attention to detail."

"You don't understand, because I've never even talked to you about this, but . . ." She hesitated, staring at him. She saw nothing in his eyes but the deep concern of a very good friend. "Years ago, as a child, I . . . dreamed things."

"All children dream."

She looked across the stables. "No. I dreamed things that had happened, really bad things. Murders. The police would come to my house and grill me about what I had seen. I could describe people, sometimes. And could generally tell them exactly what had happened."

"Did they ever catch anyone because of these dreams of yours?" David asked, his tone grave.

"I believe so."

"Then, you were doing something good, Toni."

"Maybe," she murmured. "But I couldn't live with it. And my poor parents! How they fought over it. Anyway, there came a point where I really couldn't stand it anymore. I blacked out, or something, and wound up in the hospital."

"And your folks didn't take you to a shrink?" he asked incredulously.

Toni shook her head. "There was a man, a friend of my mom's. He was wonderful. He seemed to understand exactly what I was going through. When the cops got too persistent, he came in, gentle and quiet, and calmed me down. When I woke up in the hospital, he was there. He seemed to know that my little mind was on overload. I told him that I didn't dream, that dreaming was bad."

"And then?"

"We moved. And I made it stop."

"You *made* it stop?" David said.

She nodded. "You don't know what it was like. My parents were torn apart. The dreams were horrendous. David, I could *see* murders — as they happened, after they happened, just before they happened. Then there were those people who found out about it who weren't with the police. They behaved as if I had leprosy. You can't imagine."

"Yes, actually, that part I can," David murmured. He picked up her hand. "Toni,

I don't think you should worry, not just yet, anyway. Seriously, I'm not insisting that everything in the world has a logical explanation, but we're in Scotland, and we did learn about a very similar history to the one you invented. As for seeing an ancient Scotsman in your bedroom in full fighting regalia, well, let me tell you, when the modern-day Bruce MacNiall came riding in during your presentation, that was pretty darned memorable."

"You think I'm being silly?" she asked him.

"I think that you shouldn't worry too much," he told her. He squeezed her hand. "Bruce MacNiall is still what you might want to call a variable. But don't forget that you are surrounded by friends here, friends who love you very much. It's going to be fine. Trust me. Besides, what can you do?"

"Nothing, I guess."

"What happened to the man?"

"What man?"

"The man who came to talk to you. The one who apparently controlled things and made you feel better."

"Oh, Adam."

"Adam . . . ?"

"Harrison," she said.

"Is he still alive?"

"Oh, yes. Well, at least he was two years ago. He came to see my show when I was doing Varina Davis in D.C." She smiled. "He didn't look as if he'd aged a day. He was still and straight and dignified, soft-spoken . . . very nice."

"Seeing him didn't awaken anything?" David asked.

"No, seeing him was lovely. He asked me how I'd been, applauded the play and was just as nice as could be. He even gave me his card again and reminded me to call him if I ever needed him."

"Well, there you go!" David said, as if having someone's card solved everything. "If anything too weird happens, you call the fellow. Hey, he's not an attorney, or maybe an American ambassador, is he?"

She shook her head.

"What does he do? Or is he retired?"

"He owns a company. Harrison Investigations."

"Investigations. There you go. He can investigate the scam artist who got us into this!"

"I don't think it's those kinds of investigations."

"Ah! You mean he's one of those guys who goes into haunted houses with weird cameras and tape recorders and stuff like that?"

She nodded, finding that she had to grin. "Um. I think that's exactly what he does."

"You don't think that a ghost screwed us all via the Internet, do you?"

Toni had to laugh. "No!"

"Well, then, let's wait and see. Hey, want to take a walk? It's gorgeous around here. Gina was saying that she wanted to go barefoot in one of the trickling streams just below our little hillock here."

"I think it's going to rain."

"Then getting our feet wet won't matter," David said.

She rose, turning back to draw him up. "Sure. Let's go."

She started to drag him along, but he pulled her back, giving her a hug again. "Hey, I'm here if you need me. Always."

She stepped back, eyes twinkling, and sighed. "You love me, you're here when I need you and you're absolutely gorgeous. Why on earth couldn't you have been heterosexual?"

"God knows," he said. "But I do love you."

"I love you, too."

"Anyway, let's get the other guys and go for that walk."

"You're on."

When they returned to the castle, they found the others in the hall, ready to head out.

Thayer was standing by the main doors, where a drawbridge — long gone now, as long gone as the moat — had once led to the portico entry. He appeared reflective.

"What's the matter?" Toni asked him.

He shook his head. "I was just thinking — we really were idiots."

"Why do you say that?" Toni asked, suddenly feeling guilty again.

"We didn't question anything. After we signed the agreements, we just accepted the fact that we would get here and get in. And we did, of course, because the door was open. The keys were hanging there, right inside, as soon as we came in! The door locks with a slide bolt, so we've been sliding it at night. Apparently, Laird MacNiall doesn't lock the place up when he's around. What do you think that means?"

"That the castle is a small one, which wasn't on any tour maps or advertised about at all until we got here. And that, in a village such as Tillingham, there's no need to lock your doors," Toni suggested.

Thayer shrugged. "I guess. I'm still feeling like an idiot."

"Ditto," Toni assured him.

"We ready?" Ryan asked, coming to the door.

"Aye," Thayer assured him. "So where are we going?"

"Just down the hill and into the woods a bit. Gina wants to romp in a brook." Ryan looked up. "I think it's going to rain."

"Probably," Thayer agreed cheerfully.

Kevin, coming to join them, said, "We'll probably catch the fricking flu. Do we really have to do this today?"

"If we're out on our arses come Monday, we might not get the opportunity again," Thayer reminded him.

"True," Kevin agreed. "All right, let's go frolic in a bubbling little brook."

Gina came through the door. "It will be fun. Trust me."

So they headed out. It was cool but not cold, which made the walk very pleasant. And the overcast sky was fascinating, painting the landscape around them in beautiful dark shades of green and mauve.

On distant hills, they could see an abundance of sheep. Climbing atop crags were also scattered groupings of the long-haired cattle that Toni had seen more frequently in the far north of the country. Apparently, they were popular in this area, too. Between the cattle, sheep, wildflowers, sloping hills, crags and cairns, the scenery around them was breathtaking.

"This place is really gorgeous," Toni commented.

"It is — and we would have been a real boon for its economy," Ryan said.

"Oh, yeah? There could have been a buildup of fastfood restaurants and Motel 8s all along the way," Thayer said.

"Right! Like Scotland doesn't depend on tourism!" Ryan argued.

"The world goes round on tourism, I guess," Thayer acknowledged.

"We've got a long walk back once it pours!" Kevin shouted down toward Gina, who was ahead of him along the path. She shot him the bird, and he laughed.

At the base of the hill, the canopy of trees began. The color was lighter, there, at the base, and oddly inviting. They followed Gina as she dashed into the woods. A minute later, she shouted out with delight! "There, look, how charming!"

A little curve in a brook jutted out into a dapple of light that made it through the branches overhead. Though the water was a bit dark under the threatening skies, the sound of it rushing over pebbles and stones was light and airy, and the shelter of the neighboring trees made it look like a little piece of heaven. The whole scene was charming.

Gina started hopping along in her haste to remove her socks and shoes, and keep moving at the same time.

Toni found herself staring at the trees. Deeper in, beyond the immediate area of the brook, the forest was dark. The green canopy made it appear like a dark den that beckoned and yet, somehow, warned of evil. Staring into the verdant growth, suddenly she felt herself shiver as an uneasy feeling assailed her.

It was as if the trees were breathing. As if the entire shroud of dark green were a living being, an entity unto itself, something that crouched and waited, watching. . . .

"Toni, what are you waiting for? It's great, sumptuous, wonderful, cool . . ." Gina said, her enthusiasm high.

Shaking off her unease, Toni rolled up her jeans and started to travel carefully out into the middle of the rushing water.

"Ouch! Hey, we didn't think about the rocks under bare feet thing when we agreed to do this!" David shouted, following her example.

"Ouch, indeed!" Kevin cried. He hurried past David, but then hit a sharp rock, lost his balance and crashed into Toni.

Outraged and off balance, Toni went down. "Kevin!"

They were both on their butts, soaked in a foot of water. Kevin started to apologize, but then he stared at her and burst out laughing.

"Oh, you think this is funny! Get him, guys."

At Toni's prompting, the rest of them piled on. And in a matter of minutes, the six of them were drenched, bedraggled and laughing hysterically.

At last, gasping for breath, mud from head to toe, Toni struggled to get up — and realized suddenly that they'd all fallen silent.

She tried to smooth back her muddy hair, and blink away the water and muck that was blinding her. Then she saw. Once again, the great laird of the manor had returned.

Bruce MacNiall was there, bareback on his great black, Shaunessy. He was watching them as if they were, indeed, part of a theater of the absurd. And there was the oddest expression on his face. Tension, anger? Toni wasn't sure. He looked like a thundercloud himself.

She thought that, for a moment, he stared beyond them, deeper into the forest, from . . . *from the place where the eyes seemed to watch, from where the sense of breathing and evil seemed to emanate.*

His eyes fell upon the group again.

With . . . relief? Toni wondered.

And when he spoke, his tone was pleasant enough.

"Having a good time?" he called pleasantly.

"Yeah!" Ryan said. He truly looked like an overgrown child. "It's great — wonderful. The water feels terrific."

"A little cold," Gina said. She sounded nervous, as if they had been caught doing something they shouldn't have.

"We're having a wonderful time," Toni said, staring at Bruce. Surely, once in a while, he let down that stern guard and simply had fun. "Really, you just need to have a bit of a sense of humor to be down here."

"Great," MacNiall called to them from the height of his stallion's back. He smiled. "Glad you're having a good time. You might want to watch out for the leeches, though."

They were dead still, like a tableau.

Then Kevin shrieked *"Leeches?"*

Toni didn't think that she had ever moved so quickly. The same might be said for the others as they scrambled over one another to get out of the stream as quickly as possible. She knocked into Kevin. Ryan tripped over his own wife. Toni reached down to Gina, and in his haste to do the same, Ryan knocked Toni back down. Thayer caught hold of Toni, David helped both Ryan and Gina, and Kevin was on his own. Finally, after a scene straight from the Three Stooges, the six of them made it out of the water and to the shore. And there they began to hop up and down, checking what parts of one another they could actually see.

Gina, screaming, banged at her thigh. "There's one on me! Get it! Get it!"

They ran around behind her, staring her up and down.

"There's nothing there," Toni said.

"There is!"

"No, honestly, there's nothing there. Look, let's just get back to the castle — and the showers!" Toni said. She, too, was feeling things all over.

Twenty minutes later, after a fierce pounding of hot water, Toni was sure that she had none of the little buggers on her. Wrapped in her terry robe, she emerged into her room, ready to find clean, warm clothing.

What she found instead was Bruce

MacNiall, in her room, getting the fire going. Hunched down by the hearth, he coaxed kindling and logs to flame. In the light, his hair was sleek, blue-black in its darkness. As he moved, she was aware of the breadth of his shoulders and, oddly, a sense of the power within them. It was almost as if he, too, like his long-dead ancestor, had hefted the great weight of a sword or battle-ax to gain such a strength.

She swallowed, feeling a strange quickening. It was one thing to acknowledge that he was an imposing, exceptionally attractive man. It was quite another to feel . . . such a strange affinity with him. She needed him out of the room — now.

"Hmm," she murmured, crossing her arms over her chest, leaning against the wall and forcing a pleasant tone to her voice. "Interesting. I could have sworn that I had to vacate the room on the other side of the bath since that one was *yours*." At the end, her tone had risen. She couldn't help it; she was unnerved by his appearance. It might be his castle, and he might have fallen asleep in her chair, but still . . . he had no right to be in here.

"Sorry," he said coolly, rising. "I certainly didn't mean to be intrusive. I had hoped to get this going and be out before you were finished." There seemed to be a slight smile on his face. She immediately felt even more defensive. "I thought you might want some warmth. It's chilly out there, and the rain has begun. Interesting day for a lark in the water."

"Sorry. The concept of wading through the rushing water was a bit too much for us to resist."

"*Wading* through the rushing water? That was more like a mass, a Holy-Roller baptism!"

"Yes, yes, I know. We got a bit carried away," she said. "We're silly Americans, being fools playing in the brook or the brae or whatever the hell it is. You'll have to forgive us. We were just having fun. I have heard that the Scots are just a bit dour, so you probably wouldn't understand."

"Seeing as how I lack a sense of humor, you mean," he murmured.

"Well, we're very close friends. And maybe such a thing wouldn't exactly be *your* cup of tea, but I would hope that you could appreciate a little silliness. Call it an American sense of humor."

Dark lashes swept over his eyes and his grin deepened as he gave the fire a last prod. Then he rose and headed for the door to the hall. But as he passed her, he paused.

"Yes, of course, an American sense of humor. Surely I can appreciate that. And I hope that you can appreciate a Scottish sense of humor."

"What do you mean by that?" she demanded, very aware of the size and scope of the man, and the smile that lent a certain charm to his face.

"Well, there are no leeches in that brook," he said lightly, and exited the room before she could reply.

6

Toni stood next to Gina on the upper landing while David played his role as the kitchen maid below. They grinned at one another as they heard the laughter.

"This was such a good idea," Gina murmured.

"Right. If only we really had a lease option on the castle," Toni replied.

"Under the circumstances, Bruce has been really above and beyond," Gina said.

"Oh?"

"This afternoon I showed him our papers again. He inspected them closely, then said that they certainly looked as if they were in order. He was very sympathetic. He even called his insurance company. Though he's willing to help us, he didn't particularly want to get sued."

"I thought we had insurance," Toni said.

"We did. It covered us and damage, but apparently I didn't read the fine print well enough. We also need a special clause to cover anyone who might get hurt. And we really should have more signs and warnings out. Anyway, he's taking care of it."

"All that, for just tonight?" Toni murmured.

"I'm getting the feeling that he might let us go on a while," Gina said. "Long enough to make some money, anyway."

"I guess we'll see," Toni murmured.

"David is about to introduce you," Gina murmured. "He was a bit strange about this afternoon, though, don't you think. I mean, about our foray into the brook."

"There are no leeches," Toni murmured back.

"Oh, he told us that," Gina said. "But I don't think it was actually the idea of us in the brook that disturbed him so much. It was the fact that we were in the forest. At lunch he was adamant about us staying out of the forest."

Toni felt a little shiver snake through her. She could remember how the forest had made her feel. As if it were alive. As if there were eyes. Watching.

"You're up!" Gina said.

Toni walked out to the landing in the white gown and began to talk about the great Bruce MacNiall, passionate in his defense of king and country. "There were those who called him a hero, and those who called him a monster. Be that as it may, he never wavered in his loyalty, or in his pas-

156

sion. In the end, the great Bruce, like Shakespeare's Othello, would find his undoing in his passion and in his heart. For years, he bested Cromwell's forces. For years, as he rode the countryside and fought, he loved his wife, Annalise. Yet, while he strayed far from home, rumors reached him of her infidelity. He returned, her betrayal like a blade that dug into his heart greater than the wounds inflicted by any real sword."

That night, there was no mighty bolt of lightning, no massive crack of thunder. Yet, Bruce MacNiall arrived on the great black in a stunning burst of speed and noise and perfection. He was not dressed as he had been the night before, but rather in period breeches, with a leather chest guard, his family colors apparent in the great length of tartan swept around his shoulders and pinned there with a silver brooch. A typical Scots knife was in a sheaf at his calf. His sword belt was buckled to his hip and swung with pure theatricality as he dismounted from Shaunessy.

The sight of him caused that strange quickening sensation in her again. He indeed appeared fierce.

Tonight — maybe because he'd had that talk about insurance with Gina — Ryan was there to take the great black the minute the man dismounted.

There was a roar of pleasure and then applause from the crowd as he came to the floor and looked up the stairs.

Toni still had no idea what he actually did for a living, but he could have been an actor. He ignored the crowd so completely, all those people might not have existed at all. When his eyes fell upon her, her own breath caught. And when he started up the stairs, more imposing than ever in his historical attire, she found herself taking a step back.

"Annalise!"

There was a hiss at the end of the word that sent shivers down her spine.

"Even upon the field of battle, word of your treachery comes to me!" he bellowed.

The crowd was dead silent as he took the steps slowly and fluidly.

She tried to remind herself that she was acting. "Nae, you're wrong, you're deceived!" she cried out. And as he neared her, she continued, the argument in her voice certainly sounding very real. "Would you doubt me so easily, m'laird? All these long days, weeks, months! I do naught but wait . . . for your return."

"Lies fall prettily from your lips!" he informed her, moving closer.

"Never! I do not lie! I swear it!"

"Annalise . . . !"

Again, the hiss at the end of the name. And then, he was there.

"Wife! Beloved wife!" he said, reaching out for her, crushing her into his arms. His fingers trailed into the length of her hair. "Wife!" he cried out again.

His face was buried against her throat. And when he whispered, "How am I doing?" he caught her completely off guard. She realized her own terrible tension, and the way that the bulwark of his chest felt against her own. There was something so incredibly electric and vital about him. She had become a victim of her own fantasy, caught up in the strength of his hold, the rich scent of his aftershave and the whisper of his breath against her neck.

"Uh . . . great!" she managed to whisper back.

"Beloved, betrayer!" he exclaimed then in a sudden fury, shoving her from him.

"Nae!" she shrieked, feeling a real unease for a moment.

Then his hands were around her throat, his fingers so long that he could wind them around her neck without putting the least pressure on her.

"Sweet Jesu, how could you betray me so?" His cry was full of passion and pathos.

Everyone below was dead silent, feeling the laird's pain and yet horrified at what he was about to do.

He shook her.

Toni grasped his hands, pleading, gasping. "Nae, nae, I have done naught but love you, naught but . . . love you."

He supported her as she slowly sank to her knees before him.

In another piece of perfect theater, he held her still.

His face came closer to hers.

"Annalise . . ."

His lips touched hers, just briefly.

"Before God! I cannot bear it!"

Again he pretended to shake her as his fingers tightened around her neck. Toni was stunned by the entire show herself. She managed to die in a pile of white silk at his feet. And then there was silence from below again. Real silence.

Bruce MacNiall knew how to work a crowd. He rose to his full height, gripped the banister and looked down at the silent people gaping up at him.

"Can't really throw her down the stairway, folks, she might get hurt!"

There was a burst of laughter and then the

thunder of applause. The tourists were thrilled.

David, Kevin and Thayer, down among them, were still gaping. Then David came to his senses.

"Tea and scones, ladies and gentlemen. If you'll follow me to the laird's ancient kitchen, we'll have a bit of a repast!"

Still on the floor, Toni knew she should be delighted that they were doing so very well — even if their host had stolen the show.

As the crowd filed out, she heard them exclaiming about what a great experience it had been, how real, how it was almost as if they could touch the past.

"Are you getting up, Toni?"

He was hovering over her, a hand extended. She accepted it, coming to her feet.

Gina came running out from the hallway, practically crashing into Bruce. "You were incredible! Magnificent. My lord, just phenomenal!"

"Thank you." He inclined his head, accepting the compliment.

"We didn't even rehearse anything," she continued with awe.

"Well, walking up the stairs and pretending to strangle someone is really not so hard," Bruce said with a shrug.

"But you came up with lines! Hey, my own heart was beating, and I know the story. Well, Toni's story . . . anyway, it was just amazing."

"Toni?" Bruce inquired politely. "Was everything all right with you?"

She didn't get to answer.

David, apparently having escaped tea-and-scone duty, came running up the stairs. Excitedly taking hold of Toni, he gave her a hug, then told Bruce, "Wow! You had me shaking in my boots down there. I almost ran up here to tell you that you couldn't really do it! What a fabulous laird you make!"

"He is a laird," Toni reminded him. Meeting Bruce's eyes, gray as slate, unfathomable, she added, "And I don't think the concept of strangling any of us is a big stretch." She offered him a rueful smile, thinking her words a joke. Yet, for a moment, as he stared back at her, she felt anger emitting from him.

"The concept of strangling anyone should not come easy to any man," he said. "Well, madam manager," he said, addressing Gina, "did last evening help?"

"Oh, certainly . . . Of course, we'd need to work this a long time to begin to recoup our investment, but you have saved us —

162

really!" Gina told him. "I know that you're a busy man, and that we certainly can't count on you every night, but is there a possibility that . . ." She paused, unsure of her words, then plunged right in. "I'm rambling here. Actually, what I'm doing is begging. Bruce, would you consider giving us a little run? We had nothing booked tomorrow or Monday, but our people in Stirling and Edinburgh were taking reservations for the rest of the week."

Bruce was dead still. Then he sighed.

"I would love to accommodate you, really, I would."

"Then do!" Gina pleaded prettily.

Bruce shook his head. "There's a situation going on here," he said. "I really think it would be safer if you all weren't here."

"What situation?" Ryan asked, joining them.

"There's a serial killer in Scotland, or so they believe," Bruce said.

Gina shook her head. "Yes, I read in the paper that a couple of girls had disappeared, and that their bodies had been discovered later in the woods. But I'm not sure I understand what that has to do with us and our performances."

"I agree with Gina," Toni said, looking at Bruce. "This is very serious, of course, but it's not as if we're a hotel and it's our guests who are becoming victims."

Bruce's slate eyes fixed on her.

"I think there's a bit of this story you're all missing," Bruce said.

"And what's that?" Gina asked.

"There's another girl missing right now," he said.

"But she wasn't from here, right?" Toni said. "I've seen the newspapers. He's attacking prostitutes, right?"

Bruce sighed. "You aren't understanding my point. There's a serial murderer at work. He's been taking his time, and he's been careful enough that, once the victims have been found, the police have gotten almost nothing from clues left on the remains to help them capture the man. And yes, he's been attacking prostitutes, but there's no guarantee this man won't change his choice of victim. Besides, even if you two young ladies are not in personal danger, don't you think it's rather in bad taste to stage this event when women have so recently been murdered?" he demanded.

"Were they strangled?" Ryan asked.

Bruce shook his head impatiently. "They don't know. The bodies were in such a severe state of decomposition when they were found that the medical examiners couldn't pin down the cause of death."

They stood awkwardly on the stairway. Voices began to rise from below.

"You and your friend could have been minstrels, you were adorable," a young woman was telling Kevin as he led the group back through the great hall to exit the main doors.

"Aw, shucks!" Kevin said. "Thanks!"

David turned to hurry down the stairs and help.

"We've got to go bid them all goodnight," Gina murmured. "Even if it is our last performance, we should play it out properly." She linked arms with Toni and they started down, followed by the others.

A tall, elderly fellow walked up to Toni. He spoke with an English accent, from somewhere far to the south. "Young lady, we were laughing away, enjoying it tremendously. But when you died! My poor heart just broke."

"Well, thank you."

A younger man stepped up. "Pete and me were about to race up the stairs and save you!" he told her, indicating his friend.

Pete, a blond fellow about the same age, grinned. "Yeah, but the concept of an encounter with the Bruce kind of quelled the idea," he said, causing a rise of laughter among the entire group now traipsing out.

"How could you, man?" the first fellow said, looking over Toni's head.

She was startled when Bruce set an arm around her. "Ah, well, the lass was not doing as she ought, and I'm afraid that back then . . . well, that particular Bruce was known to be loyal to a fault, good to those who supported him, lethal to those who betrayed him."

"Is the story real?" Pete asked.

"Laird Bruce MacNiall was real," Bruce assured him. "As to the disposal of his wife, no one knows. She simply fell from the pages of history, so anything about her is just local lore. Poor Bruce did meet a sad end. Since his Annalise perished tonight, we didn't include the part about him castrated, hanged until half-dead, disemboweled and beheaded."

"Ugh!" someone said from the crowd.

"Luckily, that was several hundred years ago," Bruce said.

"Luckily!" the older man said. "Honey, I couldn't strangle you, no matter what you did!"

"Thank you," Toni told him.

"I think poor Annalise was innocent. I mean, why cheat on a fellow like that?" a young woman said with awe, smiling at

Bruce. A little too wistfully, Toni thought, surprised by her own annoyance. "So . . . does the great Laird MacNiall sweep up his wife and carry her off to the master's chambers?"

A quick no came to Toni's throat. But as she'd noted earlier, Bruce knew how to play to a crowd.

"Of course," he said simply. And turning, he swept Toni off her feet as effortlessly as if she were a rag doll and started for the stairs.

Gripping his shoulders, Toni quickly queried in a whisper, "What are you doing?" Her words were a little desperate.

His eyes were lighter, amused, as they met hers. "Trying to get them all out of here. Say good-night, my love."

He turned at that, clearing his throat loudly. "A little privacy in the castle, please!"

His words were followed by laughter — and an exit.

On the landing, Bruce set Toni down perfunctorily and turned, immediately retracing his steps. Their guests were out the doors. Kevin remained in the hall.

"There's still food in the kitchen?" Bruce asked.

"Yes, certainly. And we can whip up anything you want, really quickly," Kevin assured him.

"Great, I'm starving. Get the group together when the buses are gone. We'll discuss the morning, and where we go from here."

Toni bit back her sense of extreme aggravation and followed him down the stairs to the kitchen. The "great laird" was apparently not in the mood for something as simple as scones, and quite capable of taking care of himself. He headed straight for the refrigerator, grabbing all kinds of sandwich makings, while the others jumped around to wash lettuce and slice tomatoes. The circumstances were very bad, Toni admitted, but she hated the fact that they were so obliged to Bruce MacNiall.

"So, Bruce, what do you think?" Gina asked anxiously.

"I think that you went through a lot of work, and that it looks like your papers — license, permits — are in order. And now the insurance has been dealt with. . . ." He shrugged.

"If you have to leave again, I swear, we will be so good to this place!" Ryan said. "And you won't have to stable Shaunessy anywhere else. You know that I'd just about lie down and die for that horse."

"So?" Gina persisted.

Toni was surprised when Bruce stared at her. He seemed reflective and worried.

"We began a conversation on the stairs. Women have been killed." He directed his gaze upon Thayer. "You must have known about it."

Thayer made a choking sound. "Well, yes, but . . ." He lifted his hands. "Sadly, these things happen often enough. People don't stop living because of it. We've had much worse situations, every country has. I never saw it as something that really concerned our efforts here."

Bruce shook his head, looking downward for a minute.

Gina said, "Bruce, people in the village don't seem to be concerned . . . for their own safety, I mean."

"No, I guess they don't," he murmured.

Ryan cleared his throat. "Terrible things have happened in almost every major city, and naturally, they can happen in the countryside, as well. Please . . . we'd never let ourselves be victimized." He winced, realizing that they *had* been victimized. "Gina and Toni are too smart to set themselves up for a dangerous situation. We're always together."

"The women have disappeared from the *big* cities," Thayer reminded quietly.

Bruce looked hard at Thayer. "So they have."

"Please! We're adults, and we're less naive than before," Toni added. "We'll be careful. Please, give us a chance?"

They were all staring at the man. Again he shrugged. "Let me say a tentative yes, we can give it a go. For the next few weeks, at least. There are problems that will arise. Aye, there's the fact that your 'guests' are usually from far away, and I don't know how the local population is going to take to this. The story Toni invented is too damned close to truth. There are those who think that I have an ancestor out there, running around in the forest, possibly capable of doing ill will. There are the other, very real problems — the situation at present. But we'll see. First thing Monday, we will go to the courthouse. I'll prove my ownership, and we'll get Jonathan going on finding out just who is behind the scam that took you people in."

"We would gratefully appreciate it!" Gina said.

He shrugged. "I do admit, you've done a lot for the place."

"Thank you," Thayer said, looking at him curiously. "I don't mean to be rude, but . . . but when we got here, the place didn't look very . . . lived in," he murmured.

Bruce looked at Thayer. "You are from Glasgow, right?"

"Aye, that I am."

"As the crow flies, not so far," Bruce said.

"Not so far, yet Glasgow is a world unto itself. Edinburgh, too, as a matter of fact. It may be a wee country, Laird MacNiall, but we both know that it's still very regional."

Bruce nodded. "Regional, aye. I'm just surprised that you didn't know that there was a real Bruce MacNiall."

Thayer grinned ruefully. "Maybe I owe you an apology then. But, I'm sorry to admit, I've never been to more than half my country. I made it to the Orkney Islands last year for the first time, though I've never been to the Isle of Skye."

"I see," Bruce murmured.

"Hey, I've never been to California," Kevin said.

"And I've never been to — Utah," David offered.

"Who can cover a whole country?" Ryan asked cheerfully.

"Ah," Bruce murmured. "It's just that news regarding the killings certainly reached the major newspapers. Murder may be something that happens everywhere, but in Scotland, such crimes do bear note."

Thayer appeared a bit tense, as if he'd been accused of lying.

"I knew about the murders. Everyone has seen something about them in the paper," Thayer said, looking confused.

"But you didn't notice any specific references?"

"I don't know what you're talking about," Thayer said.

"References to the area?" Toni asked.

Bruce ignored her. "Thayer?"

"I swear, if there was mention regarding this place in the newspapers or on the telly, I didn't see it," Thayer said. "I live and work in Glasgow, and as you must know, with our size and certain factors, we do have our own crime rate."

"I'm aware of the city. I've actually been there," Bruce said.

Toni was oddly uncomfortable, feeling, as Thayer apparently did, that he was somehow under attack. "In the old U.S.A., most farm boys have been to the big city. Doesn't mean all the city folk have made it out to the farm," she said lightly.

Bruce's eyes shot to hers. "I see. So we're yokels out here, are we, Toni?"

"It's small, that's all I'm saying," she told him with exasperation.

"Perhaps we should talk about this in the

morning," Gina said softly. "Tempers seem to be rising a bit."

"My temper isn't rising," Toni said, staring at Bruce. "It's just that Thayer is my cousin, and I understand completely how he might not have heard of the great and almighty Bruce MacNiall."

"Toni!" David warned.

"No, really! Bruce, please, listen to me. I'm grateful that you're being magnanimous. But if we're going to make this work, you need to trust us."

After a moment Bruce turned to Thayer. "I'm not accusing you of anything, Fraser. I'm just curious, that's all. Naturally," he said, addressing Gina, "we will have to have some kind of contract written up, but we can work that out at another time." He set his sandwich on a plate and turned to leave. They watched him in silence. At the kitchen door, he turned back. "One last thing. Stay out of the forest. That's a must." He stared at Toni. For a moment, it seemed that he was speaking only to her.

She felt almost as if they were touching. Her heart hammered, her breathing quickened. Kinetic energy seared between them, and she wanted to reach out and shake the man.

After he left, they remained in stunned silence for a minute, and Toni felt something deflate in her.

"I don't know about this," she said. "Every time I start to think he might be decent, he turns back into an ass."

"Toni, it's just you!" David said.

"He was on to Thayer!" Toni said.

"Hey, kinswoman," Thayer said lightly, "it's all right. This is Scotland. I can see where he was coming from. Aye, he got m'dander up! But it's all right. There was no revolution here, you know. There's still royalty, nobility, peerage, the whole bit. They tend to think they should be known, though, as you've seen, old piles of stone like this one tend to be all about. The bloke probably can't quite admit that this isn't exactly Stirling or Edinburgh castle!" Thayer shrugged. "We're at the base of the Highlands, you know. The Lowlanders and the Highlanders have always been a bit off. I'm fine with it all. Hey, I am a Scotsman. I should have seen to it that I knew more about the place, eh?" He walked to Toni, smiling ruefully, and gave her a kiss on the cheek. "My fierce little American! I'm all right on my own, honestly."

She nodded, liking him very much then.

Thayer's small dimples showed and his green eyes were light. With his fingers he shoved back a lock of sandy hair and said again, "Toni, I'm all right, honestly."

"Well, there you have it!" David announced. "It's late."

"Yes, if the lot of you will just get out of the kitchen, David and I will whip it all clean in a matter of minutes," Kevin said. "We can make more sense of things in the morning."

"No, we'll stay and help," Toni murmured.

"No, you will not!" David protested. "You'll make it take longer."

"You'll start breaking dishes," Ryan said.

"I will not!" Toni protested.

David came by her side, hugging her. "Toni, you're in bitch mode," he said softly.

"I am not!" she protested vehemently. Then she looked around, they were all staring at her. "I am not," she said stubbornly, but far more softly.

"It's him," Thayer said.

"You're right, it's him," she agreed, thinking, that naturally, Thayer was on her side. Then she realized that he hadn't meant the words quite the way that she had taken them, because the others were suddenly grinning.

"You noted it, too?" Ryan said to Thayer.

"The sparks that are always flying?"

Kevin suggested.

"Chemistry in the air," David said.

"Oh, no!" Toni protested.

"I'd do him in a flash," Kevin said, "if I weren't taken."

"And if he weren't reeking heterosexuality," David said pragmatically.

"Trust me —" Toni began.

"Oh, Toni! Quit being so blind!" Gina advised. "Every time the two of you talk, I'm waiting for one of you to lunge at the other and grapple on the floor!"

"I give up," Toni said, very aggravated and tense.

"You are free, white and female," David reminded her.

"Hey, might be good for her," Ryan commented. "Look how calm and sweet Gina always is! And she can thank me for that!"

"Okay, I've had it — I'm out of here!" Toni said.

To her complete irritation, they all laughed as she departed.

Upstairs, she showered and was just crawling in for the night when she heard a tapping on her connecting door. She thought about calling out, but didn't. Instead, she rose, walked across the room and opened the door.

Bruce was there, in his bathrobe, his hair

slick and black, slate eyes enigmatic. "If you're not all right, just call out," he told her quietly.

"If I'm not all right?" she murmured.

"If dreams plague you. Nightmares," he said.

She met his eyes. There was concern in them, and she was amazed at the sudden sense of *knowing* him that leaped into her heart. *Wanting him,* she thought.

He touched her face, his thumb moving gently over her cheek, rounding down around her chin. "You know," he mused softly, "it is just a matter of time."

"Excuse me?" Her words were breathless. She should have just moved away to begin with. His touch was somehow extremely intimate. She felt as if her flesh was crying out to be touched by him. All of it. The length of him beckoned — his hands, the size of him, cast of his features, texture of his skin, even the slate of his eyes.

"A matter of time," he repeated.

"Until . . . ?" she managed with a smile.

"Well, until you jump me, of course."

"Until I jump you?" she demanded, some sense of indignity coming to the fore. "Laird MacNiall, I'm afraid that you do have a rather inflated opinion of yourself!"

He was still amused. He leaned closer to

her and said softly, "I won't be stopping you, you know, lass."

Then he turned and quietly closed the door between them.

Toni kicked it.

"Call if you need me," he said.

She made a point of locking the door.

But later that night, the dream came again. She was sound asleep, or so she thought. Then she opened her eyes, and he was there. At the foot of her bed. In full war regalia, with his sword, at his side. Dripping blood.

And she began to scream.

The first scream cut through Bruce's subconscious like a razor. He bolted up, seeking the danger for a millisecond, then he burst from his bed and hurtled through the bath.

She had the door locked.

He hesitated for a moment, listening. Then, once again, he heard her scream. Swearing, he hurried back in his room and dug in the cuff-link drawer of the wardrobe for the skeleton key. Seconds later, he had the door open.

She was sitting up in bed, staring, her blond hair streaming out over the lilac print of her flannel gown. Her eyes were open, dead-set on something in front of her, something that he couldn't see but which was so very real to her.

Another scream ripped from her.

There was something achingly vulnerable, young and fragile about her at that moment. The fine construction of her features seemed more delicate, the wheaten beauty of her hair more sheer. She looked for all the world like an otherworld Ophelia.

And, like the mad Ophelia, if he didn't move, she would not be reprieved.

He started for the bed, then halted, because suddenly she was moving, no longer simply staring and screaming, but shrinking back. As if something — someone — were after her.

He flew across the room, calling her name.

"Toni, Toni!"

Falling upon the bed, he caught her by the shoulders. She was stiff and cold, as if she were nearly dead herself. She didn't acknowledge him, but neither did she look through him. She looked around him.

"Toni!" He gave her a shake, drawing her to him, determined to transfer some of his own warmth into her form. "Toni, wake up, it's a dream, a nightmare." He stroked her head, his fingers cradling the shape of her skull. "Toni!"

At last, he felt her resistance. She pulled away from him, her eyes wide and confused in the night. She said his name, but with a strange hesitance and uncertainty.

"Bruce?"

"Aye, it's me."

She still looked so wide-eyed, not so much terrified as . . . confused.

"In the flesh," he added, trying to speak lightly. He was very nearly in little but the flesh, and was glad he'd gone to sleep in boxers.

"Bruce?"

One of her hands fell against his chest. The fingers were still chilled, but the brush against him seemed to evoke a flash of fire. He caught that hand, held it between his own, rubbed it, tried to warm it.

"Aye, kid, you're having something of a poor time getting sleep in here, eh?" he asked her.

She flushed, then looked at him sheepishly again. "It's rather ironic, really. I make up a fellow, only to find out that he existed, and now he keeps appearing at the foot of my bed, with his sword dripping blood." She hesitated. "Do you think he's trying to warn me to get the hell out of your castle?"

180

They faced one another on the bed then, not touching, but very close. He couldn't help the small smile that came to his lips. "Nae," he said softly, purposely allowing the Scots burr into his voice. "Nae, fer 'tis said that Bruce were a man what loved a damselle, and wouldna hae it that one should suffer at his door."

He was glad of his speech, for she smiled, as well, and it seemed that the terror and confusion had at last lost their grip upon her. "How did Lady MacNiall feel about that? If she was running around with some local fellow, it might have been out of revenge for all the lasses he kept giving, er, sanctuary? At his castle?"

"They were different days," he told her lightly.

"Oh?"

"Well, there were a few instances in Scottish history that certainly wouldn't be the least politically correct these days. Take Robert the Bruce. His poor wife was captured by the English and held prisoner for years, just for being his wife. He loved her dearly — honestly, he did — but there were a number of children born in those days that bore the king's protection. So . . . while she was locked up for being his wife, he was still prey to manly temptation."

"So Bruce MacNiall cheated like crazy, then killed his poor wife?" Toni said, wrinkling her nose.

"You made that part up. No one knows what happened to his wife," Bruce reminded her.

"I made the whole thing up!" she reminded him with a soft groan.

He pulled her against him again, stroking her hair. "It's a castle, you invented a bloody warrior, he happens to have existed."

She leaned against him, apparently content to be there. Her hair was a velvet tease against the nakedness of his chest, the scent of her a strange and riveting intoxication in the night. She could speak with such determination, quell with a look, move with grace and dignity . . . by day. But at night, she was like a brush of pure silk, sweet smelling, lustrous, supple and . . . vulnerable. Tonight she was vulnerable.

"It's more than that," she whispered.

"What more could it be?" he asked gently.

She shook her head. He threaded his fingers into her hair, gently tugging back, anxious to see her eyes. Huge, bluer than the midnight sea, they met his. Little triggers of electricity seemed to tease both his muscles and his flesh. Something akin to pure agony clamped down upon his groin. He gritted his teeth, determined not to let her see the rise of pure carnal instinct and natural humanity.

"I . . . you don't understand. I'm afraid. Never mind . . ." she murmured.

"What is it? You can tell me, honestly," he assured her.

"Ah . . . so that you could mock an American further?"

"Americans are lovely people," he told her, smiling.

"Most, anyway, right?"

"Toni, if there's something wrong, you can tell me. I swear, I will not bring it beyond the walls of this room," he vowed levelly.

She shivered suddenly, then moved, as if pretending that she had not done so. She set her hands upon his shoulders. "You know, you're rather a lovely man yourself — but only in the dead of night."

"Ach, I'm really lovely as hell by day, as well. You're just not noticing," he informed her.

Another shiver, almost imperceptible, ran down her spine. She moved closer, resting her head against his shoulder and throat. "I have noticed," she informed him. Then she looked up. "You know that question you asked earlier?" she whispered.

Ah, and that whisper brushed his cheek, and soft and light as it was, it beckoned to an even greater desire inside, one that shrieked and cried out, in bone and sinew and blood.

"About jumping me?" he inquired.

"Yes, I would be referring to that one."

The flannel of her nightgown suddenly seemed to hug her breasts with pure temptation, concealing, too clearly giving away structure, firmness, rise. . . .

Her voice was meant to be casual, almost haphazard, but it was tremulous.

He caught hold of her chin.

"I won't sleep with you because you're frightened," he told her.

"I wouldn't dream of sleeping with any man for that reason!" she told him.

"It's all right. I won't sleep with you, but I won't leave you," he told her, stretching out on the bed, drawing her against his shoulder. "If my ancestor comes anywhere near, you can always try arguing him to death. You've come quite close with me, you know."

She thumped on his chest with a finger.

"I am not that bad. And I am not a bitch."

"Ah . . . so, your friends even know you want to jump me," he said.

She started to push away from him in a

sudden, indignant fury.

"Get some sleep!" he told her, drawing her down again, smoothing her hair as she rested her cheek against his face.

It was absurd. He'd known her so very short a time. She hadn't been so much as a figment in his mind just two days ago. And now . . .

He breathed in her scent and felt her softness, the warmth in his arms. *It was almost like forever.* He also felt the insane drumming in his groin. Lord, he wanted her. But . . . not because she woke screaming in the night, having seen *his* ancestor at the foot of her bed.

"Sleep," he murmured again.

Later, when she breathed easily against him, her every breath adding torture against his awakened flesh, it was himself he mocked.

"You are an ass!" he whispered aloud.

When daylight came, he left her once again.

Interlude

The bodies had been taken to a mass funeral pyre. It hadn't been out of a sense of brutality; they were sorry that many a good soldier with a different loyalty could not be returned to his family, could not receive honors and a proper burial. But they knew that, with so much death, flies and maggots would come in droves and the blood would taint the water and the earth. Sickness would soon follow.

The air was ripe. There was nothing so horrible as the smell of burning flesh, but there simply was no choice.

MacNiall's own men were seeing to their wounded, their own dead and their dying.

But victory had been achieved, and even among the wounded, aye, and the dying, there was a sense of justice and purpose. They had prevailed. Whiskey and beer were flowing freely — the wounded needed it, the victors craved it. Still, in the midst of jubilation, the troops knew discipline, and they celebrated in closeknit ranks.

From somewhere within the many pockets of men came the plaintive notes of a bagpipe. Despite victory, Bruce MacNiall could find no pleasure or solace that night. Secure that his scouts remained on the lookout, that the wounded had been gathered and that the ranks would not break, he went to Angus at last.

"Ye are in charge, man. I'll be gone but a day or two."

Angus shook his head. "Ye canna be runnin' off half-cocked, man. Not on the word of a liar who would see y'be the one hanged!"

"I have to go."

"Nae, y'do not!" Angus protested. "She waits, as she has always waited. She loves ye, man!"

"Aye, and that be so, she is in danger herself. I must see to her welfare. She canna stay at the castle longer. Thus far, they've ignored it. Too far from any place that counts! Fer many years, I've been the enemy, they've not taken their vengeance ta the homes. Now, with the words Grayson Davis has spoken, I canna be sure!"

"Ye canna go! I've a fear deep in me heart. Ye canna do this, Bruce."

"I must do this. As I must breathe," he said simply.

He set his arms around Angus, giving him a fierce hug. "Y're in charge, man. They'd be no other ta know the heart and soul of the men. Keep them safe, keep yerself from harm, Angus!"

He had led his great black warhorse to the copse to speak with Angus, his right-hand man, his fiercest warrior, his dearest friend. He stepped away then and mounted, swinging easily upon the giant stallion. Then he looked down at Angus.

"Ye canna do this!" Angus begged again.

"I can, and I must," Bruce said. "I wish to God that I dinna feel so urgent a need!"

Before he could swing the stallion around, Ian MacAllistair came hurrying through to the copse.

"Laird MacNiall!"

The fellow appeared stricken.

"Aye, man, what?"

"Three of the prisoners . . . have escaped."

"Now how in bluidy hell did that happen?" Angus began in a fury.

"Which men?"

"The Smithson brothers, and Lord Davis. Grayson Davis."

"He was half-dead already!" Angus roared.

"Ah, but half-dead isn't dead," Bruce said.

"How?" Angus roared again, fear in his thunder.

"They were shackled together," MacAllistair said, shaking his head. "MacIver and others watched them, but the fires were burning, the smell, the bluidy smell, and the smoke! When the wind shifted, they were gone, the lot of them!"

Angus turned to Bruce. "See there, man! Ye canna go."

"Nae, Angus, more than ever, I must! God go with ye, lads. Heal the wounded. I'll be back in a few days' time!"

He could wait no longer. From their rocky tor, the castle was a day's ride.

And so he began. Usually he scorned what major roads there were, but this time he rode the night and the darkness bold as brass. By day, he was forced to pause, forced to realize that he would kill his noble mount. And when the light came, once again, he forced himself to care. He was a wanted man, a marked man. A dead man, if his enemies were to see him.

And still, he pushed and pushed. He knew the back ways as no other man could. He could ride them more recklessly, and with his heart ruling his head, he did so.

At first, he prayed to come upon Grayson Davis. There would have been no mercy then.

He thanked God that the man was wounded, and on foot. He could not have reached the castle before him.

Rain hampered him, then cleared. By nightfall, he was nearly home.

Near midnight, the moon rose. It was full and glowing when he reached the last valley and looked up — at the castle.

Beneath the moon, the old stone seemed to glow. There was light, fires that burned to warm those within. All was well, he tried to assure himself. All was well.

The bridge over the moat was up. His men, bless them! They did intend guard against unlikely attack. They kept his vigil for him. By day, all here went about their business, good subjects of the Lord Cromwell's reign. But night, they were ever watchful, protecting their lady, as befitted her, and their absent laird. He had long ago told his tenants that no working man was to suffer for his allegiance to a distant, running king. They obeyed the laws, Cromwell's laws. And Cromwell kept care, ruling with a stern but judicial hand, ever wary that the Scots were a fierce lot, ready to rise and turn at any moment. Aye, they'd been beaten, those who honored the king. But they could rise again in mass, and that the governing powers did not want.

In the moonlight, he breathed a sigh. Pray God, it was all right. And pray God that Davis was a liar.

He spurred his horse. Shouting, he rode the distance to the castle, rising them upon the hill to the moat. The lookouts were at their station, and recognized their laird. With a great cranking sound, the bridge was lowered. He thundered over it. A groom came forward to take his horse; men gathered around. He assured them of his welfare and told them of the victory. Then he begged away, for he would see his lady. The men understood.

He burst through the front doors and stood in his great hall.

"Annalise! Annalise!" he shouted.

She was there already, standing at the top of the stairs, having heard the drawbridge, he was certain, and . . . hoping.

She had come running from the master chamber in a gown of white. It flowed about her in elegant swirls. Her delicate features were pale — had she been frightened that it was someone else? Her fingers, long and delicate, were at her throat. Blond hair like the sun at its highest point cascaded around her shoulders, swept down the length of her back.

Eyes bluer than blue were enormous in

her face as she looked down at him.

"Annalise!"

He began to take the stairs, two by two. But . . . there was something wrong, something very, very wrong. He saw it in the way she looked.

And a fury gripped him, deep and terrible.

"Annalise!"

He had her by the shoulders, longing to enwrap her, to kiss the fullness of her lips, bury himself in her, seize her up, sweep her to their chambers. . . .

"Tell me, before God, that Davis is a liar!" he demanded.

"My laird!" Trembling, her voice a whisper, she fell, shaking, to her knees. "My laird! My dear, dear Bruce . . ."

He lifted her chin, looking into her eyes.

"Before God, Bruce!" she whispered.

7

Toni awoke early; Bruce was gone. She lay quietly for several moments, wondering if he had merely returned to his own room.

She didn't think so. Oddly, she was certain that he had left the castle.

Looking at her wristwatch, she saw that it was just eight. Though she wished she had slept longer, she was antsy and anxious to be up. With a groan, she rose and headed into the shower. She hesitated at the connecting door, then tapped lightly and pressed it open. As she had sensed, Bruce wasn't there.

She showered and dressed, then decided on a cup of coffee. But going down the stairs, she realized that she was resentful. The castle was silent; the others were all managing to sleep.

In the kitchen, she put on a large pot of coffee, thinking that she'd leave it for whoever stumbled down next. The coffee had barely brewed when she heard a thunderous banging that made her jump a mile. She realized instantly that it was only the front door. Apparently the laird of the castle had remembered to lock the door when he left.

She hurried to the door and threw it open. The constable, looking quite nice and casual in jeans and knit sweater, was standing there. "Morning, Miss Fraser. Is Bruce around?"

She shook her head. "I don't think so."

Jonathan Tavish sighed. "His car isn't about, but after the drive up, I thought I should give it a try."

"Can I help you with anything?" she asked.

He shook his head and frowned slightly, looking concerned. "Everything is all right, eh?"

"Fine, thank you. It's going well. Bruce has actually been very decent."

He remained at the door. She hesitated.

"I just made coffee. Would you like some?"

"Actually, that would be wonderful."

"Come in, please."

He followed her to the kitchen and took a seat at the table. Just then David came in, yawning, scratching cheeks with a sign of morning shadow. He stopped short, seeing the constable.

"Ah, morning!" he said.

"Good morning," Jonathan said.

David stared at Toni. "Is . . . there anything wrong?"

"No, the constable was just looking for Bruce, but he's . . ." She shrugged. "He's off somewhere."

"Ah." David grinned. "Well, Constable, excuse my appearance."

"Call me Jonathan, please, and I'm the one interruptin' here."

Toni set out the coffee, sugar and cream. "I'll grab some scones," David told her.

"Thanks," she murmured. Actually, the last thing she wanted this morning was a guest for breakfast.

"Well, Jonathan," David said, stirring his own coffee, "it seems we will be around for a bit."

"Aye?" Jonathan seemed surprised.

"Our host has agreed to let us make up some of what we've spent," Toni explained.

"Ah," Jonathan murmured. "Well, then, that's fine."

"Good morning!" Gina called cheerfully, strolling into the kitchen, dressed in a robe, as well. She, too, stopped short at the sight of Jonathan. "Hi! Is . . . anything wrong?"

Jonathan smiled, shaking his head. "No, not at all."

"He stopped by to see Bruce," David explained this time.

"Who isn't here," Toni added.

"Ah, I see."

"Well, I've just heard you'll be around a bit," Jonathan said.

"Yes, isn't it great!" Gina said cheerfully. "Bruce has been wonderful, really. Not just tolerating us, but helping us!"

"I admit to being surprised," Jonathan said. "But then, as you're aware, he comes and goes as he pleases, sometimes on a whim." He shook his head ruefully. "Indeed, when I saw you all about town, I was surprised that he'd rented out the castle, but I honestly couldn't have said that he hadn't done so. Strange situation though, eh? And a bit of a frightening one. In this day and age of computers and machines, some awful things can happen. We had a young woman a few years back who was in dire trouble, indeed. Someone stole her passport, and with it, her identity. Before it was all straightened out, she was wanted for a bank robbery in Cannes!"

"Identity theft!" David said, nodding sagely. "I wonder if . . . if that's what happened!"

"We'll get to the bottom of it," Jonathan assured them.

"I hope!" Gina said. She smiled. "Bruce really has been great. All he's asked is that we make sure to stay out of the forest. He's so concerned about what's been going on in

Scotland — the women disappearing and being murdered," she murmured. "I'm afraid that, in the States, we're far too accustomed to such horrible things happening. When it's not right in your own backyard, well . . ."

Jonathan was staring at them strangely, looking a little ashen.

"What is it?" Toni asked.

"He asked you to stay out of the forest, did he now?"

"Yes. Why, is there something bad in the woods?" David asked.

"I'd have thought that y'd 'ave known," he said softly.

"Known what?" Gina demanded.

"You see, the bodies of the murdered lasses were found in Tillingham Forest." He grimaced. "Not quite the backyard, but . . . close enough," he ended softly.

Toni, Gina and David stared at one another. "Both bodies?" murmured Gina.

"Indeed."

"But the girls weren't from here," Toni said.

"No, they were not. And . . . well, they were a different sort than yourselves," he assured her. "Still, not a bad idea to stay out of the forest, as Bruce said."

"I'll stay out of it all right," Gina said.

Jonathan still looked uncomfortable.

"There's something more," Toni said, her tone determined as she watched him.

"Well, I can see why it makes Bruce so uncomfortable. Y'see, it was he that found one of the poor lasses."

Hell, it was bloody early, Thayer thought. Eleven o'clock. Well, bloody early for him to start drinking, anyway.

Fuck it. He'd already been awake for hours. He'd left himself right after he'd seen Bruce pull away from the castle, and that had been hours ago now. Early? No, plenty late enough.

"Aye, give me a pint, luv," he said to the barmaid. He'd come for the Sunday roast, or so he had thought. But he wasn't hungry, he'd discovered, once he'd chosen the Silver Crow, a dark, somewhat aging pub in Stirling. Most pubs in Stirling were aging, he determined with wry humor. But then . . . this one was struggling, he thought. It was very dark within, the floors needed to be swept and the tables all carried a thin layer of grease. And there was but the one harried barmaid, and a number of locals, demanding better service.

There was much about Stirling to be admired. It was a beautiful city, with progressive people and an air of the present. And the huge castle welcomed visitors from all over. Fairly recent improvements had made the place quite charming, in truth. Mannequins in period costume, all going about their period business, displayed some of history's darkest moments along with some of the finest.

"We were damned bloody, bloody bastards, through it all!" he muttered.

"Pardon?" the barmaid said.

"Nothing, luv, just talking to myself."

He smiled. At least the barmaid was attractive. She was in a little black halter shirt, and wore black shorts, as well. The way they hugged her rear end didn't leave much to the imagination. And what they did was mighty graphic.

Maybe that's how this place was surviving. Dingy lighting and dirty floors were okay if a bloke could have himself that kind of a view.

He looked around. The tables were mostly empty; the bar was full. Aye, folks around here came for the view.

His stomach growled. He'd taken off that morning without a bite to eat, aware that the great laird of the castle had vacated it early, as well. Hell, it seemed the man needed to escape his own place. But then again, it appeared he'd escaped it often enough in the past. Thayer looked at his hands. Raw. They'd put work into it, all right. He hadn't realized how much work there'd be when he agreed to their mad scheme. But the piano bars of Glasgow hadn't been quite a dream fulfilled. He'd had a few pounds and, under his circumstances, given his *habits,* thought why the hell not. There had been so many very interesting directions in which to take the idea.

"Think I'll have me a wee bite to eat," he told the barmaid.

She flashed him a smile. She was young, and still had a kind of innocence about her — despite the shorts.

"Good. The roast is not so bad, really, sir," she said.

Sir. He liked that.

He took a seat in the back, unnoticed by the rest of the clientele. A few moments later, the barmaid came over. She smiled at him again. Why, bless her, she was flirting. She kept flashing him something of a blush and something of an invitation as she laid out silver, a napkin, salt and pepper. He mused over his own assets. He wasn't bad-looking, really. He even had a look of his American cousin about him, since his hair was a tawny color — full and rich and all there, thank you very much! His features were not badly assembled, and he had some decent height, too, though he'd often rued the fact that his shoulders were never really going to fill out — not like those on Ryan or the great Bruce.

Pity that he had so many of the same characteristics as Toni. The night he'd met her — she with all her unbound enthusiasm to have actually found a family member! — he'd been smitten. Those deep blue eyes were something else entirely on Toni. She'd been electric, with her slim, natural elegance and her total vitality. She'd made him quicken all over. But he'd realized soon enough that she'd wanted a cousin. What he'd wanted, what he'd needed . . . The barmaid's shorts came to mind again.

Maybe that was why Toni's scheme had looked so good. He'd thought time spent with her might change the way she saw him. It hadn't changed anything for him. He'd been fascinated by her more every moment they shared. She had talent and a passion. She could dig into hard work, just as she could wane rapturously about a dream. When her hair brushed his fingers, when she gave him her smile, eyes brightening . . .

But then, there had been MacNiall. Even

as Toni faced off with the fellow, any fool could see that the sparks were about to ignite.

Fuck MacNiall. Thinking about him was damned irritating.

Sometimes Thayer hated being British, and he loathed being Scottish. Many centuries had gone by, yet too often they were considered something of a lesser country by their neighbor — good old England! Wars, and the fact that they shared an island and pacts, be damned. Underneath, it was still there. They still groveled so over any old bloke with a title before his name!

"Your roast, sir." The pretty little barmaid was back. She hovered after she put the plate down.

Not bad. Not bad at all. It was those shorts. . . .

"I'm Thayer," he told her. "What's your name?"

"Katherine," she said. "Katie, to me pals."

"Katie, then, nice to meet you."

She glanced back at the bar. Another girl had joined the workforce there. She was older, tougher looking, someone who'd worked pubs for a few years, no doubt.

"I'm on break," Katie said.

He angled his head, smiling. "So, can you join me, luv?"

Her smiled deepened. She'd been waiting for the invitation. Ah, so his shoulders weren't what they might have been, but he seldom had trouble with women.

She took the seat opposite him. "What brings you to Stirling?"

"I'm looking for a bit of excitement."

"In Stirling?"

He shrugged. "It was close enough."

"You're out in one of the villages, eh? Sounds like you come from Glasgow."

"That I do," he told her. He took a bite of his roast. It was good.

"And you, Katie? You're from Stirling?"

She shook her head. "Orkney."

He arched a brow. "Talk about a need for excitement! So, have you found any in Stirling?"

"I've only been here a few days." She leaned closer. "And the bloke what owns this place . . . what a jerk! I think I'll do better heading for Edinburgh, or Glasgow. They say there's some life going on there, at least."

"Katie, life is where we find it. All along the road."

She smiled and proved to be more of an aggressive little vixen than he had imagined. "Think that you could show me some life along that road?" she queried.

He hadn't realized that her hands were beneath the table until he felt her fingers squeezing his knee.

He placed his fork down, crossed his arms over his chest and surveyed her with definite interest and amusement. "Katie, lass, you can't begin to imagine what I can show you along the road."

"I'd love to see," she said.

He smiled, leaning back in his chair. "Maybe we could meet later."

There was a breath of excitement in her voice. "Maybe we could!" She rose quickly. "I'm off at two. So I shouldn't be seen sitting here with you . . . if we're going to get together later."

"Good thought," he told her gravely. "Very good thought."

"Meet me down by the graveyard?"

"Perfect," he told her.

Jonathan's information regarding Bruce had been accepted as it had been offered, Toni thought — as a good sound reason for them to stay out of the forest, and, as a darned good reason for him to feel very uneasy about the situation.

Toni was certain that David had told Kevin, and that Gina had let Ryan know. Thayer wasn't around, so he was the only one who didn't yet know.

The bodies had been found here. And Bruce had discovered one of the dead girls. Now they were all left a little uneasy, she thought. And she couldn't help wondering if they should just cut their losses and leave.

She was scrounging in the refrigerator, looking for something cold to drink, when Gina came into the kitchen.

"Don't get any food!" Gina ordered.

Toni closed the refrigerator and looked at her. "Actually, I wasn't, but why not?"

"Because we should go on a picnic."

"A picnic? Where?" she asked Gina carefully.

"Don't worry. I'm not going to drag anyone into the forest. I'm not sure where to go, but we'll find a meadow somewhere. With sheep."

"And sheep poop!" David added cheerfully, coming on in behind Gina and taking a seat with them at the kitchen table. He grinned at Toni. "I've already told her, Kevin and I are in."

"I guess it's just us," Gina added. "Bruce is gone, and Thayer took off this morning."

Toni looked at both of them quizzically. "You're not upset?"

"Upset?" David said, looking at Gina, frowning.

"About the bodies having been dumped in these woods, and about Bruce having made the discovery of one of them," Toni said.

David shook his head. "As long as you and Gina don't . . . pick up the trade and go running around in the forest, no. I'm sorry, of course. And I understand now why Bruce is so weird about it. But no, I'm not upset."

"We just need to be cautious," Gina added. "Women usually need to be smart about what they're doing."

Toni nodded. "Um. Good."

"Are you upset?" Gina asked.

"No!"

"Are you coming on our picnic?"

Toni was quiet for a minute. "Mind if I beg out of it myself?"

"Why?" Gina asked, sounding a bit hurt.

"I'll leave it as a romantic outing for two couples," Toni said.

"Hey, it's never like that," David protested. "We're all friends."

"But I'm still the odd man out when we're down to five."

"We've been five lots! Last trip to Scotland, we were five. And the year before that," Gina reminded her.

"You guys are all great. I didn't mean that I felt like the odd man — or woman — out when I'm with you. It's just that you should go alone. Besides, I want to go wander around the village a little," Toni said.

Gina sighed and looked at David. "I guess it's just the four of us then. And the sheep."

He rolled his eyes at Toni. "Very romantic."

"You'll love it," she told him. "I know you guys — you'll pack real plates and glasses, you'll sip champagne on a hillcrest, looking out over gorgeous hills and dales, and you'll have a great time."

"I still don't understand why you don't want to go. We've been in the village," Gina reminded her.

"Yes, but every time we've been in, it's been with a mission, buying things, getting to know the local hardware store. I'm going to explore like a tourist. They've a centuries-old church and an ancient graveyard . . . And you know me, I like to dawdle. You guys just get bored," Toni told her.

"She wants to be an isolationist," David said.

"You know you hate old churches and musty graveyards," Toni reminded him.

"I always go to them."

"Of course, you do. And then I feel guilty when I dawdle too long," Toni said.

"The sheep are going to miss you," he said.

"And I'll miss them, minus the sheep poop, of course," Toni said.

Toni had planned on taking her time getting ready, but she discovered, to her dismay, that she found being alone in the castle somewhat unsettling — especially after Jonathan's revelations that morning. Grabbing her handbag, she ran down the stairs, anxious to get out.

One of their rental cars, a minivan, was parked out by the stables. Thayer must have taken the little BMW, she determined. But the van would be fine. Any vehicle would be fine.

She quickened her steps, surprised that she was in such a hurry to reach it. Yet, as she neared the car, she stood stock-still.

A scratching sound was coming from the stables.

Of course, there are horses in it, idiot! she told herself.

But it didn't sound like the kind of noise a horse would make.

She hesitated, caught between the stable doors and the car. *What would make that kind of a noise? Someone stealing the horses?*

She stood for a moment in indecision. If

someone was stealing the horses, and she tried to stop them, she might well get hurt. No, the smart thing to do would be to get the hell out, go to town and get Constable Tavish to come back with her.

But as she stood there, the noise stopped suddenly. *She'd been seen.* Absurdly frightened by such a small thing, she started to hurry toward the car.

"Ah, Miss Fraser!"

She froze, then turned. Eban Douglas was standing in the shadowy doorway of the stables. The wizened little man was wearing his customary grin. An eerie grin, she decided.

"Eban!" she said, trying to sound cheerful. She didn't know why, but today, his presence made her uneasy.

"Seein' to the lads, I be," he said, indicating the stables.

"Yes, thank you!" Toni said cheerfully.

"The rooone . . . he's lookin' a bit weathered."

"Excuse me?" Toni said, then realized that he was saying "the roan."

"Oh, well, Ryan will look in on him later," she said.

"Y'don't want to give the boy a look yerself, miss?"

Go into the dark stables with only Eban around for miles? Not in a thousand years!

"Um . . . I'm afraid I wouldn't know if he was ailing or not, Eban. Ryan is the one who knows about horses. If you think he's really ill, though, we could call a vet?"

"I'd not feel right, mum, callin' in the doc withoot one of ye seein' to the boy."

"Eban, trust me, you have my permission to do so," she said. She felt as if he was pressuring her. *Pressuring her to go into the dark of the stables.* If he didn't look so strange, would she have thought anything of it?

Yes! Because women had been murdered around here. Their bodies had been found in the forest. And like it or not, this little man was weird!

Bruce MacNiall and Jonathan had done a fair job of scaring them all, she thought. Still, she wasn't going into the stables.

"Eban, I'm asking you to please call the vet out. And thank you so very much. I've got to get going."

Whatever it was that unnerved her, she was hard put *not* to run to the car. With a forced smile and a friendly wave, she hurried her footsteps.

Old habits died hard. She raced for the left-hand door, then felt like a fool, remembering that she was in Great Britain.

She grimaced foolishly as he watched her, and walked around to the right door.

"Mind ye, keep yer eye on the roads!" Eban called to her.

"Yes, I will, thanks!"

In the car, she switched on the ignition and started down the rocky driveway. Angry with herself, she stopped the car near the point in the forest where they had gone into the canopy to find the stream and wade in the water.

Her hands were shaking.

She put the car into Park, telling herself that she was being ridiculous. So much for priding herself on the fact that she didn't have a prejudiced bone in her body! Eban had frightened her — because he had such a strange look.

Then again, she didn't really know Eban. He was just . . . around. *Caretaking.* He'd helped them out several times when they'd been working. They'd seen him . . . and they hadn't seen him. Yet, when they hadn't seen him, he still must have been around, watching them.

She took a breath, ready to put the car back into gear, really beginning to feel a bit ridiculous.

Eban worked for Bruce MacNiall, keeping an eye on the castle. It would have been his job to report to MacNiall, they just hadn't known it.

Then something caused her to look toward the forest.

Bruce was there, on his huge black horse, right at the point where they had entered to reach the stream. She shaded her eyes from the morning sun, trying to get a better look at him. He was waving to her, beckoning, and he looked impatient.

"What?" she murmured aloud. "He insists we stay out of the forest, and there he is, waving me into it!"

And then, there had been Jonathan's words that morning. . . .

Frowning, she got out of the car, wishing that she'd remembered her sunglasses. He waved again. The great black turned and went down the path.

"What the hell . . . ?" she muttered aloud.

He'd disappeared down the trail, expecting her to follow.

"All right. Great!" she said. Maybe it was safe to go into the forest as long as she was with him. But he'd found one of the two bodies dumped in the forest! she reminded herself.

"I'm only going so far!" she said, and realized that she was still talking to herself. But even as she approached the first canopy of trees, she felt again the strange hesitance she had felt the day before. And she had been with a crowd of people then! And that was before she knew about the bodies!

This was insane. She shouldn't trust him. And yet . . . she did. Somewhere in her heart, she'd felt a deep unease regarding Bruce. But even as she'd felt it, something in her soul had rebelled.

And now, for some reason, she was compelled to follow him.

As soon as she came into the field of trees, she was blinded again, having gone from surprisingly bright sunlight to a dark expanse of green.

"Bruce!" she called out, irritated. "I am not coming any farther —"

He had dismounted and was in front of her again.

"Bruce, dammit!" she told him.

Come, please.

She thought he said the words softly, yet she questioned her own sanity because she wasn't certain that they had been real words.

She thought about just turning and running, but for the life of her right then, she couldn't do it. Nothing had changed. She had to follow. She was drawn.

"Stop, then, wait up for me!" she said, her words angry. She was starting to feel like an idiotic teenager in a bad B horror movie, who's in the very spot where the maniacal killer always strikes.

But that was insane. Bruce was right in front of her. Sanity be damned. Instinct assured her that he'd never hurt her.

She didn't want to rely on instinct; she didn't want to dream. She never, ever wanted to admit that she hadn't shut down the visions that had haunted her with such vivid brutality . . .

"Bruce! Damn you, wait!"

But he wasn't waiting. And she couldn't turn back.

She started to hurry, walking quickly to catch up, stumbling slightly as she reached the soft, rocky embankment of the brook. She stubbed a toe and stopped, swearing. She rubbed her foot, really angry then, ready to tell him to go right to hell. Yet, when she looked up, he was nowhere to be seen.

And she had come much farther into the forest than she had imagined.

The trees seemed to be surrounding her, massive, so deeply green, in an eerie darkness. And there was a sudden hush all around her. No birds chirped, no insects buzzed.

It was as if the world was waiting.

"Bruce!" Her voice wavered, shocking in the stillness.

And then . . .

She had followed the trickle of the brook, but not even that sound seemed to be able to pierce the stillness. Ahead of her, water dashed and jumped over little rocks and fallen branches. She tried to remember playing in the water with her friends, how they had soaked one another, how they had laughed. She tried, desperately, to keep that vision in her mind.

But she could not.

She saw the large, downed branches, the blanket of green that was oddly out of place on the water. It was out of place. It was a piece of the forest, yes, but . . . set as if by human hands.

No! A voice inside her shrieked out.

Fear gripped her. The silence remained, as if all the forest, trees, bushes, fish, fowl, insects and even the air itself stood still and waited. And watched.

She knew, long before she actually found the strength to propel herself forward, what she would find. She knew, yet she didn't want to know. Then a calm settled over her and the blind fear abated.

She walked purposely, steadfastly forward and lifted the branch. It was heavy, heavier than she had expected.

She dragged it but inches.

A scream formed in her throat, but it never left her lips.

Bones. She had found bones.

8

"Ah, a hill full of long grass and flowers, a delightful breeze and bubbly! What more could one ask?" Kevin said, leaning back on the blanket.

Ryan sipped his champagne, wishing that he could feel as relaxed as the others seemed to be.

"A beer, maybe. A Bud. Cold," Ryan said.

"Aren't we grouchy," David said.

Ryan shrugged and rose, stretching. "I wish Toni had come with us," he murmured.

"Well, of course, I wish she'd come, too," Gina said. "But . . . why?"

"I don't know. I guess I'm worried about her. Rambling around in that castle alone . . . and going to the village alone," Ryan said. "Who knows what she's up to? Maybe she's asking too many questions . . . irritating people."

Kevin laughed aloud. "Oh, my God, Ryan! You're making it sound like the Village of the Damned, or something of the like!"

He turned and looked at them. "Maybe it is."

"Oh, Ryan! I thought you loved it here," Gina said.

"I do."

"Then . . . ?" David demanded.

Ryan shook his head. A restlessness was sitting upon him. He gazed at Gina. She knew him, knew his moods, and she didn't look happy. She touched his arm. "We're out for a picnic with friends now, Ryan," she said.

"Right."

"And everything is going well — as well as can be hoped, under the circumstances," David reminded him.

"Yeah, great! A tall guy on a fantastic, huge horse rides in and we discover we've been gypped out of our life savings. Then we find out that this same guy has found the body of a murder victim in the woods. And now Toni is alone at the castle. What if MacNiall returns before we do? We don't really know a whole hell of a lot about him," Ryan finished.

"He's the laird," David said.

"Yeah? And Countess Bathory sliced up virgins and bathed in their blood," Ryan said.

Gina was staring at him hard. Warning him? he wondered.

"The laird has been damned decent," David said.

"What? Do you think he'd chop us up in his own castle?" Ryan said.

"Oh, Ryan, stop! Please." Gina begged.

"I like the guy, honestly like him," David said. "And Ryan, you've been riding with him, have talked horses with him. You seemed to be his biggest fan."

"Yeah, that's true. He came on like a warrior lord of old that first night, but, hey, we were in his castle. And he's damned good with horses. Sure, I like him," Ryan said. "Respect him," he added thoughtfully.

"Me, too. He demands a certain respect, but he's been damned decent to us," Kevin agreed. "Look, he probably wasn't even in the country when those girls disappeared."

Gina shivered violently. "Maybe he wasn't, but . . ."

"But what?" Kevin demanded.

"Nothing," Gina said. "Nothing, really."

"I know what you were going to say," David said, staring at Gina. "*We* were in the country, probably, during the time of . . . well, at least two of the disappearances."

"What the hell does that mean?" Ryan demanded.

"It means I'm damned glad that we stick

together," David said. "That we watch out for Gina and Toni."

"Well, it probably helps that we're not streetwalkers," Gina said pragmatically.

"True," David agreed.

"Hey, can we get back to the beauty of the day, the champagne and all that?" Kevin demanded.

Ryan was still tense, but he joined Gina on the blanket, sat back, closed his eyes and let his wife work the knots out of the muscles in his shoulders.

Toni could see the skull protruding from mud and rock, and bits of flesh, she thought, blackened by the soil. There was also a length of hair and pieces of cloth, all but glued or fused with the bone, or plastered to it by the mire, the very dark muck that formed on the banks of the little brook or stream.

Get away! a voice of self-survival cried in her head. *Scream, just start screaming, and run as fast as you can!*

And still, she didn't scream. There was no need to look farther. Whoever this victim had been, she had been here some time. There was certainly no need to feel for a pulse, to attempt to drag her from the water. None at all.

Get away! the voice repeated.

Yes! Now!

She thought that she would run then, able to scream and shriek at last, in the darkness of the eerie forest. But she didn't. Instead, she stayed, trying to ingrain every detail of the moment in her mind. It might be important.

The water was no more than two feet deep here, and the skeleton was lodged against a large rock. Until she had moved it, the huge branch had all but hidden the corpse. People could have walked right by without seeing it, for a very long time. How long had it been there? Had the rains carried it from elsewhere, or caused the earth to shift so that they were dug up after a long period of time?

She turned then at last, slowly. Running could cause her to trip on the underbrush and hurt herself. She was deep into the wood, having followed the brook quite far in her attempt to catch up with Bruce. But she didn't think she'd get lost. All she had to do was follow the water.

She didn't dare think about fear. Fear could cause panic. If there was one thing she didn't want, it was to fall, sprain an ankle and remain in the forest as darkness fell.

She'd been shouting before, convinced that Bruce was ahead of her; now she was silent, careful in her footsteps.

She still felt . . . watched. Yet, strangely, that sense didn't create a rise of . . . terror. The trees would not come to life, branches like arms, and suck her into themselves. She was simply being watched as she left.

That woman had been hidden long before they'd come to Tillingham.

She kept her eyes looking forward, afraid of what she might see gazing out at her from the green darkness.

Straight ahead! Look straight ahead. Walk, don't run. Steady, steady, follow the brook, get out!

And at last . . . she did, emerging in the same area where she had entered.

She half expected her car to be gone, but it wasn't. And as she crawled into it, she realized just how frightened she'd been. Other bodies had been found in Tillingham Forest. Had she just stumbled upon the first of the killer's victims, perhaps? A woman never reported as missing? Someone lost to society, and then life?

Fear began to seep through her then, a very real fear. This was a killing ground. Yes, women were abducted from other places. But they were brought here.

Did that mean the killer knew this area very well? Knew that disposing of a body here meant that chances of discovery were small, or that this type of environment would play such havoc with a body that no clues would ever be left?

Her hands were shaking as she gripped the steering wheel, trying to decide what to do. It would be quickest to go back to the castle and call until she got someone on the line.

But Eban was at the castle! She felt a surge of hysteria at the thought of the man. Could he have done something like this?

He never seemed to leave. And if he did, she didn't think he ever went far.

But what if, when no one knew, he silently took a car and drove off, drove out to the big cities, where no one knew him. Where women who worked the streets for their income were accustomed to servicing men who were sometimes less than attractive?

Suddenly remembering that her cell phone was in her purse, she turned to scramble for it, only to hear a tapping at the driver's window.

Startled, she turned.

It was Eban. Face pressed far too close to the window. Macabre through the glass.

Fear, blind and, perhaps, unreasoning, let

loose within her system and she let out a scream at last. She tried to twist her keys in the ignition, but they weren't there! Staring at the man, she fumbled on the seat for them. He backed away, looking puzzled.

She found the keys. After three tries, she got them into the ignition.

When she floored the gas pedal, he literally hopped away.

Without looking back, she sped all the way into the village.

Detective Inspector Robert Chamberlain was thirty-five, tall and wiry, with dark hair already showing signs of serious silver — brought on by his work, he had long ago told Bruce.

They had known one another forever, having met in the service. For a while they had worked for the Lothian and Borders Police in Edinburgh together, until Bruce had left and Robert had moved on. Throughout the years, they had remained friends. A year ago, when Bruce had found the body in the woods, he had been appalled by the lack of technique displayed by Jonathan and his men upon their arrival at the scene. Granted, they had never dealt with such a situation before. But since they hadn't, the proper steps to take would have been to alert the authorities with more expertise. Despite the fact that Bruce had long ago left the police force, Robert often discussed cases with him. On occasion, he had been able to trigger the right hint, clue or information to help Robert solve a case. And both were now deeply concerned about the disappearing girls and the murders.

Robert sat with Bruce in a pub in Edinburgh close to the Greyfriar's churchyard where the famous Bobby — the terrier who came to his master's grave to sit vigil for a decade — now lay buried alongside the man to whom he had been so loyal. Robert looked particularly glum.

"Jonathan has told me that he's had men out," Robert said, referring to the Tillingham constable. "They've combed the woods, but not discovered a body." He ran his fingers through his graying hair. " 'Tis difficult. So far, we've a woman missing for about a week, we think. In fact, she might well have disappeared just after you reached Edinburgh. I knew I needed you back here. And I'm grateful that you came."

Bruce shrugged. "I was restless. Needed to come anyway," he told Robert. "And, as it happens, it was a good thing I did return."

Robert nodded. "With Annie we're just

guessing. We don't really know when she disappeared, because none of her 'friends' kept tabs on her." He pushed the file on the table between them toward Bruce. "Annie O'Hara. Northern Irish, came over from Belfast about five years ago. No known employment — legal employment, that is. She's been arrested three times in those years. Drug abuser, but not the haggard-looking desperate kind as yet. She was picked up twice working the Royal Mile, and both times she was released — you know how that goes. Anyway, one of her friends realized that she was gone after five days or so and reported her missing, but she had no idea how or when Annie disappeared." He shrugged. "Who knows? She might have headed on back to Ireland, but since Helen MacDougal disappeared in like fashion a year ago, and was found by you, and then Mary Granger, just six months ago, and found by that fellow, Eban, in the forest, as well, I think there's a real possibility that Annie'll be found, too, and sadly, found deceased."

"In the forest," Bruce murmured bitterly.

Robert shrugged. "Maybe not. Maybe the killer will find a new place to dispose of the bodies."

"Why would he bother? Jonathan Tavish

isn't too concerned. He doesn't consider it his problem at all — because the women have disappeared from Glasgow, Stirling and now Edinburgh."

"Well, he has a point in that the killer has to be operating out of the big cities."

"We don't actually have a 'red light' district in the village," Bruce said. He was irritated with Jonathan, though. His old friend seemed to be more suspicious of his activities than worried about the fact that a real psychopath was on the loose, and probably growing more dangerous with each passing day. He'd run into him in the village, just before leaving. Apparently Jonathan had been looking for him, wanting to know if he'd lost his wallet recently, if there was any possibility that he might be a victim of "identity theft." Actually, he had to admit that Jonathan might have a point there. How else could he explain how his castle had wound up listed as being for rent. According to Jonathan, there was no Web site for the castle, and, thus far, the legitimate ones he had checked had never had a listing for the place.

Even seeking out the case of fraud, though, Bruce would have far more faith in Robert's knowledge — and, naturally, the fraud department of a major force — than he would in Jonathan. He understood Jonathan's resentment, but it didn't change the fact that Tillingham was small, and major crime was not a frequent event there.

"No. Of course, this is far more serious than Tavish is willing to admit," Robert said. "I don't blame him for not using all his local funds to mount an inch-by-inch combing of Tillingham Forest, not when we've got a disappearance with no guarantee that any foul play happened to this woman."

Bruce sat back, shaking his head. "The killer will return with his victim's remains to Tillingham. If we'd found just the one girl, then it might have been merely a convenient place for him to dispose of the body. But a second corpse discovered? He's using Tillingham as his personal refuse property, and he's going to keep at it. I even think there may be a 'why' behind it."

Robert shook his head. "Now, Bruce, y'are taking this far too personally. Tillingham is lush and deep. We've not got a thing on the killer yet because of the advanced stage of decomposition of the bodies by the time they were found. We don't have hair, fibers, semen, anything. There's nothing personal about the fact that the bloke is hiding his heinous crimes there. It simply puts him in the classification of an organized killer, a fellow who thinks it out and knows how best to keep himself from being discovered."

"I suppose I do take discarded bodies in what is very nearly my backyard personally," Bruce agreed. "It means one of two very bad things. Either we have an organized psychotic on a methodical killing jaunt dumping bodies once he's had his jollies, or someone in that area knows that it's the perfect dumping site and is traveling farther from home for his victims."

"You should have stayed with the force, Bruce," Robert told him, shaking his head. "You were good. We'd have never gotten the Highland Hills killers without you, you know. It was uncanny, the way you could read the fellow's mind."

"Behavioral science," Bruce said, waving a hand in the air. He didn't like remembering the massive hunt they'd had a little more than ten years ago, seeking out a man who was kidnapping teenaged girls, raping them and leaving their mutilated bodies strewn across Edinburgh and its outskirts. Four girls had died in all; it had been a heartbreaking assignment. "We were able to get something from friends back then. I'd have never realized that there were two people involved if one of the witnesses hadn't mentioned that the last time she'd seen her friend alive, she'd been giving directions to a lady on the passenger's side of the car. Even then, I doubted myself at first."

He hadn't; he was lying. It had been frightening, how much of a connection he'd had with the killers. There was a point, on a day when they had stood on a hillside just outside of the city, when he had suddenly known that the killer couldn't be acting alone, known that there had to be a woman involved, as well. How else could the killer have managed to lure girls who knew to be on the lookout for any strange *man*. From then on, little clues fell into place. Tire tracks had indicated a return to the city. The area around one of the schools had provided one pub, and he had taken to spending his time there, watching. A handsome young couple who held hands across the table and whispered constantly like foolish, snickering lovers had garnered his attention. He was never sure if he heard their conversation, imagined it or recreated what it might have been in his own mind. But suddenly he'd been certain, so he'd followed them.

One afternoon he tried to imagine the

route they'd take if they had, indeed, been stalking the girls together. Getting his car, cruising the area of the school, he put himself into the man's mind, made himself think and feel as the killer had done. There had been the thrill of the chase and, aye, some brutal treatment to his wife.

Eventually he was certain he knew just how and when the couple had moved. How the wife, claiming to be lost, would lure the girls, ask directions, come back once the girl was on her way home, alone, and coax her into the car. There she was drugged. Traces of morphine had been found in the body, so he didn't consider that any great divining work on his own. Then she was taken to their flat, a ground-floor apartment in a working man's area where the husband wouldn't be noted taking in a roll of bedding or carpet. Inside, the woman had held the girl at the man's command. And after he abused the terrified child, he'd have sex with his wife, as well, the girl still alive but unconscious. Then the poor wee lass would be taken into the bathroom and killed in the tub, so that the blood could be washed away.

He gave the scenario to his superiors who thought that he was daft. And even if he wasn't, they couldn't arrest a couple because he'd seen them in a pub and followed them to their flat.

But after a storm, he'd gotten a friend to take a cast of the tire marks left by the couple's car near the pub. They matched those found at the site where the girl had been found. It was not enough for a conviction, or even a trial, but enough to get them what they really needed through the court system — a DNA sample. The case had taken months, eating into his soul — and into his last precious moments with Meg.

Her illness had been the reason he had given for resigning. His proximity to the mind of the killer had been the reason he had never gone back.

"Aye, who would have figured that such a man would have a wife just as eager to perform that kind of cruelty on another." Robert shook his head with disgust. "They had a case like that in Canada, not long ago. The wife got ridiculous leniency. Her defense attorneys claimed she was a victim herself. Looks like no one is accountable for his or her actions anymore. Even in the Highland Hills case, the husband was locked up for good but his wife may be out in as little as ten years! But the point is, *you* made the difference in that case."

Bruce felt a moment's severe discomfort.

"Back then, the authorities were on it with a passion. Robert, you know as well as I do that if these were prominent lasses, the press would be having a stink and Jonathan wouldn't be halfheartedly sending a few men out to look around in the forest."

"That's sad, and always the case," Robert agreed, drumming his fingers on the table. "Aye, for a small country, we've had our share of loonies." He lifted his hand, indicating the town. "Edinburgh. It's where Burke and Hare practiced their ghastly trade, killing when they found out just how profitable it could be. Five years ago a fellow on the outskirts of town was killing one immigrant a month, in honor of social justice, so he claimed! He didn't like the fact that we weren't so 'pure' anymore. Tillingham, though . . . there's not been much violence there in centuries, as you are well aware. And what tragedies took place there always had to do with war, or feuding clans. This is definitely not clan retribution. Although . . . Jonathan does seem to have his share of troubles when it comes to that forest. At least a dozen teens, intent on some hanky-panky, have come out of it screaming their fool heads off, convinced there's someone, something, there. The superstitions grow. The local forces don't like going in there, so they only halfheartedly look for anything. Look, I'll see that the central office gets a crew out to search the forest. Will that give you any reassurance?"

"Aye, it will," Bruce told him.

"Now, as to the other . . . your American invasion?" Robert asked.

"They have rental forms and permits that look as legal as an international peace accord," Bruce told him, grinning. "I'm wondering if they're still not halfway convinced that I've been deprived of my land through some nonpayment of taxes and can't accept the fact that it's no longer mine."

"No!" Robert said, laughing.

"Yes, actually. Just such a scenario was suggested by one lass."

"They don't know what you do, or who you are?" Robert queried.

"No, not even the Scotsman among them. Frankly, I found that rather suspicious."

Robert shrugged. "In this day and age? Maybe. And maybe not. In Glasgow, folks tend to get into being . . . well, from Glasgow."

Bruce arched a brow at him.

"Now, Bruce, you know my own hometown by the Loch — 'tis nothing there!

Longing to be a police officer, there was nothing for me to do but come to the city. You know that's true. But don't worry on that front. If he's a Scotsman, I can trace his past for you by tomorrow. Actually, I can run traces on your entire group, though it might take a wee bit longer with the Americans. And once I've gotten copies of their documents, we can set the boys in the white-collar crime units on the trail of whoever is renting properties and taking euro-checks for them. Euro-checks, eh?"

He shrugged. "That's what she said."

"Not pounds sterling?"

"I didn't pursue that yet. My hearing is quite good, though, and she did say euro-check. This agency has probably purported itself to be something of a European finding facility, so I doubt that the use of a euro-check — even for a property in Scotland — would have seemed that strange."

"And you didn't send them packing immediately?" Robert said.

Bruce shook his head. "It was late Friday night when I found the folks putting on their show."

"Actually, it's a rather clever idea," Robert mused. "They're making a mint on graveyard tours and the like here, you know. People are ghoulish, that's a fact. They like a nice little chill, with the safety of knowing that the evil fellows practiced their wicked deeds centuries ago."

"I believe they were in Edinburgh when they got the idea," Bruce said.

"And how long ago was that?" Robert inquired.

"I don't really know."

"So these folks have been to Scotland before?"

"Aye, so they have. Why? Is that important?"

Robert shook his head. "Just a point of interest. I suppose there's no reason to think that they'd know much about the wee hamlets and villages, even if they'd been several times before. And from what you say, they've done well. Your castle was in need of serious repair."

"Aye, I've let it go. But every time before . . . well, it had been Meg's dream to go with all guns blazing and make it a showplace. When she was gone . . ."

"That's been more than a decade."

"I know, and I don't need any speeches. I've gone on with my life. I function well. I travel the globe. I do my best to steal from the rich and give to the poor. It was just the castle where I fell short."

"So your guests — for want of a better description — don't know what you do, who you are or that the castle isn't really what you call home?" Robert said.

"No."

"Are you keeping these things a secret for some reason?"

"Not really. No one has asked. I don't know. Maybe," Bruce said, correcting himself. "We might all be a bit wary of one another. They certainly appear to be exactly what they say. Still . . . let me tell you, it was strange to come home and hear what they were up to, then to have Toni Fraser tell me that she had made up her story, but even the name of Bruce MacNiall's wife was exact."

Robert waved a dismissive hand in the air. "That happens all the time. People hear things, forget them and then think that they're original thoughts."

"Well, that's what one would assume," Bruce agreed. "But I've talked to her, rather extensively. She's convinced that she made it up. And something more."

"What?"

"She's scared by it. She's having nightmares about my ancestor standing at the foot of her bed with a dripping sword."

Again Robert was unimpressed. "That's easy enough. She's in the old laird's castle."

"Easy enough — unless you've been there

and seen the way she looks when she wakens from such a dream."

Robert arched a brow at him. "She's an actress, right?"

"Aye."

"Do you think that maybe, just maybe, a scam is being played on you?"

"Not unless it's the best one in history."

"Granted, you're not the kind to be taken," Robert mused. "A lot of this is outside my jurisdiction but, naturally, I'll get on it."

"Thanks."

Robert's phone went off, and he excused himself to answer the summons. Bruce watched his friend's face go from surprise to concern.

He clicked off, staring at Bruce.

"I'll head back with you right now," he said.

"What's happened?" Bruce asked, an uneasy feeling already seeping into his bloodstream.

"They've found a body."

Bruce's blood chilled. And yet, he wasn't surprised!

"Is it — Annie O'Hara?"

"I don't know. One of my sergeants saw the alert and called me right away. Jonathan and the medical examiner are heading out to the scene now. Even if the body is not at a severe stage of decomposition, I doubt they can be certain until they've brought it out and performed an autopsy."

"Oh, God. They've found her in the forest?"

"Aye. More than that." He was looking at Bruce strangely.

"What?"

Robert shook his head, rising. "I'll tell you on the way. I want to get out there before they botch anything up."

"Dammit, Robert, what is the 'more'?" Bruce demanded.

"She was found by your guest. Miss Fraser."

9

A strange calm had descended over Toni. By the time she'd reached the village and a lazy deputy had accepted the fact that she wasn't hysterical and had contacted Jonathan Tavish, she was already ruing her actions in regard to Eban. There was no reason to suspect the fellow. Away from the green darkness of the forest — and the sight of the pathetic remains — she felt stronger.

When Jonathan arrived, she gave him a description of walking into the woods, seeing the branch and moving it. They sat in his office. He was just feet from her, looking almost like the boy next door in his casual Sunday attire.

"Toni, lass, what were you doing walkin' so deep into the woods on your own? I explained this morning why you shouldna be doing so."

"I saw Bruce," she said.

Jonathan shook his head. "I don't think so. After I left you earlier, I saw him in the coffee shop. Said he was taking the drive to Edinburgh to have lunch with a friend."

His comment chilled her, but it didn't

create the panic it might have just hours before.

"Well," she murmured, letting her lashes fall over her eyes. "I thought I saw him."

He sighed. "I hate to ask this of you, but you'll have to come back into the forest with me. I need you to guide us to the site."

"Certainly."

So she wound up not in the minivan, but in the constable's car with him and one of his deputies. Another car following behind them was filled with police tape and other paraphernalia needed to protect the integrity of the site.

At the scene, photos were taken before anyone touched the remains. The medical examiner — an almost absurdly kind and jovial-looking little fellow named Daniel Darrow — carried a small recorder and made comments into it as he made a preliminary inspection of the site and the skeletal corpse.

Toni stood some distance away, glad that the area was teeming with people. Even then, she felt as if she were being watched, and she kept herself from looking into the trees, somewhat afraid that she would see eyes observing her. Watching. Waiting. *For what?*

She heard Dr. Darrow speaking with Jonathan. "Well, it's not the missing Annie O'Hara. That's for certain."

"No?" Jonathan said.

"Definitely not."

"Aye?" Jonathan said. "How can you be certain?"

Darrow nodded. "This lass, if I'm not mistaken, has been here for centuries."

"Centuries!" Toni heard herself say.

"So I believe."

"And you know it's the body of a woman? If it's been here centuries, how do you know?"

Darrow smiled dryly. "Well, there are remnants of clothing left, even now. Don't think we had too many drag queens back then, eh? Then there are the medical reasons, as well, Jonathan, the pelvic bones of a woman being entirely different from those of a man, the delicate nature of the facial bones, stature, breadth of the ribs . . . Don't worry, we'll do all the proper procedures back at the morgue, but I think I'm safe in referring to our poor corpse as a lass! I'm going to try to excavate a bit here, rather than just remove the corpse. And we'll have to have a forensic anthropologist in. This is really most remarkable. She must have been buried deep in the muck to be as preserved as she is. Oddly enough, the lass's means of death is rather apparent."

Toni and Jonathan both stared at him blankly.

Darrow nodded, using a stick to point to the corpse.

"See there? It's a scarf, ascot, handkerchief . . . something of the like, used as a ligature. Poor wee thing was strangled."

Toni wasn't sure that she saw, but then, Darrow certainly knew this business better than she did.

Jonathan sighed. "At least it's not Annie O'Hara, though I don't know whether that's good or bad."

Darrow looked at him sharply. "I thought you'd searched the woods for Annie O'Hara? You might have discovered this old grave site."

"We did search for Annie O'Hara," Jonathan said flatly. "As you'll note, this is a dark area. And I'm certain that only the recent rains could have caused this — these remains — to suddenly rise to a point of discovery. And Miss Fraser reported that she only discovered the bones when the branch was moved. Hell, Daniel, I'd need more men than I have here to move every branch in this forest!"

Toni was impressed with Daniel Darrow. Details had gone into his recording, and, despite the fact that it seemed she had found an ancient corpse, he made a point of keeping everyone else out of the immediate area.

She had no idea how long they had been at the site when Bruce MacNiall came striding to it with a grave fellow in a suit that identified him immediately as a professional lawman of some variety.

The men stopped at the yellow tape stretched around the immediate area. Bruce looked as imposing in the forest as ever, and yet somewhat haggard. His eyes pinned first on the cordoned area where the remains lay, then on Jonathan. Then he looked around until his gaze fell on where she stood by the trees.

"Toni!" His voice was harsh, yet there was an underlying emotion to it that she found gratifying. His long strides brought him to her in seconds. His hands fell on her shoulders; steel-gray eyes assessed her with pointed concern. "Are you all right?"

She nodded, glad of him there, wishing that his presence didn't make her feel a sense of tremulous weakness again. "Of course," she told him.

"I'll get you out of here," Bruce told Toni. "Can you give me another minute?"

"Bruce, I'm fine," she said. "I'm the one

who came upon the remains, and I've seen quite a bit already, as you can imagine. And Bruce, this isn't a recent victim of a serial killer. Dr. Darrow says that she's been here for centuries."

His brow furrowed and the muscles in his face tightened in confusion.

She nodded. "Centuries," she repeated.

He turned away from her, striding toward the others.

"Bruce," Jonathan said, his tone wary. "I'm here. Daniel is here. And now Robert is here, as well. You don't need to be."

"Aye, I do," Bruce said harshly. "The castle is the closest location to this forest. This corpse is ancient?" he asked, looking at Darrow, both incredulous and relieved.

"I believe. I'm not an expert, but I'd wager she was put here hundreds of years ago," Darrow told him. "I told Jonathan, what we really need is an excavation." He glanced at Toni, and she wondered if she had been staring at him with horror or dismay, because he quickly added, "We'll not be leaving her here. No, we'll see that she is brought out intact — as intact as possible — with the muck, as well, so that the experts will have all this to help them determine just what happened." He offered Toni a smile. "Miss Fraser, you've given a hand to history here today. This lass was strangled, that's a fact."

"Annalise!" Jonathan said suddenly, staring at Bruce. He seemed almost pleased. "Looks like the hero of many a Royalist battle might have strangled his wife after all!"

"Maybe, and maybe not," Bruce said evenly.

"Centuries old, so Dr. Darrow says," Jonathan persisted.

"Aye, but that doesn't mean the laird did her in, even if it's possible to prove that this is Annalise. The autopsy will take place in Edinburgh," Robert said.

"This is my jurisdiction," Jonathan replied testily.

"And it's a national situation," Robert reminded him.

"You're not the one to make that call," Jonathan said.

"Now, Jonathan, it's the right call, and we all know it," Daniel Darrow said evenly. "This really is a piece of old history we've found here. Naturally, with what's been happening . . . well, we all thought that Miss Fraser had stumbled upon someone else. And even though this pathetic wee one isn't who we thought, it's pretty evident that we have something very serious on our hands."

Darrow's voice made it clear that no one could fault Jonathan for being frustrated — or for a lack of investigative technique. Everyone involved had been tense, certain that the discovery would be a recent victim of violence. But Jonathan apparently felt under the gun, nevertheless.

"For now," Darrow continued, "I'll get the boys to help me dig her out and get her to the morgue. Perhaps, Jonathan, Robert, y'll both give me a hand. We need to see to it that an expert is brought here."

Toni didn't know much about the laws regarding jurisdiction over a corpse — especially a centuries-old corpse, or the remains of one — but Darrow's solution seemed to satisfy everyone. In fact his calm approach somewhat soothed all tempers — if only as far as professional and outward appearances went.

Bruce didn't go past the tape, but he hunkered down at a distance again, looking at the remains.

Toni's own gaze was drawn to it then, and her stomach catapulted.

Death was never kind. The angle of the skull made it appear as if the neck had been broken, as if she had been left in pieces, as if the violence done to her had continued — even after death.

She couldn't help but look, though empty eye sockets stared back at her.

"How is that she is in pieces, and yet there are bits of flesh and bone?" Bruce asked.

Darrow hunkered down next to him. "I'd say that she was buried deep. The muck preserved her."

" 'Tis a pity it didn't do so for our more recent victims," Jonathan said.

Darrow looked around. "The air is what often causes decay. If the recent rains shifted an old grave, she's not been exposed long. Aye, poor lass! Certainly looks as if she met her end by strangulation. The marks and —" He produced a small flashlight. "There! Y'can see how this was tied about her." He flicked off the light. "Pity! I can tell more on this lass already than we've gleaned at autopsy on the girls killed within a year or so!"

Bruce stood. Whatever he had seen, it had been enough. "I'm getting Toni out of here," he said, looking around to adamantly defy anyone who might protest. No one did.

"Aye, good," Jonathan said simply. Toni wondered if he really thought it was such a good idea that she be taken from the area, or if taking her out meant that Bruce would be out of his way, as well.

Robert turned to Toni then, offering her a hand. "Robert Chamberlain. Detective Inspector Robert Chamberlain. Strange circumstances here, but it's a pleasure to meet you, Miss Fraser."

"Toni," she murmured, taking his hand. "Please. And yes, it's a pleasure, Detective Inspector."

He offered her a wry smile. "Robert, if you will."

"Robert," she murmured.

"I'll come to the castle before I leave," Robert told Bruce.

"Aye, and thanks," Bruce said, slipping an arm around her shoulder and leading her from the site.

They walked in silence along the brook, exiting to the road area where there were now at least a half-dozen cars parked, along with the medical examiner's hearse.

It wasn't until they were out of the woods that Bruce said suddenly and angrily, "What in God's name were you doing in there — that deep, especially! — in the first place? I told you to stay out of the forest."

She stared at him, startled, feeling a tinge of anger herself, ready to tell him that she had followed him. But he'd call her a liar, or worse, say she was mad. And she was feeling somewhat insane herself. If he'd headed

252

straight for Edinburgh that morning, he couldn't have been on his horse, in the woods, beckoning her to come.

But what if he had purported to be making the drive to Edinburgh, then doubled back, taken the horse out, lured her into the forest, left her there and driven on to Edinburgh? Was the timing possible? Maybe. Just maybe.

And far more probable than seeing a phantom on horseback!

"I thought I saw you," she said simply.

"Me?" he demanded.

She shrugged. "I must have been mistaken."

"Why would I lure you into the forest when I keep telling you to stay out of the damned place?" he demanded angrily.

"Hey! I thought I saw you. I was mistaken," she said, shaking off his touch.

Evidently he caught hold of his temper. "I'm sorry. You've been through a lot."

"I haven't really been through anything," she said softly. "It's not as if I found . . . please, don't treat me like a frightened child. I'm all right." She felt a twinge of anger, as well. "And you might have explained to us that the bodies had been found in Tillingham Forest — and that you were the one to discover a victim."

"I had thought it would suffice to make your group understand that there were murders taking place. I had also assumed that, since it's my castle and I'm allowing you to stay, my directive to keep out of the forest would be respectfully observed," he said.

"Bruce, honestly, I thought you were there and that you were calling me in."

"Don't follow anyone, even me, into that forest."

A strange surge of unease filled her, teased along her spine, then disappeared. She couldn't believe that he intended any ill to her.

"You're trembling," he said.

"I'm fine."

"Are you? Perhaps you didn't come upon Annie O'Hara, but such remains are still . . . disturbing. And I assure you, I wasn't so 'all right' the day I found the first body in the woods," he said.

"That was different."

"This was pleasant?"

Her lashes fell over her eyes. "No! Of course not! Okay, I'm shaken. But I'm all right."

"Let's get back to the castle," he murmured, indicating his car. "How on earth could you have thought that you saw *me?*"

"I was mistaken!"

She felt stiff, even awkward as she walked the few feet to his car and got in. *So . . . she was lying now. Well, not really. She had followed someone she thought to be him into the woods. Maybe she should have told the constable that. Maybe there was someone who looked like Bruce MacNiall, who was playing games, luring people into the woods, for a psychotic reason all his own. Or maybe it had been Bruce!*

But she couldn't really believe that. And just as she had felt earlier, a strange calm descended upon her.

"Please believe me, I'm okay. Yes, it was startling. Scary. But now, more than anything, I just think it's very sad," she told Bruce, looking at him as he drove. He nodded, but his features were still tense. Despite the niggling suspicion of *possibility* that teased at the back of her mind, she found herself admiring the hard, sculpted line of his profile, the determined set of his jaw and the gravity with which he considered the situation. He might have let his castle go to hell, but he had a deep concern for this, his home territory, and a decent and humane care for those found here who had suffered so cruelly.

He was also upset, she thought, because of Jonathan's certainty that they had found

Annalise and that she had, indeed, been killed by her husband all those years ago.

In a matter of minutes, they pulled up to the castle.

Gina, Ryan, David and Kevin came bursting out the front doors. Gina rushed for her first, exclaiming, "Oh, Toni! You poor dear!"

David was behind her, hugging her. "Eban came and told us all about it."

Ryan brushed back a thick strand of his long brown hair, hovering awkwardly by her side. "We wanted to come to you, but Eban said the authorities were with you and that they wouldn't want anyone traipsing through the woods then. At least, I think that's what he said."

"Toni, how about a drink?" Kevin suggested. "I think a drink would be the best thing in the world right now."

Toni took a deep breath, offering a rueful smile and returning the hugs. "Guys! Honestly, I'm fine. Please, I'm not a hothouse flower."

"Neither am I," Gina said. "But still, I can't imagine . . . Bruce, we're so sorry, by the way. Such things are always so horrible."

"Sorry?" he said.

Gina looked awkward, uneasy. "Well . . .

we hadn't realized that the murder victims were discovered right here, in Tillingham, one by you and one by Eban. And though he was relieved that the corpse didn't belong to that missing girl, Eban indicated that the discovery probably means that a sad part of your family legend is true. Either way, we're really sorry. I guess our murder scenes have been in bad taste. And, of course, we will stay out of the forest — as Toni should have done."

"Aye, everyone needs to stay out of the forest. Except for the police," Bruce said. "As for my family legend, finding a body doesn't prove how it got there."

David slipped an arm around Toni's shoulders. "Toni! Seriously, young lady! What were you doing so deep in the forest? Laird MacNiall told us to stay out of it!"

She inhaled very deeply. She'd be explaining this forever, she thought. "It was a mistake, that's all. A trick of the light. I thought I saw Bruce there, beckoning to me."

They all stopped, staring at her. "Bruce left very early this morning, Toni," Gina said, looking at both of them. "I told you that, remember, when we were planning the picnic. You did leave, right, Bruce?"

"Aye."

"Hey, it's a forest, a trick of the light!" Toni repeated, and headed inside to get away from their questioning stares.

The others followed, automatically heading into the kitchen, where it seemed they always gathered. Kevin immediately went about preparing drinks. "This is one of those occasions that calls for tea and whiskey," he said, as the rest of them took a seat around the table.

"Thayer hasn't come back yet?" Toni said, suddenly noticing that her cousin was absent.

"No, he's still off," Gina said.

"He's got his cell, so we could call him," David said. "But we thought we'd let him finish out his afternoon before telling him about . . . this."

She realized then that the group was once again nervous about Bruce, and the ramifications of what had happened that afternoon. He had been concerned about their show, and the fact that very real murders were occurring, but he had allowed them to stay so they could make some of the money they had poured into the place. Now it seemed that they had found Annalise.

Bruce, too, realized what was weighing on their minds. And he wasn't the type to keep anyone in suspense. "You can continue your tours," he said, eyeing them all one by one. "But no one strangles anyone, is that clear?" He stared at Toni. "There will have to be a new spin on your 'history.' Figure it out, and all will be well."

Gina cleared her throat. "Bruce, do you think that the bones Toni found could have belonged to MacNiall's wife?"

Bruce sighed. "The bones may prove to be Annalise, and they may not. My ancestor may have killed her in a fit of rage, and he may not have done so. I hate assumptions, that's all. And while the tests and research are going on, I'd just as soon not capitalize on the sensationalism, even if we are trying to make some of your money back."

A collective sigh could be heard around the table.

"Thank you," Ryan said simply.

Bruce nodded, then he finished his drink in a long swallow and rose. "Gina, when you have a chance, get all your documents together. I've a friend coming who is with the force in Edinburgh. I'd like him to see them. Naturally, his office and his resources are better equipped to deal with an international fraud situation than the department here."

"Yes, of course," Gina said. She, too, hopped up.

"We can hold dinner for your friend," Kevin said. He was of the firm belief that a good meal, served well, could help solve all problems.

Even Bruce quirked a smile at that. "We'll see if he can stay," he told them. "And now if you'll excuse me, I'll be in my room if you need me."

When he departed, they all talked at once.

"Thank God!" Gina breathed.

"He really is a great fellow," David said.

"You poor thing!" Kevin said, shaking his head sympathetically at Toni. "It's so terrible, what happened to her. It was chance that you found her, certainly."

"Toni, are you all right with all this, after . . . ?" Ryan asked.

Toni rose, feeling the weight of having gone through the forest, the bits of mud that had stuck to her that she hadn't noticed before. The tea and whiskey had been good, but more than anything, she wanted a bath.

"Guys, I'm fine. Thank you all for being so caring. But I've really got to clean up! I'll be back down in a bit."

"And I've got to get back out and see to the roan!" Ryan said. He shook his head. "I don't know what on earth could have made old Wallace so ill!"

Toni paused. She had forgotten about

260

Eban telling her that the horse was doing poorly. "The vet came out?"

Ryan nodded. "When we came back from our picnic, he was here. He's doused the fellow, but he seemed a little confused himself. Said it must be something the horse ate. But Wallace is in there with Bruce's stallion, and Shaunessy is doing just fine. I only bought the best — you know how I feel about horses."

The roan had been another investment, but of course, he was much more. And although she hadn't Ryan's expertise or knowledge, she had been the one to choose the horse with him. Ryan had looked for all the good points in a horse, for what they needed — a docile nature being among them — whereas she had simply liked the roan because he had liked her and he loved to have his nose stroked. Besides that, his name had been Wallace, which was wonderfully historical for their venture. He'd seemed like an omen of good fortune.

"I'll go out and see him later, too," she said, feeling troubled.

"The vet is excellent, at least," Ryan said. "I guess out here they have to be top-notch, since folks depend on their livestock."

"That's good to hear," Toni murmured. "I'll be back down soon." And she left

261

them, hurrying up to her room.

The door to the bath was closed. She knocked gently on it, but there was no answer, so she opened the door. Glancing across, she saw that the door to Bruce's room was closed, as well. Not locked, but closed.

She made the conscious decision not to lock it as she poured herself a hot bath.

Stripping off the clothes she had been wearing, she knew that she was never going to wear them again. Leaving them beneath the sink, she added bubble bath to the tub and climbed in.

Grateful that no one else had taken a shower or bath lately — and used up the hot-water supply — she sank back and let the heat soak into her. She hadn't realized just how damp and cold she'd felt. The water was good. The steam rising around her seemed to permeate the icy feeling in her bones.

She closed her eyes, resting her head on the rear of the tub, and before long she was back in the woods.

She saw again the man beckoning to her, saw the bubbling water, the tiny whitecaps formed when it struck upon the rocks. Then she saw herself coming upon the branch again, lifting it. Tension gripped her, but she couldn't escape the image she was suddenly seeing. For it wasn't that of ancient bones, the remains of a centuries-old crime.

She pictured a different body. Complete, intact. The body of a young woman, naked, facedown in the mud and water, hair encrusted with the black muck, tendrils of it betraying that once it had been blond and long.

She pictured herself turning the body, seeing the face. Pictured the eyes looking up at her, glazed with horror. And she wanted desperately to escape the grasp of the vision, but she could not.

Suddenly Toni had an image of the girl that haunted her as she had been in life, standing on a street corner in Edinburgh. She vaguely recognized the locality, not on the Royal Mile, but a street that was off the main drag, very dark, shadowy, the lights flickering. From somewhere she could hear the sound of music, muted as it came from a pub. There was also the sound of laughter, voices, distant, as well, merrymakers drinking quite a bit. She could see the girl's face, the eyes, and almost enter her mind.

Money. She needed money. And standing on the street corner, she wondered if she should go back in the pub and seek out a man there . . . except that she had been in the pub already and had seen no familiar faces. And no prospects. She had chosen a working man's place that night, and the fellows had all been the kind down with the economy. So she had come to the street. She had to be careful, of course — she didn't want to advertise to any of the bobbies who might be cruising about — but she also had to stand in such a way that the right fellow would know . . .

She was dressed in a plaid miniskirt to show off her legs, which she knew were very good. And her blouse wasn't ridiculously low-cut, but low-cut enough.

She hesitated, wondering if she had chosen the right street corner. For a moment, a brief moment, she wondered what she was doing. How on earth had she chosen this way of life? Then she knew. She hadn't really chosen this life. She had just known that she had to get out of the life she would have lived, scrubbing floors, working in a factory or serving burgers in a fast-food dive. She had no real education, and she would have married some fellow who would also take a menial job. She would have had a dozen children and lived in poverty.

She still believed that with a little more money — and learning to stay out of the

pubs! — she could make it down to London.
And once there . . . well, something would
work out.

She shouldn't be doing this, but she
didn't have a whole lot of options. Besides,
she had learned . . . even with an ugly,
smelling, fat old fellow, all she had to do was
close her eyes, get it over with. Then it was
done. And she had learned how to forget.

Maybe tonight she could find one who
wasn't quite so fat, so gross, a fellow who
didn't smell of stale whiskey, or worse yet,
sheep.

Maybe there would be no one. . . .

She heard the car before she saw it. It
drew up next to her. She bent down, looking
into the window and her heart soared. He
was really quite a handsome brute. Great
smile.

She climbed into the car.

"Toni!"

Her eyes flew open. She jerked up. All
images faded in a snap, as if they had never
been. Only a whisper of unease remained
with her, a slight trickle of fear.

Bruce MacNiall was just inside the
doorway, a deep frown creasing his forehead. She stared at him, aware that the bub-
bles around her were dying and totally

heedless of the fact.

She had consciously made the decision to leave the door open. At the moment, though, she barely remembered that as she tried to recall what she had seen in her mind's eye.

She had clearly seen the girl's face, her eyes, with far too much detail! And she had felt things for another, stepped into a different life.

"I'm sorry, I didn't mean to intrude," Bruce said, his voice deep. "I was afraid you were drowning in here."

She was suddenly so glad of his appearance that she could hardly bear it. She scrambled to her feet, almost tripping in her haste to leave the tub, startling him when she flew, soaking, into his arms.

"Hey!" he said, very softly and apparently heedless of the water that soaked from her naked body onto him. His arms wrapped around her for a moment, giving her all the warmth, security and live, vital reality that she so desperately needed. Then he drew back slightly, lifting her chin.

"I thought that you were all right?" he queried gently.

"I am," she said, and she was. At that moment, in his arms, she was fine. When he held her close, she was not afraid. She did not become blind to her visions, nor did she forget them. But she felt a sense of well-being. And more. Suddenly, despite what she had seen — or perhaps because of it — she wanted to feel all the heat and eroticism promised in the electricity that burned between them every time they spoke, every time they touched.

He arched a brow, then said, "If you're afraid, Toni, I'm pleased to protect you, to offer whatever company you may need. But don't come to me in such a way unless it's what you really want."

She nodded, and a wistful smile came to her lips. "I need you."

"Aye, and I'm here."

The curve to her lips deepened. "I know that you'd . . . keep me company with nothing more required. And this may sound very strange indeed, but I'm not afraid anymore. I want to be with you. So . . . you know that thing about me jumping you? Well . . . ?"

He hesitated for a minute and a wave of uncertainty washed over her, almost a sense of panic. He would push her away, she thought; she was acting like a fool.

But then he lifted her chin and met her eyes with an intensity burning in his own. "I just don't want you jumping me because . . . because you need someone to sleep with."

She stared up at him, shaking her head. "Not *someone*. You."

"Ah," he murmured, still studying her.

"So . . . you *don't* want me jumping you?" she queried.

"Aye, lass, that I do," he said, and the ragged tremor in his voice alone sent shock waves of hunger and anticipation streaking through her. "I do, that I do. I want you jumping me because you just can't stand it anymore. Because you're thinking I'm the sexiest thing that's ever walked into your life. Because you want my hands all over you, everywhere. Because your every thought regarding me is totally sensual, simply carnal." His voice deepened still further, and the steel of his eyes was silver, the heat in his hold, in his body, almost staggering. "I want you jumping me because you're dying to get your hands on my bare flesh, because you're absolutely fascinated by what a Scotsman's got under his kilt."

"You're not wearing a kilt."

"Ah, lass, if this is really what you want, I don't intend to be wearing anything."

She reached up, stroking his cheek, marveling at the texture of his flesh, wondering, in that moment, how she had kept so long from doing this. She breathed him in, feeling the deep-seated power in his chest and everything that was so strikingly male about him — the sense, the feel, the color of his hair, the set of his features and all that she couldn't quite touch.

"I want to crawl into your skin," she whispered honestly, meeting his gaze.

He stepped back, and for a moment again, she felt the vulnerability of having laid her heart on the line. Or the absolute extent of her desire, at the very least. She felt her nakedness then, and her eyes betrayed a need too deep.

But he hadn't left her. He was simply getting out of his shirt so quickly that a button went flying.

"My skin is all yours," he said. "All of it."

She smiled, throwing herself against him once more, taking a moment to delight in the feel of his flesh against her own, her breasts pressed hard to him, the erotic pressure of muscle, the tease of dark hair upon his chest. His hand, massive, the fingers so long, caught beneath her chin, lifting her face to his. His lips formed upon her own, his tongue bold. The first kiss was no gentle sway but a staggering force that eclipsed the world and created a staggering acuity in her senses. She was so keenly aware of where he touched her, and where he did not. And every inch of her naked length longed to be stroked by him, longed to come closer and closer. His tongue entered her mouth with a thrust and power that created a staccato pulse of all that was to come. She seemed to lose air and all thought of breathing. She felt like a bow, stretched tight and quivering, and she was afraid her knees would give at any moment.

Maybe he knew. . . .

He lifted her against him. Again, every brush of sensation seemed to be acute. The feel of the fabric of his jeans, his belt buckle, his hands, his flesh, the force of his erection against the denim. It occurred to her vaguely that she'd known him two days' time; it seemed like forever. His naked chest against her flesh was hot with a fever that seduced and entered into her soul, exotic, overwhelming. He laid her upon the ancient tapestry of his bed, beneath the brocade canopy, and when he moved to doff his shoes and jeans, she was bereft, left cold and aching. In seconds he was back, upon her, straddling, creating a new wave of frenzied fire as she felt the bareness of his sex against her flesh. *Then* would have been fine. She had never wanted anything more. But he leaned low, eyes meeting hers again, fingers finding her arms, tracing their length, drawing them above her head as his lips found hers once again.

And from there . . .

The wet pressure of his lips, tongue, mouth, the feel against her breasts, nipples, was almost more than she could bear. His hands slid down to caress her torso; her fingers threaded into his hair. She writhed beneath him, gasping. "I am supposed to be jumping you!"

For a moment, his eyes touched hers, steel and silver, both hard and bright. "Ah, but jumping on me now could cause serious damage, and not further the cause at all." His face burrowed against her belly then, his tongue teasing her navel. Lower. Laving the hollows of her hips. And his hands . . . between her thighs. His fingers . . . a stroke never hesitant, a touch . . . followed by his kiss. . . .

She cried out, stunned, catapulted to an urgency that was pure anguish. Reeling with the impact, the sensual sensation so staggering, she jackknifed beneath him, reaching a climax that rocked through her with astonishing speed, staying with her, gripping her. . . .

And feeling him again, the slide of his body against her own, the insinuation of his sex and the length of it within her, so that before she had drifted down she was soaring up once again. She was moving with him in a state of blind, desperate bliss, so very aware of his scent, his heat, his vibrancy and every detail of the sheer physicality of their union. Heaven and earth seemed to fade away. There was nothing but entwining arms, limbs, the slick feel of naked flesh, the rise within her and the pounding, pulsing desire to reach the pinnacle once again.

She had thought herself stroked, sated, to the point of wild ecstasy before, had thought that nothing could ever shock or exhilarate her to such a fantastic sensual delight and combustion again. She had been wrong. His ragged pulse, stroke, thrust, touch, evoked and elicited a wildness in her she had never dreamed. Cries escaped her; she clung to him, writhed beneath him, arched and thundered, indeed, as if she could get into his skin . . . and the wild violence with which she exploded then into climax was shattering. As it ripped through her again and again, she trembled, awed, weakened, shaking, barely aware of the world around her. He held her still, damp, hot, the pulse that had thundered through the beat of her heart, slowing, bit by bit. . . .

His arms, fast around her, his hair, a tangled thicket of ebony over his forehead, his eyes . . . silver, so sensual. His words . . .

She waited, barely breathing, longing to know what he would say.

And then . . . they both heard it — the rapping on the door.

"Bruce? You in there?"

The flicker in his eyes became one of resignation and amusement.

"Robert Chamberlain," he murmured with regret. "I told him to come by."

She certainly wasn't a child, had every right in the world to do what she was doing, to be where she was. Yet Toni found herself leaping to her feet, offering him a grimace. "Right," she said simply, and fled through the connecting bath.

10

Darkness had descended and done so deeply by the time Thayer returned. As he headed up the driveway, he slowed, noting the cars at the foot of the hill by the forest, all with law enforcement markings on them. There was the constable's car, and a few from farther afield — as far as Edinburgh and Stirling.

It didn't take a rocket scientist to figure out what had happened.

Still he slowed the car. An officer in uniform seemed to be standing vigil out by the cars. He walked to the driver's door of Thayer's vehicle as he slowed.

"Evening, sir!" the officer said.

"Evening."

"Heading for the castle? If you're here for one of the tours, I'm afraid there isn't one tonight."

"Actually, I'm with the folks giving the tours."

"Ah!" the fellow said. He peered more intently at Thayer.

"Heard it was Americans, giving tours on Scottish history. You from Glasgow?"

"Aye, that I am. Kin to one of the Americans. They're giving good tours," Thayer said. He didn't know why he was sounding defensive. He certainly didn't want to be challenging any law officials. Especially with what he had in the car.

"What's happening here?" he asked the officer.

"The news will be gettin' out soon enough, I wager," the officer said.

Thayer tensed.

"They've . . . found a body?" he asked.

"Aye!" the officer said gravely.

"In the forest again, eh?"

"Aye, again!"

"So . . ." Thayer said slowly, feeling a sheen of sweat break out on his upper lip. "They found the missing girl?"

The officer suddenly frowned, shaking his head. "Is that what you thought? Ach, well, and why not, since the other poor wee lasses were found here," the officer said. "Nae, what they've found is a very old corpse . . . well, bones and pieces, at the least. They're thinking she was the wife o' the laird of the castle, but there are fellows in there now from the university, as well as from the law! That's all I know. So, if you've legitimate business up at the castle, you go on up. Take care around here, eh? They haven't found the poor lass gone missing last in here as of yet, but with the discoveries made of late, well, they still may be doin' so. Aye, and if you can think of anything that you've seen around here out of the ordinary — other than a flock of Americans! — you be sure to tell the constable right away."

The officer thought that he was amusing. Thayer cracked a weak smile.

"Seriously, report anything suspicious right away," the officer said.

"Aye, right away," Thayer promised him.

The officer patted the car's hood. Thayer gave him a wave, put the car into gear and started up the path to the castle.

He parked in the driveway and hesitated. He hadn't realized that he was sweating, that his palms were clammy, that he had been shaking inside, right down into his boots.

Did he look as flushed as he felt? he wondered. And why not? He'd just been told that a body was found in the woods.

He sat a second longer, then exited the car. He started toward the castle, then turned back and stared at the vehicle, and made sure that the locks had clicked.

He slicked back his hair, and started on in.

Actually, he told himself, there was a bit of a thrill to it all.

★ ★ ★

"I didn't catch you sleeping at this time — and under these circumstances?" Robert said, looking up as Bruce made his way down the stairs.

"Sleeping?" Bruce repeated. "Ah, no." *Frankly, old chum, you just interrupted one of the finest moments in my life,* Bruce thought dryly. Then again, he'd asked Robert to come by. "Shared shower these days," he said briefly. That kind of explained, with a grain of truth. He wasn't so sure Toni would want their intimacy either known or broadcast at this moment, so he went on quickly. "Have you met the others?"

"I have," Robert told him. "Including Miss Fraser. She's the one with whom you share the shower?"

"Ah, yes." Bruce grimaced. "Where are they off to at the moment?"

"In the kitchen. The Glasgow fellow, Thayer, just returned. Everyone is talking at once in there, trying to tell him what's happened, and why the base of the hill is covered with police vehicles. When it winds down to a soft roar, Gina Browne is going to copy the documents and give me the original ones. She's trying to pull up the corporation on the Internet again, but naturally, there is no such place anymore, so we'll have to get the cyber experts on it. You were right, their papers look absolutely legal and authentic, but I suppose that's not a difficult thing to accomplish, if you're of a criminal bent."

"They're making copies here?"

"I guess you haven't wandered into Mrs. Browne's domain," Robert said. "She has a computer, printer, fax and mobile phone line. Quite an amazing display of 'have electronics, will travel,' actually."

Bruce nodded, not really surprised. "They trust you, then, I take it?" he queried.

Robert's eyes sparkled for a moment. "Well, there is the fact that I'm accepted by the dozen crime-scene experts down the hill, though I'm pretty sure that Mrs. Browne called Edinburgh and checked on my credentials."

Bruce smiled ruefully. "Well, good. I think they really believe that I own the place now, too."

Robert arched a brow in amusement.

"Was anyone able to glean anything more from the site?" Bruce asked him.

Robert shook his head. "Not at the moment. It appears that the remains must have washed up very recently. Darrow is actually excited, which is something I don't think he gets to feel often when he's found a body — or pieces of one. Due to our discoveries of the past, I made a very thorough search of the area myself. I guess I was actually hoping to find Annie O'Hara, but there was no sign of her — or anything else, for that matter. As for footprints, I could follow those of Miss Fraser, and the tracks of our officers, but nothing else. They were still scouring the area when I left — since all those men are there, it seemed a fine time for a very thorough search — but so far, nothing. Not a cigar butt, a broken branch, nothing. Darkness is on us, though. The woods do need a good scouring, but Jonathan is right about one thing — it's a damned big forest."

"That it is," Bruce agreed.

Robert angled his head, regarding Bruce carefully.

"Jonathan got your goat tonight, didn't he?"

Bruce offered his friend a slow, wry smile. "The rumor that our local hero murdered his wife in a fit of rage and jealousy has been around for years. Perhaps it's true. Maybe these bones will turn out to be those of one of my ancestors. It's only Jonathan's pleasure at turning my blood kin into a monster that riles me." He shrugged. "We're still friends, I believe. Have been, all these years."

"He's jealous of you, always has been."

"That's foolish. I may own a derelict castle and bear the old title, but it doesn't mean all that much these days."

"I don't think it's the title that bothers him," Robert said.

"Then what?"

"Your reputation," Robert said. "For solving a national mystery, all those years ago."

"I've been out of it for a decade."

"And he's still a small-town constable."

"Well, if he harbors ill will, it's his problem, and his foolishness," Bruce said, shaking his head.

"So you won't be greatly disturbed . . . if this proves to be the long-gone Annalise?"

"A mystery will have been solved," Bruce said simply. "Whatever it was, I can't change history."

"Nae, not a one of us can do that, ancient or recent," Robert said with a sigh, and Bruce knew he was thinking that if they could only catch the killer, they might well change the history of life for many a poor lass. "I've been invited to supper," Robert told him suddenly. "I was sent to retrieve you."

"Ah."

"But Miss Fraser is still upstairs?"

"I believe she'll be right down."

"Is she doing all right?" Robert asked.

"Yes, she seems to be just fine. Come on, we'll head on into the kitchen."

Robert was watching him somewhat strangely, but Bruce ignored the look and led the way. By the time they reached the door that led through the secondary hall, they could smell the succulent aroma of the meal. Pushing through the doorway to the kitchen, Bruce found the table handsomely set, Gina pouring wine, Ryan at her side, Kevin carving the roast and Thayer and David rushing about to find the proper bowls for the accompanying vegetables. With a tray of meat and tiny pearl onions in his hands, Kevin turned and saw Bruce.

"Laird MacNiall, thanks for coming down. I know it's been a sad and traumatic day, but while we live and breathe, we have to eat, right?"

"Right. It looks like a fine supper, Kevin," Bruce said.

Kevin set the tray on the table.

"Where on earth is Toni?" David fretted, setting down a plate of broccoli, then running his fingers absently through his dark hair.

"On her way, I'm certain," Bruce assured him.

"I think we'll really have to start without her," Gina murmured. "It will all grow cold."

"I think I should go up," David said.

Kevin set a hand on his arm and nodded. "You should."

"They'll just take longer, chatting up there together," Thayer warned as David started out.

"David is very dear to her," Gina said, finishing with the last glass, surveying the table, seeming pleased. "If she's at all upset . . . well, David is close to her."

"We're all close to her!" Ryan protested, staring at his wife.

"Yes, dear. But David and she . . . just let David handle it," Gina said. "Inspector Chamberlain, we're so pleased that you could stay!" she added, smiling at Robert as he walked in.

"Not to mention, grateful for your help," Ryan said. "Especially when the fact that we've been fleeced can hardly mean much in comparison to the plethora of bodies to be found about."

"A plethora! Ryan!" Gina said, horrified by his choice of words.

"I'm sorry. I mean, bodies . . . in the forest. Ancient, new. . . . Sorry!" Ryan said again.

Robert waved a hand in the air. "Actually, I won't be handling your problem myself — we have people who specialize in computer fraud and international crime. And you needn't be grateful to me in any capacity. Enforcing the law is my work, in no matter what capacity. We'll get your case into the right hands, which, admittedly, are not my own. The supper smells delicious."

"Thank you!" Kevin said, beaming.

"Actually, he's the meat wizard," Ryan protested. "Potatoes and broccoli are creations perfected by my lovely wife," Ryan informed him.

"To everyone involved in the effort, it looks — and smells — quite divine," Robert said. He flashed a glance at Bruce, indicating that he considered his household of Americans quite an amusement.

"Robert, we put you here, opposite the laird of the castle!" Gina said, trying for a light note.

The group assembled, minus David and Toni for the time being. Kevin cleared his throat. "Shall we say grace?" he asked, looking at Thayer for guidance.

Thayer offered an amused smile. "If you wish."

"Um . . . sure," Ryan murmured. He lowered his head, but his eyes were open as he looked around.

They were a fairly spiritual group, Bruce thought, decent folk, but not necessarily the ones in the front of the church every Sunday morning. Like Thayer, he was slightly amused, and yet he admired the group for trying to gage the proper etiquette for a Scottish Sunday meal.

But no one spoke.

Kevin looked around, apparently a bit panicked, since it had been his idea.

"Um . . . is it proper for the laird of the castle to speak?" he inquired.

"I think it would be quite proper for the American cook," Bruce said.

"Ah," Kevin agreed. "Okay. Dear Lord, thank you for this meal, for the generosity and kindness of our host and for the help of our host's friends. We're aware that there is famine and real tragedy in the world — like the poor old soul found in the forest this time, and those other girls — but please, oh, Lord, help us in our endeavors, as well. We really meant all the best. We love Scotland! We mean to help —"

"Amen!" Gina cut in firmly, glaring at Kevin.

Robert simply laughed out loud. "A lovely grace, Kevin," he said. "But don't you have the same one in the States that we have here? Simply quicker. 'God is great, God is good, thank you God, for this food. Let's eat.'?"

Kevin flushed as the rest of them laughed.

"Let me pass the meat!" Gina said quickly.

Toni had just set the hair dryer down when she heard the knock at her door and David's voice. "Toni?"

She opened the door. "Hey, I'm sorry. I've taken too long, huh?"

"Kid, you can take all night if you want. I came up to make sure that you were all right. The concern about a hot meal doesn't really compare to the discovery of bones in the forest," he assured her sympathetically.

"I keep saying this, though no one seems to believe me, but I'm all right," she said. "It's just . . ."

"Just what?" he asked gently.

She walked on into the room and sat on the side of the bed. He joined her, slipping an arm around her shoulders.

"Are you still envisioning a long-dead Scotsman with a bloody sword?" he asked.

She shook her head quickly, but then flashed him a glance.

"David," she murmured.

"Talk to me," he said. "That's why I'm

here. Look, you're a good actress. You have everyone else convinced that you're relieved because it wasn't that missing girl, turned up dead. But I know you, and I know you're upset about those bones."

"She's dead," Toni murmured.

"What?"

She looked at his handsome, caring face and shook her head. "Nothing."

"Toni! Please, you know I never repeat a word you say to me."

"But do I know that you won't have me committed to an asylum?" she asked.

"Never," he assured her.

She inhaled deeply. "David, I could have sworn that I saw Bruce go into the forest."

David frowned. "Toni, he did leave the castle very early."

She nodded. "So I've been told. And I know travel here can take some time, but still . . ."

"Did you ask Bruce?"

"He was in Edinburgh. With his friend."

"And you trust in that, of course."

"There's something about him that . . . yes, I trust him."

"Then . . . ?"

"David, I think I'm seeing things again." Her words suddenly started to pour from her. "This afternoon . . . if it wasn't Bruce, then it was the man that I invented, that Bruce from centuries ago. Or else, someone who dresses up like him and has access to a big black horse. Or else, I'm going crazy."

"Toni," he said slowly, "you're not going crazy. We'll rule that out right off the bat. When you came in tonight, you said something about it being a trick of the light. Isn't that possible?"

"I suppose," she murmured.

"But you don't believe it."

She shook her head. "There's more."

"Go on."

She shook her head. "When I was taking a bath . . . David, it was suddenly as if I was *her*."

"Toni, you're losing me. Her — who?" He shook his head. "The long-gone Annalise?"

"No. And that's what one would have thought. I mean, after everything else I made up that turned out to be true, I should have been imagining what it had been like for Annalise. But no, it was suddenly as if I were . . . the missing girl."

"Annie O'Hara?" he said with surprise.

She nodded gravely.

"What do you mean?"

"Well, it was as if I was where she had been, as if I could follow her thoughts the night she was taken. And killed. I could see outside a pub where she was drinking. She was even weighing in her mind what she was about to do. And then a car came up, and she was pleased and excited, because it wasn't some creepy old man about to pick her up."

"Did you see him?" David asked sharply.

"No." Toni shook her head. "No, I didn't. I — I was distracted. I don't know if I would have seen the fellow or not."

He sighed, rubbing her shoulders. "Toni, you do know that the mind can do bizarre things — especially under the stress of suggestion?"

"Yes, I know. Oh, God, David! Don't you think I'm looking for every possible rational reason for what I'm thinking, feeling . . . doing?"

"Toni, please don't go getting all paranoid. Honestly, think about it. Everything happening here is very suggestive. And hey, maybe there is some idiot in the village who hates Bruce MacNiall and is trying to get the man into some serious trouble by dressing up like him."

"You think someone else might have a big black horse?" she queried.

He smiled. "I sure as hell think that's possible. They breed horses all around here. And big hairy coos!" he added, trying to get her to smile.

She did smile, but the effort faded quickly.

"Ah, Toni!"

"I'm still . . . scared. Well, not exactly scared, but worried. Unnerved, I guess."

"Toni! You found a body, the human remains of someone. That's pretty traumatic."

She shook her head. "No, you don't understand. Yes, it's horrible and disturbing, and I think I've had the reaction most people would — out-and-out pain and sympathy for the poor girl. And I also feel that distance most people would. Whoever she was, she died years and years ago. But it's this connection I feel to Annie O'Hara that's so unnerving! I don't know how to explain it."

"Still, it's natural that you would feel for another soul, and that your mind might play tricks," David said.

"David, I told you about the things that happened when I was a child. I had pushed it all back — so far back! — for years. It's terrifying to see these things."

He was silent for a minute. "Toni, don't say this to anyone else."

"They'll see that I'm locked up, right?"

He didn't smile or even reply right away. "No, that's not what I mean. It's just . . . you shouldn't say things like this to anyone else. It could get out."

"I don't intend to! I didn't even intend to say anything to you. But if you're not worried about them all thinking that I'm crazy, what are you worried about?"

He hesitated. "Toni, you might have stumbled upon old bones, but there is a very real killer out there. He's probably a psychotic and far away, but people talk."

"So?"

He exhaled and looked straight at her. "Toni, people like wild stories. Newspapers will pick up anything. And whether they think you're a crazy, headline-hunting American or not, they could print something. Most people will think you're nutty. But there is a killer out there, and if you scare him, make him think that you can see things others can't, then you could be considered a real threat."

She stared at him, slowly understanding just what he was saying.

"A threat, Toni! Do you understand? You could put yourself in danger!"

She shook her head at first, in denial, then she felt the chills snaking down her spine.

"Don't worry," she whispered after a moment. "Trust me, I won't say a word to anyone, anyone at all. As I said, I didn't even mean to talk to you."

"But I love you, and I'm your best friend," he reminded her. "Well, Gina likes to claim that she is, but we both know it's me," he teased.

Toni laughed. "You're both the best friends in the world," she assured him.

"You can talk to me whenever you're feeling frantic, and I promise, I'll never make you think that you're crazy. I'll always be around when you need me," he said, giving her another hug.

"Thanks!" she whispered, and hugged him back fiercely. "Okay, I'll give it to you this time. You're the best friend in the world!"

"I'm the best friend, but Laird Bruce is still the hottest guy around, huh?" he teased.

She felt a flood of color soar to her cheeks.

"Hey! I have hit on something there, haven't I?"

"We'd best get downstairs," she said.

"I told you, he is a hottie," David said, watching her with keen interest now, a curious light in his eyes.

"Yes, yes, he's attractive," Toni murmured. "Shall we go down?"

He agreed, and rising, he took her hand and escorted her toward the door. When they reached it, he turned back, looking around the room. "Hmm. The bed is way too neat," he said. "And there I was, thinking that . . . But wait! There is another room, right? Through the bath?"

He started to walk back into the room, but Toni caught him by his shirt. "Out! You — we — are not going snooping into his room!" she said, trying to put some indignity into her tone.

"Snooping? I don't think you were snooping earlier!" David teased.

She groaned aloud. "Downstairs. Food, dinner, remember?"

"I want details!" he teased.

"You're not getting any."

"Aha! So there are details to be gotten?"

"Dinner!" she insisted.

"That's okay, I'll make up a better story than you could give me," he said.

She paused for a minute, aware that he was making her squirm — and laugh. He really was the world's best friend.

"There is no better story!" she said, putting up a hand. "And that's all you're getting! Let's go down."

Laughing, he followed her as she hurried toward the stairway.

"There's really a lot of activity in the forest," Thayer said, taking a piece of the meat and passing it on. He watched Bruce MacNiall, and the new man, Robert Chamberlain, with interest.

He'd heard of Chamberlain, of course. The man was ostensibly with the Edinburgh police, but had been called around the country often enough, and was held in high esteem by the government and his fellow law-enforcement officers. From what Thayer had read about the fellow, he'd thought the man a better diplomat and politician than detective. That evening, he felt as if he might have been wrong. There was something about the bloke.

"And judging by the number of cars, they've called in people from all over. It's funny, but I got the impression that the constable is a little proprietorial."

"Jonathan is all right," Robert said, glancing at Bruce.

"There is simply no way for a village such as this to have the kind of technology available in the larger cities, obviously," Bruce said.

"So," Thayer continued, "the folks out there now combing the forest are specialists? Forensics fellows, lasses, whichever?"

"Yes," Robert said.

Bruce nodded. "I think they were contacting the university, hoping to get out some anthropologists and specialists."

"Aye, then, that's good," Thayer said. "Maybe, while they're digging up old bones, they'll find out more about the fellow killing girls now, and be able to put a stop to the bloke."

"We will put a stop to him," Robert said.

"Pity that Toni didn't stumble upon Annie O'Hara," Thayer said.

They all stared at him.

"Sorry! I didn't mean that I'd wish such a thing on my own kin, or that we should give up hope that the girl is alive. But . . . if she'd been found, it may have helped the effort to catch the killer, right? It's bad business. No one even knows if Annie O'Hara is only the third victim."

"We don't know that she is a victim," Robert said.

"Has this guy been at it for such a long time?" Ryan asked with a frown. He flushed slightly as he looked over at Bruce MacNiall. "That sounds so callous. I'm sorry. I guess I just didn't really realize how long it's been going on. I don't know why it surprises me — we've had serial killers at large for years in the United States. Nowadays we're always hoping that they're . . . well, caught quicker. If you watch CSI back home, you get the feeling that a crime can be solved in a night."

"Sadly, it doesn't often work that way," Bruce murmured.

"The first woman disappeared over a year ago," Robert said, glancing at Bruce. "She was found in a sad state of decomposition. The second, just a bit more than six months ago. She was also found in a very serious state of decay. We've had little, if nothing, to go on."

"Dead men do tell tales," Kevin murmured.

"It's definitely true that the dead can speak, through medicine and science," Robert said. "But to make comparisons, you have to have a suspect."

Kevin set down his fork.

Bruce MacNiall stared at Thayer. "Surely, Thayer, you might not have heard my name — or known anything about the castle or the forest here — but you must have heard about this killer? When the first girl went missing, there was barely a notice, until her body was found in the forest, by me. But there was national coverage when the second girl went missing, and then when she was found in the forest, this time by Eban."

Thayer was alarmed by the strange chill that snaked down his spine. What did MacNiall think this was, a bloody game of Clue? "Aye, *I've* heard about the killer. I do read the papers. But we've had other crimes, as well, about the country."

"But you didn't remember the name of the forest?" MacNiall persisted.

"This was advertised as Castle Keep," Thayer said, trying hard not to sound defensive. "Nothing in the documents we all read and signed mentioned anything about Tillingham Forest."

"I see," MacNiall murmured, not sounding convinced.

Toni walked into the kitchen then, followed by David, who was grinning broadly, until he sensed the tension in the room. "Is everything all right?" he asked.

"Yes, absolutely," Thayer said, thankful for the interruption. He lifted his glass. "We should be toasting Kevin's fine meal. And our host, Laird MacNiall, and his good friend, Detective Inspector Chamberlain."

"A toast!" David said. "Yes, indeed." Still standing, he lifted his wineglass. "To Kevin, great meal."

Gina cleared her throat.

"To Gina," David said, laughing. "Great veggies, as always! To Detective Inspector

Chamberlain, with our deepest thanks, and to our host, more gratitude and admiration than he can ever imagine!"

"Here, here!" went around the table.

Then Thayer watched as Toni took her seat next to Laird Bruce MacNiall. He saw the flash in her eyes and the smile that curled her lips. And he saw the way that MacNiall looked back at her. Though it was subtle, it was still one of the most telling exchanges Thayer had ever seen.

Something had changed between the two. It wasn't a great mystery. His muscles clenched and tightened. His stomach hurt. So . . . they'd slept together.

Toni, with her huge, deep blue eyes, generous, sensual lips, damned plethora of blond hair, lithe height, supple curves, intoxicating laughter and scent . . .

Thayer could be nothing but her cousin, her friend. They were far too close, she said. Like hell. He remembered when they had met. He could have told her the truth — the real truth. Instead, he had tried to emphasize just how many times "removed" they were as relations. But it had done no good.

Face it, fellow, he told himself. *She just didn't find you attractive. You might as well have been a eunuch — or of another persuasion, like Kevin and David. You fool. You've* dreamed, you've drooled. You thought you'd give it time. And there she is, sleeping with the bloke after only forty-eight hours?

His fingers knotted around his wineglass.

He could see the two of them, Toni, with those eyes on him, his eyes somewhere else. Hell, the great MacNiall, the fellow with the castle, the title, the fookin' bulging biceps and castiron chest.

Suddenly the glass snapped in his hand.

"Thayer!"

Toni was the first to jump up with alarm, running to his side, her napkin in her hand.

"It's all right, it's all right!" he said quickly.

Her eyes were on his, deep with concern. "Must have picked up the handle wrong!" he muttered.

"You're bleeding. Let me make sure there's no glass in it," Toni said.

"I'll get the first-aid kit," Gina said.

"No!" he said, standing.

It had been a bark, he realized, for everyone in the room was staring at him. And was there suspicion in the eyes of the great Detective Inspector Chamberlain, and those of the even-greater Laird MacNiall?

He forced a wry grin. "Sorry, I'm feeling the worst fool, such an oaf," he muttered.

"Thayer, it's all right," Toni said, still

concerned. "But you are bleeding."

"A scratch. If you will excuse me, I'll just see to it. Ach, I hope I didn't get glass in any of the food," he said, causing them all to look at the table.

"None of it even near any food, old chap!" David said cheerfully.

That damned David, always working to make everything fookin' copasetic! he thought.

"Thayer, are you sure you're not cut deeply?" Gina asked, concerned.

He shook his head. "Embarrassed is what I am," he said. "I'll be back in a moment."

Gina and Toni were picking up shards of glass.

"I really don't think we have to worry about any of the food," Gina murmured. "I think we're getting it all."

"Aye, don't worry none," Robert said. "If there's a shard there, your host will be seein' it."

"Good eyes, eh, Bruce?" David said.

Thayer found himself pausing just beyond the doorway, ignoring the blood that dripped from his hand.

"His eyes are the best," Robert informed them all. "Hell, when he was with the force, Bruce was run ragged. We dragged him in on everything."

There was a startled silence.

"You were a *cop?*" Ryan said to Bruce.

"Aye, for a time," Bruce said. There was a slight edge to his voice, as if he hadn't particularly wanted the information known.

Thayer remained in the hall, feeling as if he was very nearly baring his teeth. *Aye, the fellow was a copper! You never knew, you fools. Never suspected.*

But how would they have known? Only a Scotsman would have read all about it.

11

Gina tidied up the business area in the bedroom she and Ryan had chosen. She'd liked it especially because of the large expanse of window it offered, looking out on the valley. Probably, at an earlier date, the room had been the domain of a chief guard, or something of the like. The window — evidently put in sometime after the turn of the nineteenth century — looked out over the hillside. From this vantage point, any invader seeking to come upon the castle would have been in clear view.

She stacked the copies of their documents and at last turned off all the machines.

Ryan was already in bed. She gazed at him with a deep and abiding love. She had known from the moment she met him that he was all she wanted in life. He could be fun, sweet — and aggravating at times. And though it appeared he deferred to her, it was only because she really did have an incredible business sense. But beneath it all . . . Ryan ruled the roost. He always had.

His hands were folded behind his head as he lay on his pillow staring up at the ceiling.

The white sheets of their bed were drawn to his waist. His shoulders and chest were bronze, and she felt the thrill that she always did when looking at him. She truly loved everything about him.

It should have been their day for total relaxation, but it just hadn't gone that way. She was tired, anxious to crawl in beside him. He was pretty damned cool beneath the sheets, as well.

She walked to the doorway and turned off the main light. With the moonlight that filtered in, there was just enough light to . . .

She paused at the foot of the bed, feeling the need for intimacy, and ready to play with it. In that mood, she slowly shed her shirt, then her bra, and made a real act of shedding her jeans and panties. Ryan should be both amused and titillated.

Coming around the bed to crawl in, she realized that he hadn't even glanced at her — not once.

He turned to her then, frowning.

"Just what the hell are we going to do?" he demanded.

"Do? We're 'doing' it," she reminded him.

He shook his head.

"What the hell are we going to do about *Toni?*" he demanded.

She felt her blood grow cold.

"What do you mean . . . about Toni?" she said with a swallow. "She's — she's just Toni. There's nothing to *do* about her at all."

"There has to be!" he insisted angrily.

"Why?" she whispered, frightened by his tone, knowing it all too well.

"Because she's dangerous," he said flatly, harshly.

The chill in her bones deepened, and it seemed that her blood turned to ice.

Toni went up first that night, leaving Bruce still talking to Robert Chamberlain. She found herself industriously brushing her teeth, washing her face . . . and finding the white nightgown, aware that it kept her covered, but not all that covered.

She had made the first move, and it had been far from subtle — since catapulting yourself out of a bathtub, naked and dripping, into a man's arms could really never be considered less than big-time brash. Certainly he would come to her tonight. He had to!

He was slow in coming up. She lay on her own bed, torn. He couldn't feel quite the way that she did — desperate to feel again what she had just experienced — and linger so long. He was unique in her eyes. Maybe she wasn't so special in his. Hell, a naked woman throws herself at you, what else would a red-blooded male do?

She flushed, wondering if she hadn't made a fool out of herself, wondering if he wasn't downstairs pondering how to extricate himself from any further intimacy with her.

She closed her eyes and gritted her teeth, wincing. There was more to it. She didn't want to be alone. She didn't want to dream, imagine, envision or see things. And there was something about him that was rocklike and solid, something that defied fear and mist and things that could go bump in the night.

But that wasn't the only reason she had gone to him.

Like David teased, he was . . . hot. Those eyes, a slate enigma, searching into her, sweeping over her, his hands touching her . . . the set and structure of his face . . .

She tossed and twisted around. How long had she been up here? An hour, more?

She rose, walked to her door and cracked it open, trying to ascertain if she could still hear voices from below. She couldn't. Looking up and down the hall, she saw that it was empty.

Cautiously at first, not wanting to run into anyone else and appear foolish, she made her way down the hall to the second-floor landing. She stood in the spot she took up when she told her tale about Cavalier MacNiall, the great hero, the battle laird who, it now appeared, had come home from victory to murder his wife.

Then she saw him.

He was standing at the great hearth, leaning against the mantel, looking pensively into the embers of the fire. For a moment, it didn't register that he had changed, that he was no longer in the jeans and tailored shirt he had worn at dinner. He was in a kilt. A swatch of his family plaid was stretched over his shoulder, held in place by a large crest brooch.

He must have sensed that she was there, for he looked up at her and smiled slowly.

Any words she might have said froze on her lips. She felt as if she were on the outskirts of the woods again. She didn't think that he really spoke, yet she heard him clearly.

Come, please. I need you.

Instinct warned her not to go, to remain where she was, but there was no denying the flutter in her heart, the compulsion to follow.

She started down the stairs. As she neared the bottom, he turned away from the great hearth and started toward the secondary hall.

"Bruce!" she managed to say.

He hesitated before disappearing, pausing to beckon with his hand.

"Damn you!" she breathed, following, even though she knew it was insane. She was more frightened for herself than ever, not because he might lead her somewhere terrible, but simply because she was seeing him. And because she had to follow.

"Stop, please!"

But he didn't. He disappeared, and she fled across the expanse of the great hall to the secondary one behind it.

He was there, waiting at the rear of the room where there was an ancient door with rusted hinges. It had been bolted tight, so that they hadn't bothered with it. It led underground, probably, Thayer had told them. A castle such as this one would have a crypt — or simple basement space.

Toni was now certain that it was a crypt, because the door was open, and she could see the winding stone stairs that led below.

She walked to the doorway and took the first step. It should have been dark, but there was a glow of light. And in that glow, she could see Bruce MacNiall, heading down the stairs.

She took a step . . . and then another step. She expected dust and cobwebs. Rats, even. But no spiders clung to tenuous webs in the rafters. There were no old, musty rushes on the floor, no dirt or dust. It seemed it had been kept clean — far cleaner than the main castle.

There were a number of corridors and alleyways, all with arched ceilings overhead, as if she had entered the ancient catacombs of an old church.

"Bruce?" she whispered. Then she saw him. He was down one of the corridors, watching her. Waiting.

She started to walk toward him, but he kept going, into the shadow at the end of the hallway. She hurried along, swearing again beneath her breath. She came to the end of the hallway, and only then realized where she was and what lined the walls.

Tombs.

There was nothing really eerie here. There were no bones turning to brittle dust on family shelves. Every member of the family had a marble flat across their final resting place. Their names were then engraved upon them, along with inscriptions in Gaelic. Wives were proclaimed with their own clan names, as well. *Mary Douglas MacNiall* was inscribed on one freestanding sarcophagus; she had died in the early eighteen hundreds, and she had been, according to her inscription, born to the great family of Moray.

Turning slowly, Toni realized that tombs surrounded her. She couldn't help the natural fear that came from being alone in the dark and the shadows with the dead.

When she turned again, she could see the end of the hall more clearly. There was a nook there, and in it a grand tomb with a marble effigy atop it of the laird, arms folded across his chest, his great sword at his side. A severe tremor shook her, turning her blood to ice. The effigy was so good. She could see the cheeks she had so recently stroked, carved in marble. It was Bruce, the Bruce she knew. . . .

How could any man look so very much like an ancestor? A stone ancestor at that!

Another tomb was at its side, but there was no effigy. And though bold words proclaimed Bruce Brian MacNiall, Laird of Tillingham, victor against all tyranny, the great laird of the true Scots and the true king, there was nothing at all on the other tomb.

She stared at the grave for long moments. The cold in the crypt seemed to creep around her. The light was fading. The shadows, as if they were living beings, began to creep across light once again.

"Bruce?" she called out. Her voice was definitely tremulous.

She turned and ran back down the long hallway of the dead, racing for the stairway. In her wake, shadow covered all that had been light.

She ran up the stairs, terrified that she would reach the doorway and it would be bolted again, shut tight on its rusty hinges. She felt a sense of hysteria coming on then. *What if she was locked down here? What if the shadows kept coming, if they swallowed her, if they sucked her into a miasma of the death and terror and tragedy that had come over the centuries?*

She rammed against the door — and went flying into the open space of the secondary hall, spinning, stumbling and landing on the floor.

With a deep breath, she got hold of herself. Then she was angry.

She stood, looked ruefully at the tear in her gown, and swore that she wasn't playing this game anymore. It was Bruce who had lured her down. It had to have been. And

Bruce had been in the forest earlier. Maybe he wanted to get even with them or teach them a sick lesson, so he was seducing her and tormenting her at the same time!

Furious, she started up the stairway to the second-floor landing. Her strides were long as she walked the hallway to his bedroom door.

She didn't knock, just burst in. And then she froze.

He was there, seated in the chair by the hearth, studying a book, in the jeans and shirt he had worn to dinner.

Eban Douglas stood outside the castle, down the driveway, looking up. He cocked his head, as if listening.

"They've found her!" he said, his voice a half whisper, half cackle. "They've found yer bride, Laird MacNiall. The wee lass. A horrid sight, so they say. Bits o' hair and flesh and . . . well y'd not want to be hearing that, wot, eh? They didna let me see her. Me, who might care for her so tenderly!"

A wind seemed to rise as he stood there. Clouds raced over the moon, throwing it into shadow.

He cast his head back and began to laugh. "Aye, the lasses, the lasses! They be in the forest, them, all of 'em strangled and gone, pretty, pretty maids . . . but with wicked ways. Ah, Laird MacNiall, I be beggin' yer pardon. Fer she was maligned, eh? Yer lady wife, she were. But not the others. Nae, not the others."

He shook his head sadly. "Poor wee sinners! Lost and alone."

Tears suddenly fell down his cheeks. "Nae, not the others!" he whispered.

Then he sighed. His shoulders fell. Dispirited, he turned away from the castle on the hill and started for his cottage, his own wee cottage where he lived, thanks to the kind graces of the great Laird MacNiall. He'd do anything for the great MacNiall. Aye, anything. Things, maybe, MacNiall didn't even know that he needed done himself.

He'd lie, steal or cheat. Indeed, he'd kill for MacNiall, he thought.

Ruefully, he smiled to himself. Aye, that was that. Time to retreat to his little cottage, where he was a little man living a quiet and secretive life, barely even noted by others.

Toni felt as if she hadn't moved in hours, as if she had just stood there, frozen in time. And yet . . . could it have been so long?

He rose, his eyes on her. Tenderly? she wondered. Or mockingly?

"There you are," he said quietly, and

smiled. "What were you doing? Raiding the refrigerator? Actually, I was about to come searching. You weren't here, and you weren't in your bed." His smiled deepened. "Or in the bathtub."

She couldn't move. Or speak. Her mind raced.

He was just a damned good shyster, tricking her downstairs, then running back up, changing clothing again. Was he trying to scare them out of his castle? And why would he? He seemed to have the legal right to it. All he had to do was tell them that they had to go!

It couldn't have been Bruce by the fireplace. But it had to have been — or else she was seeing ghosts.

His eyes narrowed sharply as he stared at her. He snapped the book closed and walked over to slide it into a drawer of his desk. Then he walked across the room to her and took her by the shoulders, staring into her eyes, his own a silver sheet of concern. "Toni? What's wrong?"

She shook her head, unable to speak for a moment. She was going crazy. No need to tell him so. It was unlikely that many men wanted to have an affair with an insane woman. Or was she just giving free vent to imagination? Was it all *suggestive,* as David tried to assure her.

She blinked, trembling, knowing that nothing mattered when he came to her, when he looked at her that way, when she felt the security of his hands upon her.

"Toni?"

She shook her head, gaining strength. She was an actress of some merit, wasn't she?

"I . . . was thirsty," she lied. "I went down for a drink."

He shook his head, frowning. "Toni, I have drinks up here. Not just brandy and such — there's a mini refrigerator, water, some sodas."

She moistened her lips. "I didn't know."

"You're white as a ghost," he said.

"Am I?"

He was still staring at her with the greatest concern.

As if . . . she weren't all there.

Subtlety be damned.

"I want something," she whispered.

"Aye?"

"To be with you."

"I've been doing nothing but waiting," he said, the words so quiet, and yet so sincere, that they were like a caress against her.

She wasn't aware that she moved, or that he did, either, but she was suddenly melded against him. He was very much alive, a vital block of heat and fire, warming the ice that had seized hold of flesh and blood and bone. Her head fell back and she met his eyes just a split second before his mouth descended to hers.

This time, he stripped back the covers before he laid her down. And as he moved away, she rose back up herself, tearing the gown from over her shoulders, making her way on her knees to the place where he sat at the foot of the bed, shedding clothing. She edged against his back, lips, kisses, tongue falling against the breadth of his shoulders. And when he turned to her, naked at last, she could not be held away, but continued her wild, near frenzied search and exploration of his flesh.

He caught her by the midriff at last, pulling her against him, and she felt the full force and passion of his kiss, as driving as any power or rage of lust. They fell back together, entwined, hands and mouths seeking as if they were both mad. She tried to crawl against him, and he murmured to her, his voice deep and husky, "Ah, careful, lass. With that jumping, we're bound to have something bent or broken!"

She found herself laughing, still desperate, smiling as she was drawn beneath him, then breathless and silent as he thrust into her with a strength she sincerely doubted could ever be bent or broken.

She vaguely felt the sheets beneath her, the softness of the bed, vaguely heard the crackle of the dying fire. The room was bathed in a red and burnt-orange light, and it flickered upon his face and shoulders and chest. Then everything seemed to blur into a shadow blaze as the need within her spiraled and rose and, once more, seared into her with cataclysmic wonder.

She was wrapped in his arms, aware again of the feel of the sheets, damp now, the sound of the fire, a softer rustling still, and the glow of the embers. His weight eased from hers, but not his hold. No, never, please God! she thought. He pulled her against him, flush with his form. She was aware of his chest, chest hair, breath, the cradle of his hips, the now flaccid pressure of his sex against her. His fingers smoothed back her hair.

Time passed in a glory of soft sounds, gentle caresses, light . . .

"You are . . ." he murmured.

She waited, but nothing came. Then she smiled. "You are, too," she whispered.

His arms tightened. She felt the way their hearts beat then, almost together, just enough out of sync so that she knew there were two.

When she slept, it was without dreams. And when she woke in the night with a start, she felt his arms around her still. So she closed her eyes again, and her sleep was deep and restful.

"He's weird, and that's all there is to it," Gina said, shivering.

"Eban?" Toni asked, startled.

They were in town. Despite the fact that Robert Chamberlain had the original documents, they were taking a set of copies to Jonathan. Though they had more faith in Robert Chamberlain, they had a bit of sympathy for Jonathan, as well. The castle, and the forest, fell under his jurisdiction.

At the moment, they were seated at a wrought-iron table in the garden section of a pub known as Angus's Alley. It did a fair business, drawing a luncheon crowd from tourists and folks visiting from the larger cities. Bruce wasn't with them; he'd left early on business. They were their own little sixsome again, which was pleasant because, among one another, they didn't have to take care regarding what they said.

And Gina wasn't hedging her opinion at the moment.

"Eban, yes!" she hissed. She jerked her head to the right. He was not far from them,

316

just off the road, feeding a dog. He was talking to the animal.

Ryan winced, his eyes light as he looked at his wife. "I talk to horses."

"Yes, and Toni talks to any animal she comes across. I've seen the two of you."

"So what's the difference?" Kevin asked her, biting into a piece of steak. "Yummy. There should really be more gourmet Scottish restaurants in the States."

"There is one in New York," David told him absently.

"What's the difference?" Thayer said, repeating Kevin's question, and staring at them as if they were a bit daft. "Don't you all ever let anyone answer a question before you go on into another train of thought entirely?"

Kevin shrugged.

"The difference?" Gina said. "Watch Eban! It's as if they're communicating back to him. Yes, Ryan, you and Toni speak to any mammal you come across, but you don't expect the animals to give you answers back!"

" 'E's just a wee bit touched in the head," Thayer said. "I feel sorry for the poor old boy."

"I don't," Gina said, not even attempting to hide a shiver. "I feel . . . scared."

"I'm sure he's harmless," Toni said, yet she remembered how terrified he had made her, just the day before. But that had been because her imagination had gotten the best of her.

Had last night been her imagination, too? Or insanity. That morning, the door to the crypts had been bolted, just as it had always been. But she knew, if she insisted it be open, that she would find everything below just as she had seen it.

"Eban works very hard. We've seen him work!" she added.

"Thank God, I'm married," Gina murmured. "I think I'd be scared in my castle room if it weren't for Ryan."

"Great," Ryan said. "She keeps me around because she's scared."

Gina flashed him a warning stare, but Ryan just grinned.

"Eh! If the old man starts giving you too much trouble, lass, remind him I'm around!" Thayer said, winking.

"There you go," Gina told Ryan.

"Well . . . if worse came to worst, David and I would let Gina have the old Duncan Phyfe sofa that's in our room," Kevin said.

Gina shuddered. "I don't think I could take the activity in your room!"

"All right, all right, the lot of you! Break

up the lust fest. A few of us —" Thayer paused, glancing at Toni. "Okay, maybe it's only me these days, but there's no one sleeping in my room, so I'd rather not hear about the writhin' and strainin' going on around me, eh?"

Gina burst out laughing. "Thayer, you could have your pick of girls! I've seen the way they look at you when we go in pubs and the like."

He shrugged.

"You're too picky," she told him.

He was thoughtful for a minute. "That I am. And I've decided I want an American lass."

"And why is that?" Toni asked him.

He shrugged. "I like the American way. Free from the shackles of tradition, and all that rot."

Gina laughed. "But you were willing to go in with us on the castle?"

"Well, in truth, that's all changed now, hasn't it? It seems like we're on a borrowed pound at a roulette wheel, eh? Just trying to make back our bet."

"We'll make it back," Gina said determinedly.

"Thanks to the largesse of our host," David murmured, and he stared across the table at Thayer suddenly. "Hey, did you know that he'd been a cop?" he demanded.

"How could he have known he'd been a cop?" Toni demanded. "He hadn't even known that he'd existed."

"Oh, yes, right," David said.

"You're starting to sound British!" Kevin told him. "Right-o, cheerio and all that!"

David looked at him and sighed.

"Well, when in Rome, you know," Ryan offered.

"But Laird MacNiall — a cop!"

"*Was* a cop," Gina said. "I wonder what he does now," she mused, looking around at all of them.

"Hey, don't ask me!" Kevin said. "I didn't know that lairds were . . . well, anything. I just thought they sat around being . . . lairds!"

"I don't think it works that way anymore, does it?" Toni asked Thayer, smiling.

"Well, these days, anyone who owns enough land collects rents," he said.

"Does he own a lot of land?" Gina asked.

Thayer shrugged, still looking at Toni. "The constable said that Laird MacNiall owned half the village, remember?"

"Hmm," Gina murmured. "So . . . he's simply rich."

"Strange, if he has money you'd think

there would be servants swarming around the family home," David murmured.

"And instead, no one," Ryan mused.

"There's Eban Douglas!" Kevin reminded him.

"And he's weird!" Gina said again.

"So we're back where we started," Ryan said, standing. "Gina, we should get those documents over to Jonathan's office."

"We were supposed to see Laird MacNiall's deed today, remember?" Thayer murmured. "I guess now we just have to accept that it's legit, huh? After all, he wound up not being with us."

Gina sighed. "Ryan and I will go to the constable's. I'm sure we have to fill out a police report, as well, but I imagine that, for the time, one of us giving the information and signing the report will be all that's required."

"Two of us," Ryan reminded her.

"Two of us. The rest of you can wander. Toni, you said that you wanted to walk around the old kirk and graveyard, right?"

David groaned. "Don't you want me to take the documents to the constable's office?"

Toni stood up. "David, go shopping. And Kevin and Thayer . . . you can sop up some more ambience at the pub, if you like. I'm fine on my own."

"I would like to see if we can't find some . . . classier paper products for our tea and scones," David said.

"They're definitely not into paper plates the way we are in the States," Kevin agreed. "But they've lovely shops. Maybe we can find something."

"I don't mind going with you, Toni," Thayer said.

"You sure?" she asked him.

"Not at all," he assured her.

"Well, then . . ."

"Hey! Someone remember to pay the bill!" Gina said. "And don't take more than a couple of hours. We'll meet at the pub at the base of the hill at four, okay?"

They all started out in their different directions. Ryan and Gina headed west, in the direction of the village square. David and Kevin went no more than a few feet before being caught by a store window, and Thayer and Toni headed east, slightly up a hill, toward the kirk and the surrounding graveyard.

Thayer seemed distracted. Toni set a hand on his shoulder. "You all right?" she asked him.

He flashed her a smile. "Aye, fine, why?"

She shook her head. "You've just seemed . . . not you, lately."

"Since our bubble was burst?" he asked.

"I guess."

He smiled, and pointed toward the kirk. "I can give you some local history. It was begun in the twelve-hundreds, and the current structure and form dates back to the fifteen hundreds. Naturally, it was built as a Catholic church, and is now a part of the Church of Scotland. It has some remarkable stained-glass windows. It also has some beautifully carved tombs on the interior — Italian artists were brought in to honor various statesmen, poets, knights and ladies, and so on. In the truly dour days of Cromwell, the reverend was a plucky fellow who managed to hide most of the treasures, so little was destroyed."

She smiled at him, impressed. "Have you seen it, then? I thought you'd never been in this area before we arrived."

"Never been in it in m'life, cousin. I looked it up on the Internet. They've actually got quite a decent Web page."

Toni laughed. "Great."

A small stone fence surrounded the kirk and the graveyard, and there was a white picket gate, which Thayer swung open for Toni.

When they entered the kirk itself, she was awed and amazed. For such a small village, it was really phenomenal. The stained-glass windows surrounding the length of it were in blues that would have done Tiffany's proud. Picking up a flyer at the rear as they entered, Toni read that the pulpit had been carved from a single huge oak in the 1540s, and she walked to it, marveling at the intricate lion designs that graced it.

"Incredible workmanship, huh?" Thayer whispered to her.

She nodded. "Gorgeous."

"Come see some of the MacNialls buried here," he said.

"I thought . . ." For a moment she hesitated. "I thought that they were buried in a crypt at the castle," she said.

He shrugged. "I'm sure some are. But come here. Look." Pointing, he showed her a fairly modern tomb that occupied space against the western wall. "Our MacNiall's grandfather, or a great uncle, certainly. 'Colonel Patrick Brennan MacNiall, RAF, born April 15, 1921, died June 8, 1944, on distant shores, serving God and Country. May he fly with the angels now.'"

"He must have died just after the D-day invasion in World War II," Toni said. "How sad."

"Very. For thousands of men," Thayer commented. "Look, here's an older one. 'Laird Bruce Eamon MacNiall, a great protector of men and honor, born October 4, 1724, and gave his life for right and freedom, Flodden Field.' "

"They had a tendency to be on the wrong side of a battle, huh?" Toni murmured.

"History always decides the wrong side of a battle," Thayer murmured.

Toni nodded. "Quite true. And we have a tendency to romanticize many a lost cause."

"Shall we wander around outside? Or did you only want to look for MacNialls?" Thayer asked.

Toni was startled, but when she looked in his eyes they seemed guileless.

"I'd love to wander around outside."

"What's your fascination with cemeteries?" he asked her, and grinned. "I did this with you in Glasgow, too, remember?"

"The art, I think. And the poems and epitaphs."

"Like at the theme parks? 'Dear old Fred, a rock fell on his head, now he's dead, dead, dead,' or something like that?"

"Not that bad!" Toni protested. "The problem is, time erodes stone, lichen sets in and they're often difficult to read." They were outside now. The graveyard was the kind that always fascinated, with beautiful marble funerary art and huge stones rising at awkward angles created by the passage of time. "Here's one!" she told Thayer, rubbing the mold from the stone to read it better. " 'Justin MacClaren. Once I ran, fast and hard, had a wife, ignored the lass. I gave all strife, ne'er went to mass, and now, lonely to this grave, I am cast.' "

"Hmm. That's almost as bad as dear old Fred with the rock on his head," Thayer said, making her laugh.

"But that's just it — they really give a little slice of life, as it was," Toni told him and smiled. Two young women had just entered the cemetery, wandering as they were, one a pretty redhead, her friend a brunette.

"Hello," Toni said pleasantly. "Good afternoon."

"Ta!" the redhead said cheerily. "You're American then, are you?"

"I am," Toni said. "Thayer is from Glasgow."

"I'm from Aberdeen myself, but I've taken a cottage here for a while," the redhead said. "I'm Lizzie Johnstone. And this is my friend, Trish Martin, up from Yorkshire to spend her holiday with me."

"Lovely," Toni murmured.

"Ah, the English are invading again," Thayer teased. He offered a hand to Trish first. She was very pretty, with large dark eyes, long pale hair and a beautiful peaches-and-cream complexion. He was, however, equally polite when he turned to Lizzie, who looked far more Irish with her wild red hair, spattering of freckles and bountiful smile.

"Thayer Fraser here. And the American invader," he added teasingly, "Toni Fraser."

"Ah, a couple are you then?" Lizzie said, obviously a bit disappointed.

"A pleasure to meet you," Toni told them. "And no, we're not a couple. We're cousins."

"Ah!" The young woman looked at Thayer with renewed interest.

Thayer smiled. It was a slightly awkward moment in which body language was too easily read. Lizzie liked Thayer. Thayer liked the blonde.

"So you like poking around old grave-yards, too?" Toni said.

"You'd think I'd tire of them, but I never do," Trish said. "Much more interesting than the ancient sites that everyone is all atwitter about these days! They're nothing but rocks in the ground, while these old places . . ."

"They tell stories," Toni said.

Trish gasped suddenly. "I know who you are! The group doing tours at the castle!"

"Indeed!" Lizzie said.

Thayer nudged Toni. "We're famous!" he teased.

"Or infamous," she murmured beneath her breath.

"Oh, no! There was a bit in the Edinburgh paper today . . . y'can buy it down at the Ioin's place, that little newsstand-café down at the base of the hill, if you wish to see it," Trish said. "It's a good blurb, I believe you'd like it. Says you do a lovely little piece of drama while bringing back the past, and suggests that even locals would enjoy the fun of it. You'll have to get the paper. I'm afraid we've left ours at the café."

Toni looked at Thayer and shrugged, a smile creasing her lips. There was pleasure and wry regret in her expression. "Thank you for telling us," Toni said.

"Didn't know we had a reporter in either of the two groups we've taken through so far," Thayer said.

"Well, now," Lizzie said, "a reporter would want to slip in unknown and unnoticed, right? Get the same treatment as everyone else, eh?"

"Now, that sounds true enough," Thayer agreed. "I'd thought our folks were all Americans, though. We've been working with a tour company that does the promotion and packaging. They just book the tours, but they've been targeting Americans."

"What? Just because we've grown up with the history, it means we don't enjoy a good time?" Trish said, batting her lashes at Thayer.

"Well, now, we all enjoy a good time, don't we?" Thayer said, his voice soft and a little husky. Toni was glad for him. He seemed to be enjoying this flirtation with the attractive women, even if they happened to be in a cemetery.

Toni had noticed an older woman, slightly humped over with the beginnings of osteoporosis, making her way through the crooked stones and monuments. The others noticed her, as well, and fell silent.

Toni stepped back, realizing that although they stood among weathered markers that might have been about for hundreds of years, there were new plaques around, as well.

The woman was heading their way with a

bundle of flowers.

"I believe we're intruding," she murmured. Thayer took her elbow, and they edged farther out of the way. They remained silent with respect, rather than make an obvious departure that might be loud and distracting.

The old woman was followed by a younger couple, a slightly balding man and an attractive, slender woman of about forty-five.

"Afternoon," the man said, nodding to them. The old woman ignored them, but the man's wife offered them a pleasant smile.

The old woman bent down with her flowers, and said her prayer by the grave. Then she rose slowly, using a headstone to help herself up, and turned, acknowledging that they were there.

Toni noticed that the woman's eyes, a faded blue set in the time-worn creases of her face, seemed to fasten right upon her.

"Yer from the castle," she said. It wasn't a question, it was a statement of fact.

Toni and Thayer nodded. Despite the interruption, they were still basking in the pleasure of having heard about such a good review of the tour. But as those faded blue eyes assessed her, Toni felt a sure stirring of unease.

The woman pointed a long bony finger at Toni.

"Y'know it, don't ye?"

"Pardon?" Toni murmured.

"There's greater trouble ahead, eh? They've found the lady, missing all those years. Disturbed the past! Dug up a ghost. And they wonder wot's goin' on in that forest! He killed once, and set her in the ground. Now she's dug up. He'll kill again, and again, and again. *We've* known that he roamed here all these years. Aye, that we have! Roamed his castle and the woods, betrayed and seeking his vengeance. Now he's risen, and he seeks it about the countryside. You!" Her finger shook in Toni's direction. "You know it! Know that he is up and about, wakened and furious! You know it! Bruce MacNiall is up and about, and killin'. And if ye tread upon the past any longer, y'll be the lass in the water. Aye, y'll be the lass in the water!"

331

12

Bruce arrived at Darrow's office not long after noon, surprised by the urgency and excitement in the message the man had left on his cell phone.

It was quite a mystery, since Daniel hadn't left any details about why he was concerned that Bruce come in. And though Bruce should have accompanied the group into town, gone straight to the office of records as planned and shown them the deed, there really seemed little urgency to do so anymore. They had accepted the fact that he indeed owned the castle.

And Darrow's message had been just too intriguing.

Tillingham was one of those places where, most often, death came naturally, and to the aged. The surrounding countryside, at the base of the Highlands, was rich farmland. Those who hadn't made their way into larger cities or towns earned their living by producing some of the finest wool, dairy products and beef available. For the most part, they loved their corner of the earth, the land and a way of life that was almost ancient, yet far better than what it had been in centuries of servitude and strife.

Bruce owned large tracts of land and a number of the buildings in town where merchants sold their wares, but his holdings hadn't all been inherited. An education in the States at UCLA had taught him a great deal about the American stock market, and he had gambled — for that's what he considered it — well over the years. Even in hard times, he'd had luck with getting in and getting out. Still, his father had ingrained in him a certain tradition. Heredity — and the return of Charles II to the throne of England — had made them lairds. That meant a responsibility to the village of Tillingham.

There was another factor, of course. The area was home. He loved it. There were still thatched-roof houses that served as cafés and shops, apartments and single-dwelling residences. The farmland wasn't far from the center and the castle sat atop a hill as it had for centuries. Whatever the history associated with the place, good and bad, it was his.

Darrow's facility was on the square, near the constable's office and the beautiful old medieval building that housed the records and licensing bureaus, among other legal offices. When he had decided to hurry on down to see Daniel Darrow, he had refrained from mentioning that he'd be near the group, intrigued to see the medical examiner on his own.

Rowenna, Darrow's secretary, greeted him pleasantly, and with a little sparkle to her eyes. "He's agog with excitement!" Rowenna told Bruce, rising to lead him into the mortuary room, where Darrow tended to the dead of Tillingham and the surrounding areas. "He hasn't even told me what's got him so excited," she said.

He thanked Rowenna when she opened the door to admit him to Darrow's work area, and she gave him another wave and smile as she closed the door behind her.

The M.E. employed two assistants at all times, but most often they were temporary, eager to work their way to larger facilities or higher positions in other small villages. Neither of them seemed to be about that afternoon. Bruce realized that this must be something of a pleasant change for the man. Darrow had a very different case of a discovered "body" on his hands.

Darrow was wearing a headlight and huge glasses, studying the remains that were stretched out in proper form on the autopsy table before him. He looked up, seeing that Bruce had arrived, and his eyes seemed enormous behind the glasses. In his lab coat and paraphernalia, he gave the appearance of a mad scientist.

"Bruce!" he said with pleasure. "You're here?"

"How could I resist such an invitation?" Bruce said.

Darrow nodded and said, "Well, my good lad, if you've ever loved me before, yer about to adore me now."

"Oh?"

He beckoned Bruce closer.

It was a strange feeling to look down at the remains. On the one side, all that time had rendered had taken away something of the humanity that once belonged to the woman. The empty eye sockets were eerie, as were the remaining tufts of hair and mummified flesh. Some bones were not actually attached, yet they had been laid out in anatomical order. Blackened pieces of fabric gave an odd cast to what she must have worn during her last moments of life. The skull itself was devoid of flesh in places, while in others, that fragile bit of her one-time life remained.

Time could play good tricks with the mind, as well. He couldn't feel what he had experienced when he found the body of the murdered girl in Tillingham, because her life had been far more recent, far more real. And yet it occurred to him that this was one of his ancestors, and that if it hadn't been for her life, he would not have had his own.

"She's truly an exquisite find!" Darrow said, studying the upper region of the remains again.

Bruce cleared his throat slightly. Darrow looked at him and then seemed to realize the association. "Sorry, dear boy. I keep forgetting . . . well, centuries have gone by, you know."

"Aye, of course," Bruce said.

"It's the state of preservation," Darrow said. "Well, we've some naked bone, but I haven't actually cut into her, taken samples. We do have experts on the way."

"Daniel, what is it then?" Bruce said, afraid that the doctor was getting so involved in his discovery again that he was going to forget to explain.

"There!" Darrow said. He focused the lights of his headgear on the ligature that remained around the neck.

There? Bruce stared, but he saw only the muddied and blackened ligature, nothing else.

"I'm sorry, Daniel. What are you showing me?"

Daniel let out an exclamation of surprise. "Now, I'm not giving it to you that easy, boy! You were a detective once."

Bruce looked up at him, arching a brow, and then back to the remains.

And then he saw it.

It was impossible to decipher the weave of the cloth tied around the neck; the rich mud had seen to that. But it had once been emblazoned with a raised crest, embroidered into the fabric. And it wasn't the MacNiall crest.

Though it took a moment's study, the encrusting mud had actually made the crest and surrounding letters more visible beneath the light. He couldn't guarantee it, and wouldn't bet on it, but it seemed that elaborate letters, *GD*, sat above a peregrine falcon atop a sword. Bruce instantly felt a thrill of excitement himself.

Any schoolchild who had grown up anywhere near the village was aware that the *GD* with the peregrine on the sword had been the battle emblem chosen by the traitor, Davis, who had brought down the great MacNiall.

"So . . . !" Bruce said.

"Aye, quite so!" Daniel said cheerfully. "Looks as if Grayson Davis did in the Lady

MacNiall, and not her laird husband. Well, certainly, there could be those arguing that Bruce did it with Grayson's colors, but what would Bruce have been doing with such a garment from his enemy? Nae, now, I'm no historian, but it seems as if our local hero has been vindicated!"

Bruce looked up, smiling. "Well, we'll see what your experts have to say, Daniel."

Daniel nodded.

"You're definitely right about one thing," Bruce told him.

"Eh?"

"Well, I've always loved you, Daniel, old boy. But I do adore you now."

"Ach, now, Ma!" the man said, stepping forward to take the old woman's arm. "Now I know y'see the old fellow about now and then," he said, tenderly bringing her to him. "But y'll be scaring away these fine folks!" He rolled his eyes at the group around him.

"They don't be seein' it, none be seein' it!" the old woman said.

She was still staring at Toni, her watery, faded blue eyes seeming to see things that no one else could.

"Y'must take care!" she whispered feverishly.

Toni nodded, her throat tight, dismayed

by the chills that iced her limbs and bloodstream. The old woman was senile, she tried to tell herself. A victim of superstition, of a way of life.

Thayer's arm came around her shoulder. Even Lizzie and Trish, whom she barely knew, seemed to be standing closer to give her assurance against the strange onslaught.

"Ma, come away, now, the flowers be at Da's feet," the younger woman said, flashing them an apologetic smile. "I'll get y'some o' the fine scones down the street. We'll have a wee spot o' tea, eh?" With a last look of apology, she gently became the escort, taking the old woman's arm. She started from the cemetery, looking over her shoulder to smile at the group, that simple look explaining all.

The old woman was daft but theirs, and they loved her.

"Enjoy your tea!" Toni said, feeling the chill the old woman's words had given her fade, and anxious to say something just to let her daughter or daughter-in-law know that it was lovely the way they guarded and cared for the woman.

The man lingered a moment, shaking his head. "Finan MacHenry," he told them. "And I do apologize, miss. Ma can give one the willies, sure enough. But take no note, please. I am so sorry. The townsfolk here, well, we've done a bit o' watching — no one here could reckon with the fact that Bruce had rented the place! — but y're doin' us all a service here, and we're pleased." He grimaced ruefully. "I own a pub, and yer tour folks have spent a good deal there, just in the few nights' time. Please don't be listenin' to me ma. She's always thought she saw Bruce MacNiall — not our current laird, but the old Cavalier — in the forest. And she's a wee bit disappointed, being of the thought that he was innocent. Now, with the bones found and all . . ."

"Thank you, Mr. MacHenry," Toni said, extending her hand. "You and your wife and your mother seem very dear, and we're grateful that you've taken the time to tell us that you're glad we're here."

He inclined his head. "My pleasure. And again, I'm so sorry about Ma givin' ye that kind o' fright. She's —" he didn't say *off the wall, daft* or *crazy as a loon*. "Ma's just old, and she's really dear. I imagine she was just thinkin' y're a fine young woman and worryin'. Well, I'll let you folks get back to yer day. I'll be havin' me tea and scones then," he said. "Good day!"

"Good day," they called in unison as he departed.

"Well, that was interesting," Thayer murmured. "Toni, you all right? It was strange as bloody hell, the way that she looked at you!"

"She's just old," Toni murmured, repeating what Finan MacHenry had said.

"Aye, and a bit daft. But it was unnerving, to say the least!" Trish offered.

"Giving you the evil eye, or whatever!" Lizzie said, and shivered. "I'm glad she didn't look that way at me! Oh, I am sorry."

"It's all right, really," Toni said. "Actually, it was quite touching, to see the way that they take care of her."

"Well, that's the Scottish for you," Lizzie said. "A bit of the superstitious and whimsical, and then the good hard logic that we're famed for, as well. Let's be putting it behind us. Honestly, we'd certainly love to be part of a tour, though, even if we're not American, and can't quite make it on a bus from elsewhere!"

"Tomorrow night. Come a bit early if you like," Thayer said.

"I'm not the management end of things," Toni said, "but I'm sure we can arrange something special for you both."

"We've got to catch up with 'management' soon," Thayer said. "Why don't we head to the pub now. We'll buy you lovely ladies a drink, and we can talk about to-morrow?"

Lizzie looked at Trish, and Trish looked back. They must have come to a silent agreement because they both looked at Thayer. "Why, that would be lovely."

"I think I'll let the three of you go on," Toni said. "I was going to wander around here a bit more, if you'll allow me to beg out."

Thayer looked at her with a slight frown, as if he were afraid the ladies would beg out also if she didn't come with them.

"I'll be right along, of course, and our other friends will be arriving bit by bit," Toni added quickly.

Trish shivered. "You want to stay in an old cemetery alone, after that?"

"I like these places," Toni told her.

"All right, then," Thayer said, anxious to move on with the women. But he had come with her, so he hesitated one last time. "You're sure? You're sure you're all right?"

"Absolutely. We are just right off the street. If a hand shoots out of a grave, or the like, I'll be out of here faster than a speeding bullet."

The three laughed.

"Shall we order you anything?" Lizzie asked.

"No, thanks. I'm sure service is quick enough," Toni said.

"Well, then . . . shall we go?" Thayer asked.

"Oh, aye, then," Lizzie said. "See you in a bit, dear!"

When they were gone, Toni felt a shudder seize hold of her again. So much for being right off a main road. She couldn't even see anyone on the streets, and the day was darkening early. This was insane. She should catch up with Thayer and the girls, and hurry down to the pub where the beer was warm, but company and hospitality warmer still. After all, here she was in a cemetery, filled with the long dead, and she already thought that a ghost was leading her around a castle.

Then she gave herself a shake. She was fine. She'd wanted to be alone, and she was *not* going to be afraid. This *was* the type of place she had always loved, the very old combining with the present, a piece of living history, since the kirk offered Sunday services now just as it had for centuries. So she turned back to look through the graveyard, absolutely determined to put the old woman's strange actions and words behind her.

One monument in particular had caught

her eye earlier. Usually she was drawn to the very old, but this one was new, and more ornate — and functional — than most. At the base, it created an arched, marble seat that faced a garden well tended by someone. At the top was a magnificently carved, flying angel. When Toni came closer, she marveled at the detail in the sculpture. The angel's face looked down in sadness. Below it, etched in large letters, were the words *Margaret Marie MacMannon, beloved daughter of Rose and Magnus, departed this for a better world far too soon, yet the memory of her goodness remains.*

She had died at the tender age of twenty-three, just a bit more than ten years ago, Toni discovered, reading the smaller print. That she had been a teacher and a lover of history, music, dance and mankind was also immortalized.

As she sat and continued to read, Toni was surprised to find, in very small print, that the kirk thanked Laird Bruce MacNiall for the garden and memorial, to be kept in perpetuity.

"So you like old kirks and cemeteries, as well as castles!"

Spinning around, Toni was startled to see none other than Bruce MacNiall coming toward her.

He was wearing a leisure suit that day, and had doffed the jacket, which he carried casually under his arm. He was wearing sunglasses, as well, so his eyes were unfathomable, and his ebony hair was slicked back. He could have just walked off a page of *GQ*, rather than out of a crumbling stone castle seeped in history and lore.

"Bruce," she murmured, feeling as if she had been caught looking into someone's private diary. "Hi. Did . . . did you know I was here?"

He shook his head, joining her on the bench. "Actually, I didn't. But I'm glad to see you."

She smiled, still feeling a little shy. Then she decided simply to ask, "Who was Margaret?"

He didn't seem disturbed by the question. He simply looked up at the angel, as if he could see something that went far beyond it, then shrugged slightly. "The great love of my youth," he said softly. He looked at Toni, though she could still see nothing of his eyes beneath the dark shades. "She was a local girl with a great love for people, life . . . children. We were engaged, but never married."

"What happened to her?" Toni asked, afraid that she was prying too deeply now, and was about to hear a horrible story.

"Leukemia," he said. "I never knew anyone with a greater love for the simplest things in life. The sky, the hills, grass . . . trees. Children. She adored children. She wanted a dozen, and always said it would be fine because we were very wee in numbers here, and the world needed more Scots."

"I'm very sorry," Toni said. "It sounds as if she was really a lovely person."

He nodded and looked away. She thought that he had decided to say no more, but then he looked at her again. "That's why I rather let the castle go, I'm afraid. She loved it. She wanted to bring life back to it. She had a way of just making you glad that you were alive and breathing and . . . well, it seemed such an irony that her own life should prove to be so fragile."

"I am so sorry," Toni repeated.

"Thanks. She's been gone a very long time now. No excuse for me, really, to have let things go the way that I did." His lips curled into a dry smile. "Did you visit the rest of the family?" he asked her politely.

"I saw a few MacNialls in the old kirk, yes."

"And you're here alone?"

"We're all meeting at the pub at the base of the hill at four," she told him. "Ryan and

Gina took copies of the documents to Jonathan. David and Kevin are shopping. And Thayer and I just met two lovely lasses in the cemetery, so the three of them headed on to the pub already."

"Good. I'm glad there's a bit of excitement for your cousin," he said. And he smiled broadly at her. "I've had a bit of my own today."

"Oh?"

"I've been at the M.E.'s," he told her. "And we think we've made a discovery that will vindicate my ancestor."

"Really?" Toni said.

He nodded. "Looks like she was strangled with a scarf that belonged to his archenemy, a man named Grayson Davis. The fellow hailed from around here, but he wasn't the kind of man to fight for a losing side for long. It wasn't really such a terrible thing for men to be on opposite sides — throughout our history, Scots have fought Scots almost as much as they've fought the English. The thing with Grayson Davis was that he turned coat, and turned in many a man he had once called his friend. He was the one who brought down Bruce MacNiall, catching up with him in the forest and giving him a mock trial then and there. And well, you know the rest."

Toni looked at him with surprise and murmured, "I wonder . . ."

"You wonder what?"

"Nothing!" she said quickly, shaking her head.

He took her hand, his thumb massaging the palm with an absent tenderness that stole around her heart. "You've done the family a great service, you know, finding Annalise. I've been telling you this all along, you know, but . . . I really do owe you."

"I'm delighted," she said, a little afraid of being so close to him and not sure why. "We really need to tell all this to an old woman who was through here a while ago. Apparently, everyone in town knows that Annalise was found. This lady was very upset, certain that your ancestor was running around, going off to the cities to abduct other women and strangle them in the forest, as well."

He frowned sharply. "What?"

She shook her head, startled to have gotten such an intense response from him.

"It was nothing to take seriously," she said quickly. "This old woman knew we were at the castle, and apparently, she's deeply distraught that Annalise was found in the forest. She wanted to believe that your ancestor was a hero, not a wife killer. Apparently she believes that Bruce MacNiall still roams the land."

He let out an impatient and irritated sound. "Elwyn MacHenry!" he said.

"Yes. She was with her son and daughter-in-law. They seemed like very nice people."

"They are, but Elwyn is more than 'touched,' as they call it here. She's been raving about Bruce MacNiall roaming the countryside for years." He looked at her with a trace of amusement. "However, he just used to ride in the moonlight. She never accused him before of going from town to town to strangle others, as he had supposedly strangled his wife."

"Elwyn will be happy then to learn the truth," Toni said.

He rose suddenly, drawing her up. "I love this place, but enough is enough. Let's go join the living, eh?"

The afternoon spanned into the evening. Bruce remained in an exceptionally good mood, and Thayer was riding high as well, enjoying the company of Lizzie and Trish. Gina reported that Jonathan had been cordial, and he had told them it was good that they had given the original documents to Robert Chamberlain, since his resources were so great. In fact, they'd saved him the trouble of having to do it. And he was pleased to tell them that the locals were cheerful about the tours. The buses had stopped in the village both nights, and the tourists had bought all manner of T-shirts, stuffed draft horses, jams, jellies, jewelry, tartans, cashmere, ties, brooches, snow globes and miniatures of the castle.

Kevin and David had spent their hours in the shops looking for plates and plasticware, and they were delighted with all their little purchases.

Gina decided that they had to have haggis, since it was the national dish, but Bruce begged out of it being the meal for the entire table.

"Hate the stuff," he told her.

"But it's the national dish!" she protested.

"Aye, it's the national dish, and do you know why?" he asked her, eyes sparkling. "It's made from the cheapest pieces of meat —"

"Body parts," David put in.

"Aye, body parts, because we were too broke here most of the time to be using the best cuts ourselves. But, by all means, Gina, have the haggis. They actually do an excellent sirloin here, and the lamb chops are phenomenal, especially considering that we're in a local pub," Bruce finished.

Toni opted for the salmon, while Thayer, David, Ryan and Kevin went along with Bruce, ordering the sirloin. Lizzie and Trish decided to try the lamb chops.

"Sure you want haggis, Gina?" Ryan asked. "I'm not trading my meal with yours!" he told her.

She made a face at him, but when it came her turn to order, she asked their waitress, "What do you think of the haggis?"

The woman glanced at Bruce. "Should I be tellin' her the truth, Laird MacNiall?"

"Indeed, Catherine, aye," he said gravely.

"I think we keep it on the menu for the tourists," she said, causing everyone to laugh. Gina switched to the sirloin.

By the end of the evening, Thayer had planned to spend the next Monday driving Lizzie and Trish down to Glasgow to show them some of the sights there. Kevin and David were planning holiday decorations for the castle. Gina was ever so slightly crocked and affectionate in her husband's arms. And the light in Bruce's eyes offered amusement and a flicker of intimacy that Toni found both touching and seductive.

Whatever ridiculous doubts and fears she had regarding him — and the ghost of his ancestor — seemed to have dissipated completely. She couldn't wait to be back at the castle, and back in his arms.

But it wasn't to work out that way. When they arrived, Eban was there to meet them. The roan had taken another turn for the worse, and he'd been out with the animal, doing his best to keep him up and walking, but he was wearing himself out. Toni was ready to run out with Ryan, but Bruce stopped her.

"I'll tend to the roan with Ryan," he said.

"But it sounds as if Wallace is really sick," she said, upset. "And I didn't see him at first when I should have —"

"I'll be calling the vet, Toni. It will be all right."

"How are you going to get a vet at midnight?" she asked.

"The rewards of a small village, where everyone knows everyone," he told her. "It's all right. Toni, trust me, I know something about horses."

"Toni!" David set an arm around her. "It's best if you let them handle this, you know."

He was right. She would be emotional, and maybe in the way.

Bruce took her arm, leading her toward the castle. "Wait for me?" he queried.

"Well, get some sleep, if you can . . . but in my bed?"

She looked into his eyes and nodded. The excitement she'd been feeling was definitely tempered now with worry for the horse, but there was something more that he gave her with his words and the gentle brush of his eyes — comfort and assurance.

"The doc will take care of old Wallace," he said.

So she went on upstairs and showered, then slipped into a gown and into his bed. Restless, she stood up and looked out the window. The lights remained bright in the stables.

She went back to bed, where she tossed and turned, her mind filled with the events that had occurred since their arrival. An hour passed, and she was still staring at the ceiling. Finally her eyes closed, and she slept. Then . . . she felt a touch. She opened her eyes, and he was there — at the foot of the bed.

His sword was not dripping blood this time. Instead, it was sheathed in the belt and holder that sat around his hip, on his plaid.

She sat up, staring at him, wishing that she could scream, make someone come running, making the apparition disappear. And though his face was Bruce's, she no longer thought that he was the Bruce she knew.

Staring into his eyes, she ran her hand over the sheets at her side, praying that maybe Bruce had come up while she was sleeping. But he wasn't there. And with the man at the foot of her bed looking so exactly like him . . . she began to question her sanity again. And to question the man with whom she was falling in love.

"Don't do this to me!" she whispered.

But he remained, turning and heading for the door.

"No!" she said.

He waited at the door until she rose and followed. Then he headed down the hall to the stairway.

Toni came along, barefoot, shivering in her gown. She didn't understand why she didn't scream then, or call out, waken someone else. If they didn't see him, then she was crazy.

But at least she would know for certain that he wasn't the man she knew, flesh and blood, playing tricks on her.

Yet, if they didn't see him, then she was following a ghost.

He paused at the landing, and a fierce tension suddenly gripped his features, as if he found it painful there. Then he looked back, as if to assure himself that she was following.

"You know," she said quietly, "you have a descendant here. You couldn't just appear before him, huh?"

There was no response. He started down the stairs.

Her heart was pounding. *Cry out!* she told herself. But still, she didn't.

He came to the great hall and waited again. When she neared the bottom of the stairs, he walked on to the secondary hall, and from there . . . to the door leading to the crypts.

"No, please!" she told him.

Nae, lass, the "please" be to you.

Did the ghost speak, or did the words just somehow echo in her head?

"I really don't like the crypts!" she whispered.

The door, bolted and rusted by day, was open. He went down the spiral stone stairs, and she followed. Once again, he led her to his grave. And then he was gone.

In the shadows, in the must and darkness of the dead, she spun around, frantically searching for him. "What do you want? Just what is it that you want? Annalise has been found. And they know . . . they know you didn't do it!"

But there was no answer, and she felt again as if the light began to disappear as soon as she lost him. She was incredibly frightened, and furious, as well. Why did he bring her here, then leave her alone in the shadows and cold, desperate to get back up the stairs?

She ran, nearly tripping in her scramble to regain the level of the hall. Once there, she burst out the door, across the smaller hall and then the great one, and up the stairs. She hesitated on the landing, thinking that David and Kevin would have to screw their sex life or intimacy that night because she was going to burst in on them and tell them that they were getting out of the castle then and there.

But as she stood on the upper landing, she heard someone humming. Looking down, she saw Ryan coming out of the kitchen with a cup of coffee in his hands. He looked up and saw her.

"Toni?" he said, and frowned.

She must have looked wild, she was certain. With him in the living flesh, walking across the hall, her panic subsided.

"I, uh, how is Wallace?" she asked.

"Fine for the night. The vet is convinced he's getting into something that's making him get this colic, though he can't figure out what. But he's good, Toni. Honestly, I wouldn't lie to you. You could have asked Bruce. He's up there now. In fact, he's been in for a while. You can go to sleep, and rest assured, old Wallace is doing well."

She smiled, glad to realize that he thought she was standing barefoot and in a nightgown on the landing because she was so worried about the horse.

"Good night, Ryan. And thanks," she said.

She turned and fled back down the hallway, bursting into Bruce's bedroom. He had showered and was in a towel. He seemed distracted, and when he looked up and saw her, his face was filled with tension.

"I was about to gather a search party," he said. "I told you that I'd tend to the horse, Toni. And he's doing well."

She nodded. "Yes, thanks."

She was still standing in the doorway.

"Are you coming in?" he asked her.

She nodded, but didn't move.

"Toni, what on earth is the matter with you?"

She swallowed. "Bruce, you weren't standing at the foot of the bed in a kilt about fifteen minutes ago, were you?"

"What? I was out with the horses, with

Ryan." He sighed. "You're dreaming again?"

She shook her head. "No . . . no, I don't think that I'm dreaming. I think that I'm seeing the ghost of your ancestor." She gritted her teeth, watching the astonishment and total incomprehension that spread over his features.

"Toni, ghosts don't exist," he said.

"I'm seeing the ghost of your ancestor," she said firmly. "And he keeps taking me down to the crypts."

"That door is bolted," he said harshly. "I keep the only key."

"Come with me," she told him.

"Toni, I'm wearing a towel. I'd have to get dressed. You're barely dressed yourself, you know. That thing is entirely see-through."

"Come now," she insisted.

"In a towel?"

"We're the only ones up," she said, and turning, she went back down along the hallway.

"Toni, dammit!" he said, but followed behind her.

She realized she was almost running. He caught up with her on the stairway, swearing as he gripped her arm — he'd almost lost the towel.

"Toni, this is insanity."

"I'll show you!"

She wrenched free, and tore through the main hall and the secondary hall. At the door to the crypts she stood dead still. It was closed.

She grabbed the handle and tugged, but it was firmly bolted. She felt him behind her, felt his doubt and skepticism. And then her own.

She turned into his arms. "I saw him!" she insisted. "He opened this door, I went down it!"

"Toni, please, let's go to bed?" he said.

She was shaking, cold as ice. He lifted her, hugging her close to him as they traveled back the way they had come. He tried to tease her. "Don't wiggle too much. I'll lose the towel."

She wasn't wiggling. She wasn't moving.

"Toni . . . !" he murmured, distressed by her fear. She shook her head, curling her arms around his neck.

He opened the door, still ajar, to the master's chambers with his foot, and closed it the same way. He laid her upon the bed and told her, "I'll get you some tea . . . brandy? Something?"

"No!" she said, rising to throw herself into his arms again. "No, no, don't leave me, even for a second."

"Toni, it's all right here —"

"No, just hold me. Make love to me, be with me, alive, vital, flesh and blood. Do what you do so well, make everything else in the world fade away!"

"Toni!" he whispered again, his slate eyes searching her own.

"Now, please!" she begged.

And with that, he complied. His lips found hers, and tonight they were gentle, slow, even hesitant. But she wouldn't have it. Not that. She was fevered, clinging to him, pressing the kiss until it became one of the most volatile passions. She ripped away his towel, frantic to be against him, to rid herself of every barrier between them. She was frenetic, electric against his flesh, needing every bit of heat and warmth, fevered, chaotic. . . .

Until he caught hold of her, bore her down, gripped her wrists and began a far slower, far more sensual seduction, bathing her flesh with fire, with the brush of lips, teeth, tongue, hands, all eliciting a deep, slow hunger and anguish, and making her feel cherished, taken. . . .

And as she had longed for, ached and needed, the world faded. Every thought was gone except for the perfect fit of his body to hers, the thunder of heartbeats, the drive of his sex, his hips, the frenzied arch and writhe of her own.

She soared, flew and exploded beneath him, then felt the burst of searing warmth within her that was his climax. And still, there was the feel of him within her, growing softer, a part of her . . . his arms, holding her.

"Toni . . ."

"No, not tonight. Please, don't talk tonight!" she begged. "Just . . . hold me."

And so he did.

Interlude

"Bruce, please. Before God, I do not know what this man has said to you, but you are my life, and I'd not betray you, ever. Dear God! I love you, Bruce!" she whispered.

And looking down into her eyes, those pools of blue, sapphire with sincerity and the sweetness of the bond that had been theirs forever, he knew that she spoke the truth. He drew her to her feet.

"Ah, so he lied, and has not come as yet. But he will come, Annalise. Perhaps the Lord Cromwell has not taken to ordering the demise of the families of men such as myself, but neither would he punish a man, here, in what he considers the wilds of Scotland, a land of savages, who took a captive . . . and misused her. Our son is safe enough, following the young king in France. You can stay here no longer."

"Where would you have me go?" she whispered.

"To the Highlands. To the clansmen there, honorbound to protect you, my love."

"We could bring danger upon those men. And here, the castle — our son's inheritance

— could fall to the enemy."

"A castle is mortar and stone, no more. And though no troops have come, in their eyes, the property is confiscated by the government, as it was. Nae, our hope is in the return of the king. And whether we are here or not, the day the king returns in triumph as Charles II of England will be the day we are justified, and all is restored."

She shivered suddenly. "What if that day never comes?"

"It will," he declared staunchly. He stroked her chin, reveled in the soft feel of her flesh and the beauty of her fine features. And more. Something that transcended anything mortal. The way that she looked at him. And all that they shared.

"I must get you away. Tonight."

"As you wish," she told him.

He held her against him, taking a brief moment to feel the heat between them, the beating of their hearts, a pulse that slowly melded, as well. He inhaled the scent of her, and thought that this, being together so, loving a person with such great passion and being loved in return, was heaven. And he was humbled.

He pulled away from her.

She smiled, her lips damp, wistful and sensual.

"There's not so much as a night we could spend together first?"

"Not in this house," he told her, ruing the words. "We must get into the forest."

She nodded. "I'll get my things. . . ."

"Bring little. We must travel fast."

She was quick, and she knew that his words were wise. As she prepared, Bruce spoke with his steward and his men, explaining that he was taking his lady away, and that, until the world was right again, the people mustn't give their own lives in a battle. But if they came, to allow the troops of the Protectorate in, let them do what they would, take what they craved, even unto the very stone of the castle. When Annalise came down to ride with him, many wept, but she gave them her cheerful, beautiful smile, swearing that all would be well.

And they rode together, both of them upon his great black mount.

He brought them into the forest. Finding a cove deep in the security of ancient oaks, he laid out his mantle, and there, surrounded by the softness of the night's breeze, the verdant richness of the woods, upon a bed of pines, he made love to her. As the moon waned high above them, he held her against his heart. Entwined, they found a night's rest, beauty and peace.

As the sun rose, he heard the snap of a branch. Leaping to his feet, he grabbed his sword. Somehow, they had been betrayed.

The sound was distant still, so he fell to his knees, waking her, his finger to his lips. "Dress, quickly. I'll leave the stallion. Take him ever north and westward, climb to the Highlands and await me."

"Where are you going? What are you doing?" she demanded with alarm.

"Leading them astray."

"No!" She threw herself against him.

"Annalise! I wage battle constantly, I know what I'm about. You must be away. Please, if I know that you are safe, I can fight any man!"

She rose, finding her clothing, scattered about, as he kilted himself into his tartan in silence. He held her then, once more. One last kiss.

"Go!" he urged her.

He bent low and moved silently, at first, until he had put distance between them. Then he let his presence be known. And he heard the activity in the forest, heard the horses, moving now far more carelessly through the trees.

He knew that his enemy waited before him, and his path veered just in time for the men to jump out from their hiding places too late.

His sword felled them both with a mighty swing.

But there were more.

Suddenly he was surrounded.

He found a path through the trees behind him, drawing them on. He was caught, and he knew it, but he fought like berserkers who had long ago come to Scotland, joining their Norse and Danish blood with that of more ancient tribes. He fought, not for his life, but for time — time for Annalise to depart to champions in the north.

That day, he brought down man after man. Yet, to no avail. For his enemy had amassed quite an army, and the men were bitter and incensed at the losses they had sustained in previous battle. Alone, he bore their assault, sustained wound after wound, and battled on.

Finally he stood in a field of corpses, but his great sword had been broken, and he was on his knees, blood dripping down his forehead into his eyes. The men around him backed away as Grayson Davis strode into the copse.

"Not such a hero now, are ye, man?" he demanded.

MacNiall looked up. "A hero? Always. For a man who believes in his ideals, and does not shift with the winds of fortune, will always be remembered as such."

Davis strode closer to him.

"Do you know how you are about to die?"

"Aye, that I do."

"You will scream with pain, beg for mercy, before I am done. I swear it."

He further inflamed his foe's wrath by smiling. "There is nothing you can do to me now that will cause me to cry out."

"Nae?" Grayson said. "Well, then, let me show you what you must see before you even begin to die!"

13

By morning, Toni fully intended to talk to Bruce. Despite the fact that she was going to sound crazy, she meant to tell him that she was definitely seeing his ancestor, that a ghost had led her into the woods and was now leading her down to the crypts. But when she awoke, he was already gone.

David, sipping coffee and reading the paper in the kitchen, told her that he'd gone into town to see Jonathan.

"You all right?" he asked her.

"Yes . . . why?" She glanced at him, helping herself to the coffee.

"Why?" He shook his head and looked toward the doorway, assuring himself that they were alone. "Because you're seeing . . . entities. Ghosts. A disturbing presence, or something." He cleared his throat. "And Thayer told me that an old woman gave you some kind of look yesterday, and then said something absolutely horrible about *you* being found in the forest."

"She was just an old, superstitious woman," Toni said.

David set his paper down and patted the

chair next to him. "Sit. Talk to me. So, she didn't scare you at all, huh?"

"She put the fear of hell and damnation right into me!" Toni said, laughing. "But only for a minute. She has cataracts, so her eyes were a little . . . eerie. After she was gone and we talked with her son . . . well, I was fine. Even stayed in the cemetery by myself."

David smiled. She decided not to tell him about her nocturnal trips to visit more grave sites deep in the bowels of the castle. He was too worried about her already.

"Laird Bruce is certainly in a fine mood, so it seems," David said.

"Well, I don't suppose the old legend had much bearing on his day-to-day life," Toni said. "But yes, I guess he's really pleased to find out that his famous ancestor most probably was innocent of the murder of his wife."

"And, apparently, we are good for the village." He was silent for a moment, studying his cup. "You know, I had been afraid that we'd be somewhat ostracized here."

"For being American?" Toni said.

David winced. "No, not exactly. And when I said 'we,' I meant Kevin and myself. For being of a different persuasion," he said lightly. "But people are wonderful. We had a great time in the village yesterday. Certainly, some of the older folks, gents, mainly, looked at us with a great deal of curiosity, but . . . everyone was curious and intrigued. We're actually going to get a lot of the locals up to the castle to see what we're up to, I think."

"That's good. I'm glad."

"But we don't really have a right to the place, so who knows how long Laird MacNiall will let it go on?"

Toni looked downward. *Yes, how long could it go on?*

"Well," she said, looking up. "In light of Laird MacNiall's pleasure over the vindication of his ancestor, I've thought of a way to change that particular bit of history in our tour."

"Oh, yeah?"

She nodded. "We have the great laird ride in just as before. He climbs the stairs to meet Annalise. It's glorious, a dramatic confrontation. Annalise pleads her innocence, then the two come running down the stairs — just as the bad guy rides in!"

David arched a brow to her. "Oh, Lord. Don't make me be the bad guy!"

She grinned. "No, it has to be Ryan. He's the only one with a prayer of controlling Wallace when Shaunessy is in the hall." She frowned suddenly, starting to jump up.

"Wallace is . . . better, right?"

David nodded. "Sit. Finish your coffee. Wallace is right as rain this morning."

She sat. "Well, what do you think?"

"I like it. And MacNiall will like it. Ryan will love it. He'll have a chance to play the knight again."

She nodded. "I've got to run it by the others. And Bruce, of course."

Kevin came walking on in.

"What are you running by the others?"

With a sigh, she went through her idea again.

"Works for me!" Kevin said. "Want breakfast? What have we got? You know, David, we bought all those supplies yesterday and what we really need is to go grocery shopping for ourselves again."

"There's eggs," David said. "Plenty of them."

"Omelettes then."

"Um, want help?" Toni asked.

"No!" both of them said in unison.

"I'm not that bad a cook!" she protested.

"As long as we're not getting too elaborate," David said, "Kevin and I work best alone. Go on out and see old Wallace, why don't you? Assure yourself that he's doing all right."

"Good idea!" she agreed, and started out.

The morning was crisp, clear and beautiful. As Toni walked from the castle to the stables, she found herself looking around, hoping that Eban wasn't about. She hated herself for still feeling so uneasy around the man, but she did. She was always ready to defend him in public. But inside, he made her uneasy.

She didn't see Eban as she walked on into the stables, but Shaunessy was gone. Bruce must have taken him. Wallace, however, was in his stall. Standing. He snorted as she walked toward him, and she thought that the horse was glad to see her.

She patted his nose, looking at his eyes, checking out his length thoroughly. "You're looking good this morning, fellow!" she told him. "Very good, as a matter of fact."

He stuck his head over the stall gate and pressed his nose against her chest, pushing her, as if he were looking for some kind of a handout.

"No, I didn't bring anything for you, boy," she told him, patting the downy nose. "We don't know what's making you sick! Maybe you're allergic to apples or carrots. Hmm. I wonder if that's possible. I haven't met this vet of yours yet, but when I do, I'll have to ask him about that."

The horse's huge brown eyes were on her, as if he really listened. He prodded her chest again with the tip of his soft nose, as if saying that such delights as apples and carrots couldn't possibly cause a problem.

"You are such a sweetie!" she told him.

She was startled when his ears suddenly went back flat. Turning around, she saw nothing. But she couldn't believe that the horse had suddenly become angry with her!

Then she heard a noise, a scraping sound from the rafters above her. A tingling of instinctive wariness vibrated throughout her limbs.

A ladder led up to the rafters. It was between her and the exit to the stables.

She inhaled deeply. *So? Someone was up there. So what?* It was probably just Eban, shelving hay, or . . . doing something.

The sound stopped, but she was still on edge.

"Well, Wallace, dear boy, I'm going to leave you to . . . enjoy your time off, stand around, do whatever horses do in their stalls," she said aloud. But she didn't walk out. Instead, she silently slipped the latch and entered the stall, standing by the horse's side. Still. Waiting.

At first, there was nothing at all. Then she

heard movement above her again. She remained where she was, not breathing. Someone was coming down the ladder. She stayed hiding behind the horse, watching.

From around Wallace's flank, she saw a man coming down the ladder. He was in jeans and a casual denim shirt. She saw the back of his head first, his sandy-colored hair.

Thayer.

He jumped the last few feet to the ground, dusted his hands on his jeans and looked around. He seemed to sigh with relief. Then he walked to the stable doors and hesitated, looking out. After a moment, he made a quick exit.

Toni remained with the horse for a moment, puzzled. Why should Thayer be nervous about being in the stables? He had as much right to come out here as any of them.

"Good boy," she murmured, patting Wallace's neck. She slipped back out of the stall, walked out down the aisle of stalls and found herself looking up the ladder.

What the hell had he been doing up there?

She was just about to set a foot on the first rung of the ladder when she was startled by a voice.

"Eh, he be lookin' well and fine this

mornin', miss, don't ye think?"

She swung around, almost in a panic herself. Eban was just inside the doorway, looking toward Wallace's stall.

She swallowed hard, forced a smile. Despite herself, she noted that he blocked the doorway.

"He looks very good, Eban. Thank you for watching him with such concern. He's really a wonderful horse."

"Aye, that he is," Eban agreed.

He didn't move from the doorway. If she was going to make an exit, she would have to walk by him.

"Well, thank you again," she murmured a bit awkwardly, striding toward the exit. She passed him, painfully aware of his presence. She was afraid that he was going to reach a hand out, stop her.

But he didn't. Instead, he caused her to pause with his words.

" 'E's trying to talk to ye, miss, ye know."

She felt almost as if she had been physically gripped. And so she turned back to him.

"What?"

"The laird. Not everyone is able t'see him. But ye . . . y've got the way, y'know. The touch."

He came closer to her and whispered, "Aye, y'must take care, grave care. Don't be

378

lettin' 'em all know it. There's those out there, always, who would do evil. But the laird . . . the laird would tell ye things."

She felt every hair on her body stand on end. Her smile was about to crack.

"I don't know what you're talking about," she said firmly, and turned.

Her footsteps were slow, but, by the time she neared the castle, she was nearly running.

As she entered the main hall, Ryan was coming down the stairs. "You went to see Wallace. Isn't it great, the old boy bounded back like a trooper!"

"Right. It's great."

She started up the stairs, anxious to hurry past him.

His hand fell on her arm. He stared at her quizzically. "Where are you going now? Kevin just shouted up to say that breakfast was ready."

"I — I just want to wash up," she said. "I'll be right back down. Don't wait for me, though. Everyone just eat, okay?"

Almost jerking free, she ran past him. She went straight to her room and found her purse. She dumped the contents on the bed, heedless of any mess. She dug into her wallet and found the card she had carried with her always, swearing that she would never use it.

She looked around, glad to realize that she'd remembered to plug her phone into the wall with the European adaptor on Saturday.

She punched in the country code for the United States, hesitated, looked at the card and then dialed.

"I've heard about the great discovery old Doc Darrow has made," Robert said, greeting Bruce as he came into the pub. "Congratulations!"

Bruce took his friend's hand and shook it as he slid into the booth. They were in Stirling, on Robert's suggestion that they meet there.

"Might be a bit absurd to feel so elated about something so long ago, but . . ." Bruce said with a shrug. "Sure, I'm happy. It's a fine thing to discover that your heroic ancestor wasn't a wife killer."

Robert grinned.

"Why Stirling?" Bruce asked.

"Didn't want to make you come to Edinburgh. I had some business here, and I don't really want our man Jonathan to know that I'm meeting with you so often. Don't want to step on his toes there, you know? We need too much cooperation."

Bruce nodded. "Well, then fine. So?"

"Want to order first?"

"Sure," Bruce said, glancing around with a slightly arched brow. The pub was rather dingy, considering that Stirling offered a lot of really fine establishments. Actually, Bruce considered the city a true gem of the country.

"They have the most delicious fish and chips in the world here. Full of fat and cholesterol," Robert said. He grimaced. "Service is slow today. The old fellow who owns the place has lost another waitress. They all quit on him. He's a bloody bugger, he is. Still, the fish and chips make it worth the wait."

"How long a wait?"

Robert grinned. "Not too long for me. He knows who I am." To prove his point, he lifted a hand. A fleshy man in an apron made his way over.

"Aye, then, what'll it be, Detective Inspector?"

"Fish and chips for me." He looked at Bruce.

"Fish and chips, and a stout," Bruce said.

"I'll be puttin' a rush on it," the man said, and he shook his head. "Lasses these days! Dependable as shite!"

"Lost another one, did you, George?"

"Came in Sunday mornin', took off Sunday afternoon, haven't see the lights o' her eyes since!" Muttering, he walked away.

"Someone should just tell him one day that he's a nasty bastard," Robert said.

George came back swiftly, nearly throwing a pint of stout down before Bruce.

"So?" Bruce said, when he was gone.

"Actually, I didn't dig up much. It's rather the coincidence of things that made me call you so quickly," Robert explained. "First, our Glasgow fellow, Thayer Fraser. The man has a record."

"Anything serious?"

"Some busts for drugs when he was young. Clean slate for the last several years. Played with a band, the Kinked Kilts, and his last gig was at a piano bar."

"As he said," Bruce murmured.

"He worked some shady places," Robert said. "Suspect, but not criminal."

"That's all on the man?"

"Aye, so far."

"And the others?"

"What I've gotten in from checking legally accessible records is rather strange. Apparently they're all exactly what they appear to be. I've found the college records from NYU, and some references to work. Not one of the Americans has a police record of any kind. But, as a point of interest, two of them are natural computer whizzes."

"Lucky for them," Bruce said. "Which two? And why is that important?"

"Well, we're following two mysteries here, wouldn't you say? For them to have gotten the permits and licenses they have, there had to be some truth to their rental agreements. That means that someone did have a hell of a lot on you, such as information regarding your actual title, your numbers in our old British society . . . information that only you, as an individual, should have had. A crack computer hacker can get all kinds of information on someone, which is why identity theft is getting to be such an issue these days."

"So, in other words, you're telling me that one of them might have known about me, gotten into my records, faked being me and rented the castle to them?" Bruce asked.

"Well, it's a possibility."

Bruce shook his head. "But whoever did must have known that I'd eventually show up."

"Right. But if the person had done it just to get money out of the others and knew how to make the computer site disappear . . . well, what would he, or she, care at that point?"

"What about Thayer Fraser?"

"So far," Robert said, "I only know that he has one hell of a Web page — oh, and that he's big into computer gaming. Medieval game playing on line, you know, the kind that goes on forever and forever, with one guy at a computer in Glasgow playing with someone in London, New York, Moscow . . . or maybe just in Stirling."

Bruce nodded, taking in the information. "Still, none of the Americans has a criminal record. That is a piece of good news."

Robert parted his folded hands, refolded them. "Aye, sure. But then there's this, as well. And . . . this probably doesn't mean a thing. I just found it interesting."

"What?" Bruce said.

"Well, there's a strange time line here. It has to be a coincidence, I imagine."

"What?" Bruce said, exasperated. Robert didn't often beat around the bush.

"Helen MacDougal disappeared from Glasgow on June third, a year ago."

"And I found her on August thirtieth, in the water," Bruce said, frowning.

"Mary Granger disappeared November eleventh, last year."

Bruce's brows furrowed to a deeper degree. "Aye, Eban found her in early January. In worse shape."

"January tenth, to be precise."

"Robert, what are you getting at?"

"Annie O'Hara disappeared, we think, just a week or more ago."

"Aye . . . so? Are we goin' somewhere here, Robert? If so, I don't see where," Bruce told him.

"You know hotels ask for passports when you check in," Robert said.

"Aye, of course."

"Well, your friends — Toni, the Brownes, Kevin and David, at least — were in a hotel in Glasgow, June of last year."

Bruce frowned. "They've said they've vacationed here, many times."

Robert nodded and drew out a folder by his side, flipping a page. "November last, Mary Granger disappeared from Stirling."

"And you're going to tell me my friends were in Stirling?"

"No. Glasgow."

He accepted that, frowning. "And two weeks ago?"

"They were back in Edinburgh, making the arrangements for licenses and the like."

Bruce shook his head. "Robert, if you're trying to draw a connection here —"

"I'm not. I'm just letting you know what I found out. And the coincidence regarding the dates just happened before my eyes. I'd be remiss not to mention it to you."

"Aye, you're right, but —" Bruce shook his head. "Think about them, one by one. Toni? A murderess of prostitutes? Kevin and David — they don't fit the profile at all. Gina and Ryan? Frankly, I just don't see it."

"We don't actually have a profile —"

"But we know what it would be. White, heterosexual male, young, twenties to thirties, day job, probably menial, maybe even a wife or steady girlfriend."

Robert nodded. "Aye, you've a point there. But profiles have been off. You know that yourself. Remember, years ago? What profiler, no matter how good, would have come up with the real scenario, a husband and wife *killing team?*"

Bruce shrugged. "Robert, I think we're grasping at straws here. If we had to go through a roster of every foreigner who happened to be in the country at the times of the murders — or disappearances — I think we'd have some numbers to go through. And if we're looking at opportunity, I'm afraid we've a nation full of people to look through, as well."

"Bruce, you don't need to be defendin' the crew. All I'm telling you is what I happened to see when I made inquiries —

which I did at your behest."

George hurried over, nearly tossing down their plates. "Damn, but if I could just get meself a decent lass!" he swore.

Bruce frowned suddenly, catching the man's arm when he was hurrying to move on.

"George?"

"Aye? Sir, be quick, would ye?"

"Your girl just walked out on you? Or just didn't show up? She didn't quit, I mean, let you know she was leaving?"

George waved an impatient hand in the air. "She was another wanderer on the loose. Strange accent — looked more the Norse type, which she should. Lass came down from Orkney. And quit? Resign? Have the courtesy to let a fellow know she wasn't coming back? Are y'jestin'? Hell no! She didn't show up, and that's that. Got herself enough money and hurried on to the next town, no doubt. Now, sir, I've got food piling up in the kitchen!"

Bruce stared across the table at Robert. "You might want to make some inquiries here," he said softly.

Robert looked down at the table and shook his head. "Aye," he said, and pushed away the plate of fish and chips he had been so anticipating.

Toni called the number she swore she'd never dial, only to find that Adam Harrison was out of town. When the young man answering the phone asked if she'd like to leave her name and a message, she nearly hung up. But she had her own cell phone with her — it wasn't as if he'd call back and leave a message on a line that anyone might answer. After hesitating, she left her name and phone number.

"Oh, hi!" the voice on the other end said. "Toni Fraser . . . Adam said to pay sharp attention if you ever called. Someone will be right back with you."

Someone?

Toni didn't feel particularly comfortable with that information, but she thanked the young man anyway and rang off.

For a moment, she pondered her next move. She nearly jumped sky-high when her cell phone, still in her hand, began to ring. She fumbled with the little buttons, nearly hanging up on the caller.

"Hello?"

"Hi. Toni?"

The voice on the other end was feminine.

"Yes?" she said carefully.

"My name is Darcy. Darcy Stone. I work with Adam Harrison."

Toni was silent. It had been one thing to contemplate talking with Adam, a man who knew her. The gentle soul who had been there when a young child's world had fallen apart. The man who had come to see her one-woman show, but didn't press it when she said that she was just fine, not having any more nightmares, no more visions. . . .

"Toni?"

The woman's voice was crystal clear; she might have been in the next town.

"Yes, I'm here."

"Listen, please don't worry, Adam isn't shuffling you off to anyone. You can speak with him in a few hours — he's on a plane right now. It's just that he has your name on a special list, and he's always said that if you called in, we were to get back to you immediately. Please, nothing you say to me will ever go any further than me. And again, no matter how insane it might sound, don't be afraid to say anything. Anything at all."

Toni stared at the phone slightly skeptically, as if by looking at it she could somehow fathom the truth of the words being said.

"Let's start at the beginning," Darcy Stone said, from across the miles. "Where are you?"

"Scotland. A small village known as

Tillingham. At — at the castle there."

"A castle. In Tillingham?"

"Yes." Toni took a breath. "I think I'm seeing a ghost," she said.

"Then you probably are," came the matter-of-fact answer.

"I am?"

"Yes." Darcy chuckled. "I'm sorry, I'm afraid you'll hang up on me when I say this, but . . . I see many ghosts."

Toni *was* tempted to hang up.

"Please, don't hang up, and do talk to me," the woman said, as if entirely aware of Toni's every thought and action.

"I rented a castle with friends in Scotland, rented with a lease option to buy," Toni said. "Except it turned out that we didn't really rent it, at least, not from the owner. We were told the family had died out, but there's a very current laird. I made up a story about an ancestor of his, and it turned out to have happened, right down to the name of the laird's wife." She hesitated. "I dreamed, or woke up, a ghost. The man in my nightmares, or ghost in reality, is the exact image of the living laird. I thought at first that maybe I was being taken, as we had been taken in by the corporation supposedly leasing the property. But then, there are the murders."

"The murders?"

"Women have been disappearing. Three to date, I believe. And two have been found in the forest bordering the castle. I went into the forest one day, led by the . . . ghost. I found bones. Everyone assumed it was the third victim, but it looks as if it's the old laird's lady, dead now for centuries. He wasn't an old laird, he just lived in the sixteen hundreds. I'm not making any sense at all. I'm —" Again she hesitated, thinking that she really was losing her mind. This wasn't even Adam she was talking to, and she was spilling out way more than she had ever planned. "I've quickly fallen into a certain involvement with the young laird, the *contemporary* laird, who certainly has been decent enough about this whole thing. We rented, or thought we rented the place to do theatrical tours —"

"I saw your production of Queen Varina," the woman interjected. "It was wonderful."

Toni had never liked to think that she overreacted to either criticism or praise. But at that moment, she decided that she definitely liked the woman on the other end of the phone.

"Thanks," she said softly. "Um . . . he — the laird, that is — doesn't see ghosts. Or the ghost." She hesitated. "There's only one."

Darcy was silent for a moment. "Women have been found in the area, dead. But the ghost brought you to the remains of his long-dead wife?"

"Yes."

"Have you seen him since?"

"Yes. Now he keeps leading me to the crypts."

There was no way she could ever describe this conversation to anyone.

"There's a simple answer," Darcy Stone said from the other end.

"And that is?"

"He wants her by his side. Now that you've found her, he wants her buried where she should be — at his side."

Toni was startled to feel a rise of excitement. Lord, yes! That would make so much sense. Well, if the fact that she was seeing a ghost made sense, then his leading her to the crypts after she had found the bones would definitely align, at any rate.

"Yes," she murmured.

"Of course, it might *not* be that simple," Darcy warned.

"Now that you've said that to me, it has to be!" Toni said. "I saw him at the foot of my bed, and then going into the forest. And then . . . into the crypts. Oh!" She groaned.

"What?"

"They think she's an incredible historic find. His wife, the lady I found. I'm afraid they'll want to study her, put her in a museum."

"Well, that's easy enough to handle. And I don't think this is one you're going to have to worry about at all. Her descendant just says no! But still, there might be a lot more going on there."

"Not in this residence," Toni said. "There are terrible things going on —"

"The victims found in the forest weren't associated with the castle?"

"No, definitely not. They were part-time prostitutes at the very least, and kidnapped from three major cities, Edinburgh, Glasgow and Stirling."

"You're certain there can be no association?"

"That would be impossible. Really. We haven't been here that long. And aside from us, there's the laird and a fellow who works for him."

"I see."

Toni hesitated, aware that she should mention the fact that Eban scared the wits out of her. And that, at times, she'd almost convinced herself that the current laird was dressing up as a ghost. *She had never seen the both of them at the same time!*

"I can come right over."

"What? To Scotland? That's not . . . necessary," Toni said. She was ready to groan out loud. What had she done? If she brought anyone else in here — especially some kind of an occultist who claimed to speak to lots of ghosts! — they'd definitely be thrown out. She couldn't begin to imagine Bruce MacNiall standing for such a thing.

"Your situation sounds a bit complex." Darcy hesitated, then her words spilled out. "Toni, Adam has talked about you. He's says that you're . . . you're one of the most amazing mediums he's ever encountered."

"Medium!" Toni said, shocked.

"You see things," the voice on the other end said.

Toni gripped the phone so tightly it might have snapped. She swallowed hard, forcing herself to breathe. "I'm sorry," she said then. "This was . . . a mistake. I'm not a medium. I had a few unusual — very unusual — dreams as a child, but I am not a medium. I don't want to be a medium. And please, do not — I repeat — do not come over here. We're in a tenuous situation, at best. I appreciate your time. I'll see to it, somehow, that the woman is buried next to her laird. Thank you for all your help. It's truly appreciated. But do not come here! Thank you and goodbye."

She hung up the phone, threw it on the bed and stared at it as if it might turn into a serpent and bite her. She waited, half expecting the woman to try to call her back. But the phone lay on the bed, silent.

She turned and hurried out of the room. One of their group had to be somewhere about. She wanted company very desperately. Someone among . . . the living.

14

It was time for the buses to come rolling up, and Bruce had not returned.

"You had it all figured out!" Gina said with dismay. "Now what are we going to do?"

"Someone else will play Bruce's part, that's all," Toni said.

They were standing in the great hall, dressed for the various roles they were going to play. Everyone stared at Toni.

"What?" she said.

Kevin cleared his throat. "Really, no one else can play Bruce's part."

"He's not even an actor!" Toni protested.

"That's just it," David said. "He *is* the great MacNiall."

Toni shook her head. "Come on, guys! We never planned on having him to begin with. He's worked with us, but he's not on the payroll."

"We don't exactly have a payroll, right now, do we?" Thayer inquired.

"Thayer, you can be Bruce," she said.

"I can't ride that horse."

"And now," Ryan said, "I'm supposed to

be the bad guy. I've been practicing my evil sneer all day."

Toni sighed. "He isn't here. So we have to do something else."

"I know!" Ryan said. "Okay, here's the deal. I'm not so sure I can ride his horse, either —"

"You can ride any horse," Toni protested.

Ryan shook his head. "That fellow *knows* his master. But Wallace is right as rain now. I'll ride him in, then I'll come up the stairs as the very personification of good and evil. You know, a dramatic Jekyll and Hyde number. I fight with Toni, and myself. It will be great."

Again, they were silent, staring at him.

"Thayer," Toni said, staring at her kinsman, "you'll have to be Bruce — without the horse. Burst into the castle on foot, run up the stairs. Ryan will come riding in as the bad guy."

"We could just do it the way we had originally," Gina said.

"That's a definite plan," David said. "It's actually the most logical."

"It is," Kevin agreed.

Toni shook her head stubbornly. "We can't go back, because now we know that we were maligning someone."

"Toni, we were never maligning anyone, because we didn't know he had really existed!" Gina protested.

"But now we do," Toni said. "And I don't want to play it the way we had it originally. Guys, we know the fellow was innocent."

"Well, we don't *know* it," Kevin said.

"Yes, we do," Toni insisted stubbornly. "So, Thayer walks in, and Ryan rides in. Agreed?"

"Sure," Thayer said.

"I don't know," Ryan protested, shaking his head. "I think my Jekyll and Hyde thing could have been really, really good."

"Alas! We'll never get to know!" Gina said, and winked at Toni.

There was a knock at the door.

Kevin clapped his hands. "Places, everyone. David and I get to open the doors now!"

"No, no! Not yet," Thayer protested. "It's just Lizzie and Trish. They were coming early."

He went to answer the door. It was indeed the girls. They came in, exited and exuberant, oohing and aahing over the castle alone. "And you all are living here! How wonderful," Lizzie said.

"Actually, yes," David murmured, looking around. "We should be grateful, for whatever time we get, huh?"

Ryan sighed. "We thought we'd have it for all of our lives."

"Or as long as we wanted, anyway," Gina said.

"Well, it's lovely, truly lovely," Trish said, catching Thayer's arm and squeezing it. "You're lucky, for whatever."

"Yes, I guess we are," Gina said.

"Buses!" Kevin said. "I can hear them. Let's move, children. Trish, Lizzie, just follow the crowd around. We can all chat when the last bus leaves."

Toni disappeared up the stairs, awaiting her cue. Leaning against the wall, listening to activity below, she smiled, pleased to hear the audience reaction as they played out their parts and gave their histories. She didn't know if the fact that Lizzie and Trish were out there, determined to have fun, spurred their tour to greater enthusiasm, or if they were just all getting into it so deeply that they naturally brought their listeners along. But the night was going wonderfully.

When she came out on the landing, clad in her white gown, ready to become the Lady Annalise, she found that she was "on" that night herself, wound up by the stories the others had told. Her voice rang through the hall. Her passion for the heroism of

Laird MacNiall was strong. And when she announced his return, she was stunned when Bruce came riding in on Shaunessy, perfectly on cue.

He strode up the stairs in anger as he had before. She found herself falling to her knees, and to her own ears, it sounded as if she really begged for her life.

Then his anger abated. If she hadn't caught the flash of humor in his eyes as he fell to his knees before her, accepting her words of loyalty, denying any fault thrown upon her by others, she would have thought the passion and ardor that he offered were real.

Ryan came riding into the hall with an expert display of horsemanship. Bruce rose, striding down the stairs to battle with Ryan.

Toni was amazed herself. Ryan, of course, had used swords in his previous work. It didn't seem a shock that Bruce might have learned something, as well. But they had never practiced. And usually, such a display was meticulously choreographed.

They were wonderful. They shouted back and forth, playing off one another's ad libs. And in the finale, a strike by Bruce's sword brought Ryan's flying across the floor — toward the hearth, away from their group. Bruce left Ryan for dead on the floor, coming back for Toni. As he reached her, Ryan slowly rose. With Bruce's back to him, he staggered up the stairs, catching Bruce by the shoulders, throwing him downward. Then he put his hands around Toni's neck. He winked as he strangled her.

After all that she had witnessed, she sprang into character, making her death scene as spectacular as the fight she had just witnessed. She lay dead on the stairs. Ryan fell at the feet of them.

Silence reigned in the hall.

Then, Lizzie, bless her, yelled out "Bravo!" And the room burst into applause that never seemed to end.

"Tea and scones! Into the kitchen, everyone!" Kevin commanded.

"This way!" David said, helping move them all along.

Toni sat up. Ryan and Bruce both were rising. "Oh, my God! We pulled it off!" Ryan said. "I thought you were crazy, suggesting that we could do this without a single practice. But that was incredible."

"I'll second that," Thayer said, coming forward. Gina, too, was running down from her place at the landing. She jumped up and down, kissing her husband, then planting one on Bruce's check before settling down in embarrassment. "Sorry, Laird MacNiall!"

"Nae, now, it was a lovely moment, Mrs. Browne," he told her, then turned to Toni. "Sorry I was late. I was — tied up."

She shook her head. "Why on earth would you want to be sorry? That was really phenomenal. The two of you . . . together. Purely amazing."

Bruce inclined his head to her. "Thank you, Lady Annalise."

She smiled but gritted her teeth, aware that no offense had been intended, but she was uneasy being called by the name. The strangeness of the day came rushing back to her — and the memory that, just that morning, she had so desperately wanted to talk to him.

Instead, she had called an agency that investigated ghosts.

She looked into his eyes. There had been laughter in them, and fun, but she was surprised to realize that he actually seemed a little distracted, as well. She had thought he was entirely into the act, but maybe he had just been going through the motions.

She turned away, disturbed. "I should really give Kevin and David a hand," she murmured, heading toward the kitchen. "We've an incredibly full house."

"I'll take the horses," Ryan said.

"Look after Wallace. I'll tend to

Shaunessy," Bruce said.

Gina and Thayer followed Toni into the kitchen. Since there were so many people there, Toni was glad they'd come in, though Kevin was so well prepared that he probably could have handled a crowd of a hundred. The scones were in baskets, there were a number of stations with cream and sugar, and he'd had the tea prepared well before the crowd came filing in.

The crowd was always eager to talk, but tonight, more so than ever. News about the discovery of the ancient remains had traveled fast, and the group was excited to be the first ever to see their little drama played out with the great Laird MacNiall portrayed as innocent.

Finally the buses left, but Lizzie and Trish remained. And after everyone pitched in with the cleanup, Toni decided that Thayer was going to have to be his charming self and deal with their guests. She excused herself and went upstairs.

"Have you ever seen anything like it?" Ryan said.

Bruce, putting up the last of Shaunessy's tack, glanced over at him. Ryan was patting the roan's nose, studying his eyes and the great head of the horse.

"Quite frankly, I haven't," Bruce said, realizing himself for the first time that it was the absolute truth. He knew horses, and he'd never seen anything like this. The vet believed that the roan had gotten into something. Eban had seen to it that the stables were swept completely, lest it be some kind of infection caused by molding hay or bad grain. But only the roan had been infected. The vet had commented that it was akin to a child eating something disagreeable, having a bad night and clearing his system, waking up just as good as ever.

He walked over to study the roan himself. Wallace's eyes were clear and sharp, a sure sign that he was over what had plagued him.

"He's doing well now, it seems," Bruce said. He patted the horse. "Good lad," he murmured, then told Ryan, "I'm thinking, come the weekend, we'll move him. You did a damned good job here of cleaning the place out, and Eban came in and did more, but we might move both the boys and I'll get a real crew out here. These days . . . well, you get some kind of a germ or bacteria and you can't tell quite what's going on. The vet took some blood samples, too, so maybe we'll know more soon enough. Good thing is, he's looking fine right now."

Ryan grinned suddenly. "Hey, speaking

of fine, we were something, eh? In the States, we couldn't have attempted such a thing! If one of us had nicked the other, there would have been law suits and all that. Where the hell did you learn to do all that?"

"Well, over here, we have mock tournaments and such, just like you have Revolutionary and Civil War reenactments."

Ryan grinned. "Well, I don't mean to brag, but damn, were we good!"

"Aye, that we were." Bruce gave him a wave and started back to the castle. He looked at the stone, climbing to the night sky, and realized that he had something very special. Time and reality had made him lose his appreciation. The Americans had brought it back.

Ryan followed him, and when they entered the castle, they could hear laughter coming from the kitchen — not surprising since the car belonging to the two women they'd met in the village remained in the driveway. Bruce had actually enjoyed the night, but he wasn't anxious for any more company.

"Sounds as if we still have company," Ryan said.

Bruce nodded. "Well, enjoy," he murmured, heading for the stairs. It was his castle; he could opt out.

He entered his room to find Toni sitting by the hearth, staring at burned-out embers. She was wearing a contemporary cotton T-shirt nightshirt, her blond hair caught by the light, her features grave. When she saw him, she brought a pensive smile to her lips.

"What's wrong?" he asked her.

Her smile remained uncertain, though she shook her head. He came to her, taking a seat on the side of the bed. He tried to calculate the time he had known her. A speck of dust in the span of his life. But it seemed natural that she was there, and beyond the obvious of a great sexual relationship, there was something better in the fact, as well. He'd known he'd come up the stairs and find her waiting. And he'd liked it.

Apparently she tried to shake off whatever was bothering her. "You and Ryan . . . wow. You played off each other unbelievably," she told him.

"It wasn't half bad, was it?" He picked up her fingers, idly stroking her hand.

"Of course, if you'd worked for me in the States, I would have fired your ass," she told him, eyes sparkling as they touched his. "You were very late."

He arched a brow. "I got held up with Robert in Stirling."

"Oh?"

He offered her a grimace. "We were at a pub and found out that one of the barmaids had failed to show. The fellow who owns the place is a bit of a bastard, so he wasn't in the least concerned, but we felt we had to look into it. We found out where she'd been living. It seems she packed her bags, so . . ."

"I'm glad," Toni told him. "Luckily, you don't need much rehearsal."

"We both know what we're doing."

"Apparently," Toni agreed.

"So that, in a nutshell, was my day. Thinking something might be wrong, finding out we were both getting a little punch drunk due to events. So, I repeat, what's wrong?"

She didn't answer right away, but stared back at the dying embers. "Bruce, is this place supposed to be haunted?"

He laughed, then sobered when she stared at him. Still, he couldn't quite help the smile. "It's a castle. Centuries old. What do you think?"

She flushed. "Well, it is haunted, you know."

He sighed. "Toni, I let the place go to hell. Aye, that I did. But from the time I was a wee lad, I knew the place was mine. I have spent a great deal of time here. Not a single ghost has ever darkened my door."

"I see your ancestor a bit too frequently," she told him.

He groaned. "Toni, I know the dreams are plaguing you, lass." He shook his head. "Is the castle supposed to be haunted? Aye, definitely. Bruce MacNiall supposedly rides the forest and wanders these old halls. There are other tales, as well, and we do have one bloody history. But that's just it. Somewhere in the past, you heard the stories. I believe with my whole heart that you came here *thinking* you made up the past. But there are all kinds of books out about Scottish ghosts. They're as prevalent as Scottish sheep. And someone may not have gotten the names or the place right, but the story has probably been written up. You simply heard about it."

She bit her lower lip lightly. "Haven't you ever . . . felt something? Had a sense of déjà-vu, a premonition?"

A premonition? Aye, and it was you in the water, facedown so I couldn't see your face, just the trail of your hair, and my heart was in my throat. And worse. Once, when I was a cop with the Edinburgh Police Department, working a sad case indeed, I was able to crack it because I could put myself in a fellow's shoes.

"Toni. . . ."

She pulled her fingers from his light touch

and gripped both his hands.

"Bruce, I need you to take me to the crypts."

"What?"

"Please!"

"Toni, I think it might be better if I don't take you to the crypts."

She shook her head. Her eyes were a true sapphire, touching his. Earnest, sincere and alarmingly desperate.

"Look," she said. "We haven't known one another long, but I admire you, and I've come to respect you tremendously. I've come to care about you, too, and I believe that you feel something for me. So I'm begging you . . . please, please, just humor me on this. I know it sounds crazy. But you have shown me a great deal more than simple tolerance regarding my strange dreams. You've helped me, been with me, made me feel sane. Help me with this, now . . . I'm begging you!"

"Take you to the crypts . . . *now?*"

She nodded. "I've been there at night."

"Toni, I keep that door locked —"

"I've been there," she insisted. "Bruce, I can describe it to you! There's a winding stone stairway almost immediately after the door opens. Then there are arched hall-ways, like in the catacombs of a medieval church. And there's a tomb and monument to Bruce MacNiall, the king's loyal Cavalier, at the end of one of the hallways. I'm assuming it was designed sometime years after his death."

Bruce stared at her with certain astonishment. It wasn't impossible that the group might have gotten in to the vaults, but . . .

"I don't particularly want a circus made out of the family crypts," he said.

"Surely even Thayer has let those girls leave by now!" she said, smiling. "I'm afraid he's been the odd man out here," she added. "We both used to be a bit on the loose, but since you returned to the castle . . . well, Gina and Ryan are as close and old hat as Ma and Pa Kettle, David and Kevin have one another, and once you arrived . . ."

He noted that she didn't say *And I have you.* But Toni wouldn't. She would never be so presumptuous. And yet . . .

He reached out and smoothed a tendril of sunblond hair.

"All right."

She smiled, her appreciation evident, and he thought he actually heard a thump in her heartbeat.

"Thank you," she said.

"Think we've given them enough time to

clear out?" he asked.

"We can see."

He nodded. "I'll need the key." The great skeleton key was kept in a drawer in the wardrobe. The thing was ancient, as old as the door and the metal bolt.

He joined her, grimacing, and took her hand as they left the room and started out. They moved silently along the hallway to the top landing, then paused.

"Hear anyone?" he asked softly.

She shook her head. "They could still be in the kitchen," she said.

"We'll check it out. However," he reminded her, "they are my crypts." She smiled at that.

They walked down the stairs and into the kitchen. It was spotless — and empty.

"Want a brandy first?" he asked her.

"I'm all right, really," she said.

"I'm not."

"Okay, then I'll have a brandy."

He poured them each a small snifter, watching her as she sipped the fiery liquid. "There's something more you want," he said.

"I'll tell you when we get down there," she said, sipping the brandy. Again her eyes touched his, searchingly. She cast her head slightly at an angle. "You don't dress up like an ancient laird and run around in the middle of the night, right?"

He arched a brow. "Nae, lass, I really don't."

She swallowed the last of her brandy, then waited patiently for him.

"You really want to go down to the crypts in the middle of the night?" he asked.

"I really don't. But . . . I don't suppose I could make you understand. I can't make myself understand."

"All right, then." He set the glasses in the sink. "Shall we?"

He offered her a hand again and they went back into the secondary hall, to the door that led downward to the crypts. She winced as the old metal scraped and groaned. He pushed the door inward. "It is a winding stairway, with very old stone. I'll lead. Be careful."

"You still don't believe me, but I've been here," she whispered. Though there was really no need for a voice so soft, the night, the circumstances, seemed to demand it.

Bruce started down, hitting the light switch on the side of the wall. They moved down carefully. But at the foot of the stairs, Toni paused.

"What is it?"

"Nothing . . . well, there weren't cobwebs

before, and I had no idea there was a light switch."

"We've had lights down here since the nineteen-thirties," he told her with a trace of amusement. There weren't, however, terribly powerful bulbs lighting up the place, and the medieval arches led to a natural state for shadows.

Moving slowly, they walked by shelves and effigies, until they reached the end of the hallway where the man history had recalled as the "great" MacNiall had been laid.

"You know what actually happened to him," Bruce said. "He met what they called the 'traitor's end.' But his execution was carried out by a mock court right out in the forest. When Charles II returned to claim his throne, he ordered that Bruce MacNiall's body be recovered from the forest and that a tomb be made. The king even paid for the marble and the artist's work."

Toni stood pensively for a moment, staring at the tomb.

"It's you," she whispered.

"I beg to differ. It's not me. I'm right here," he told her.

She flushed, glancing at him. "But it is uncanny. There are hundreds of years between you, and yet . . . the resemblance is so great."

He shrugged. "Maybe we see more than there is."

"I don't think so," she said.

"Genetics can be very strange."

"True," she murmured. "And yet, does it ever make you feel . . . ?"

"Uneasy?" he asked, slipping an arm around her shoulders. "Never, since I grew up here. And I used to love to bring friends down. We'd tell ghost stories ourselves and run up the stairs screaming, and my da would get mad. We were typical kids. But the great MacNiall isn't still with us, Toni. He lived out his life. He lived hard, passionately, and he arrived here, as all men will. I like the history. I like the fact that the family he served with such ardent loyalty returned that favor in the person of Charles II, restoring him to his home. It's legend, Toni, history and myth, nothing more."

She smiled, inching just a bit closer to him, still staring at the grave and the marble effigy of his ancestor.

"Bruce, there's a second sarcophagus behind the first."

"I suppose they believed that one day they would find the bones of his beloved."

"They've been found now."

"Aye. But who knows when the forces that be will release the remains, eh?"

She turned to him, solemn, deeply concerned.

"Bruce, she needs to be given a proper burial, here, with her laird."

"Well, lass, I'm sure that she will be. In time."

Toni shook her head vehemently. "They may try to keep her. The levels of preservation were rather bizarre. Someone may want her in a museum. Bruce, you can't let it happen!"

He looked down at her, smiling a little. "Ah, Toni, so you think my ancestor comes back, hauntin' your dreams at night, to have his lady buried at his side? They'll want a bit of my blood, you know. To verify that the lady was my great, great — whatever! — grandmother. And then she'll come home. When it's proved she is my ancestor, I'll bring her home."

"I'd really like it if we could rush them as much as possible," she said.

His smile deepened. "All right, but . . ."

"But?" she queried.

"I've a bit of problem with it all, you see. I haven't always been the most religious of men, but I do have a rather deep-set belief that there is a greater power — God. And perhaps, because like all men, I don't want to consider myself merely mortal, I do believe in an afterlife. But I also like to believe that beneath it all, we're something finer than the weakness of flesh and bone. And that being the case . . . well, Bruce MacNiall did not want his bones to lie here for him to be legend, to find his peace in death, or whatever. And though, certainly, I'd not want the remains of an ancestor treated with anything less than respect, I cannot believe that an ancestor of mine would haunt you, tease or torment you, over earthly remains."

"Maybe he doesn't think he's tormenting me," Toni said. "He just wants to make sure that the remains of what was once the living, breathing woman he loved are treated with the due respect to which you refer."

He swept his arms around her tightly, caught, even here, in the realm of the dead, by the sapphire sincerity within her somewhat anguished gaze.

"We'll see to it, eh?" he said softly. "Now . . . if you don't mind, it has been a bitch of a day. Shall we?"

She nodded, smiling, and led the way out of the crypts. But at the base of the winding stairway, she paused.

"What now, Miss Fraser?"

She flashed him a smile, and shook her

head. "I . . . nothing."

"What?"

"No, nothing, really. Just a sense of . . ."

He sighed. "Toni!"

She exhaled. "Just a sense that someone was behind us!"

"Shall we walk back?" he asked.

She shook her head. "No."

They proceeded up the stairs. He followed her, watching the way the cotton clung to her curves. At the top, she stopped again, looking back at him.

"What?" she asked, perplexed.

"Keep going," he said.

Outside the door, he paused to close and lock the door. It creaked loudly.

"I did know what it looked like, exactly!" she whispered. "I told you, right? And I knew that the tomb would be there, knew that the old Bruce and you were spitting images of one another."

"Aye," he said.

"Well?"

"Well, what?"

"I don't know . . . exactly. Aren't you going to admit there's something a bit weird about it?" she queried.

He shook his head.

"No?" she said.

"Not tonight."

"Then why were you staring at me?"

He caught the innocent confusion in her eyes.

"I hate to admit to having feelings of a rather base inclination at the moment, but frankly, Miss Fraser, I was watching your hips, the machinations of the way you moved, and thinking I wanted nothing more to do with the dead, the old, the past. I find that my concern right now is extremely focused and has everything to do with the present. The immediate present. Dare I be crass? Madam, I was watching your ass."

The confusion left her eyes. She laughed softly, a breath of anticipation, of excitement in the sound that stimulated every sensual essence in his being.

He drew her against him then, allowing his fingers to ripple down her back and form around her buttocks as he drew her close. "This is my castle, and as laird here, I do have the right to every sexual fantasy known to man, as far as mind and place are concerned. Before the great hearth, in the kitchen, on the stair . . . But the place is filled with your associates, and God knows, they may well wander at night. And, truthfully, stone is quite hard on the back and the bones, so . . ."

"You do have a great bed," she mused.

"And you have a great — great assets," he assured her teasingly.

She escaped his hold, scampering ahead of him up the main stairway. In the hallway of the upper landing, she waited, looking back. Her smile was still in place, her eyes bright, her hair like a halo in the dim light. He was rather certain that she had chosen the cotton gown with the full intention of getting him to show her the crypts that night, that she had worn it in case they had, indeed, run into any of her friends.

She couldn't know how the soft fabric molded to her with sheer seduction, or that he would find her as appealing in burlap. Or that, even standing in the hallway so, she could arouse him to a staggering heat and hunger.

She turned, heading for the room, and he caught up with her just as she plunged into it, drawing a little cry of surprise from her. With her in his arms, held against him, he kicked the door closed, turned and found his way to the bed. They fell heavily upon it, and in moments, were tangled together.

That night he loved everything about her. It wasn't just that she was made beautifully, with the right assets, curves, flesh, breasts, skin, face, lips, or her innate ability to use all to the most erotic levels. No. Her seduction was in her laughter, the husky, silver whisper of it, and her eyes, conveying an excitement, a thrill, that elicited a masculine response of ego, that sheer, pulsing, hard, desperate, devil-may-care arousal.

Neither her gown nor his clothing actually left their bodies as they came together in a wild clash of fabric and flesh that needed no play, for that had come before, in the simple act of getting up the stairs and closing the door. In a smile, in a whisper, in the sapphire pools of her eyes. That time.

Then there was laughter as they untangled themselves from wool and cotton, kicked away sheets so that they could be drawn back up. There were the jokes about kilts, more words whispered, the sweetness of being close in the aftermath, eyes touching again, hands against one another, naked flesh against naked flesh.

It occurred to him then, almost in a corner of his mind, that he never wanted her to leave. Sex was easy to come by. She was not. Only once before had he felt . . .

Not at all ready for them, he pushed such thoughts aside. And when he made love to her again, it was slow, painstakingly slow, for himself, and yet . . . his fingers idled over her flesh, teasing long before she turned back to him, snaked herself against his body, moved down against him, caused him to erupt to fire again.

He thought that it was late, very late when they lay together and started to drift to sleep. But just when the darkness was about to overtake him, he opened his eyes. He didn't know what he had heard, but he had been attuned for years to listening. And he had heard . . . something.

He rose carefully, silently, taking up his swatch of tartan and quickly wrapping it about himself. Bare chested, he silently opened the door and started along the hallway. His feet made no sound against the stone.

He came to the top of the stairs and looked down to the hall.

Nothing.

He shrugged. One of his guests must have arisen and then gone back to bed. Until he'd had his "guests" here, he'd never even bothered to lock the great main doors. Tillingham had never really had such a thing as a crime ratio. None of the local teens would break in. If they were of that bent, they'd want to hit a store with a cash register. It was true, as well, that there were those who swore the place was haunted. Who wanted to chance the anger or vengeance of such a bloody legend as Bruce MacNiall?

He hesitated, then walked down the stairs. The doors were locked, as they had been when he and Ryan had come in after seeing to the stabling of the horses. So he walked back upstairs and slipped silently into the room, and next to Toni.

He pulled her against him. She sighed softly in her sleep. He let the silk and fragrance of her hair tease his nose, and he closed his eyes.

Toni didn't know why she awoke. She had been sound asleep, but suddenly she was wide-awake, staring. A chill gripped her. She wondered why, when she was in Bruce's arms, held tight against him.

She winced and stared toward the foot of the bed.

He was there.

That other Bruce. Come back, from a long ago time.

He stood staring at her, his features hard and tense with what looked like sorrow . . . or concern. *Fear.* For her?

She exhaled. "Not tonight!" she whispered out loud. "Please, please, not tonight!"

She closed her eyes tightly, praying that

the vision would go away. And when she opened her eyes, to her amazement, the vision was gone.

"Toni?"

The living Bruce, vital flesh and blood at her side, touched her, whispered her name. She snuggled more deeply against his chest. He absently stroked her hair.

They both slept.

15

Bruce's phone rang first thing in the morning. He reached over from the bed to find it, thinking it was in the pocket of his jeans. But he'd come in with the swatch of wool around him he'd used for the tour, and his jeans were around somewhere. Not wanting the sound to wake Toni, he stumbled up quickly, and went searching around to find them. He fell upon them, and after some swearing and mishap, found the phone and answered it.

"Bruce." It was Jonathan.

"Aye, Jon, how are you?"

"Good, good. I've some information for you."

"Oh?"

"Can you come to the office?"

"Sure." Somewhat bleary-eyed, he tried to read his watch. It wasn't quite eight. "There's nothing you just want to say over the phone, eh?"

Jonathan sighed. "I'd rather you come in. What I've to say . . . well, I don't want to be coming there, and I think y'should come in."

"All right. I'm just out of bed. Give me time to shower." He rubbed his jaw. "And shave."

"I'll have coffee ready here," Jonathan said.

He hung up and glanced over to the bed. Toni seemed to be sleeping deeply, and he was glad. He frowned slightly, worried about her.

Strange that she had known the outlay of the crypts. He kept the door locked — and always had. It was one thing for locals and tourists to wander into the castle area, but another entirely for someone to come in, trip down the spiral stairway and lie injured in the cold, damp corridor of the ancient and the dead. But there were certainly plenty of people who knew what the crypts looked like. And every man jack from the village to the surrounding miles knew that the "great" Laird MacNiall lay at the end of a corridor, immortalized in marble by decree of the good old restored Stuart king, Charles II.

He showered, shaved and dressed quickly, quietly leaving Toni sleeping. As he closed the door behind him and hurried down the stairs, he could hear activity in the kitchen, but no one was in the great hall so he hurried on out and headed for his car. As he drove down the hill, he noticed the forest to his right, and felt again an anger and a conviction that they would eventually find the remains of Annie O'Hara there. And if they did not, she was there anyway, somewhere.

The remains of Annalise had gone undiscovered for centuries.

Parking, he looked up at the statue of his famous ancestor and shook his head. "You know, old fellow, if you are somehow haunting my American lass, I wish to bloody hell you'd stop!" he said, then became irritated with his own whimsy.

He strode on over to Jonathan's office. The constable was in his office, waiting for him.

"What, do you grow a beard all over your body?" Jonathan demanded.

"You woke me," Bruce told him with a shrug. "I'm here, what is it?"

Jonathan ran his fingers through his sandy hair. "Maybe nothing. Maybe a lot. I got this in from a computer fellow with the Lothian and Borders Police. Thought you might find it quite interesting, and that you'd be best out of the castle when you received it."

Bruce frowned, scanning the report.

The "corporation" the group had

"rented" the castle from had a post office box in Edinburgh. But the computer site advertising his castle had been conceived and implemented from Glasgow.

He looked up at Jonathan. "Aye, so, it would appear the crooks are based in Glasgow."

Jonathan arched a brow. "Look into the next folder."

It was information Bruce actually had already. About Thayer Fraser's past. He tossed the folders back on the desk, grimacing. "Ah, Jonathan! The fellow has a shady background. And microchips are telling us that a person or persons committing fraud are based in Glasgow. We can't arrest a fellow for that."

"I know. But this, in itself, is damned suspicious. This fellow from Glasgow, a Scot, born and bred in the country, comes here with a group of Americans and claims he's never heard of you, that he has no idea there's a living MacNiall who owns the castle at Tillingham."

"It's a small castle."

"Ach! Bruce, you don't want anything to be wrong with the fellow, since he's the lass's kin, and that's a fact."

"True, maybe," Bruce admitted.

"Well, there's more. And I didn't actually

get the 'more' legally. The fellow has a bank account with over a hundred thousand pounds."

"It's not a crime to have money, either, Jonathan," Bruce said. "And how did you come about this information?"

Jonathan shook his head. "No way that can be traced, should we go to court against him. I spent some time calling the banks, pretending to be a credit investigator."

"I see," Bruce said.

Jonathan shook his head, looking down at his desk, then back to Bruce. "You're my friend, Bruce. I took a few risks. Make some calls yourself, if you wish. Nae, there's no way I can arrest the fellow now, as is. But the fellows into microchips will be comin' up with more, I think. So, I wanted you to know. And not when you were in the damned castle with the fellow."

Bruce didn't let a flicker of emotion into his face. He nodded gravely. "Thank you, Jonathan."

"Keep an eye on the family silver," Jonathan said. "Or throw the lot o' them out. You've the right, y'know."

"Aye." Bruce rose. "But I think not, not yet. After all, if the computer fellows can get something real on him, we won't want him to have bolted on us, eh? As long as he thinks he's covered his tracks, he'll sit tight."

Jonathan agreed. "There's something about the fellow I never liked. Takin' up with Americans who think they can tell Scottish history!"

Bruce laughed. "Actually, they didn't do a bad job."

"What the fellow did was a serious crime, Bruce."

"What we think the fellow may have done is a serious crime."

"How else does a no-good bloke playin' a piano bar get that kind of money?"

"Well, we don't hang fellows in the square on suspicion anymore, Jonathan. I appreciate you calling me, and I thank you for the information. We'll sit tight and see."

He left the constabulary and decided to pay another visit to Daniel Darrow's office.

Rowenna greeted him in reception. "We've a team here, t'day, Bruce. Seeing to the lass from the past," she told him.

"The lass from the past would be my kin, Rowenna," he said lightly.

"Oh, aye! I meant no disrespect, Bruce, truly."

"I didn't think you did, Rowenna."

"They'll be glad to see you. Daniel said something about wanting a blood sample from you."

"I assumed they'd want one. My veins are ready and waiting."

"They've machines going in there. They're doing an MRI or the like on her, trying to see what they can before cutting up what tissue they've got. Mind waiting?" Rowenna asked.

"Not at all."

As he sat, he noticed the day's paper, and the headline. Still No Clues To Missing Girl. He picked up the paper and quickly read the article. It rehashed old news, then made mention of some of the old cases being reopened. Cold-case detectives were bringing up cases from as far back as 1977, trying to ascertain similarities to current crimes. But before he could read further, Rowenna came back into the room.

"Could you go in, Bruce? There's a Dr. Holmes from Edinburgh in with Daniel. She's an anthropologist, but qualified to stick needles in your arms, as well!" Rowenna said cheerfully.

"Aye, I'm happy to bleed for you all, Rowenna," he said, and tossing the paper back down, he went in to do just that.

★ ★ ★

"Will you look at this!" David said, pouncing as soon as Toni walked into the kitchen. He had the Edinburgh paper in his hand.

She glanced at the headline, then at David and Kevin. The two had been alone in the kitchen.

"They haven't anything new," she said, staring at the two.

"Read," Kevin advised her.

She arched a brow, then read as Kevin brought her a cup of coffee. She thanked him while trying to decipher what they were so excited about.

The article was mainly about new technology being used by detectives so they could go back to old cases. In 2002, the South Wales police had at last identified the murderer of three girls who had been killed back in 1973, using a Familial/Sibling Swabbing science technology.

There were sad statistics on the number of heinous crimes never solved, and then a reference to the work by police that could be attributed to their dedication and professionalism — something that science could never go without.

The article went on to talk about Laird Bruce MacNiall and his time with the

Lothian and Borders Police. It described the victims and the horrors of their deaths, and it commended Bruce. She read on, stunned to discover that the brutal slayings had been committed by a husband and wife, and that, in that instance, an officer's insistence on following his gut instinct had led to the solving of the crimes.

She looked up at David and Kevin. They were both staring at her, waiting for a reaction.

"We knew he'd been with the police," she said.

"Did you read the whole thing?" David demanded.

"Most of it."

Kevin sighed. "You didn't read the last paragraph? At the time, he'd told his superiors that he'd 'gotten into the head' of the man! Thought like him . . . moved like him!"

She looked at both of them a bit blankly. "Okay, isn't that what FBI profilers say they have to do when they're trying to solve crimes?"

"It's scary! That's what it is," David said.

"David! The guy was a good cop!"

"So why did he leave?"

"I don't know. Maybe he didn't like being in the head of a serial killer!" she said.

"Or maybe . . ." Kevin murmured.

"Maybe what?"

"Maybe it was too much like his own," David said.

"Oh, please!" Toni said, tossing the paper down.

"He found the first body," Kevin said.

"And the second body was found in the forest, as well," David said.

"You're sick, both of you!" she accused them.

"Maybe," David murmured. He hesitated, looking at Kevin. "But . . . he's a local hero-type here, Toni. I mean, if he was up to something, everyone in this village would protect him. Maybe he doesn't even know he's a lunatic."

She stared hard at both of them, then tapped the paper angrily with drumming fingers. "It seems to me that he saved a number of young lives. And with very hard and painful work. Good Lord! He caught a *couple*. Can you imagine that, a husband and wife working together, luring innocent young victims!"

Unfortunately Ryan and Gina chose that precise moment to come walking cheerfully into the kitchen.

" 'Morning, all!" Ryan said, then stopped dead, his expression quizzical as he realized that the three were staring at them.

"What are you all doing?" Gina demanded.

"Reading the paper," Toni said.

"Seems our host captured some really serious killers at one time," Kevin said.

"A married couple."

Gina turned to the three of them, outraged. "So you're looking at us as if . . . as if being married makes us guilty of something?"

"No, don't be ridiculous," Toni said.

"That would be damned ridiculous!" Ryan said. "What? Gay people never kill other people?" he demanded.

"Sure, they do," Kevin said calmly, grimacing. "Statistically, they kill other gay people."

Toni groaned. "Don't worry, the Keystone Cops here aren't after the two of you. They're convinced now that I have to be careful around Bruce."

"I was just thinking that maybe you shouldn't be quite so close to him," David said with a sigh.

"As in sleeping with him on a nightly basis," Kevin added.

"I thought that he was the one who *caught* the killers?" Gina said.

"He was," Toni said flatly.

Gina arched a brow and looked at David and Kevin.

David threw his hands up. "Look, what do we really know about this guy?"

"Oh, let's see!" Toni said. "He's rich, owns half the village. People here are very loyal to him. He was with the police. And he's been damned decent to us, since he could have thrown us all out on our butts!"

David looked down his nose at her. "My dear, Toni! We know that you're solidly infatuated with the man. But let me ask you this. If he's so rich, why does he own a ramshackle castle?"

She sighed. "You two, it's just silly to be so worried about this guy. All right, let me fill you all in on something, having to do with the state of the castle. He was engaged once to a woman who was in love with the place. It was her dream to fix it up again, make it magnificent. She died, and he lost heart. And that's why he's ignored it. It's probably why he still spends so much time out of the area, even out of the country."

"It sounds . . . reasonable," Gina said.

"Oh, yeah, I just about hear violins," Ryan murmured.

"Hey! That borders on the entirely insensitive!" David protested.

"How do we really know anything around

here, though, especially when it comes to our host?" Gina murmured.

Kevin glanced at David and then at Toni. "You've got to admit, we really don't know much of anything. And then . . . well, you do see the guy with a sword in your nightmares."

Toni instantly stared at David. "You — you traitor! You weren't supposed to say anything about things I told you in confidence."

"I didn't! Well, of course, I talk to Kevin. Especially when I'm really worried about you!" David said, defending himself.

She groaned.

"Now I really don't know what any of you are talking about!" Gina exclaimed.

Toni groaned again, laying her head on the table.

"Somebody better tell us," Ryan said.

Toni lifted her head, not about to let David do her explaining. "I've had some nightmares, very real nightmares, about the legendary Bruce coming back and standing at the foot of my bed with a sword, okay?" She glared at David. She didn't want anything else about her past spread any further than it had already gone.

"And see, there's the thing. Thayer told us about the old woman in the cemetery the other day," Kevin said softly.

"Now Thayer has a mouth on him, too!" Toni muttered.

"Oh, yeah! That's right!" Ryan said. He looked at Gina. "Remember? He was talking about how he and Toni had just met Lizzie and Trish, and then this weird old bat comes in with her son and daughter-in-law, and rambles about the old Bruce being up from his grave, running around the country-side, finding women and strangling them as he had his wife."

"Dammit!" Toni said. "We know now that the old Bruce didn't strangle his wife, one of his enemies did it."

"We don't *know* that for a fact," David said softly.

"Right. Before he gets chopped to minced meat himself, he asks his executioners for a woolen scarf so that he can kill her first?" Toni said sarcastically.

"No, but maybe he stole his enemy's scarf."

Toni threw her hands up. "You're being ridiculous," she told them. "I can't listen to this anymore!"

"Toni!" David said. "I'm sorry, honestly! I'm just afraid for you, that's all. Maybe you don't have to . . . to sleep with him. Well, sleep with him, but don't *sleep* with him.

Not until we find out a little more about him."

She shook her head with disgust and exited the kitchen.

Bruce wound up staying far later than he had intended at Darrow's office; it was impossible not to do so. With a full team in tiny Tillingham, fascinated with the discovery of Annalise and armed with modern technology, he found himself involved. He looked at half-a-dozen scans, and was there when they painstakingly removed the ligature from around the throat of the remains. The scientists were fascinated with the quality of the weave; he couldn't help but remain pleased with the evidence suggesting that his ancestor had *not* been the one to murder his wife.

When he returned to the castle, it was afternoon. He looked in the kitchen and found David and Kevin working on costumes. They looked at him like a pair of cats that had just filled up on canaries. But when he questioned them, they both said that they were fine — a little too quickly — and went back to work, telling him that Ryan was probably out on Wallace somewhere and Gina was upstairs working with the numbers to find out just what it would take to get them out of the hole. Neither of them had seen either Thayer or Toni for hours.

He couldn't find Toni upstairs, so he headed out to the stables. Shaunessy greeted him with a whinny.

He heard someone working above him and backed away, trying to see who was in the rafters. Eban was there, studiously working hay piles.

"Ah, Laird MacNiall!"

With a smile, the funny little man dropped his rake and came down the ladder. He was agile and quick, dropping the last few feet as easily as a monkey.

"Afternoon, Eban," Bruce said.

Eban gave him a gamine's grin. "The roan is doing fine. I bin keepin' an eye on him, now, I'ave."

"Thank you, Eban."

"I bin thinking, y'see, that someone is walkin' round," Eban said gravely.

"Walking around?"

"There's them that say it's yer ancestor. Y'know, *the* MacNiall."

Bruce exhaled with patience. "Ah, Eban! The dead don't walk around."

"And they don't go making a healthy roan sick, either, so they'd say!" Eban muttered, shaking his head. "There's someone walkin', and that's a fact."

He set a hand on the man's shoulders. "Myth, Eban. Legend. Good stories for a dark night. If *the* MacNiall were about, don't you think he'd be pleased to see his castle so well tended?"

"As y'should ha' tended it all these years."

"Aye, Eban. True."

"She sees him, too, y'know. 'Tisn't just me, Laird MacNiall."

"She?" he asked.

Eban nodded gravely. "The lass, the American lass. A fellow such as me, I see it, I do. I see it in her eyes. She be one of the 'touched.' "

"Eban, you know I don't believe all that."

Eban grinned. "Believe or nae, what is, is. Anyway, I just wanted y'to know, the roan will be well. I'm watchin' now, I am."

"Thank you, Eban. You do good work."

"Ach, Laird MacNiall! Like the days of old. Y'give me a home. A place. Others might not ha' been so kind. And I know it." With his strange little smile in place, he started back for the ladder. " 'Tis like the days of old. Whether the eyes see or not, what is, is," he said, shaking his head as he went back up to the rafters.

A noise at the door alerted Bruce to the

fact that someone was coming into the stables. He turned quickly. Thayer.

He felt his mouth tighten and his muscles tense. He might have refused to let Jonathan see any of his concerns regarding the man, but he felt them, just as he had from the beginning. He didn't think it was ego to wonder how the man could have lived in Glasgow and never heard his name — or known that he existed. And if he had been living with his head in a pint, he should still have known something once he heard the name of the property his group was renting.

"Bruce, you're back," Thayer said.

"Aye."

Thayer looked uncomfortable. He hadn't expected to come here and find his host.

"Well, I was just going to look in on the roan," Thayer said.

"He isn't here. Ryan must have taken him out. But actually, I'm glad you've come. I've gotten some news. I thought I should share it with you first." He meant to take grave care with just what words and what information he "shared."

"Oh, aye?" Thayer said carefully, hovering in the doorway, as if he could make a quick escape.

"They've traced the origins of the Web

441

site that advertised this castle," Bruce said.

"Aye?"

The man looked as tense as a drawn bow.

"Glasgow."

"Glasgow?"

Bruce nodded, watching the man.

Thayer shrugged. "Well, then. That would explain a bit of it."

"What do you mean?"

"Well, there were advertisements about, as well. Flyers in a few local pubs, you know, like broadsides on walls, at bus stops, I think."

"Ah," Bruce said.

"I'm glad. I hope like bloody hell they catch the bloke," Thayer said, staring straight at Bruce.

Actors. It was a crowd of actors, Bruce told himself.

Thayer frowned suddenly. "Ryan isn't out with the horse," he said. "At least, I don't think, anyway. I saw him upstairs in his room, talking with his wife, not twenty minutes past."

"The horse is gone," Bruce said, frowning, as well. Then he realized that Toni had the horse out, and an unreasoning sense of panic set into him.

Thayer, too, seemed alarmed for reasons of his own. "Toni!" he said.

"I'll find her," Bruce told him, already turning to lead Shaunessy from his stall.

With landscape and terrain this beautiful, Toni wasn't sure why she hadn't been out riding before now.

One benefit to growing up in rural Maryland had been the little pinto her father had bought her. But as an adult working in the city, she'd had to leave Barto, now twenty-two, with her old neighbors. It was good for Barto, though. He was hardly ever saddled, was loved like an old dog, and given the best of everything.

She seldom saw him, and with the move to Scotland, she had given up the idea of ownership altogether, and given him to the Andersons' granddaughter. He was a gentle soul by then, just right for a child, as she had been.

Wallace was definitely a fine fellow, heavy enough for Ryan with his armor and weapons, and still sleek enough for a good ride. Whatever had ailed him, his recovery had been all but miraculous. He wasn't just glad to be out; he was feeling his oats.

Her mood had been angry and wild, so she hadn't bothered with a saddle. She'd just slipped the bit into his mouth, the bridle over his head, and chosen a path down the hill. There was plenty of country-side. Beautiful spaces. They passed slope after slope, scattering a few sheep as they raced along, but the longhaired cows they passed didn't seem to mind.

She wasn't sure how far she'd gone when she noticed that a white car marked Tillingham Constabulary was parked by a fence. Curious, she rode in that direction, and saw Jonathan out in the field. He appeared to be inspecting one of the sheep.

Nudging Wallace, she rode down the little slope that led to the valley where the car was parked. Jonathan heard the horse, looked up, released the sheep and dusted his hands on his uniform pants as he walked toward the fence, calling out a cheerful greeting. "Aye, now lass, good t'see you. That is the way to really enjoy this countryside," he told her.

"Hello! And, yes, it's really beautiful. How are you?" she asked him.

"Well and fine enough, Miss Fraser. So . . . all is working well for you? Your friends were in, you know. And though I've not the resources of the big department, we are working hard for you, through the folks that know their business. I just told Bruce this morning, they've traced the site on the Web page to Glasgow."

"Really? I haven't seen Bruce today," she told him. "Glasgow," she repeated. "I'm delighted, naturally, and grateful that they've traced it so far already, but I suppose they'll need to learn much more to actually catch someone."

"Aye, Glasgow," he said. She thought that he was looking at her strangely, as if that should mean something.

"It's a very big city," she murmured.

"Aye, that it is." He was still staring at her strangely.

"I'm sorry, should that fact mean something to me?" she asked him.

"Your cousin is from Glasgow," he reminded her.

She instantly felt defensive bristles grow up around her. "It's a very big city," she reminded him.

What was it today? Was there something in the water? People attacking everyone who meant something to her?

"You're right," he acknowledged. "A very big city. I just thought that you wanted the truth. No matter what the truth may be."

"We do want the truth. Sorry, I didn't mean to bark. But I don't think the fact that something originated in Glasgow is any aspersion on Thayer at all. That would be like me being guilty of something because it happened near Washington, D.C."

"D.C. is much bigger than Glasgow," he said with a rueful grin.

"Still the point," she said.

"And well taken," he told her gravely.

"Well, I do thank you. Very much."

"You're quite welcome, but it is my job to uphold the law, even if it falls into unfamiliar realms. We've good police here in the old country, y'know. I feel somewhat guilty, I do. I should have known, before your group put the work into the place, that he'd have never rented out the place. But then, he hadna' been about himself for some time, so . . . it would be his right to do it, had he chosen."

"Please, there's nothing for you to feel guilty about. And actually, he's been quite wonderful."

Jonathan glanced down. "Oh, aye, the fellow is . . . magnanimous, isn't he?" he queried, looking back up at her.

She nodded, not wanting to go any further in that vein. "Are these your sheep?"

"Aye, that they are."

"You've beautiful land."

"Well, quite frankly, it's not my land. But I pasture here. Heard there's been some trouble with that roan there, but he looks fine to me. I thought I'd be wise to take a look at these fellows and lasses, assure myself nothing was getting into the herds."

"He's fine. The vet said he must have gotten into something, but he's come through just great. Like a little boy with a bellyache who'd eaten too much candy, I guess," Toni said.

"Well, you're right, must have been something . . . Anyway, the sheep look fine and healthy, too, lass. I guess I'd best be getting back into town."

"It was nice to see you!" Toni told him.

"Enjoy your ride!" He waved and started toward his car. Toni headed Wallace back up a slope. He seemed to want to run again.

She let him do so, mulling over her encounter with the constable. On the one hand, it seemed that he did want to do what he could for them. But on the other hand . . . he seemed more concerned with how their business affected him. The foreigners have a sick horse, so he checks *his* sheep?

Then, of course, there was that ridiculous conversation she'd had with the others back at the castle, and . . . there was the ghost. A ghost that should be happy now! A ghost who kept appearing at the foot of her bed.

She leaned low against Wallace, and let the wind rip by her. She wanted *not* to think for a while.

She didn't know how long she traveled the hills and valleys before she realized that, even if Wallace was feeling frisky, she might well be pushing him too hard. After all, they'd had to send for a vet to see him twice in the past week. Patting his neck, she slowed him down, leaped off for a moment and came around to take a good look at his eyes.

He stared back at her and snorted, sending a sneeze and some mouth foam flying over her. "Wallace!" she chastised him. "Ugh! How could you do that to me? There are times when you *should* do it to Ryan, but I'm your friend. I think I am, anyway. You need a drink. Well, we should walk a bit and then get you a drink."

She looked around, trying to ascertain where she was, then wondering how on earth she could have turned herself around so badly. Although she could still see sheep, there was no sign of a house, a cottage or even a road.

Listening, though, she could hear the bubble of a brook. It was to the right, through a field of trees — and the path — a great canopy of trees arced over pine needles — looked inviting. "We'll wander in and find the water, eh, boy?" she asked, rubbing his nose.

As he tended to do — with true love and affection, she was certain — he nosed her in the chest, gently prodding her, as if he understood her words.

Plenty of light dappled through the trees. The shadows and patterns that fell around the trees and bushes were quite beautiful. The trails seemed broad and well used, yet when she followed the sound of the water and came to it at last, she felt like a fool.

"You know what? We're back in *the* forest."

It was all right. She definitely hadn't come that far, walking the horse. All she had to do was retrace her steps. She wasn't frightened, and she wasn't even worried. When Wallace had drunk his fill, she'd start back. But just when the horse lifted his head, the rain came.

"Son of a bitch!" she swore out loud, drawing a snort from Wallace.

It wasn't the rain. She didn't care much about getting wet. But the air was cold, and she hadn't set out with any kind of jacket, waterproof or otherwise.

"You know, it rains a lot here!" she told the horse, angry with herself for not being better prepared. But she'd left the house angry and disturbed, and decided on taking a ride on the spur of the moment.

In seconds, she was soaked. And what had been light and beautiful was now gray and . . . murky.

She determined to go back the way she had come. It should have been easy, but it wasn't. In a matter of minutes, she was entangled in the trees.

She looked at Wallace. Surely, it was close to feeding time. If she just gave the horse his head, he'd take her home.

"It's up to you, buddy," she said.

By the time she had leaped up on his back, making three attempts — because of the slickness, she told herself, not a lack of coordination — the rain had slackened. But the gray and the murk remained, and there was a low ground fog, as well. The whole atmosphere was . . . creepy.

"No!" she said aloud. Because now, she was feeling the eyes again, the eyes of the forest, watching her.

"Home, Wallace!" she said out loud, hoping the words would dispel the sense of eeriness that had crept around her. She *was* being ridiculous. These were *trees*, for God's sake! Trees, bushes, natural bark, leaves, the sound of rushing water. . . .

Given free rein, Wallace simply stood dead still.

"Traitor!" she told him.

He whinnied and shifted weight from hoof to hoof.

"What kind of a horse are you? You're supposed to know the way back to the barn!"

The eyes . . . she could feel them.

"All right, forget it," she said, and gathered up the reins. She didn't know how far it would be, but since there was only one forest, she could hope there was only one stream. She'd follow it out.

The water was very shallow. She led the horse straight through it, then along the embankment when it deepened. She tried whistling, but she couldn't keep her lips wet enough. And as she rode, she fought a sense of sheer panic that could do her no good. But images kept floating before her mind. A picture of a man, a warrior, a Cavalier, in armor, kilted, dirty, worn, tired. . . . A sword that dripped blood in his hand. The same man, standing before the hearth, watching the flames, then beckoning her down into the crypts.

Yesterday. The voice on the phone. The word *medium*.

She gritted her teeth. She was not some kind of a vessel for horrid messages about things that she could not change or see through! Unlike the girl on the phone, she had no desire to see lots of ghosts!

She bit into her lower lip. The rain had stopped completely, but the mist continued to rise from the forest floor. She was soaked to the bone, completely chilled. And she continued to feel watched. *Stalked.*

Each time she hesitated and looked around, she saw nothing. The forest was big. Hadn't she heard many people say that? She glanced at her watch, again, seeking a sense of normalcy in the action. Yes, the forest must be very big. She'd been following the stream, she estimated, for nearly two hours, and suddenly realized that she wasn't just stiff, she was in agony.

She turned, setting a hand on the horse's rump, trying to see anything that she could behind her. Any movement. But all she saw was the fall of shadows.

"Hurry it up a bit, shall we?" she murmured.

They trotted forward, and when she looked back, the feeling that a darkness followed her, reaching out, started to recede.

Finally she could take it no more. She had to stretch, change her position. It might have been a nice day to choose to take a saddle, she reflected, but it was too late for that, far too late.

"Whoa, boy," she told Wallace, reining in

lightly. She looked behind her uneasily, thinking that if she saw anything, anything at all, she could turn, slam her knees against Wallace and race away. But there was nothing, just the coming darkness.

She needed a quick moment's rest, then she needed to move again. So she slid from Wallace's back, wincing slightly. She walked a few steps, stretching. "I guess it is a big forest, if troops, outlawed by the powers that be, used to hide in here," she murmured. She led Wallace over to a large oak set up on a little hillock of grass, just above the stream, and sat down, leaning against the tree, ruing her stupidity.

"Wallace," she said, "you really aren't much help."

Still, she was very glad of the horse. He seemed to be her link to reality, to normalcy.

Tired, she closed her eyes for a minute. When she opened them, Wallace suddenly lifted his head, his ears pricking as he stared off toward her left. The horse was still, yet it appeared that his flanks were trembling. He snorted. She stared at him curiously, the animal's fear snaking into her, and realized, too late, that he was about to bolt.

With another snort, he did so, leaping forward like a show jumper. The reins, held too loosely in her one hand, snapped free from her hold in seconds.

She leaped to her feet. "Wallace!" she cried angrily. Then she fell silent, aware that the animal had run because something had frightened him. She stood very still, feeling the odd awareness, the *fear,* which the animal had passed onto her.

She listened. She could still hear the echo of the horse's hoofbeats. And then . . . the cry of a bird. And then . . . a rustling.

From somewhere far away, the faint wail of a bagpipe sounded, but not loud enough to dampen the sound of twigs snapping. Someone was near.

She moved against the oak. Then . . . she could see a figure, a man with a dark tam, his head down. He wore an old suede jacket.

She stayed still, not daring to breathe. But a sound of surprise came to her throat as the man stopped, dusted dirt from his hands onto his pants and looked around. She saw his face clearly. It was Eban.

Call out! He'll get you home, she told herself. But something warned her to remain still. *What had he been doing in the forest? Burying the remains of some poor girl? Was that why his hands were dirtied?*

No, stop! She told herself. She was being cruel, judging when she shouldn't judge.

But no sound would come to her lips. She remained quiet. Only when he was gone — gone, way past her — did she start walking again, following the stream. After a minute, she quickened her pace. If she'd seen Eban, she had to be close to the castle.

"Toni!" she heard her name called. There was thrashing ahead of her. Someone was in the forest, looking for her.

"To-ni!"

"Here!" she called out.

"Toni!"

That time, the sound of her name seemed to come from behind her. The voices, she realized, looking around, could have been coming from anywhere, she was so disorganized. She started to run, directly in the stream, which was shallow enough here. Water kicked up around her. It didn't matter in the least.

"Here!" she cried again, then paused suddenly, startled. The light was bad, very bad. The silver mist still lay close to the ground. But ahead of her, maybe thirty, forty feet, there seemed to be something in the water. She blinked, looking that way.

There was a thrashing sound ahead of her.

No, behind her . . .

She started to turn.

She saw the branch . . .

Saw it, tried to turn from it . . .

And went down, her skull filling with pain.

Her vision filling with the mist . . .

And then darkness.

And something else.

Interlude

Grayson Davis's man had Annalise by the hair, dragging her into the copse. She did not come easily.

Bruce's heart cried out as she was thrown down upon the ground, a cry wrung from her lips as she went to her knees where she was cast, sliding until she came to a stop before Davis. *Ah, and there she is, yer lady, Laird MacNiall. Filled with foolish pride, as ye would be. Ach! Y'd thought y'd bought her time, out of the forest, eh? Nae, foolish fellow. So now it is time fer heroes and legends to die, and fer rich men to die poor.*

Her eyes met his. He pleaded with her silently, begged his forgiveness. *Do whatever he asks. Live. The day will come when you will be set free. . . .*

She smiled at him and shook her head slowly.

"Annalise!" Her name was a cry of anguish.

Grayson Davis swaggered before him, gripped Annalise by the elbows and pulled her up to face him. "Ah, Annalise. We have come to a moment of truth. Will it be the laird there, half-dead as we speak, with none but torture ahead, or . . . they can take you from the forest before it begins. You can await me."

"Obey him!" Bruce pleaded. "Before God, obey him!"

She looked at Davis, as if weighing his words. She had never appeared more beautiful, proud or elegant, despite the mud caking her clothing, the scratches upon her cheeks, the wildness of her hair.

She seemed to deliberate long and carefully, then she looked back at Bruce and smiled again, a slow, sweet, wistful smile.

"Time, my love. Time will tell the tale," she said. Then she spit in Grayson Davis's face.

He struck her. Bruce roared with rage, but to no avail. The force of the blow sent Annalise down again, but her head remained high.

"Bitch!"

She smiled, eyes even, leveled upon him.

"Y're judged! He is judged. Condemned."

She shook her head. "Ah, Grayson, what a fool. There is a far greater judge. And my laird husband and I can truly be judged in His eyes alone."

"Not on this earth. Not on this earth! You

had your chance!"

"And chose not to take it."

"Annalise!" Bruce cried again.

But her eyes, her steady gaze, had been the last straw against Davis's temper. He wrenched the colors from around his shoulders and drew them around Annalise's neck. Her fair neck. Slender, graceful, delicate . . .

"Nae!" The great MacNiall, humbled, hung back his head, bitterly fighting the arms that held him, nearly fighting off the men. He watched as she gasped, choked, shuddered, jerked . . . death brutal despite pride. He struggled free from the arms that held him. He raced forward, then staggered in the mud, almost reaching her.

An ax had landed in his back.

But he did not die. Not quickly enough. He saw as Grayson Davis picked up his wife, limp as a cloth doll, and cast her facedown into the stream. He cried out in anguish and in rage, saw the blood before his own eyes . . .

"Fool! Who put that ax into him? He mustn't die, not yet!" Davis commanded. He walked to where Bruce had fallen at last, arms outstretched in the mud. He rolled him, forcing the blade more deeply into him, relishing his enemy's anguish.

"First, castration. I want you to live for that! Then yer innards, great laird! Set to blaze before yer eyes. Eventually . . . yer head. And if y're living then, I'll see that the blade is dull and moves slow."

He stared at Davis, shaking his head. "It matters not what y'do to kill me. I am already dead. And yet, I will live Davis, fer y're cursed now, and I will live to see you fall!"

"Cut him!" Davis roared.

Mercifully, the ax had done its damage.

The great MacNiall stared into the trees as the blood blurred his vision. But in his mind, his heart, he was with her already.

16

Bruce was deep into the forest when he heard a heavy thrashing.

"Toni?" he called.

From a deep thicket, the noise continued, as if someone was hurrying toward him. He reined in on Shaunessy and waited, watching the area of lush growth. The green waved and jiggled. And the roan, Wallace, appeared. Riderless.

He quickly dismounted from Shaunessy, hurrying over to the roan. There was a scratch on his nose, but that had most probably come from a brush with a branch. The horse seemed all right, just spooked.

"Did you throw her, boy? Did you throw Toni?"

He shook his head, looking in the direction which the horse had come. Toni could be out there, unconscious, bleeding. He gauged the direction; she'd been trying to follow the stream.

"Go on home, boy. Go on home," he said, giving the horse a sound smack on the rump.

Quickly remounting Shaunessy, he drove through the thicket at the spot where

Wallace had just appeared. An overgrown, slender trail brought him back to the embankment.

"Toni!"

He felt his sense of panic rising. Nudging his horse's flanks, he quickened his pace, mindful of the rocks, stones and slippery embankment.

Ahead, he could see that the mist was still high over the bubbling water. He reined in, eyes narrowing. There seemed to have been a shadow moving through the mist. A shadow . . . in human form. Then he heard the sound of a grunt.

"Toni!"

Dismounting from Shaunessy, he hurried on foot through the mist and water.

"Toni!"

He heard a soft groan. Then . . .

"Toni? Bruce?"

Disappointment, dismay, washed over him. Thayer. Thayer was ahead of him. Still, he kept going. "Aye, I'm here. Toni!"

The mist still lay before him. And the water.

He suddenly saw her, saw her . . . as he had seen the body of the dead girl. Facedown in the water. Long trails of blond hair no longer lustrous, but caked in mud and grass and tangled with twigs.

No! That was only in his mind's eye, a remnant of a dream.

"Toni!" His voice ricocheted through the woods, vibrant, loud.

"Bruce?"

Her voice was barely discernible in the rush of water and whisper of breeze.

"Where are you?" he cried.

"Toni!" From somewhere, he could hear Thayer's voice, as well.

And then he saw her. She was seated on a fallen log, drawing back sodden tendrils of her hair.

She wasn't facedown in the water. She was seated, alive and well. A bit bedraggled, nothing more.

He let out his breath in a rush of relief. His knees were weak, and his voice came out like crackling thunder. "Toni!"

Then, just seconds after he had seen Toni, Thayer came crashing through the brush from the opposite direction. Seeing Toni, and then Bruce, he, too, went still.

"Toni!" he breathed.

She rose, distracted, offering Bruce a weak smile and then a quick defense. "Bruce!" She turned. "And Thayer. Thank God. And wait, please, no one yell! I probably should have spent some time riding with someone else before taking old Wallace out on my own. I didn't come into the forest on purpose. I wound up riding some fields on the other side and didn't know where I was. Then it started to rain, as you can see," she put in wryly. "Actually, I think I would have made it out eventually, except that Wallace decided to desert me, and I walked smack into a major branch over there, and . . ." She was looking from one of them to the other. "Hey! Bless you both, thanks for coming!" She gave Thayer a quick hug first, then turned to Bruce, a question in her eyes.

He reached for her. She came into his arms. He felt the air wrap around them, and felt the chill in her body.

"Let's just go back now, eh?" he said. Then he drew away, looking at her. She was somehow reserved, despite the look she had given him and the way she had melded to him.

"You're really fine?" Bruce said.

"Nothing happened?" Thayer asked.

She looked at them both and shook her head solemnly.

"The horse didn't throw you?" Bruce demanded.

"Wallace? No, Wallace is a love. I was off of him, stretching." She winced. "I haven't been riding in a while, I guess. Didn't bother with a saddle, so . . . did you see him? Is he all right?"

"He's on his way back to the stables now, I'm pretty certain," Bruce said.

"Well, that's what I assumed he'd do in the first place!" Toni said. She pressed her fingers against her temple. "I think I need some aspirin."

"Let's get back," Bruce said anxiously. "Come here, I'll lift you up on Shaunessy."

"No, no, that's all right," she said, flashing a smile toward Thayer. "We'll all walk out together."

"Toni, I can get out on m'own," Thayer assured her. "But you're soaked!"

"As I have been for hours," she said lightly, then added firmly, "We'll walk out, all together."

For a moment, she thought that Bruce toyed with the idea of arguing with her, even taking a medieval stance and simply throwing her over Shaunessy's haunches.

It wasn't a matter of the total political incorrectness of such a gesture that stopped him; it was Thayer. He was hesitant about leaving the man behind, when, despite her words, there was something strange about Toni, about the way she had been sitting on the rock, and the way she had touched her forehead.

"Fine. We all walk out together," he said. "I'll just lead Shaunessy."

As they started back, he pulled off his jacket and set it around her shoulders. She flashed him a smile of gratitude.

"Darkness is coming quickly," she murmured.

"And the buses soon, too soon," Thayer murmured. He looked at her. "You should rest. Gina can take on being you tonight. You could wind up with your death of a cold."

"I feel fine," she assured him.

"He may be right," Bruce said.

"When I'm not fine, Gina can run around like a madwoman. Right now, I'm fine." She glanced at him, her smile sweetly suggestive, her tone specifically for him. "Absolutely nothing that a hot bubble bath can't take care of."

"Ach, do I have to hear this?" Thayer demanded.

Toni laughed. "And I thought I was being so subtle." She stumbled slightly; the terrain wasn't level as they followed the brook. The rain had left exposed roots, and flooded some of the embankment.

"Man, this is quite a place!" Thayer murmured. "The friggin' forest primeval!"

"Aye, that's why people should stay out of

it," Bruce said. He glanced at Thayer. "I'm amazed that you stumbled upon Toni as I did . . . and as quickly," he added, watching the man's reaction.

"So am I. I thought I was lost myself," Thayer said. He pushed a tree branch out of the way for the others to precede him.

"Look how quickly it gets dark in here!" Toni marveled. "Seriously, thank you both so very much for looking for me. I think I would have made it eventually, but I'm awfully darned glad not to be here alone, now."

"Aw, shucks!" Thayer teased.

Minutes later, they'd broken through, reached the bottom of the hill and were on their way up. The others were waiting anxiously by the stables. Ryan had Wallace by the reins.

"Toni!" Gina came rushing down the hill, hugging Toni, then drawing away. "Ugh! You're soaked."

"Toni!" Ryan was right behind Gina, hugging Toni, as well, then demanding to know, "What did you do to Wallace?"

"What did I do to Wallace?" Toni demanded. "He deserted me!"

Ryan looked from her to the horse. "Wallace! Shame on you." He looked back, glancing anxiously at Bruce. "Really, what the hell were you doing?"

"Getting lost, nothing more. And I'm fine," Toni told them.

David and Kevin were both there now, looking at Toni worriedly.

"I'll make tea," Kevin said.

"With a shot of something," David said.

"We have about an hour before the buses show," Gina said, sounding very much like the business manager. "So we need to hop to it." She glanced at Bruce and swallowed a little uneasily. "Um . . . Bruce, are you still willing to play this with us?"

"Who else could better do the old great MacNiall?" he asked her, allowing his own accent a practiced strength.

"I'm going up," Toni said, and she flashed him another quick glance that was almost a question. Was he going to follow?

Oh, aye, beyond a doubt!

As if on cue, Eban came striding out from the barn. "Eh, Bruce, shall I be taking Shaunessy, setting him up for his grand entrance?"

"Aye, Eban, thank you."

"Well, Wallace, I'll be cleaning you up a bit!" Ryan said.

Bruce left them and walked toward the entrance, aware that they watched him in silence as he departed.

★ ★ ★

Toni sat in the tub, simply glad of the steaming water that soaked into her, pure bliss after the hours of cold. But her mind was racing. I'm on overload! she told herself.

So much had happened, yet no matter how hard she tried to recall those moments in the forest, she couldn't. Something had struck her. When she'd risen after falling, she'd thought she hit a tree branch.

But had she? Because it had happened right after she had seen . . . something. Something ahead of her in the water, gone when she had found her seat on the rock, gone when they had walked back following the stream.

Then there was the time — seconds, minutes, longer? — she had been out. Knocked out or just . . . out. Seeing a picture of the past, coming alive in the forest. She'd seen . . . Annalise, on her knees. Bruce, shouting, raging, straining, anguish written into his features.

And in the vision, she had been screaming herself, just as she had when she'd been a child. She'd been so desperate *not* to see more, praying, please, God, don't let me see the execution. . . .

There she was, half in the water, half out,

her temple killing her and the rock before her. And as she found her footing and then sat, she heard Bruce and Thayer again, calling to her. The forest had been as it was, trees, pine carpet, bubbling, beautiful brook.

"I'm losing my mind!" she whispered aloud to herself. But she wasn't. And she remembered the woman's voice over the phone. *Medium. She was an incredible medium.*

No!

But she knew that denying something couldn't make it change. Maybe she had put it all past her for years and years, so far behind her that she'd never expected to know that kind of sensation again, that kind of fear. And yet, if she just accepted some of it, would the fear recede?

I talk to lots of ghosts, the woman had told her.

There was a tap; the bathroom door opened. Bruce came in, hair damp and raven dark, features taut and concerned, chin hard-squared, eyes slate and sharp. For a moment, she saw the distant MacNiall, saw him as she had in the very strange interlude amidst a field of trees. The ferocity, the rage . . . and the undying devotion he'd given his Annalise.

She bit into her lower lip, watching him, and the warmth of the water was nothing compared to the searing tempest she felt when he was near. She started to rise from the water very slowly, stepping from the top, coming to him.

"Lass, you've been soaked. A bad day . . ."

"Then make it better," she whispered.

He cocked his head slightly. "There's not much time."

"Then we'd best use it well."

He wrapped his arms around her. For a moment, he held her tight, her frame taut to his. She felt the changes. And yet . . . it was as if he waited, waited to know what she really needed.

And then . . . he gave it to her. All that she wanted. A total abandonment of thought and worry, fears and visions. Reality, flesh, the senses . . . the feel of his hands and lips, body heat emanated, damp and slick, pure physicality, grinding, meshing. She had the longing again to crawl into his skin; they couldn't be close enough. And then those seconds of total constriction, the soaring, the touch of Elysian fields.

The man at her side was real, flesh and blood.

He stroked her hair for a moment, pulled her closer.

"The chill is gone?"

"I could never feel the slightest chill with you," she told him.

"It's not my show, you know," he reminded her gently, "but your buses are coming."

"I know," she said, but didn't stir. She waited a moment, thinking there was a tension about him, that he was about to say something. But he didn't.

So she did.

"I saw . . . what happened, in the past. Today, in the forest."

"What?" She felt his withdrawal, just slight and not physical.

She rose on an elbow, looking into his eyes. "I really didn't mean to be in the forest. I was furious with myself for being lost, but I was doing all right, except that that traitorous horse spooked at something and took off on me. Still, I was all right. I think I heard your voice first, maybe Thayer's, too. I turned to find you . . . and smacked into a branch. I saw stars, mist, darkness. Then — I know how this sounds — but it was as if I was back in time. Bruce, it was vividly real. There were these men, so many of them, and they had your ancestor.

They dragged in Annalise, and the fellow strangled her there, in front of him. He broke free, but someone threw an ax, and he fell. They were about to do other things, but then I heard your voice."

He was staring at her as if she were stark raving mad. *Well, what the hell had she expected?*

"So you did bump your head!"

She sighed. "Bruce —"

"A conk on your head, and you . . . dreamed."

"No! That wasn't it."

"I knew you'd hurt yourself, the way you kept feeling your forehead," he murmured, thumb on her cheek then, shifting her head, looking for damage.

"Bruce —"

"My ancestor is not a ghost, a presence, ranging the forest, looking for victims!" he told her.

"I never said that —"

"Toni, you're dreaming, and that's all."

She turned away from him, rising, heading back to her own room.

He followed her. "Toni! Don't be angry with me. I'm trying to help you," he said, following quickly behind her.

She had the bathroom door halfway shut, but he stopped it from closing.

"Excuse me," she said coolly, "did you want the bathroom first?"

"I want you to listen to me!" he said. "Toni, suppose there was . . . a ghost. We all know that history was tragic. Okay, he led you to a tomb. He wants Annalise in it. So, we'll get her in it. I was at the autopsy today and I made it very clear that once my blood proves her my ancestress, I want her back. She'll lie in the tomb next to the great MacNiall. So why would this ghost still be haunting you?"

"He wasn't haunting me. He was showing me what happened."

"Why?"

"So that we know."

"Once they found the scarf, the truth was fairly evident."

"Maybe he just wanted the full story known. Bruce! It tore my heart out, really. When he was threatened, it didn't matter. He said that he was already dead, because his Annalise was gone. And he said something about vengeance, even though he was half-dead already."

"Dead men don't find vengeance, Toni."

"Damn you, I was glad that I saw it! I wasn't afraid in the forest then."

"You should be afraid in the damned forest. Someone — who isn't a ghost! — is killing women and discarding them there," he said. "Toni, your imagination is very vivid —"

"Do you know what?" she interrupted. "You're right. It's late. It's always your own business if you care to join us or not, but I owe a lot to this group. It is time I got ready."

"Toni —"

"If you're going to mock what I'm saying, or tell me that my imagination is too vivid, or that I'm losing a grip on sanity, you can just let it wait. Now, we do need to be ready. I repeat, did you want the bathroom first? It is your castle and your bathroom."

He didn't reply, but he closed the door sharply on her.

Toni winced at the anger she felt from him. Gritting her teeth, she turned the water on high and stepped into the shower, letting it cascade quickly over her. *Never! She was never sharing any of this with anyone, ever, ever again!*

Once again, his castle was full. Standing outside with Shaunessy, decked out for their grand entrance, Bruce looked at the tour buses with amazement. He'd have never believed that people would flock out like this — and pay the price charged — for a living history tour. But they did.

It still made him uneasy. But then, it had been a long time since he hadn't been uneasy, with regard to the castle — and the forest.

Shaunessy pawed the ground, as if he, too, was anxious to be at it, and over it.

"Hey!" Ryan came from the stables, leading Wallace. "I'm sure we've told you, but it really is damned decent of you to let us do this — and to pitch in." He cleared his throat. "We should probably do a legal contract with you, though. I mean, you didn't get the money, so we do owe you, but we can't pay you unless we're making it. Which we are. Gina has been meaning to talk to you. She just hasn't had the chance." He smiled awkwardly.

Bruce understood. Aye, he was helping them. But then, it was his property, wasn't it? And he could change his mind at any time.

"I'm sure we can work something out," he told Ryan.

Ryan let out a sigh. "I was so afraid I'd offend you," he murmured.

"I'm not offended."

"Good, thanks." Ryan inhaled deeply again. "I'm just thanking God old Wallace here has come through okay. If we'd lost our money on the castle, and then on the horse, too . . . well, it would almost seem as if someone was out there to get us!"

"Aye, it would, wouldn't it?" Bruce murmured.

A white flag was suddenly waved out the doorway.

"My cue," Bruce murmured.

"Go for it, man," Ryan said.

And he did.

There was always a fine line between acting and truth, he thought, as he played out the role, mounting the steps in a fury. Her words were right, her plea, brilliant. A pin could have been heard dropping from below. But her eyes . . . Aye, she was pleading all right. And she was still furious. He suddenly felt a great weight around his shoulders. He was sick to death of the myth and legend surrounding his ancestor, because it would start up all the rot about Bruce MacNiall roaming the forest. And since he and his ancestor were supposedly spitting images of one another, there would be those who stared at him, superstitious, thinking that the sins of the past were coming alive through him.

Except that she hadn't been unfaithful. And the great MacNiall hadn't killed her.

Staring down into Toni's eyes, re-creating history, he wondered if it had been like this. Had Annalise looked up at her husband all those years ago with eyes this blue. . . . Challenging and angry?

Ryan made his entrance then and they went into their mock battle. Soon, the tour group was moving on into the kitchen. Ryan, deeply pleased, clamped a hand with Bruce's. "Damned, but we're good. And we still haven't had a chance to choreograph anything. Toni," he said, looking up the stairs, "weren't we phenomenal?"

"Absolutely," she said, but she was hurrying toward the kitchen. "Big group. I'm going to give the boys a hand."

"She pissed at you or something?" Ryan asked Bruce.

He shrugged. "You can tell?"

Ryan grinned. "I know Toni. Actually, I thought you were going to be angry with her. For being in the forest again, I mean." He was studying Bruce's face intently.

"The remains of two murdered women have been found in those woods," Bruce said.

"Three, if you include your ancestress. She was murdered, too. Why, I'll bet you the place is full of bodies, considering the history here! Oh, man, sorry. I mean, I hope it doesn't have any more bodies."

"Thanks, Ryan. I hope it doesn't, either," he said. "I'm going to take old Shaunessy out and put him up for the night. Then I'm to bed. You can tell the others good-night for me, all right?"

"Yeah, sure. And thanks."

He departed, anxious to have his horse bedded down and himself upstairs before the tour group began filing out. He wasn't much in the mood to be pleasant to strangers.

In his room, he started a fire, stripped down and stretched out in his bed, lacing his fingers behind his head as he watched the logs catch.

Should he relent? Just say, I've had a few moments like that myself. It's all right. Hell, no! He'd never seen his ancestor prowling the place.

She was getting too carried away. It was dangerous. There were bad things happening, really bad things. Ryan's words came back to him — *It was almost as if someone wanted them all to go down* — and then his conversation with Jonathan Tavish that day.

Glasgow. It had all originated out of Glasgow. And Thayer was from Glasgow. Thayer had been in the forest. Helping him find Toni? Or trying to make sure that he didn't find someone — or something — else?

Toni had noted the couple in their tour group right away, simply because they were so attractive. She looked like she belonged on the cover of a magazine, and he was the tall, rugged-looking sort who could have walked through a Western and been instantly perceived as the real thing. And though they walked the tour with the others, there was something about them that struck Toni.

So she wasn't at all surprised when the woman followed behind and stopped her, catching up with Toni at the bottom of the stairs as she tried to make her escape.

"Toni!"

"I'm sorry, but if you'll excuse me, the others will help you. I had a — er — fall today, and I've got a terrific headache," Toni said, eager to keep going.

"I'm Darcy," the woman said.

"Darcy?" Even as she repeated the name, Toni knew who the woman was. Dismay filled her.

"Darcy Stone, we talked on the phone —"

"I know who you are!" Toni said, shaking her head. "But I told you not to come here!" Despite herself, she looked around. All she needed now was to have Bruce think that she was going to fill his castle with ghost hunters!

"I know. And please don't worry — we've not let anyone know who we are."

"We!" Toni gasped.

"Just me and my husband."

"Look, I'm certain you went through tremendous trouble and expense to get here, but I can't . . . you can't be here!"

"We've taken a little rental cottage in the village. Adam tried to reach you himself, but he wasn't able to get through. He's eager to talk to you. He's also afraid that things may be very serious if you've actually tried to reach him. So . . . here we are. It wasn't really such a bad trip. We made it in this morning."

She had a level tone, a sweet smile and a certain down-to-earth manner that belied her sophisticated looks.

"There is a presence here," she said.

Toni stiffened.

"Look, I'm leaving. But, please, I'm certain you need to talk to someone."

"I can't talk to you here, now," Toni said.

"I understand. Can we meet?"

Tourists would be pouring out from the kitchen at any minute. "Lunch, tomorrow," Toni said. "There's a pub at the bottom of the hill in the village. You can't miss it. Meet me there, say, one o'clock? And if anyone asks, I'll tell you frankly, I intend to lie. You're someone I met in the States."

"I did see you do Queen Varina," Darcy said with a smile. She glanced over her shoulder, aware they were going to be interrupted any moment. "Please, don't stand me up. Honest to God, I think I can help you."

"I'll be there," Toni told her. "But, please . . ."

"Good night," the woman said calmly.

Her husband was the first one to return to the hall. He glanced at his wife, and she gave a slight nod. The man then offered Toni a quick smile, slipped his arm around his wife and started for the main door.

Toni turned and fled up the stairs as quickly as she could. She went for Bruce's door and then hesitated. She was the angry one! She backed away and went into her own room. She tapped at the bathroom door, but there was no answer, and the door to his bedroom was closed, also.

Turning away, she brushed her teeth, washed her face and found her nightgown. She hesitated again. She could just go in, but what if he was angry now?

She turned, went back to her own room

and crawled beneath the sheets. Fear suddenly set in. What if the old Bruce, with his bloody dripping sword, appeared again tonight?

The solution was simple. She was going to go to bed, close her eyes and not open them again until morning.

But sleep didn't come easy. She spent the first minutes wishing that Bruce would suddenly come into her room. And finally, she drifted off.

Then she awoke. Don't open your eyes, don't do it! she told herself. But she opened them anyway.

She expelled her breath with a sigh. The room was empty. And yet . . . there was a *feeling* in it, a feeling of . . . sadness?

She sat up, remembering that, just after she'd *seen* what had happened, she hadn't been afraid.

Though she couldn't see her visitor from the past, she still somehow *felt* him. And she just wasn't ready to deal with it.

She rose, walked into the bathroom, hesitated, then opened the door to his room. She walked to the foot of the bed, biting into her lower lip, trying to see in the deep shadows. He was probably sound asleep. Should she dare take the next step and just climb in next to him?

"Are you coming in here?"

His voice, out of the darkness, caused her to jump.

"Well, are you coming in, or do you just intend to spend the night there at the foot of the bed, staring at me?"

"I'm coming in," she said. Her voice sounded ridiculously prim and sharp.

She crawled in, and his arms came around her.

"Toni —"

"No! Don't talk. Please don't talk!" she said.

"Toni —"

"Please!"

"Anyway you want it," he whispered. And he, too, sounded ridiculous, sharp and cold, especially considering the way he held her.

17

The couple were already seated in a booth at the pub when Toni arrived, and the lithe blonde introduced Toni to her husband, Matt. It might have been just a lovely meeting of Americans in a foreign country, where even casual acquaintances could suddenly become best friends.

"So you're Toni," the man said. And though the smile he offered her was warm and encouraging, she still didn't feel terribly assured.

"You saw Queen Varina, too?" she asked him.

He shrugged, looking at his wife with a half smile. "I am the Southerner," he said.

Toni shook her head. "You both came to the show with Adam?"

"Yes, actually, we did," Matt said.

"Adam has talked about you a lot," Darcy said.

"So I gathered," Toni murmured.

"And then, of course, when he discovered the castle was here, and that the owner was Laird Bruce MacNiall . . ." Darcy said with a shrug.

"Wait a minute. You're going to tell me that Adam knows Bruce MacNiall, too?" Toni demanded.

Matt Stone inclined his head and she realized that the barmaid had come to stand before them. "I'll take a pint of anything," Toni said, noting that the two were drinking beer.

"Lamb is great today," the barmaid suggested. "And there's a lovely chicken entrée."

The three opted for poultry, and the barmaid smiled and moved on.

"Adam knows Bruce?" Toni repeated.

Matt inclined his head again; her beer was coming. She decided that, with his smooth, cultured Virginian accent, he might have made an interesting twist on James Bond.

She thanked the barmaid for her beer.

"Please. Are you going to answer me?" she asked.

Darcy smiled. "He doesn't know Bruce MacNiall. He knows *of* him. He's been watching him. Bruce is actually on our register, as well."

Toni stared at the two of them with a certain outrage. "He's on the *register?* This is beginning to sound a lot like Big Brother!"

Darcy shook her head. "I never do begin well, do I?" she said to her husband, who smiled. She looked back at Toni. "It's nothing like that, honestly. Adam is the most humane, caring individual I've ever met. His son was incredibly gifted, so Adam started doing research. Most people who have . . . well, I guess around here they call it 'the touch,' others call it a gift and many call it a curse. Call it what you will, most people who have it are afraid of it. And they don't want to use it."

Toni inhaled, watching her silently.

"Like you," Darcy continued. "What child could endure such things happening, seeing such things in dreams? Adam said that you retreated, but that you were incredibly strong-willed and appeared to have put it all behind you. However, he always felt that you would call one day."

"As I did," Toni murmured.

"So," Matt said. "Want to give us the whole story?"

"In a minute," Toni said, still wary. "What were you talking about regarding Bruce? You said that he was on the register."

Matt leaned forward. "There was a case here, years ago —"

"Yes, I recently heard about it. He'd been a cop. His work led to the arrest of a serial killer. I think that means he must have been a good cop."

"An excellent cop. And according to him, he simply used the methods employed by profilers."

Toni nodded, looking at him expectantly. "So?"

"There were some articles written at the time that drew Adam's interest," Darcy explained. "Apparently, he actually managed to *think* as the man."

Toni frowned. "So," she said, still skeptical, "there must be a lot of good cops on that register."

"Oh, there are," Darcy assured her.

Matt smiled. "You're still looking at us as if we're crazy. But that's what you want to think, isn't it? Toni, if nothing else, we'll listen to you *without* staring at you as if you're mad, and we may really be able to help."

She drew her finger along the line of her beer mug, as if it were frosty, which it definitely wasn't. She'd actually grown accustomed to warm beer.

"If Bruce has any of the touch, he certainly denies it," she said, hoping that her voice didn't sound angry or bitter. "He thinks that I have nightmares, that I hit my head . . . anything but that I might really have seen a ghost."

Matt lifted his hands and grimaced.

"Guys don't like to admit that they see ghosts," he said simply.

"I don't think that he does see this one," Toni said.

"Different people have sight in different ways. I think that when he was on the force, Bruce wanted to catch the killer— or killers — so desperately, that he was able to call on reserves he'd never want to acknowledge he has," Darcy explained.

"And probably never will again," Toni said.

"You never know," Darcy told her. "So . . . please, try to tell us more."

"Well, for one, they have a very contemporary problem here," she said. "There's a serial killer on the loose. He abducts prostitutes from the cities and dumps them in Tillingham."

"Yes, we know," Matt said.

"Tell us more about the ghost," Darcy said. "Especially if anything new has happened since we spoke on the phone."

Toni arched a brow, staring at the woman. "Actually, something very new happened yesterday afternoon, not long before the tour."

"The entrées are coming," Matt warned lightly.

So Toni waited. And once the food arrived, she started talking. And to her amazement, she talked and talked.

"A ghost is usually trying very hard to say something," Darcy told her when she was done.

"Let's say I buy into that," Toni told her. "That I can even understand it! History didn't pinpoint him as his wife's killer, but legend and speculation certainly abounded. So now Annalise has been found. They're doing DNA tests, and if it's proved that she is Annalise, she will come back to the castle and be entombed next to her laird. He'll be vindicated. She'll be at rest. So this ghost should be happy and quiet now, right?"

"He should be," Darcy said.

"Unless . . ." Matt murmured.

"What?" Toni demanded.

Darcy exhaled softly. "Apparently, there's something else bothering him. And if you really want him to be at peace, you'll have to figure out what it is."

"We've company," Matt murmured suddenly.

Toni turned to find Bruce coming into the pub with Jonathan Tavish. They both looked grim. Toni felt guilty instantly, although she wasn't sure why.

Bruce saw them and headed toward the table.

"Hi!" she murmured, trying to sound casual.

"Hello," he said, and looked to the couple across from her. "I saw you two last night, right?"

"Yes. Strange, isn't it?" Toni said cheerfully. "Matt and Darcy Stone, this is the real Laird MacNiall. Bruce, Matt and Darcy."

"Nice to meet you. Our constable, Jonathan Tavish," Bruce said, and Jonathan, too, exchanged pleasantries.

"Did you know one another in the States?" Jonathan asked. To Toni's ears, he sounded suspicious.

"Toni didn't remember until I talked to her last night," Darcy said easily. "Matt's family home is in northern Virginia, so we often go into D.C. for the theater. We were there for one of Toni's performances of Queen Varina. We're staying in this delightful village for a few weeks, so, naturally, I begged her to join us for lunch."

There wasn't a lie in her words. Toni admired her smooth narration.

"Ah, so you're joining us in the village for a wee bit?" Jonathan said, pleased.

"It's gorgeous," Matt said.

"We've rented the Cameron cottage," Darcy told him.

"Well, we'll let you get back to your meal," Bruce said.

"Join us," Matt suggested.

"We've a bit of business," Jonathan said, "so we'll be beggin' out, if you don't mind. Another time?"

"Certainly," Darcy said politely.

"Seems the castle is bringing in the lunch-time rush," Bruce murmured.

Toni twisted in her seat. She was surprised to see Thayer just a booth away, lunching with Lizzie and Trish. And three booths back, Kevin, David, Ryan and Gina were biting into what looked like servings of lamb.

"See? It's all good for business," Jonathan told Bruce.

"Apparently," Bruce said pleasantly. "Well, excuse us, then. We'll say a quick hello to the others and have lunch, as well."

With a wave, he turned. The barmaid apparently knew both him and Jonathan well, for she jovially told them that their "usual" booth was available.

"Hail, hail, yes, the gang is all here!" Toni murmured as he moved away.

"Great," Matt said. "I'm anxious to talk to them all. So is Darcy, right?"

"Oh, yes," Darcy said. "Definitely."

★ ★ ★

Bruce let it go for the evening, and all through that night's performance.

But after he'd stabled Shaunessy, he went upstairs, built a fire and sat before it — waiting.

In time, Toni came into the room.

"What's wrong?" she asked him.

He turned to her politely. "Friends from the States, eh?"

"Yes," she said carefully. "Well, acquaintances, you know."

"You called a *psychic?*"

"What?" He could see her mind racing as she tried to figure out how he could possibly know.

"Small place," he told her, deciding to spare her and cut to the chase. "Jonathan looked them up."

"Jonathan looked them up?"

"Passports," he reminded her. "You are all visitors in a foreign land," he reminded her. "And with computers these days . . . well, it can be quite easy to find out almost anything."

"I didn't call a psychic and ask her to come," Toni said.

"You didn't?"

"Well, I called her. Actually, I didn't call her, I called a friend. And —"

"Planning on adding tarot readings to the tour?" he demanded. She was floundering. She had done it.

"You're being sarcastic and — and horrible!" she told him. She was staring at him wide-eyed — caught, one might say. And yet those sapphire eyes accused him. She was still Annalise, dressed in the ancient white gown. A flicker of something passed through him then. *She must actually be a lot like Annalise was, slim, blond hair cascading down her back, those eyes. . . .*

He brushed away the thought, angry again that she was so convinced there had to be a ghost. The damned place wasn't haunted. Although he was glad his ancestor had been vindicated — and he didn't mind a good historical place — he sure as hell didn't want the family home to be ridiculed, chronicled on *Ripley's Believe It Or Not* or a novelty in a ghost segment of the Travel Channel.

"This is still my property, my home," he said icily. "And I don't want a séance here, or a woman reading a crystal ball, or anyone making light of the history of my home. Do you understand what I'm saying?"

"Yes, I understand," she said. "Don't worry. And don't blame the others. I'll see to it that neither Darcy nor her husband ever darken your door again. Frankly, they're here to help. But then, you don't need any help, do you? After all, you were a great cop. You've got a friend who's a constable, and another who is a detective. So, what the hell, you would never need the help of anyone who might in the least tamper with the great dignity of the place! I understand. But if you had even begun to understand me, and taken the slightest chance of *believing* something that I said, we wouldn't be having this conversation now. But like I said, there's nothing to worry about. I'll never mention the word *ghost* to you again, or your ancestors, as matter of fact. Hell, do what you want with the remains of Annalise! Sell them to a museum, indulge posterity, whatever. You've no right to be angry with me because you really don't understand anything at all!"

"They were here, weren't they?" he asked.

"Yes. But I didn't ask anyone to come here. In fact, I specifically asked that she not. We all know that we've kept this going by your great bounty alone," she said, and there was definite sarcasm in her tone. "I don't know why I'm bothering. Obviously, you don't believe anything that I'm saying."

"Should I believe you?" he asked. "On what basis? I mean, do we really even know one another?"

She stiffened. "I thought I knew you," she said.

"And I thought I could trust you."

"Trust me? You know you can trust me! And if you were willing to take the least chance on me — and yourself! — you'd give me the benefit of the doubt. Apparently there have been times in *your* life when some kind of a sixth sense kicked in. That's why you were such a great cop."

"What?"

"Are you afraid to admit there just might be something in the world beyond what you can see?"

He was going to get angry. He was going to deny her words again. And yet . . .

Dammit. He didn't want to remember what it had been like when it had seemed that he had entered the mind of another man. A killer.

It was all bunk. Shite. In his rational mind, he had to believe that there was reason, and nothing else. He denied himself. No wonder he denied her, too.

"When you choose to," she said coolly, "you'll trust me. Because when you choose to look at the truth, you'll know, beyond all doubt, that you can."

She spun around, leaving him. He heard the bathroom door slam — his side first and then the other. He stared at the fire, still seething — and sorry.

But neither did he want to be a fool. These people had invaded his home . . . well enough, they'd been taken, he'd understood. But he hadn't thrown them out. Instead, he'd let them work — even when it was beginning to appear that one of their number might be guilty of the fraud from the start. Credit cards had been involved, and they were being tracked now. But in doing background checks, Jonathan had informed him, they had discovered that Thayer Fraser reported a bank card missing just before it had all begun.

"Aye, it could have been stolen," Jonathan had told him. "But don't you think it's rather a coincidence if it was the one used with the Internet providers?"

"Maybe too much of a coincidence," Bruce had told him.

"Meanin'?"

"Could he really be that stupid?" Bruce had asked.

Jonathan had shrugged. "He's a Scotsman, Bruce. And, aye, it might well have been a Scotsman to have way more information on you than anyone else. Bruce, it's lookin' as if someone's really pretended to be you."

"They took my identity, but the Internet site was a total setup!"

"Aye."

There were still discoveries to be made. But they would be made.

He sat in front of the fire awhile longer. Jonathan had told him who the people having lunch with Toni that afternoon were. He'd done the research on them himself, and he'd been astonished. Low-key, low profile. Harrison Investigations didn't advertise on television, didn't promise to fix anyone's love life or connect anyone with deceased relatives.

Still, they investigated strange and unusual occurrences, trouble spots. Ghosts. Hauntings. No matter what the hell they wanted to call it!

As if they hadn't enough real problems around here! He could be glad that a family mystery was solved, but there was fraud in his own house. A killer, leaving victims in the forest. And the last damned thing he wanted around was a psychic!

He could hardly kick the pair out of the village, but he damned well could make sure that they weren't invited into his home! Yet as he stared at the fire, nothing of logic, truth or the simple fact that he did own the property seemed to mean anything. Her last few words stung. *I thought I knew you.*

She had been the one angry before, but she had come back. If he just waited . . . maybe she would come back again. Because she was frightened? he wondered, mocking himself. Ego or not, he couldn't accept that she had come back into the bedroom the night before out of fear.

He *could* go to her. Actually, he could *apologize. Except that he wasn't in the wrong.*

The fire continued to crackle. Time passed and he was still there, staring at the flames. At last he rose, turned out the lights and went to bed. But he didn't sleep. He realized that he wasn't sleeping because he was waiting. And after a while, he realized that she wasn't coming.

Donning his robe, he went through to the bath. She hadn't locked the door on her side of it. He tapped lightly. There was no answer, so he opened the door and walked over to the foot of the bed.

She slept, her hand curled beneath her chin, hair splayed around her. He wouldn't wake her, he decided. But as he stood there, she suddenly bolted upright, staring at him with alarm.

"It's just me," he said. "Real. In the

flesh," he added. She still stared. "Not a ghost," he told her.

She nodded after a minute, still staring at him.

"Do you want to be alone?"

"Is that an apology?"

"Did you apologize last night?"

"Was I wrong last night?"

"Am I really wrong now?"

She looked down for a moment, lashes sweeping her eyes, the fall of her hair concealing her features. "Does it really matter?" she said very softly.

Those words touched him in a way he couldn't quite fathom, and did more than any argument. "I'm sorry," he murmured.

"For what?" she asked him, looking up.

He crossed his arms over his chest. "I really don't want a psychic here. I hate it when you see those programs with cheap special effects as a handheld camera follows a purported medium around a house. I think we have enough problems here. I'm sorry I spoke the way I did. And I . . . I wish I could believe you. I believe that you believe your dreams are very real."

She rose, brushing by him, heading for the connecting door. There she paused. "You really do have the better bed," she told him. He followed her.

They were awake another hour. Then, they both slept.

Toni awoke thinking that it had to be very late, or nearly morning. But the room was in deep shadow. The fire had died in the grate and the lights were out, except for one that remained on in the bath.

She felt Bruce's arm around her. But still, she had the feeling that they were not alone.

She looked to the foot of the bed. And he was there. Once again, standing, looking at her, sword hanging from his hand, bloodied. He looked at her, and she knew he wanted her to follow.

At her side, Bruce stirred. "Toni?"

"Yes?"

"Is he here?"

She didn't know if the question was mocking or not. She was staring at the apparition. She told the truth.

"Yes."

She heard a soft groan, but he pulled her closer. "Tell him to go away. Tell him that *I'm* here."

She looked at the apparition. "Go away!" she whispered. Words formed then, unspoken on her lips. *Please. I don't know what you want!*

He inclined his head, as if bowing to her desires. Then, as she stared at him, he faded until he was nothing more than a shadow in the night. She lay back down, glad, gnawing upon her lip.

There had to be something else that he wanted . . . but what? What the hell *was* it that he wanted?

Toni was determined to find out, whatever it took, wherever it led. She would swallow fear and find out why he kept coming back. . . .

With that settled, she moved in tightly next to Bruce. His breath teased her nape. His hand rested on her midriff. Her back was solidly to his chest, and he gave her tremendous warmth. Like a cascade of warm water, the touch filled her with comfort and ease. She closed her eyes and fell back to sleep. She didn't waken to darkness again.

In the morning, Bruce was up and gone when she awoke.

"You're joking with me, right?"

Bruce sat across the table from Robert Chamberlain at the pub, having received a message to meet him there at eleven. He was surprised that Robert wanted to meet in the village; he usually chose Stirling.

But he was even more surprised by his friend's words.

Robert shook his head gravely. "I've asked them to meet us here."

Bruce groaned. "I don't believe this. Not from you."

"Bruce, law enforcement has resorted to such tactics many times. I wouldn't have called over to the States myself —"

"Why should you? It's not as if we don't have our share of quacks in Great Britain," Bruce said.

Robert grinned. "I wouldn't have known that they were here if you hadn't logged on to the police line to investigate them. But since I saw your inquiry, I looked them up."

"Harrison Investigations," Bruce said, shaking his head. "They go into places where unusual events have taken place."

"They're discreet, but not secretive," Robert said. "There's no sensationalism regarding the corporation. They've been called upon by law agencies in many places. They've worked for congressmen and senators, even a U.S. president —"

"Whoever said that men and women in the government were sane?" Bruce asked him.

Robert shrugged. "Bruce, you have told me a dozen times yourself that we should be tearing the forest apart, looking for the remains of Annie O'Hara."

"The last two victims were found there," Bruce said. "That's logic, not intuition."

"I still think it was more than logic when you nailed the killers ten years ago."

Bruce shifted uncomfortably. "It seems to me that there's a great deal more we could — sorry, the law could be doing without resorting to . . . mumbo jumbo."

"Be polite, please."

"Hey, times have changed. I'm not the ruler of my own little kingdom. I own the castle and a lot of property. I have the title, but you can buy a title on the Internet these days. I can hardly order these people to get out of my village by sundown," Bruce said.

"On a more realistic note," Bruce said, "I met with Jonathan yesterday. The boys in computer tech are apparently having some pretty good luck tracking down information on the phony corporation that rented the castle."

Robert nodded. "I've seen the reports. I've kept out of it. Jonathan is the local constable."

"He's got it out for Thayer Fraser, I'd say."

Robert shrugged. "We can't make any arrests on what we have right now. But the man's bank account pretty much matches the amount the Americans put up. And he reported a bank card stolen. If it proves that the bank card was used at the Internet Café in Glasgow where the site was formed . . . well, then we'll have to bring him in for questioning, at the very least."

"Doesn't make sense. He'd have to know he'd be caught."

"Aye, but there's a certain defense in that, too. They're trying to track his money now, as well. That will help. Naturally we need legal resources to do all that." Robert leaned back. "You won't see this one in the papers, because we've been keeping the inquiries quiet, but I've had my men go a lot deeper into the disappearance of the barmaid in Stirling."

Bruce frowned. "She'd cleaned out her room. She was packed up, bag and baggage."

"But no one knows where she went. She didn't take a bus or a train. She's just gone. Annie O'Hara could have gone back to Ireland, but I don't believe that. And our boy, Thayer, was seen with the bar maid that same day."

"Wait, you're accusing him of fraud — and of being a serial killer?"

"I'm not accusing him of anything," Robert said. "I'm telling you what we've got."

"It doesn't gel," Bruce said. "It sounds like grasping at straws."

"Straws are all we've got."

"With a good attorney, the man could skewer the force," Bruce warned.

"We can't make an arrest. But since the fellow is living in your castle . . ."

Bruce shook his head. "The fraud is one thing. But to assume the man might be a killer because he was in a pub . . . that's pushing it, don't you think?"

Robert didn't answer. "They're coming," he said. He and Bruce stood as the handsome American couple strode over to the booth.

"Hello," Bruce said, shaking hands along with Robert. "What did you think of the tour at the castle the other night?"

"It was quite remarkable," the woman said.

Bruce stared at the man. The fellow didn't look like a quack. "So, did you feel anything in the castle?" His words were polite, but he couldn't keep his tone as cordial.

"No, but then, I'm not the one who would," the man said.

"Matt is actually the sheriff in a town named for his family," Robert explained.

Bruce cast Robert a dry stare. *Might have mentioned that before, old chap!* But of course,

Robert had refrained on purpose.

"I didn't ask them to meet about the castle," Robert said.

"No, of course not."

"It's a beautiful place," Darcy told him. She wasn't obsequious, just pleasant. Still, he knew he had a chip on his shoulder regarding them.

"Saturday, I've got men coming in from a number of the surrounding areas," Robert explained. "We're searching for the body of a woman almost certain to be a victim of a serial killer. I was hoping that you would be willing to search with my men."

"Of course," Darcy said, glancing at her husband.

"Naturally." Matt glanced at his wife.

Robert nodded. "Naturally," he agreed.

Darcy Stone looked across the table at Bruce. "You'll be there, won't you, Laird MacNiall?"

"I will."

"Of course," she said. "You feel a responsibility."

"The forest borders my castle."

She nodded. "It's interesting, Laird MacNiall. You really haven't spent much time at your castle in the last decade or so."

He arched a brow.

"Well, there's the place you have in New

York and the horse farm up near Loch Ness. You even have an interest in a breeding facility in Kentucky."

Bruce stared at her levelly. "All that," he murmured, "and you didn't even ask to see my palm."

He started to make a move, but she placed her fingers on his hand.

"We, too, have access to the Internet, Laird MacNiall."

"Ah," Bruce murmured, wondering why the couple made him feel as if he should be wearing full body armor. There really was no call for him to be rude. Robert wanted to see if they could help. It was on the wrong side of good sense as far as he was concerned, but they certainly appeared respectable enough. The woman was hardly dressed in black with a veil, nor did she carry a crystal ball. There was no reason to be so instantly hostile.

He wasn't so sure he liked the scrutiny they had put on his life though. And he didn't like the idea that Toni had called Harrison Investigations in the first place. Despite the fact that he believed her conviction that she'd never heard the story about the great MacNiall before, he was sure there was a logical explanation. There was surely even a logical explanation for her knowledge of the crypts. And it was pure luck and circumstance that she had come upon the remains of Annalise after the rainstorm.

After all, it was luck and circumstance that he had caught the husband-and-wife team of killers, all those years ago.

"The castle is your ancestral home," Darcy Stone mused, "but it does seem as if you've spent years running away from it."

That was it, his cue to leave. He rose.

"It's been a pleasure," he said, "but you will have to excuse me. I have some business in town. I'll see you both Saturday, then. Robert, keep me informed."

He shook Matt Stone's hand and strode out of the café, suddenly wishing to hell that he was in New York right then, on the streets somewhere, watching a flood of living, breathing, pierced-tongued, green-haired teens and young adults walk by in a hurry to get their next tattoos.

Beyond the café, he paused. It felt as if he had shed a heavy overcoat, just being in the air again. He glanced around, considering a drop-in at Jonathan's constabulary, then a visit to Daniel Darrow. He eschewed both ideas, staring up at the statue of his ancestor. Marble, some steel and God knows what else went into a statue.

"Get out of my life!" he told the statue.

"So, the old laird is in your life," a soft voice said.

He spun around, damning himself for not moving more quickly. Darcy Stone had followed him out.

"Mrs. Stone, if you'll forgive me —"

"Please, just give me a moment of your time."

He crossed his arms over his chest. "A moment, then."

"First, Toni Fraser didn't ask that we come."

"Why did you?"

She wasn't ready to answer that one. "There is a presence in your castle."

"There are a lot of presences. Americans," he said.

She smiled. "Laird MacNiall, you made one of the most brilliant cases and arrests in the crime annals. And then you left the force. Why?"

He lifted his hands. "Because the work absorbed my life. I put off my wedding. My fiancée became terribly ill and died soon after that case was solved. I decided that I had put a little bit too much time into man's inhumanity to man. Not that it's really any of your business, but then, you seem to know everything else about me."

"Might that be only part of the reason?" she asked.

"I don't know what you're talking about."

"I think you do. I think you had a few moments during that case when you saw too clearly what the killers were doing. Maybe you even got into their skin — into their hearts and minds — far more than you wanted."

"Murder is ugly, Mrs. Stone."

"That's why it should be stopped, whenever possible. Why killers should be taken away from the public, locked up," she said.

"Is that all, Mrs. Stone?"

"No. I just wanted to say that if you want to talk, if there's anything I can do . . . well, I would really love to help you."

He wanted to tell her that he didn't need her help but he refrained. "I'll keep that in mind."

"I really would love to come back to your castle."

"I'll consider it," he told her. "Is that it?"

She shook her head. "Just one more thing."

"Aye?"

"You . . . you have real capabilities, I believe. If you'd let yourself use them."

"I'll keep that in mind, as well, Mrs. Stone. Now . . . if you'll excuse me?"

And he made a point of getting into his car.

18

Gina was in the kitchen with David and Kevin when Toni came down. The three of them were studiously poring over a document.

"Toni," Gina said. "Want to take a look at this? I've written up a new rental agreement. Well, it's not exactly a rental agreement, since MacNiall will apparently be staying on his own property. And, of course, there's no telling how long he'll be willing to play his ancestor with our presentation. Anyway, I'm asking him for a six-month run. If we keep doing as well as we've been doing, we'll be able to pay him for the facility — and even give him a cut for his participation — and come out with enough to look into going home and getting new work, or looking for another property."

Toni poured herself a cup of coffee, then leaned against the counter and said, "Gina, I'm sure you've written up a good agreement. But what we have to do now is get it to an attorney — and past Laird MacNiall."

Gina chewed on a thumbnail, reading over her own document. "I hope he'll go for this. Otherwise, we're just living day to day."

"Actually, we all just live day to day, no matter what," Kevin said.

"Sage, very sage," Toni told him. "Where is everyone else?"

"Bruce went somewhere in the car this morning, but he came back and went riding," David told her. "Thayer muttered something and went out. Ryan is upstairs — he wants to drive into town and buy some kind of polish for his swords. Eban is . . . well, he's being Eban, out doing whatever he does."

Gina glanced at her watch. "We should get going. We always spend more time in the village then we intend. Toni, want to come with us?"

"No, I think I'll hang around here."

David frowned at her. "You should come."

She smiled. "I'm fine. Really."

"Ah, the nights are not enough!" he teased. "She's awaiting the return of Laird MacNiall."

She forced another smile. "I have a book I want to read," she told him.

"Um," Kevin teased. "The book of man. And it's partially in braille."

"You two are terrible," she said.

515

"I'd rather thought last night that there was some trouble in tranquil waters," Gina said, looking at her somewhat sharply.

That caused David and Kevin to study her, as well.

"Oh?" she said.

"I heard your voice when I came up. You sounded a little sharp," Gina said. "Are you two arguing?"

Toni shook her head.

"Because we really need him to sign this agreement," Gina reminded her.

She sighed. "He will sign it, or he won't sign it. I'm not arguing with him."

They heard singing and Ryan came bursting into the kitchen, doing a version of "Oklahoma." He seemed cheerful. They all stared at him; he wasn't known for his vocal ability.

He stopped and stared back. "What?" he demanded. "Okay, so this is Scotland. Brigadoon! I feel a new song coming on."

"Let's get out of here, please!" David begged. "Toni, come on. I'll go read more headstones with you, if you want."

She laughed. "I'm fine here alone. I'll walk you to the car."

They started to trail out, but when David opened the front door, they were startled to find Constable Jonathan Tavish standing

516

there. He looked grim.

"Constable," Toni said. "Hello. Can we help you? Bruce isn't here."

Jonathan shook his head sadly. "I'm sorry. I've not come to see Bruce."

"Then . . . how can we help you?" Ryan asked.

"I've come for your cousin, Miss Fraser." He hesitated a moment. "I'm truly sorry. I've come to arrest Thayer Fraser."

David was the one to gasp. "Why? For what?"

Jonathan Tavish shifted uneasily on his feet. He truly looked miserable. "Fraud," he said.

"Wait! Please, explain this!" Toni said.

"Is he here?" Tavish insisted.

Toni shook her head. "He may be about . . . we don't know where he is. But —"

"I'm sorry to say this, folks, but he engineered the whole deal. Set you all up. He created a fictitious corporation on the Web and arranged for the box as an address. He probably presumed that you'd all be out after the MacNiall returned . . . you'd have to go home, broke, and he'd have managed to make himself long gone. It's quite a surprise that he hasn't flown already, but maybe he thought he'd covered his tracks."

"Thayer!" Toni exclaimed.

"Your cousin?" Ryan said.

"Now, now, we may be able to retrieve a bit o' the money," Jonathan said consolingly.

Toni shook her head. "I don't believe it."

"You don't want to believe it," David murmured.

"What kind of proof is there?" Toni demanded.

"Enough for an arrest," Jonathan told her quietly.

"I still don't believe it," Toni said stubbornly.

"Y'are not certain the chap isn't about?" Jonathan asked.

"He could be. We don't know," Ryan said. He stepped back. "Come in . . . I can check his room."

"I'll take a look around upstairs," Gina said, "while Ryan goes to his room."

Toni stood awkwardly for a moment, then thought that she might know where Thayer was. The stables. Up in the rafters. She didn't know what he did up there. *And maybe she didn't want to know.* But she did want to see him before the constable got to him, though.

"I'll . . . look around outside," she said.

She walked out the main doors, gazing toward the stables. Despite the fact that he'd actually warned her just yesterday that a trace had been made to Glasgow, she was stunned. *You don't want to believe it!* That much was true.

As she started across the grass, she saw Thayer. And she was certain he had been up in the rafters of the stables. He was walking toward her casually, though, smiling, taking long strides, his arms swinging, as if he hadn't a care in the world.

She stood still, feeling the cool breeze lift her hair from her forehead. "Top o' the mornin' to you, cous— ach! That's Irish, eh?" he said teasingly. Then he stopped, seeing her expression. "Toni? What's the matter?"

"The constable is here."

"Aye?"

"To arrest you."

"Arrest me?" He appeared honestly stunned.

"For fraud."

"What?"

"For fraud. For taking the lot of us."

He looked toward the door. Something else passed over his features. Turning, she saw that Jonathan had come out.

"Bloody hell!" he muttered, and took off running.

It must have been a moment of blind

panic for him, for there was really nowhere to run. Or maybe there was. If he could have gotten down the hill and into the forest, he might have managed a real disappearance. But he didn't.

Jonathan Tavish could run. Seeing Thayer's intention, he came out with a startling flash of speed and athleticism. Thayer hadn't gone more than twenty yards before the constable tackled him. "This is bullshit! Bullshit!" Thayer roared as the two scrambled on the ground.

Tavish was the stronger man, broader, and in better shape apparently. The scuffle didn't last long. Thayer was quickly cuffed. Dusty and disheveled, he was dragged to his feet.

As Jonathan led him toward the patrol car, he looked at Toni. "I didn't do it! I don't know what kind of crazy proof there is against me, but I didn't do it. Toni, you've got to help me."

"Tell it to the judge!" Jonathan muttered, shaking his head wearily.

"I need help, Toni!" Thayer called to her. "Legal help. I swear, I'm not guilty!"

"We'll get you a lawyer!" she cried out. "A solicitor . . . whatever you need!"

The arrest was not like on a cop show. Jonathan didn't protect his suspect's head and put him into the back. Instead he opened the passenger door of his vehicle and shoved Thayer in.

Thayer's eyes remained on Toni's, silently begging for help.

David, Kevin, Gina and Ryan were there then, aligned on either side of her. "My God!" Gina breathed.

"Well, Constable Tavish said that we could get some of the money back," Ryan said.

Toni spun on them. "He says that he's innocent!"

David looked at her sadly. "Toni, most people don't go around yelling out that they're guilty, you know."

She shook her head. "I believe him. And we've got to get to the bottom of this! He needs legal aid — whatever it is over here."

"They have a fair and judicial legal system," Kevin told her sympathetically.

"We should have never trusted an outsider," Gina murmured.

"Right, he's my cousin, my fault," Toni said angrily. "What if he's innocent?"

"Toni!" Gina argued, but gently. "They couldn't have arrested him without some kind of proof."

"I want to know what proof!" she said. "And I want him to have legal help, right away."

"Well, that's just great," Kevin said.

"Why?" Toni demanded.

"Because we're all broke!" he reminded her.

"Look," David said calmly, "we need to find Bruce. This is his place, and he always knows more than we do. We can get hold of his friend, Robert. He can tell us, I'm certain, what they really have on Thayer. Let's hop in the car and drive around until we find him."

"Great," Kevin said with a sigh. "We're going to try to help the guy who screwed us all royally."

"Whatever happened to innocent until proven guilty?" Toni demanded.

"We really need to put all this before Laird MacNiall," Ryan said.

"Could he have *ridden* down to the village?" Gina wondered.

"I suppose you can ride anywhere around here," Ryan answered. "Hey, David and Kevin — you two take the minivan down to the village, ask if anyone has seen Bruce. Gina, Toni and I can hop in the car and try driving around these roads, cover the farm paths and all that."

Toni backed away. "Thank you," she murmured. "But I'll stay here, in case he's not in the village, and you miss him on the roads."

"You're going to stay here? By yourself?" Gina asked her.

She shrugged. "Eban is around somewhere."

"Oh, great. Eban! That gives me a real sense of security for you!" Gina said.

Toni shook her head. "It's all right. It's broad daylight. I'll be fine."

"I don't like it," David said.

"Oh, for the love of God, will you please go! If Bruce doesn't come back soon, or if you guys don't find him, I'll just hop on Wallace and come down to the village," she said. "Please, let's all move. I doubt if they'll be keeping Thayer in the village. They'll want to take him to a jail in one of the larger cities. We really need to move on this."

"All right," Gina said. "But, Toni, you've got to accept the fact that he might have done it."

She nodded, then backed away, toward the castle. But when both cars had started down the road, she walked resolutely toward the stables.

Entering, she noted Wallace in his stall, walking to the gate, expecting her to come and rub his nose.

"Sorry, boy!" she murmured, heading straight for the ladder. She climbed quickly to the rafters and looked around. A layer of hay covered the floor. She walked the planked surface, thinking this was foolish. She couldn't find something — whatever it was that brought Thayer up here — if she didn't know what she was looking for.

Then she heard whistling and stopped short. Eban. She listened as he strode into the stables, walking straight over to Wallace. "He y'be, lad, yer special treat!"

He was feeding the horse something. But what?

It occurred to her then that the strange little man may well have been feeding the horse something that made him sick. After all, Shaunessy had never been taken in. But why would Eban do such a thing? To sabotage their efforts? Or maybe he thought, as Bruce had originally, that they were mocking Scottish history.

She held very still, listening.

"Ah, there, lad, aye, eat it all up!"

She forced herself not to move, not to breathe. She waited. Eventually, she heard him leave the stables. Even then, until the sound of his whistle was long gone, she waited. Then, in a fury, she began to kick the hay around, desperately . . . searching.

"You'll not get me on this!" Thayer told

Jonathan. "I didn't do it."

"You should be ashamed! A Scotsman, doing such a thing!" Jonathan said.

"Listen, I'm telling you —"

"Don't be tellin' me!" Jonathan warned him.

"Listen to me —" Thayer began.

"I'm warnin' ya!"

"Aye, and I'm beg—"

The constable had no more patience. He lifted his elbow as he drove, slamming it against Thayer's head.

The blow hurt. Like bloody hell! Stunned, Thayer reacted to the strike. He swung his elbow back, and caught the constable on the side of the head. Jonathan's skull crashed against the glass. He lost control of the car. It began to careen down the hill.

Jonathan swore just as the car hit a large boulder — and flipped.

Toni kicked up a lump of hay and saw it — a plastic bag. She crouched down and picked it up, looking at the contents. Grass?

Running her hands over the floor, she found a second bag. It held matches and brown cigarette wrappers. She sniffed the first bag, no longer puzzled.

So Thayer had been coming to the stable

rafters to smoke weed. It seemed evident, but it wasn't the answer she'd been looking for. She'd wanted something to either convict him or exonerate him on charges of fraud!

Sighing, she returned his stash, thinking she sure as hell didn't want to get caught with it herself. Rising, she walked gingerly to the ladder, not wanting to run into Eban again. She crawled down quickly, then made a detour to Wallace's stall. She eyed the horse carefully and critically. He whinnied. "I don't have anything for you. And if that man is giving you anything bad at all to cause a colic, I'll punch him out myself, okay?"

She glanced at her watch. Though it had seemed like she'd spent aeons in the rafters, only fifteen minutes had passed since the others left. She hesitated for a minute, afraid, and then she purposely walked back to the castle.

She resolutely made her way upstairs, into Bruce's room, and sat in the chair by the cold embers in the fireplace. Then she closed her eyes and spoke softly.

"If you're here, this would be a great time for you to appear," she whispered. "Please, we're alone now. And . . . I'm going to trust you. I'm not going to scream or panic."

And when she opened her eyes, he was there, watching her gravely, sadly.

Come.

"Yes, as you wish," she said.

He turned, tartan swaying, taking large steps with his long legs. He exited the master chamber, heading out to the hallway.

Toni moved along the hallway, following. He led her to the landing of the stairs and paused there. She waited as he looked back, assuring himself that she followed. Then he started down the stairs and she came behind.

Once again, he paused in the great hall, assuring himself that she was following still. She knew where they were going. "Down to the crypts?" she whispered. He stared at her with silent gravity, turned again, and traversed the secondary hall.

As she had feared, the door to the winding stairway down to the realm of the dead was open. Once again, he awaited her.

She stared at him, shaking her head slightly. "Why me?" she asked softly.

There was no reply; she hadn't expected one. Again he turned and started down the winding steps. Toni followed quickly. This time, however, she turned on the lights.

The lights didn't seem to help much,

though, not when she was down there by herself — with a ghost. She was grateful that the MacNialls had not chosen to lay their dead out in simple shelving, that there were no decaying shrouds resting upon bodies left to go to dust with the passage of time. Still, ancient marble and words etched in Gaelic, monuments and carvings all reminded her of where she was. There was a certain cold down here that defied all logic. And as she wandered through the crypts, alone in the castle, with only the presence to guide her, she wondered at her own sanity.

As she ventured deeper into the recesses of the hallway, the light seemed to fade. On her left, the tomb of a laird from the 1500s was adorned with the life-size figure of a Renaissance man, seated upon his coffin, head resting upon a hand, marble eyes staring. She looked away quickly, feeling as if the blank eyes were watching her. She knew where she was going — the end of the hallway in the crypt.

She arrived, and though she had followed the vision of the great MacNiall down to this point, he was gone. The far end was cast in deep shadow. She stared at the marble figure, too much like the Bruce she knew, and wondered why she was here again, what it was that she hadn't seen.

Her blood seemed to turn to instant ice as she saw what was different tonight.

The stone sarcophagus just behind his — which had been set beside his own in the niche hundreds of years ago by someone determined that one day Annalise's earthly remains would one day join those of her beloved in death — was ajar.

She frowned and whispered aloud, hoping that the ghost would hear. "But she will come home, you know. Bruce will see to it. She will come home and lie beside you!" Her voice echoed back to her eerily in the arched stone corridor.

She moved forward, stepping around the edge of the effigy of the great MacNiall in death, trying to ascertain how and why the simple slab atop the second vault had been left open.

The shadows were thick and heavy. At first she could see nothing. She started to press at the stone, thinking she could see better if she could move it, but the weight seemed far too great for her at first. Then she heard a scraping, stone against stone. It was giving, moving back.

And she saw what lay within the coffin.

A scream tore from her throat. Loud, shrill, terrible. It ricocheted off the stone and echoed with resounding horror.

Toni backed away from the tomb, turned and ran down the corridor, desperate to leave.

She had her answer. She knew what the great MacNiall had been trying to tell her.

19

There was nothing like riding, especially a horse as fine as Shaunessy. And God forgive him a certain pride, but there really was nothing as beautiful as the hills of his native land. Drawing to a halt at the top of a crest, Bruce surveyed the lands — dotted with sheep and cattle — that stretched in shades of green and purple as far as the eye could see.

It was amazing to look out over the peacefulness and tranquility of the scene below him. So much tragedy, bloodshed and pain had come before in this very area, where ancient tribes had battled for the best land, where the early nationalists had waged war against imperialism and where, in later years, men had shed their blood again and again for their loyalties, ideals and pride.

The last gave him pause, for he was disturbed, deeply disturbed. And uneasy, as well. He felt a growing sense of something . . . about to happen. Something about to break.

"Foolish, eh, old boy?" he said aloud, as Shaunessy pawed the earth.

He turned from the tranquil setting of the valley to stare into the dark green depths of the forest. Ten years had passed, yet the case he had solved still disturbed him. *Why?*

He knew why. He had entered the mind of a heinous monster, and it had scared him. It had made him wonder if, in doing so, he could become a monster himself.

I do not believe . . . ! he told himself. And yet . . . just as he had never forgotten the case, he had not, in the last days, been able to rid himself of the vision of Toni, facedown in the stream.

Ghosts and ghost-busters! he thought angrily. Aye, tricks could be played with the mind, and all of this was playing tricks with his own.

Darcy Stone had gotten to him. As had Toni. There had been such a serenity about her. No driving passion, no wild speech. And he couldn't help but wonder, as he sat there atop Shaunessy, what the hell he was doing? Because one thing was true.

The vision returned again and again, haunting him. And the sense of fatalism was growing.

Toni slammed against the door, absolutely terrified that she would find it locked. But it burst open as it had before, easily allowing her an exit.

The phone. She had to get to the phone.

Eban! Eban was around somewhere. Not in the main castle. He never came in . . . or did he?

Striding for the main hall, she came to an abrupt halt before she could turn for the stairs.

Thayer was standing in the doorway, looking dazed, wild. Like a madman. Blood covered his forehead and caked his hair. His shirt was ripped; he was filthy. The handcuffs he'd been wearing dangled from his one wrist.

"Thayer?" she said.

"There was an accident," he said.

"An accident?" she said carefully. What she had seen below was still so vivid in her mind, that she realized she didn't trust anyone. An hour ago she had been defending him so staunchly. But now, the way he looked . . .

"What happened?" she asked thickly.

"Hit . . . the constable . . . bastard . . . hit me. I hit him back."

"Where? Where is the constable?" she asked.

He shook his head. "I crawled out. I . . . Toni!" He started walking toward her. Panic seized her. She'd been too trusting. He'd been up in the rafters, smoking dope, when they'd all been in a precarious situation. Can't hang a man for that! she chided herself. But the way that he was staring at her . . .

He grinned suddenly, but it seemed lopsided and eerie. "Toni, you look as if you've seen a ghost. Been prowling around in the castle graveyard, eh?"

That did it. Screw the phone. She was getting the hell out. When he walked toward her, she pushed him. Hard. He staggered back, falling. "Toni!"

Ignoring him, she raced toward the stables, thinking to get Wallace. But she came to a dead halt. Eban was coming from the stables. He had an oilcloth in one hand and a sword in the other. He was just cleaning the sword! she told herself.

"Miss Fraser!" he said. "Coomin' to the stables, are ye? Aye, and good. Y'can see to old Wallace, good old lad!"

She shook her head, trying to appear nonchalant. *Wallace! Good old Wallace. Was the horse dead this time? Had Eban poisoned him?*

"I'm off for a bit of a walk, Eban!" she said, and waved jauntily, hoping Thayer wouldn't appear behind her right then. But . . . maybe it would be best if he did. Both men couldn't be guilty of heinous things. . . .

Or could they?

She quickened her pace, grateful that she was going downhill. A walk at first, a trot, a lope . . . and then she was running.

"Toni!"

She looked back. Thayer, menacing in his stagger and tone, was coming after her.

It was a long, long way to the village.

She paused, looking back, taking a deep breath. He might not have moved quickly enough when Jonathan was coming after him, but he was cutting some speed now.

She happened to glance to the other side of the slope and saw the constable's car, overturned, down below.

There was no other choice.

She turned for the forest, tearing into its dark shadows as quickly as she could.

Bruce rode back to find the stables empty, the cars gone and his front door open. Striding into the great hall, he shouted, "Toni? Gina . . . David! Anyone?"

A sense of emptiness was his only reply. Still, he strode through the second hall, thinking someone might be in the kitchen. But he never made it there. The door to the tombs was standing open.

His heart thundered in his chest. Damn her! Had she gone down, fallen . . . scared herself into a state of catatonia?

He took the spiral stairs at a dangerous speed. "Toni?" There was no answer, but he knew the route she would have traveled. He strode swiftly toward the great laird's tomb.

He frowned at first, seeing only that the slab was shifted over. Then he got a whiff of the sickening smell just as he looked in.

He didn't reel; didn't fall back.

He'd been wrong, dead wrong. They weren't going to find Annie O'Hara in the forest. She was here. How? his mind shrieked.

At the moment, how didn't matter. Toni was nowhere to be seen, and his sense of panic was growing.

He bolted back up the spiral stairs, feeling an urgency to find her unlike any premonition he'd ever experienced before.

Premonition. Aye! For that's what it was. That picture of Toni, blond hair trailing . . . facedown in the water.

The trees shielded her from the first second she moved into the cool green darkness. She tore across the brook, heedless of the fact that she soaked her shoes and jeans up to her knees. The cold didn't mean anything, not at this moment. Then, finding the thick trunk of an ancient oak, she leaned against it, getting her breath, trying to think rationally.

She was certain that, this time, she had found the remains of a recent victim, those of Annie O'Hara. It actually made sense; it was logical. The other bodies had been dumped here, in the forest. And now a body was actually discarded, right in the castle. Bruce's castle! That should make Bruce appear guilty. Except that . . . it couldn't be!

She heard thrashing, and she turned around.

"Miss Fraser!"

It was Eban's voice, Eban calling her.

Why? Why had he chased her in here? And where was Thayer? He had been far ahead of Eban when she had looked back. In fact, she hadn't even realized that Eban had followed her.

"Lass! 'Tis dangerous in here!" Eban called with dismay. "The laird doesn't want ye in here, y'know!"

Flat against the tree, she remained perfectly still until she heard his footsteps moving on. She started to move out from around the tree. But as she did so, she was stunned to see Thayer, frozen, dead still, standing directly in front of her.

"Toni!" he said softly. "Ah, Toni, here y'are! Luv, I've been lookin' for you. Ah, Toni! I'm sorry, really, truly sorry!"

They nearly crashed into one another. If

Kevin hadn't shouted, David never would have stopped the car in time.

Ryan braked to a halt and leaped out his side of the car just as Gina came out of hers. They both rushed at the minivan.

"Something's wrong! Really wrong," Ryan said.

"Yeah! You can't drive!" David accused, but Ryan's look silenced him.

"What? What?" Kevin demanded.

"We were at the castle maybe fifteen minutes ago. Toni is gone, the door to the castle was standing wide open and the door to the crypt is open!"

Ryan paused for breath, and Gina continued. "And the constable's car is upside down at the bottom of the slope!"

"We just came up the road — Toni isn't on it. Did you find Bruce?" David asked anxiously.

They both shook their heads.

"Neither did we," Kevin ventured.

They stared at one another for several seconds. Then they looked to the dark green canopy of the forest. Kevin groaned.

"She had to have run in there!" Gina whispered.

"All right, all right, let's go!" David said. He and Kevin exited the minivan. The four of them stood together, looking at the forest. Then they walked in.

When they came to the brook, David said, "Kevin and I will follow it this way . . . you two go that way."

And they parted.

He couldn't possibly have the strength to hurt her, Toni thought. But she dared not take that chance. She stared at him a moment, then turned to run again.

"Toni, wait! For the love of God, lass, wait!" he cried.

For the love of God!

She ran. She thought she was leaping brush and dodging trees in a race to go deeper into the forest, but she came back to the water instead. Standing dead still, trying to think of her next move, she heard a groan. Her eyes darted to the water . . . to her left. Farther to her left.

There was someone in the water. Someone. Not a body, since the person was groaning. Male, or female? She couldn't tell. She couldn't even see clearly, the branches were so low, the green darkness so vast . . .

The groan sounded again. The mass was moving.

"Oh, my God!" she breathed, and rushed forward.

He rode Shaunessy hard down the hill, reining in when he saw the cars. The two of them, almost touching. The constable's car, down the slope.

He dismounted, leading Shaunessy quickly toward the entry and the brook.

Eban came out of the forest, shaking his head. Bruce strode quickly to him, catching him by the shoulders. "Eban, where's Toni?"

"In there!" Eban said, waving a hand. "But the lass won't come to me!"

"Eban, you're certain? Who else is in there? All of them? You've got to answer me, Eban. Thayer? Thayer . . . he struck Jonathan. He's in the woods now, right? Eban, listen carefully. There's a body in the crypts. Do you know how it got there?"

Eban stared at him, then frowned. "Laird MacNiall, there be lots o' bodies in the crypts."

Bruce prayed for patience. "One of the murdered girls is in the crypts, Eban. Do you know how she got there?"

Eban stared back at Bruce, shaking his head. "Y'don't keep up the place, Laird Bruce, if y'll forgive me sayin' so!"

"Get to the castle and call Detective Inspector Robert Chamberlain. Please.

Quickly, Eban. Get him out here."

"Aye, Laird Bruce. Aye!"

Eban hurried toward the castle. Bruce cursed himself for not carrying his cell phone, slapped Shaunessy's haunches so he'd head back, as well, and plunged into the forest himself.

"Constable!"

Toni rushed to Jonathan Tavish's side, trying to help him up.

He leaned on her heavily to gain his footing. "Toni . . . Miss Fraser . . . I'm sorry, but he's a bad seed, that one, he is! Slammed me in the head, wrecked the car! And he's loose."

Toni swallowed hard. "Come on. We'll get out of here. There's much worse, Constable Tavish. The body of that last missing girl . . . I'm almost positive I know where it is."

"Oh, aye?"

He found some strength, straightening to look her in the eyes.

"In the crypt. The castle crypt," she said. "I — I don't know what it means. I can't believe that Bruce MacNiall . . . No, others had access, too."

"Aye, and who would that be? Your cousin, Miss Fraser?"

"Anyone had access to the castle," she said. "It wasn't locked when we reached it, before we knew about Bruce. And there's Eban Douglas, as well. He's a local, and your friend, but he's a strange little man. Think about it! Anyone had access."

"Aye, anyone had access," he agreed.

The sound of a twig snapping suddenly alerted them to another presence. They both looked ahead.

Thayer had found her. He looked steadier, and he stared at Jonathan with loathing.

"Toni . . . you need to get away from him."

She sighed. "Thayer, we'll still help you. We'll see that you're represented. We'll —"

"Toni! You've got to get away from him. He clubbed me in the side of the head! Law-enforcement officers don't do that!"

"You bloody bastard!" Tavish roared. "You clubbed me!"

"You're not right, Tavish! You're not right!" Thayer shouted.

That caught Jonathan's attention, and gave him back his full power. He rushed Thayer, slamming him down against the ground. She heard a grunt, saw that the wind was knocked out of Thayer, and that Tavish was about to slug him hard in the jaw.

"Constable, no!" she cried, running through the water toward him.

The blow landed. Thayer's eyes closed. Toni's heart leaped to her throat. Despite all that she had seen, something in her heart was denying it.

"We've got to get him help. You might have killed him!" Toni said angrily.

Jonathan Tavish straightened again and stared at her, brushing his muddied blond hair from his forehead. "Ah, lass!" he said, coming toward her. "Poor, wee, beautiful lass! I'd envisioned so much more for you!"

She backed away instinctively. Too late, she realized that Thayer had been right. Indeed, he'd been barely walking, but he'd dragged himself after her because . . . he had known that Tavish would be in the forest.

He took another step toward her.

Toni screamed, as loudly as she could. She screamed again and then turned to run, praying that Tavish was in worse shape than he appeared.

Fingers tangled into her hair, jerking her back. She went crashing down into the water. She tried to rise, but he had her by the throat. She desperately grasped his hands, nails clawing. He was extremely powerful. She saw the world going a darker green all around her.

Green . . . black . . .

She heard gasping, choking . . . no air.

She slammed a knee against his groin with all her strength.

Bruce burst out on the little copse that sheltered the stream. And he saw her. Toni. Facedown in the water. Blond hair trailing behind her, floating . . .

"Toni!" He roared out her name in anguish, heedless of anything else around him as he raced over rocks, embankment, and into the water, falling to his knees, dragging her into his arms. She was still, so still, cold, silent . . .

He pressed his mouth to hers, parting her lips, breathing in. He staggered up with her in his grasp, anxious to get her to the slick embankment to perform CPR. Yet even as he held her, she gasped, choked, coughed up a wealth of water. Then she opened her eyes.

"Bruce!"

It was little more than a croak, but it registered as a warning. He set her down, spun and caught the blow of Jonathan's billy club right against his temple. He staggered back, falling on his haunches, his vision fading.

"What . . . the hell are you doing, Jonathan?"

"Taking care of a bloody murderer!" Jonathan told him.

The pain in his head was staggering, the darkness, welcoming. But he fought it, fought to get back to his feet. "I didn't murder anyone, and you know it!"

"Eh? Like as not how the law will see it, Laird Bruce! There's a fresh one in your old crypt."

"Aye," Bruce said, warily meeting his eyes. "You know I did not put it there."

"Actually, I do. Y'know, Bruce, I'm a handsome fellow. But the girls never came to me quite as they come to you. And there was that castle, rotting on the hill! You never had appreciation, Bruce. Y'don't deserve such a place. Now, if I don't kill you, and your last victim, y'may wind up ruling some prison and gettin' out again. So y'll die here with the lass. I believe y've said yourself upon occasion, ye can buy a title these days. And a castle, on a hill."

"You've murdered people — to spite me?" Bruce said incredulously.

Jonathan reflected on that for a minute. "Nae, the killing came first. Or maybe not. Maybe y'were the cause of it all, Bruce, because of Maggie."

"Maggie!" Bruce said incredulously. "Maggie has been gone a very long time, Jonathan."

"Aye, a long time."

"She was my fiancée, Jonathan," Bruce said.

"But I loved her first. And there was a time when I was certain she loved me, too. But you came into the picture, Bruce, and it was as always — the spoils of life to the great laird of the castle! And then there was pity in her eyes when she looked at me. I just hungered from afar, but then . . . well, she died, and that an act of God. Still, she taught me about women."

Jonathan started to pace, getting caught up in the frenzy of his words. "You know, Bruce, I've always been a smarter man than y've ever given me credit for! I'm the clever one, always have been. You, the great MacNiall, know how to look up your stock reports! But I can do anything with a computer." He paused a moment, then continued on. "It wasn't after the first girl that I thought of what I could do. It was after the second. There were a few times when I thought I might have erred, so there had to be a scapegoat. Actually, it was quite easy. I set these people up to come. Ah, Bruce, the Internet! What an invention. I knew everything about you there was to know, and you can sell anything at all over the Web, that you can. I thought y'd really show yer temper. Who knew? You might ha' thrown 'em out right on their arses. Then again, they might ha' been around when the last body was found. The lovely Miss Fraser might ha' been spared, but now . . . well, there will be a bit of a mess to clean up here!"

Bruce locked his jaw, thinking of the dizziness, the darkness that still gripped him. His so-called friend meant to kill them, there, in the forest.

Jonathan drew a knife from his pocket, smiling. "A law officer, attacked. I did what I had to do!"

Jonathan hadn't just resented him, Bruce realized, he had hated him with a pathological conviction for years. The man hadn't acted in any mad, sudden rage. He had plotted and planned, dreamed of this.

Bruce flew at him in a desperate tackle, bringing him down hard in the water. But Jonathan had some strength in him. He forced a roll, bringing Bruce beneath him.

With a cry, Toni threw herself at the man. But he was powerful, and he heard her. Turning, he sent a fist jackknifing out. Toni went flying, falling hard back into the water.

Bruce saw the knife raised high above him, ready to plunge, and forced his shoulder to twist, throwing the man off. But Jonathan instantly started crawling through the water again, intent on getting the knife into Bruce's chest. Bruce managed to lash out with a foot, catching him in the ribs.

He fell back, but was soon up again. Then . . . absurdly, he stood in the middle of the stream and stared at Bruce, then away, then at Bruce.

"Hold still, y'bloody bastard!" he roared.

Incredulous, Bruce stared back.

Toni was on her rump, edging her way out of the water. "Which one, Jonathan? Which one do you need to kill?" she demanded.

Bruce glanced quickly and sharply at her. They were both seeing . . . *someone.*

"This one, Jonathan! This one! He's leaping at you!" Toni cried.

And to Bruce's amazement, Jonathan went charging forward, determined to wrestle thin air. He found no hold, barely balanced, and turned again, ready to reach for Toni then, the knife silvery in the green darkness, his intent fierce and brutal.

It was Bruce's chance, perhaps his only chance. He gut-tackled the man again, bringing him down hard into the stream. He heard a terrible cracking sound and winced inwardly. They'd struck a rock.

Beneath him, Jonathan Tavish didn't move. He knew it had been self-defense, but he had killed the man. There was a terrible emptiness inside.

He rolled, letting the water of the brook, icy cool and fresh, wash over him. A second later, Toni was by his side, taking his hand. Her eyes, sapphire and glittering with tears of relief, touched his. The death of any man was a tragedy. They both knew it. Yet, they had survived. For her life, he knew, he would have given his own. And for their future, he couldn't rue the fact that they had both lived.

Not without help.

"He was here, right?" he whispered to her hoarsely. "The great MacNiall. He appeared in the forest. Jonathan saw him, too, and didn't know which of us to kill?"

She nodded.

Bruce closed his eyes. "Thank him for me."

20

"It's still beyond my comprehension," Bruce said, sitting across from Robert Chamberlain at the coffee shop. "Why? Why would anyone spend a lifetime wanting nothing more than . . . well, revenge, I guess, for not being born the laird to a castle?"

"In a way, I can almost feel pity for Jonathan. Whatever his hatreds, real or imagined, they festered in his heart. Along with the sickness that tore into him. Who is to say just what caused what?" Robert asked. "It might have begun with Maggie, and it might have started before she fell in love with you."

"She never rejected Jonathan for me. There was never anything between them," Bruce said, shaking his head.

Robert sighed. "But he believed she would have loved him if it hadn't been for you. I'm no psychologist, but when he finally started killing, he might have been looking for women who somewhat resembled Maggie — in the dark, at least. Getting even with her. He chose prostitutes because they can disappear far more easily than your average office worker, wife, mother or schoolgirl. In the main cities, they would just see him for a fairly decent-looking bloke, nothing scraggly or ugly about the man. They wouldn't hesitate to go with him. Disposing of the bodies in the forest was a way to get to you. Imagine how delighted he must have been, ready to wait and watch, when he snared in that group of Americans — and Thayer. It was nothing for him to slip the money for the payment on their lease into Thayer's account, and make it look as if Thayer had been the one committing the fraud. He was good with computers. Brilliant. It's a pity he couldn't have put it to good use. The fellow is all right, by the way?"

"Ah, yes, fine. Absolutely fine. Toni was nearly hysterical to reach him, once Jonathan was dead. Then the others arrived, and he was helped out of the woods. And, well, you know the rest." He grimaced. "Here I am, forty-eight hours later, still barred from my own castle while the forensic teams finish with all their work."

"Bruce —"

"Hey, I was a cop, remember? Take all the time you need to see that everything is processed." He exhaled with a grimace. "There I was, thinking that Jonathan was incompetent when he was really a master criminal. And I was certain there was something really evil lurking in Thayer Fraser. I'm sure Toni and her friends were just about in terror of poor Eban. I even began to wonder at times if we weren't looking at another husband-and-wife team of killers. And all along I had inspired this terrible hatred myself."

"Whatever you do, don't blame yourself," Robert cautioned him. "You didn't do anything to Jonathan. No one knows what really causes that kind of short circuit in the mind and soul. Maybe he was born with a capacity for evil. Or maybe he let it grow inside. Anyway, here comes your crew. And I have work to do."

Toni and the others had arrived, having taken a bit longer to get ready. They were staying at the Thistle and Crown, just down the street, and though it reeked with charm and hospitality, it lacked a great deal in water pressure.

They all greeted Robert affectionately, but he demurred and told them that he had business when they implored him to stay.

As he was leaving, Matt and Darcy Stone arrived, and he went through a series of goodbyes once again.

About to actually depart, Robert stopped

suddenly. "Oh!" he said, offering them all a grin.

"Oh?" Bruce said.

"Now I can't believe I forgot to mention this! The barmaid, the young barmaid from Stirling we thought to be missing — do you remember?"

"Oh, aye," Bruce said.

"Indeed," Thayer muttered. "Katie."

"Well, she's not going to be found in the forest," Robert said. "Seems she turned up in London. She had a date with a young man who convinced her that she was worth more than being a lackey to a mean man. She's working in a clothing shop and going to school. She was horrified when the London bobbies stopped her. She'd had no idea she'd been reported as a missing person."

"Thank God!" Thayer said.

"Well, now, there's a truism, all right. Good news, for once. Ta, now, folks, for real."

They were all gathered at the table and the waitress came to take their orders. For several minutes, there was a certain amount of chaos, what with decisions on what to eat and drink being made. Then there was a silence.

So far, all they had done was apologize to

553

one another for their suspicions, worry about one another and talk about what had happened. But as of that night, the forest and the castle had been the domain of the police. Evidence was being gathered, and both forest and abode were crime scenes, off-limits. Even Shaunessy and Wallace had been moved to the stables in town. And Eban, loath to leave his little cottage, was now in wonder at the friendly service he received at the little hotel.

So now there was the future. It would be tinged by the past, but as always, the future would be what they made of it.

They were all staring at him.

"Here's how I see it should be done," Bruce said. "The tours will be stopped — for a few weeks. The police still have possession of the castle. And there will be articles in all the papers, so a little time should definitely pass out of respect. But then, knowing how people really do seem to love the gruesome, you'll probably be so busy, you'll be turning people away."

Gina made a funny sound in her throat. "You're . . . going to let us continue?"

He shrugged. "For about half a year."

"And then?" she whispered.

He didn't get a chance to answer, because Thayer suddenly burst out with, "Who'd ha' figured! Him, Jonathan . . . a *constable*. A man y'd know all yer life, Bruce!"

The past . . . yes, it would remain with them awhile. Even when they thought they had talked it out, it came back. Like a ghost from a not so distant time.

Toni looked at Darcy Stone. "Darcy, could Jonathan have been . . . Grayson Davis, living out another life?"

Darcy smiled and shrugged. "I don't know. Maybe, maybe not."

Matt added, "There aren't always answers, you know, from the living, or the dead."

Bruce spoke up. "Maybe he was just a man who resented me all his life — and had a penchant for power and murder, as well. There's nothing that will excuse his actions, but I can almost understand his hatred for me. I had everything he wanted — the castle, the title. Despite the fact that I was seldom here after Maggie died, I was the laird, and that meant something to the people in the village. Then there was Maggie . . . my fiancée. I'd never known that Jonathan had been in love with her. She always thought they were friends. Apparently, he thought that he'd been rejected. Maybe there's a whole slew of psychological explanations. And then again, maybe he was Grayson Davis, living a new life, without really having learned from the old."

Gina shivered suddenly and stared at David and Kevin. "And you! You little rats! As soon as you read about that case Bruce had solved in Edinburgh, you were staring at Ryan and I as if we were capable of such horrors."

"Oh, now, that's not true!" David protested.

"As if Gina would allow another woman next to me, much less find one for me," Ryan said.

Gina stared at him in reproach.

"You are jealous," he told her.

"My foot!" she said.

Bruce laughed. "Hey, come on now, Ryan. I've seen you hug Toni."

"Toni . . ." He waved a hand in the air. "Toni's my friend."

"Chopped liver!" Toni said, amazed that she could smile and laugh.

"I hug Toni, just like I hug David and Kevin."

"Ooh! Sexy!" Kevin teased.

Ryan groaned. "Ignore him, please," Ryan said to Bruce. "So . . . you'll let us stay and work for six months. And then what? Are you going to keep working with us, as well?"

"Aye, after the first month."

"After? Why after? What's happening before then?" David asked.

Bruce turned to Toni, a smile halfway curling his lip. "I thought I'd get away for a bit. And though I know Toni has a true love of Scotland, she might need to get away, too. Somewhere brand-new, very commercial, with a beach and lots of sun. Cancun, the Florida Keys, Aruba . . . Disney, maybe, though we'd definitely avoid the Haunted Mansion." He arched a brow to her.

"Toni can't go!" Ryan said. "Then all we'd have is Gina, and she can't do all the female roles. Ow!" he complained at the end as his wife elbowed him.

"There's Lizzie and Trish," Thayer said. "They'd love to be part of this, though I'm thinking of opting out myself."

"What?" The question came from around the table.

Thayer grimaced. "You know what all this has taught me? I want to be on the right side of the law. I want to clean up my act, get in some training, learn to be a cop . . . and apply to be constable here." He looked at Bruce. "All right, you're thinking I've been something of a scumbag, not worth a hoot —"

"Actually, I was thinking you might be

perfect for the job," Bruce told him.

Thayer sat up straighter, stunned and very pleased. "Aye, I'd be good, I swear it." He was quiet for a minute, staring at Bruce. "And you . . . you should go back to police work, you know. Robert told me that you were an asset he sorely misses."

"Truly, Bruce, it is something you should consider," Darcy said.

"There are many different ways in which you could put all your learned and . . . natural talents to good use," Matt told him.

"Sometime in the future, maybe," Bruce said. "Just not immediately."

"Okay, great. You're going off, Thayer wants to be constable and we get to keep doing the tours, minus half the staff!" Ryan said.

"You've got yourself, David and Kevin, Gina . . . Lizzie and Trish. And we will be back," Bruce promised. He looked at Toni again. "That is, if you're coming with me?"

"Try to leave without me," she told him.

"Still, what happens after the six months?" Gina demanded, diverting his attention.

"I think I know," Darcy said lightly, grinning. "And it doesn't take a psychic to see the future here!"

Bruce's eyes never left Toni. "Well, the

way I'm hoping it will go, there will be this magnificent wedding here. The bride will be incredible in white, the groom, traditional in his colors. And the bridal party . . . well, you all figure it out." He glared at David and Kevin. "No yellow!" He turned back to Toni, taking her hands. "I was born a privileged man. I ignored that, and my heredity, a long, long time. This castle should be a home. I want to make it so, with a wife, with children. Think about it, lass!" he said softly, his words earnest. "That poor fellow, the great MacNiall, spent all those years walking this place, watching out for his antecedents. I owe him that, don't you think? A bride as fierce, as passionate, as loyal as his own . . . and great-great-grandchildren?"

It was somehow incredibly special to Toni that he had dared to say this, before them all.

"You said you didn't really know me the other night," she reminded him.

"I was wrong. I know now — as I knew then — everything about you that I will ever need to know." He paused, now a little unsure of himself. "I'm sorry, I'm rushing you."

She shook her head. "No, you're not. I think it's the most wonderful story I've ever heard — and I didn't even make it up myself."

"Oh, my God!" David exclaimed. "Does that mean you two are engaged?"

"Aye, precisely," Bruce said.

"Ach, then! It's time for champagne," Thayer said.

And so there was a toast. And they spent most of the day together, a group that would forever be linked by the strange events they had shared.

Then night came again, and Bruce and Toni were alone at last. Cozy in their little room, he gathered her into his arms, taking her chin, raising it, meeting her eyes. "This is what I haven't said yet. I love you. It's not that I was a monk after Maggie died, nor was I a roving lecher of any kind. I was just existing. And then there was you."

"My dear, dear, Laird MacNiall!" she returned. "You do have a way with words."

"You still know very little about me," he warned her.

She shook her head, delighted just to look into his eyes. "We'll have a month in Aruba for you to tell me everything."

"And?" he said softly.

"And . . . I think I fell in love with you the moment you came riding into the hall, the great MacNiall! As you said earlier, I know everything I really need to know about you. And I love you, for everything I know, for you being you."

He smiled and kissed her. And when the kiss would have become extremely ardent, with clothing being shed, he paused suddenly, staring into her eyes again.

"The great MacNiall?" he queried.

"I don't believe he checked into the hotel," she teased innocently.

"Toni . . . is he still around?"

"He's gone," she said simply.

"You're certain? For good?"

She nodded. "He did what he needed to do. He's at peace."

"Ah. Well, peace isn't exactly what I intend to give you, you know. I have a feeling there will be plenty of tempest ahead."

"I wouldn't have it any other way," she assured him.

Then he kissed her again. And the tempest began.

About the Author

A master storyteller, **Heather Graham** describes her life as "busy, wild and fun." Surprisingly, with all her success, Heather's first career choice was not writing but acting on the Shakespearean stage. Happily for her fans, fate intervened and now she is a *New York Times* bestselling author. Although Heather and her family enjoy traveling, southern Florida — where she loves the sun and water — is home.